THE ROAD TRIP

Also by Beth O'Leary

The Flatshare

The Switch

THE ROAD TRIP

BETH O'LEARY

Quercus

First published in Great Britain in 2021 by

Quercus Editions Ltd
Carmelite House
50 Victoria Embankment
London EC4Y 0DZ

An Hachette UK company

A CIP catalogue record for this book is available from the British Library

HB ISBN 978 1 52940 905 5
TPB ISBN 978 1 52940 906 2
EB ISBN 978 1 52940 908 6

10 9 8 7 6 5 4 3

Text designed and typeset by CC Book Production
Printed and bound in Great Britain by Clays Ltd, Elcograf S.p.A.

Papers used by Quercus Editions Ltd are from well-managed forests and other responsible sources.

For my bridesmaids

NOW

Dylan

'The road of friendship never did run smooth, is what I'm saying,' Marcus tells me, fidgeting with his seat belt.

This is my first experience of a heartfelt apology from Marcus, and so far it has involved six clichés, two butchered literary references and no eye contact. The word *sorry* did feature, but it was preceded by *I'm not very good at saying*, which somewhat undermined its sincerity.

I shift up a gear. 'Isn't it *the course of true love* that never runs smooth? *A Midsummer Night's Dream*, I believe.'

We're by the twenty-four-hour Tesco. It's half four in the morning, the air thick with duvet-darkness, but the bland yellow light from the shop illuminates the three people in the car in front as if they've just moved into a spotlight. We're close behind them, both following the slow, rattling path of a lorry ahead.

For a flash of a second I see the driver's face in the rear-view mirror. She reminds me of Addie – if you think about someone enough, you start to see them everywhere.

Marcus huffs. 'I'm talking about my feelings, Dylan. This is agony. Please get your head out of your arse so that you can actually listen.'

I smile at that. 'All right. I'm listening.'

I drive on, past the bakery. The eyes of the driver in front are lit again in the mirror, her eyebrows slightly raised behind squarish glasses.

'I'm just saying, we hit some bumps, I get that, and I didn't handle things well, and that's – that's really unfortunate that that happened.'

Astonishing, really, the linguistic knots in which he will tie himself to avoid a simple *I'm sorry*. I stay silent. Marcus coughs and fidgets some more, and I almost take pity and tell him it's all right, he doesn't have to say it if he's not ready, but as we idle past the bookie's another flash of light hits the car in front and Marcus is forgotten. The driver has wound the window down, and she's stretched an arm out, gripping the roof of the car. Her wrist is looped with bracelets, glimmering silver-red in the car lights' glare. The gesture is so achingly familiar – the arm, slender and pale, the assertion of it, and those bracelets, the round, childish beads stacked up her wrist. I'd know them anywhere. My heart jolts like I've missed a step because it *is* her, it's *Addie*, her eyes meeting mine in the rear-view mirror.

And then Marcus screams.

Earlier, Marcus gave a similarly horrified scream when we passed a Greggs advertising vegan sausage rolls, so I don't react as fast as I perhaps otherwise would. As the car in front stops sharply, and I fail to hit the brakes on the seventy-thousand-pound Mercedes that belongs to Marcus's father, I have just enough time to regret this.

Addie

Bang.

My head whips up so fast my glasses go flying backwards off my ears and over the headrest. Someone screams. *Oww, fuck* – a pain shoots up my neck, and all I'm thinking is *God, what did I do? Did I hit something?*

'Shit the bed,' Deb says beside me. 'Are you all right?'

I fumble for my glasses. They're not there, obviously.

'What the hell just happened?' I manage.

My shaking hands go to the steering wheel, then the handbrake, then the rear-view mirror. Getting my bearings.

I see him in the mirror. A little blurred without my glasses. A little unreal. It's him, though, no question. He's so familiar that for a moment I feel as if I'm looking at my own reflection. Suddenly my heart's beating like it's shoving for space.

Deb's getting out of the car. Ahead, the bin lorry moves off and its headlights catch the tail of the fox they braked for. It's moving on to the pavement at a saunter. Slowly, the scene pieces itself together: lorry stops for fox, I stop for lorry, and behind me Dylan doesn't stop at all. Then – *bang.*

I look back at Dylan in the mirror; he's still looking at me. Everything seems to slow or quieten or fade, like someone's dialled the world down.

I haven't seen Dylan for twenty months. He should have changed somehow. Everything else has. But even from here, even in half darkness, I know the exact line of his nose, his long eyelashes, his snakeskin yellow-green eyes. I know those eyes will be as wide and shocked as they were when he left me.

'Well,' my sister says. 'The Mini's done us proud.'

The Mini. The car. Everything comes rushing back in and I unclick my seat belt. It takes three goes. My hands are shaking. When I next glance at the rear-view mirror my eyes focus on the foreground instead of the background and there's Rodney, crouched forward on our back seat with his hands over his head and his nose touching his knees.

Shit. I forgot all about Rodney.

'Are you all right?' I ask him, just as Deb says,

'Addie? Are you OK?' She pokes her head back in the car, then grimaces. 'Your neck hurting too?'

'Yeah,' I say, because as soon as she asks I realise it does, *loads*.

'Gosh,' Rodney says, tentatively shifting out of the brace position. 'What happened?'

Rodney posted on the 'Cherry & Krish are Getting Hitched' Facebook group yesterday evening asking for a lift to the wedding from the Chichester area. Nobody else replied, so Deb and I took pity. All I know about Rodney is that he has a Weetabix On The Go for breakfast, he's always hunching and his T-shirt says, *I keep pressing Esc but I'm still here*, but I think I've pretty much got the gist.

'Some arsehole in a Mercedes went into the back of us,' Deb tells him, straightening up to look at the car behind again.

'Deb . . .' I say.

'Yeah?'

'I think that's Dylan. In that car.'

She scrunches up her nose, ducking down to see me again. 'Dylan *Abbott?*'

I swallow. 'Yeah.'

I risk a glance over my shoulder. My neck protests. It's then that I notice the man stepping out of the Mercedes passenger seat. Slim-built and ghostly pale in the dark street, his curly hair just catching the light of the shopfronts behind him. There goes my heart again, beating way too fast.

'He's with Marcus,' I say.

'*Marcus?*' Deb says, eyes going wide.

'Yeah. Oh, God.' This is awful. What am I meant to do now? Something about insurance? 'Is the car OK?' I ask.

I climb out just as Dylan gets out of the Mercedes. He's dressed in a white tee and chino shorts with battered boat shoes on his feet. There's a carabiner on his belt loop, disappearing into his pocket. It was my idea, that, to stop him always losing his keys.

He steps forward into the path of the Mercedes' headlights. He looks so handsome it aches in my chest. Seeing him is even harder than I expected it to be. I want to do everything at once: run to him, run away, curl up, cry. And beneath all that I have this totally ridiculous feeling that someone's messed up, like something didn't get filed when it should have up there in the universe, because I *was* supposed to see Dylan this weekend, for the first time in almost two years, but it should have been at the wedding.

'Addie?' he says.

'Dylan,' I manage.

'Did a *Mini* really just total my dad's Mercedes?' says Marcus.

My hand goes self-consciously to my fringe. No make-up, scruffy dungarees, no mousse in my hair. I've spent bloody *months* planning the outfit I was supposed to be wearing when I saw Dylan again, and this was not it. But he doesn't scan me up and down, doesn't even seem to clock my new hair colour – he meets my gaze and holds it. I feel like the whole world just stumbled and had to catch its breath.

'Fuck me,' says Marcus. 'A Mini! The indignity of it!'

'What the hell?' Deb says. 'What were you *doing*? You just drove into the back of us!'

Dylan looks around in bewilderment. I pull myself together.

'Is anyone hurt?' I ask, rubbing my aching neck. 'Rodney?'

'Who?' says Marcus.

'I'm OK!' calls Rodney, who's still in the back seat of the car.

Deb helps him climb out. I should have done that. My brain feels kind of scrambled.

'Shit,' says Dylan, finally registering the crumpled bumper of the Mercedes. 'Sorry, Marcus.'

'Oh, mate, honestly, don't worry about it,' Marcus says. 'Do you know how many times I've totalled one of my dad's cars? He won't even notice.'

I step forward and check out the back of Deb's battered Mini. It's actually not looking too bad – that *bang* was so loud I would've assumed something serious had fallen off. Like a wheel.

Before I've registered what she's doing, Deb's in the driving seat, starting the engine again.

'She's all good!' she says. 'What a car. Best money I ever spent.' She drives forward a little, up on to the curb, and hits the hazard lights.

Dylan's back in the Mercedes, rifling through the glove box. He and Marcus talk about roadside accident assist, Marcus forwards him an email off his phone, and I think to myself . . . that's it, Dylan's hair's shorter. That's what it is. I know I should be thinking about this whole car crash thing but all I'm doing is playing a game of spot-the-difference, looking at Dylan and going, *What's missing? What's new?*

His eyes flick to mine again. I go hot. There's something about

Dylan's eyes – they kind of catch you up, like cobweb. I force myself to look away.

'So . . . you're on your way to Cherry's wedding, I'm guessing?' I say to Marcus. My voice shakes. I can't look at him. I'm suddenly thankful for the dented rear bumper to examine on the Mini.

'Well, we were,' Marcus drawls, eyeing the Mercedes. Maybe he can't bring himself to look at me either. 'But there's no way we're driving this baby four hundred miles now. It needs to get to a garage. Yours should, too.'

Deb makes a dismissive noise, already out of the car again and rubbing a scratch with the sleeve of her ratty old hoody. 'Ah, she's fine,' she says, opening and closing the boot experimentally. 'Dented, that's all.'

'Marcus, it's going ballistic,' Dylan calls.

I can see the Mercedes' screen flashing warning lights even from here. The hazards are too bright. I turn my face away. Isn't it typical that when Marcus's car breaks, Dylan's the one sorting it?

'The tow will be here in thirty minutes to take it to the garage,' Dylan says.

'Thirty minutes?' Deb says, disbelieving.

'All part of the service,' Marcus tells her, pointing to the car. 'Mercedes, darling.'

'It's Deb. Not darling. We've met several times before.'

'Sure. I remember,' Marcus says lightly. Not very convincing.

I can feel Dylan's eyes pulling at me as we all try to get the insurance stuff sorted. I'm fumbling around with my phone, Deb's digging in the glove box for paperwork, and all the while I'm so aware of Dylan, like he's taking up ten times more space than everyone else.

'And how are we getting to the wedding?' Marcus asks once we're done.

'We'll just get public transport,' Dylan says.

'Public *transport*?' Marcus says, as though someone's just suggested he get to Cherry's wedding by toboggan. Still a bit of a wanker, then, Marcus. No surprises there.

Rodney clears his throat. He's leaning against the side of the Mini, eyes fixed on his phone. I feel bad – I keep forgetting him. Right now my brain doesn't have room for Rodney.

'If you set off now,' he says, 'then according to Google you would arrive . . . at thirteen minutes past two.'

Marcus checks his watch.

'All right,' says Dylan. 'That's fine.'

'On Tuesday,' Rodney finishes.

'What?' chorus Dylan and Marcus.

Rodney pulls an apologetic face. 'It's half four in the morning on a Sunday on a bank holiday weekend and you're trying to get from Chichester to rural Scotland.'

Marcus throws his hands in the air. 'This country is a shambles.'

Deb and I look at each other. *No, no no no—*

'Let's go,' I say, moving for the Mini. 'Will you drive?'

'Addie . . .' Deb begins as I climb into the passenger seat.

'Where do you think you're going?' calls Marcus.

I slam the car door.

'Hey!' Marcus says as Deb gets into the driver's seat. 'You have to take us to the wedding!'

'No,' I say to Deb. 'Ignore him. Rodney! Get in!'

Rodney obliges. Which is kind. I really don't know the man well enough to yell at him.

'What the fuck? Addie. Come on. If you don't drive us, we won't get there in time,' Marcus says.

He's by my window now. He knocks on the glass with the back of his knuckles. I don't roll it down.

'Addie, come on! Christ, surely you owe Dylan a favour.'

Dylan says something to Marcus. I don't catch it.

'God, he's an arse,' Deb says with a frown.

I close my eyes.

'Do you think you can do it?' Deb asks me. 'Give them a lift?'

'No. Not – not both of them.'

'Then ignore him. Let's just go.'

Marcus taps on the window again. I clench my teeth, neck still aching, and keep my eyes straight ahead.

'Our road trip was meant to be *fun*,' I say.

This is Deb's first weekend away from her baby boy, Riley. It's all we've talked about for months. She's planned every stop-off, every snack.

'It would still be fun,' Deb says.

'We don't have room,' I try.

'I can squeeze up!' Rodney says.

I'm really going off Rodney.

'It's *such* a long journey, Deb,' I say, pressing my fists to my eyes. 'Hours and hours stuck in the same car with Dylan. I've spent almost two years tiptoeing around Chichester trying not to bump into this man for even a *second*, let alone eight hours.'

'I'm not saying do it,' Deb points out. 'I'm saying let's go.'

Dylan has moved the Mercedes to somewhere safer to wait for the tow. I turn in my seat just as he's getting out of the car again, all lean, scruffy, almost-six-feet of him.

I know as soon as our eyes meet that I'm not going to leave him here.

He knows it too. *I'm sorry*, he mouths at me.

If I had a pound for every time Dylan Abbott's told me he's sorry, I'd be rich enough to buy that Mercedes.

Dylan

Sometimes a poem arrives almost whole, as if someone's dropped it at my feet like a dog playing fetch. As I climb into the back of Deb's car and catch the achingly familiar edge of Addie's perfume, two and a half lines come to me in a split second. *Unchanged and changed/ Eyes trained on mine/And I'm—*

I'm what? What am I? I'm a mess. Every time I look at Addie something leaps inside me, dolphin-like, and you'd think after twenty months it wouldn't *hurt* quite like this but it does, it hurts, the kind of hurt that makes you want to fucking *wail.*

'Shove up, would you?' Marcus says, pushing me into Rodney's shoulder. I throw a hand out and just about avoid landing it right in Rodney's lap.

'Sorry,' me and Rodney say simultaneously.

My palms are clammy; I keep swallowing, as if that'll help keep all the feelings down. Addie looks so different: her hair is cut almost as short as mine and dyed silver-grey, and her glasses – miraculously recovered from the boot of the Mini after the crash – are chunky and hipster-ish, unapologetic. She is quite possibly more beautiful than ever. It's as if I'm looking at Addie's identical twin: the same but different. *Unchanged and changed.*

I should be saying something, clearly, but I can't think quite what. I used to be good at this sort of thing – I used to be *smooth.* I cram myself into the narrow middle seat and watch Marcus's father's car being driven away down the dark street, clinging forlornly to the tow truck's back, and I wish I could reclaim some of the cockiness I had when I first met Addie and didn't have the foggiest idea of how completely and utterly she would change my life.

'What were you doing heading off so early, anyway?' Addie says, as Deb pulls away from the side of the road. 'You hate driving early.'

She's putting on make-up, using the mirror in the sun visor above the passenger seat; I watch her blend a paste from the back of her hand into the cream of her skin.

'You're a little out of date,' Marcus says, trying to get comfortable in his seat, and elbowing me in the ribs in the process. 'These days Dylan has *very* strong opinions about why road trips absolutely *must* start at four a.m.'

I look down at my knees, embarrassed. It was Addie who taught me how much better a road trip is when you leave in the thick quiet before dawn, the day still heavy with hope, though she's right: when we were together, I always complained about how early she made us set off for a long drive.

'Well, it's a good job we started early!' Rodney chirps, checking his phone with his elbows tucked as tightly to his sides as possible.

Marcus is making no such sacrifices to my comfort: he is spread-eagled with his knee carelessly thrown against mine and an elbow half in my lap. I sigh.

'We'll be tight getting to the family barbecue as it is, now,' Rodney goes on. 'Over eight hours of driving and it's already five thirty!'

'Ah, you're coming to the pre-wedding barbecue?' I ask.

He nods. The question is a blatant attempt to work out what

Rodney is doing here, but I'm hoping it passes for friendliness. For one awful, lead-weight moment when they first got out of the car, I thought he was coming to the wedding as Addie's plus one – Cherry had said a few months ago that she might be bringing somebody. But there's no obvious sense of connection between them; Addie seems to be largely ignoring him.

She's largely ignoring everybody, actually. After those first few heart-jolting, gut-wrenching moments of eye contact, she's been studiously avoiding my gaze every time I try to snag her attention. Meanwhile Marcus is tapping a loud, inane rhythm on the car window; Deb flashes him an irritated look as she tries to concentrate on joining the Chichester bypass.

'Can we get some music playing or something?' Marcus asks.

I know what's coming before Addie's hit play; as soon as I hear the opening notes I have to swallow back a smile. I don't know the song, but American country music is undeniably distinctive – you only need a few chords to know you'll be hearing tales of late-night kisses on porches, trips to the honky-tonk, long drives with pretty girls in passenger seats. Addie and Deb have loved country music since they were teenagers; I used to tease Addie about it, which was particularly hypocritical of me, as a man whose 'Long Run' playlist is almost exclusively populated by the works of Taylor Swift. Now I can't hear the twang of a banjo without thinking of Addie dancing to Florida Georgia Line in one of my old shirts, Addie singing along to Rodney Atkins' 'Watching You' with the car windows down, Addie undressing slowly to the tune of 'Body Like a Back Road'.

'Maybe not this one,' Addie says, hand hovering over the phone.

'I like it! Leave it,' Deb says, turning it up.

'What the hell is this?' Marcus says.

I watch Addie's shoulders square up at his tone.

'It's Ryan Griffin,' Addie says. 'It's – it's called "Woulda Left Me Too".'

I wince. Marcus snorts with laughter.

'Oh, is it now?' he says.

'It's on the Country Gold playlist,' Addie says; a pale pink blush blossoms on the skin of her neck, uneven, its patches like petals. 'And that's what we're going to be listening to for the next eight hours. So you better get used to it.'

Marcus opens the car door.

'What the—'

'Marcus, what the fuck—'

There's a scrabble in the back seat. Marcus elbows me off. The door is only open a few inches but the wind rips through the car, and Rodney is leaning over me now, trying to reach the handle and pull it closed, until there's four or five hands clawing at the car door, and we're scratching one another, Rodney's greasy brown hair in my face, my leg somehow tangled over Marcus's—

'I'll hitchhike!' Marcus is yelling, and I can hear the adrenaline in his voice, the buzz he gets from doing something stupid. 'Let me out! I can't do eight hours of this! Turn it off!' He's laughing even as I slap at his hand so hard it stings the skin of my palm.

'You're insane!' says Rodney. 'We're going at sixty miles an hour!'

The car swerves. I catch sight of Deb's eyes in the rear-view mirror: they're narrowed in grim concentration as she tries to hold her lane position. On our right cars flash by in a stream of over-bright headlights, leaving yellow-white streaks across my vision.

Addie pauses the song. Marcus closes the door. Now the music is off and the wind isn't roaring through the door you can hear every noise in the car: Rodney's laboured breathing, the sound of Deb relaxing back into the driving seat. With the rush of physical adrenaline from the scuffle comes a startling desire to punch Marcus on the nose.

'What the *hell* is wrong with you?' I hiss.

I feel Addie turn to look at me then – surprised, maybe – but she's back to the road before I can meet her eyes.

Marcus swallows, side-glancing me, and I can tell he already wishes he'd been better behaved, but I'm too irritated to acknowledge it. After a moment he forces a laugh.

'We want road-trip music!' he says. 'Put on some Springsteen, will you?'

For a long moment Addie says nothing.

'Deb,' she says eventually, 'take the next services, please.'

'Do you need a wee?' Deb asks.

'No,' Addie says. 'We need to drop Marcus off. So he can hitchhike. As requested.'

She hits play on the country song again.

Addie

It turns out there are no services for ages. When we eventually reach a petrol station, I really do need a wee. And some air. This is suddenly feeling like the smallest car in the whole bloody world.

'Are we actually dropping Marcus off here?' asks a worried voice from behind me.

I'm power-walking across the petrol station forecourt to the building. The aim is to move fast enough that Dylan can't catch me up for a chat. So far I have managed to avoid direct eye contact with him since we all got in the Mini. I reckon this is a sustainable plan for the next four-hundred-odd miles.

Rodney can move very fast for such an ungainly man. I glance over my shoulder at him.

'Probably not, no,' I say. 'Marcus is prone to dramatics. Best to nip them in the bud or he'll act out all day.'

'How do you know him?'

Rodney dashes forward to hold the door open for me as we reach the services. I blink. He's so gawky. There's something adolescent about him, but he's got to be at least thirty.

'Dylan and I used to date.'

'Oh. *Oh.* Oh my God, how incredibly awkward!' Rodney says, pressing both hands to his mouth.

I laugh, surprising myself. 'Yeah, something like that.'

I grab a handful of chocolate bars from the end of the aisle. Me and Deb packed enough road-trip snacks for two, but Dylan eats like a horse. We'll run out of food by Fareham if he sniffs out the treats.

'Sorry you've got stuck in the middle of things a bit,' I tell Rodney. 'It'll be fine, though. Dylan and I can be civil for a few hours, don't worry.'

'Oh, so it all ended, you know, amicably?' Rodney asks, holding out a basket for me. I drop in the chocolate bars, plus five packets of biscuits and a bunch of grab bags full of sweets.

'Uh, amicably?'

The night that Dylan left me, I'd screamed at him. Not in the way people usually mean it – like, yelling – but actually screaming: mouth open wide, the sound clawing at my throat. I'd pounded his chest with my fists, sobbed until my whole body was wracked with it. I didn't eat for three days afterwards.

'Ish,' I say. 'Amicable-ish.'

When we walk back to the car, Dylan's leaning against the side, arms folded, staring off to the left. The sun is rising behind him. He looks like he belongs on a poster for something. An indie band or an expensive cologne. He's still scruffy and dreamy-eyed, but he's more grown-up now – his edges seem cleaner cut.

I keep my eyes on him a little too long, and he catches my gaze for just an instant before I look back down at my feet.

'Addie,' he says, as we approach.

He steps forward to help me with the bags. I twist aside, moving past him to the boot of the car.

'Addie, please,' he says, more quietly now. 'We should talk. We're going to be stuck in a car together for the best part of a day. Don't you want to – you know – just . . . make it less . . . awkward?'

I slam the boot closed. I've just about fitted the extra snacks in, but there's not much visibility out the back window now. Dylan and Marcus have packed like Mariah Carey, by the looks of things, and then there's all Deb's breastfeeding paraphernalia: two pumps, the cooling bag, bottles . . .

'I'm going to go for a wander, stretch out the legs,' says Rodney. 'See you both in five minutes?'

I shouldn't have said amicable-ish. He wouldn't have left me alone with Dylan if I'd told him he ruined my life.

'Addie . . . can you not even look at me?'

I'm honestly not sure I can. Trying to look at Dylan hurts. It feels like we're two magnets with the same force skidding away from one another. Instead I look out towards the green where a few people are exercising their dogs. A little poodle going around in circles, a sausage dog in a ridiculous pink harness. The sun is inching up behind them, drawing long shadows on the grass. I spot Marcus, crouched low to say hello to an Alsatian. I hope it's an unfriendly one. I don't want Marcus to get bitten or anything, but maybe he could get growled at a bit.

'Where's Deb?' I ask.

'She got a call from your mum about Riley.'

I glance at him. 'She told you about Riley?'

His gaze is soft. 'Just now. I thought you'd . . . I thought you would have told me, you know. Things like Deb having a baby.'

'We said no contact.'

'You said. Not we.'

I raise my eyebrows.

'Sorry,' he says. 'Sorry.'

I fiddle with my bracelets. My nails are newly painted for the wedding, but they're so short they look a bit ridiculous. Little stubs of red.

'I'm really happy for Deb, anyway,' Dylan says, when I don't respond.

'And a little surprised?'

He smiles, and I start smiling too, before I catch myself.

'Aren't you going to ask who the father is?' I say.

'I assume she didn't require one,' Dylan says. 'Like Gaea, you know, when she gave birth to Uranus?'

The smile grows despite my best efforts. 'You know I don't,' I say dryly.

'Right,' he says hastily. He brushes his hair back, like it's still long enough to fall in his eyes – an old tic. 'Greek mythology, very pompous, arsey reference, forgive me. I just meant Deb's never needed a man, has she? Not that anyone *needs* a man, but . . . ah, Christ.'

'Let's get this show on the *road*!' comes a voice from behind us. Marcus barges past and opens the door to the back seats. 'You might want to start up the engine. Rodney's coming at quite a pace.'

I turn just as Deb appears, sliding her phone into her hoody pocket. She climbs in after Marcus as I move to the driving seat. I panic: does that mean Dylan is going to sit up front with me?

'What's Rodney doing?' Deb says.

I look over my shoulder, back towards the green. Rodney is running towards us in a great flail of long arms and legs, hair flying. Behind him is the Alsatian, dragging its owner by the lead.

'Oh, brilliant,' I mutter, clambering into the car and fumbling to turn the key in the ignition.

Marcus whoops as Rodney scrambles into the back, breathing hard.

'Sorry!' he calls. 'Sorry! Sorry!'

Deb makes a squished sort of *oof* sound. 'Watch those hands, please,' she says. 'That one strayed very close to my vagina.'

'Oh my God, I'm *so* sorry,' says a mortified, breathless Rodney.

Dylan climbs into the front seat. He's trying to catch my gaze again.

'No harm done,' Deb says. 'I pushed a baby out of that thing, it's sturdy.'

'Oh, no,' Rodney says. 'Oh, I didn't – I'm so sorry.'

'I forgot how much I like you, Deb,' Marcus declares.

'Really?' Deb says, sounding interested. 'Because I don't like you at all.'

I pull out of the service station. I can't resist – for a second my gaze flickers towards Dylan in the passenger seat.

'Only three hundred and fifty-eight miles to go,' he says, quietly enough that only I can hear him.

Marcus is explaining to Deb that he is 'often misunderstood', and is 'actually in the process of reforming, much like a rake from a poorly written nineteenth-century novel'.

'Three hundred and fifty-eight miles,' I say. 'I'm sure it'll fly by.'

Dylan

We speed along the A34. Already the heat is as thick as honey, viscous and sweet. It's turning into a glorious summer morning: the sky is a deep lapis lazuli blue, and the fields are sun-kissed and yellow-bright on either side of the road. It's the sort of day that tastes of crushed ice and suntan lotion, ripe strawberries, the sweet head rush of too many gin and tonics.

'Chocolate's going to melt at this rate,' says Addie, turning the air conditioning as cold as it'll go.

I perk up.

'Chocolate?'

'Not for you,' she says, without looking away from the road.

I sag back in my seat. I thought we'd made a little progress – earlier she turned to me and offered half a smile, like the smallest bite of something delicious, and my heart soared. A real smile from Addie is a true prize: hard to win and utterly heart-stopping when it comes. Disturbingly, this seems to be no less true now than it was two years ago. But she's gone cold again; it's been thirty minutes since we left the services and she's not spoken to me directly until now. I have no right to object, and it shouldn't make me angry, but it does – it feels like pettiness, and I like to think we're better than that.

I shift in my seat and she glances across at me, then reaches to turn the radio up. It's rattling out some pop song, something bouncy and repetitive, a compromise between Addie's tastes and Marcus's; at this volume I can't quite catch the inane chatter in the back seat. Last I heard, Rodney was explaining the rules of real-life quidditch to Deb, with the occasional amused interlude from Marcus.

'Go on,' Addie says. 'Whatever you want to say, just say it.'

'Am I that transparent?' I say, as lightly as I can manage.

'Yes.' Her voice is frank. 'You are.'

'I just . . .' I swallow. 'You're still punishing me.'

The moment I've said it, I instantly wish I hadn't.

'I'm punishing you?'

The air con is a slow, warm breath frittering away on my face; I'd rather crack the windows, but earlier Marcus complained about what it did to his hair, and I don't have the patience to go through that conversation again. I shift so the lukewarm stream of air hits my cheek side-on – this way I can watch Addie driving. The tips of her ears have gone red, just visible through the ends of her hair. She's wearing sunglasses now, and her other glasses are propped up on her head, pushing her sweeping fringe back from her face; I can just see the brushstrokes of her old hair colour at the roots.

'You still won't speak to me.'

'Not speaking was never about punishing you, Dylan. It actually wasn't about *you* at all. I needed the space.'

I look down at my hands. 'I just thought you'd stop needing space eventually, I suppose.'

She glances at me; her eyes are unreadable through the sunglasses' filter.

'You were waiting?' she asks.

'Not . . . not *waiting*, per se, but . . .'

I trail off, and the silence rolls ahead of us, ribbon-like, too long. I catch sight of the expression of the passenger in the car across from us on the motorway – a middle-aged woman in a cap, staring wide-eyed at our car. I glance back at the others and imagine what she's seeing. A motley collection of twenty-somethings cheerfully crammed into a bright red Mini at half seven in the morning on a bank holiday Sunday.

She has no idea. If one could harness secrets for energy, we wouldn't need petrol – we'd have enough grudges in this car to take us all the way to Scotland.

THEN

Addie

I stare at the ceiling. The caretaker's flat in Cherry's villa is underneath the house – same size as the first floor, just at basement level. Beautiful, if you don't mind not having any windows. When it means living in the south of France all summer for free board and a few hundred euros a month, I don't mind not having windows at all.

A family arrived this morning, friends of Cherry's parents. They got a cab from the airport, which is lucky because last night me and Deb drank three bottles of wine on the balcony of the master suite and stargazed until the sky got light. I'm probably still not legal to drive and it's basically midday already.

I'm pretty sure this is the summer of my life. It's like . . . there's an epic backing track playing, or the saturation's turned up. This summer I'm not little Addie, trailing behind. I'm not the person you forget when you're telling your mates who's at the pub. I'm not the girl you ghost because you've met someone better. I can be whoever I want to be.

This is my summer, basically. Not that you'd know it right now, because I'm too hungover to move much.

I frown up at the ceiling. Something's up with this new family.

The caretaker's flat isn't soundproofed – we always have a pretty good idea of exactly what's going on up there. More than we'd like, generally. But now I can hardly hear anything. They're definitely here – the cab woke me when it pulled up earlier. And there's movement. Just . . . quiet movement. Like, one person's worth of movement.

One set of steps making its way across the kitchen to the wine cooler and back again. One shower running. One window left open so that a bedroom door slams when the mistral blows through.

I wake Deb at quarter to two in the afternoon. She shuffles into the kitchen in sagging knickers and a French band T-shirt she picked up on a one-night stand in Avignon, then pauses, listening.

'Where are they all?' she asks.

'No idea. I'm pretty sure there's just one guy here.'

She yawns and takes the mug of coffee I hold out for her. 'Huh. Weird. Maybe this guy killed all his family on the journey over.'

We can always tell if it's a man or a woman from their footfall. Men are stompier.

'That's your first thought?' I say.

Deb shrugs and begins sawing at yesterday's bread. A spattering of crust fragments go flying like chippings in a wood shop.

'What else have you got?'

'Maybe they're all coming later,' I say. 'Maybe they stopped off in Nice to see some pals, yah.'

This is one of those summer things that won't be funny next year, but cracks me and Deb up right now. Ever since we got here we've collected the phrases we hear through the ceiling or drifting over from the terrace: *pals*, *décor*, *blotto*, *divine*. I've never met people like the Villa Cerise guests before. They don't ask the price of stuff before they buy it. They drink champagne like it isn't even a thing. They own multiple houses and animals and have opinions about literally everything. It's almost too easy to mock them.

'Cherry's mum would've texted if they were coming late,' Deb points out.

I pull a face, like, *Oh yeah, true*. Deb spreads butter on to her bread, laying it on as thick as a slice of cheese.

'I don't think he's old, you know,' I say. 'He walks too fast.'

Deb's eyebrows go up. 'Maybe he's staff?'

This is another new phrase we've learned. *Staff* as a job title.

Our mysterious solo guest moves into the kitchen, directly above our heads. We pause, me with a glass of orange juice halfway to my mouth, Deb with butter on her nose.

The fridge upstairs opens. Something clinks. The fridge closes.

'A day drinker,' Deb says. She pauses in thought. 'If there's only one guy here all week, do we really both need to be here?'

'Are you ditching me again?'

Deb looks at me, frowning, trying to guess if I really mind. I'm not sure, to be honest. It was always the plan that while we were here, we'd each go off to explore France when we could. As it's happened, though, Deb's gone adventuring more than me. I do get it: she's more easily bored than I am. And I love this villa – the infinity pool, the vineyards, the way the air smells first thing in the morning. Deb's not sentimental like that. It's just a house to her, albeit a big one.

Sometimes I like the extra space when she's gone. But I also kind of hate being the one who's left behind.

'There's a guy outside Nîmes with an empty house. Kind of a commune thing,' Deb says. 'But like, a party commune. Not the nun kind. Do you not want me to go?'

She's never really got the concept of half-feelings, Deb. I turn away, irritated, and shoot 'Of course you should go' over my shoulder as I stare vaguely at the contents of the fridge.

'If you need me here, you know I'll stay,' she says.

I glance back at her. Her expression is totally open. It's impossible to stay irritated with Deb. She's just got someplace else she wants to be, and in her head, why would that affect me unless I needed her here?

'No, you go,' I say, closing the fridge. 'Find yourself a sexy French hippy.'

We pause again. Upstairs our solo guest has walked out of the kitchen and on to the terrace. He's speaking. Muttering. I can't quite catch the words.

'Is he talking to himself?' Deb asks, tilting her head. 'Maybe a madman's found his way in. Maybe we've got a squatter.'

I move closer to the door to our flat and crack it open. The villa's built on a hill – our door is tucked away to the right of the building, hidden from view under the walkway that leads from the kitchen to the raised terrace with its infinity pool.

Through the gap in the door, I can see the guest's lower half passing the balustrades around the terrace. He's wearing stone-coloured shorts and no shoes. A half-drunk bottle of beer taps against his thigh as he paces. His legs are tanned pale brown. He doesn't look like a squatter.

'What—'

I shush Deb and try to listen. He's reciting something.

'Upon a great adventure he was bound, that greatest Gloriana to him gave . . .'

'Is he reading out some Shakespeare or something?' Deb asks in my ear. She shoves me aside and opens the door wider.

'Deb, careful,' I hiss. Caretakers aren't meant to spy on guests. This job is the best summer gig I could have imagined. Every so often I'm hit with a pang of fear that one of us will screw up so badly someone'll notice and call Cherry's parents.

'To win him worship, and her grace to have, which of all earthly things he most did crave, and ever as he – even as he . . . Fuck.' The man stops and lifts his beer. 'Fucking shitting fuckity shit.'

He's posh – he sounds like Hugh Grant. Deb covers her mouth

to stifle her laugh. The man stills. I breathe in sharply and pull her back from the doorway.

'Come on.' I drag her back through to the living room. 'Let's not piss him off on day one, whoever he is.'

'I think he's fit,' Deb decides, flopping down on the sofa. Like most of the furniture in the flat, it lived in the main house once, then got downgraded when Cherry's mum fancied giving the place a new look. It's dark pink velvet and has a massive red wine stain on the right arm – nothing to do with us, thank God.

'You got that from his feet?'

Deb nods. 'You can tell a lot from feet.'

This is the sort of Deb comment I've learned to just skim over, because you get into a whole world of weird if you start asking questions.

'You going to stick around then? Now you've seen his sexy ankles?'

Deb pauses in thought, then shakes her head. 'I can get posh boys in chino shorts back home,' she says. 'I fancy myself a long-haired French hippy.'

'You think you'll ever get bored of it?' I ask her, hugging a cushion to my chest.

'Bored of what?'

'You know – only ever having flings.'

Deb stretches her legs out on the sofa. Her toenail varnish is chipped and there's a bruise on each of her long brown shins. Deb inherited her dad's skin tone – her grandfather on that side was Ghanaian – while I got the pasty white skin of mine. I find it irritating when people say we're *half-sisters*. Deb's my soul sister, my other half, the only person who understands me. I'm her anchor, the one she always comes back to. There's nothing half about us.

When we were growing up, I always hated it when Deb's father visited. He'd take her off somewhere, just the two of them, a trip to the park or the bus into town. Dad would look pinched and sad until Deb came home and wanted to build model trains with him and he'd light up again. As awful as it sounds, I was glad when Deb's father argued with Mum and, eventually, when I was about eight, he stopped coming altogether. In classic Deb style, she's written her biological dad out now. Deb doesn't really do second chances.

'Why would I get bored?' she says. 'I have endless variety.'

'But don't you want to settle down one day?'

'Settle what down? What is there that needs settling? I know who I am and what I want. I don't need some guy to make me complete, or whatever it is they're meant to do.'

'But what about kids? Don't you want them?'

'Nope.' She scratches her stomach and lifts her head to stare at the ceiling. 'That's one thing I know for sure. No babies. Not ever.'

I wave Deb off as she heads to Nîmes in her dodgy banged-up rental car – I only know she's going because I hear the car engine starting. Deb doesn't really do goodbyes. She hates hugs, which has put her off the whole goodbye thing, since people always seem to expect them. Ever since we were kids, she and I have said goodbye on text, after the fact. I kind of like it – we hardly ever text the rest of the time, especially now everyone uses WhatsApp, so our text conversation is always a string of nice notes.

Bye, love you, call me if you need me, my message to her reads.

Ditto, kiddo, says hers. *You need me, I'm there.*

Usually me and Deb introduce ourselves to a guest as soon as they arrive, but this time I decide to wait until the evening, once she's gone. No need to confuse matters by giving the impression of two caretakers when one of them doesn't plan on sticking around.

I make my way up the servant's entrance to the villa. There's a cramped spiral staircase that leads from our flat to a small hallway just outside the villa's kitchen. The door between kitchen and stairway is locked from our side, but I knock loudly anyway. I've been burned before, just walking in: I caught a beer-bellied Scottish guest helping himself to some crackers in the nude.

'Hello?' I call through the door. 'Mr Abbott?'

No answer. I unlock the door and step through gingerly. Nobody here. The kitchen's a tip: baguette ends, empty bottles, rinds of cheese, a whole slab of butter sweating in the evening sun. I tut, then stop myself, because tutting is exactly what my mother would do.

I gnaw at one of the baguette ends as I tidy. Whoever this guy is, he's used to someone else clearing up after him. And he's drunk, judging by the number of bottles. I swallow the last of the bread and pause in the middle of the floor. It's quiet except for the constant static of the crickets outside. I'm not used to quiet up here in the house. Sometimes a family go out for the day, but they're usually around in the evenings, and most of the time I have Deb with me anyway.

I'm a little spooked. Just me and a strange drunk man in the house. I count bottles. Five beers, a half-drunk bottle of wine.

I check the kitchen once more, poke my head out to see the terrace, then wander through into the villa's grand entrance hall.

'Hello?' I call, more quietly this time.

It's cooler here, with the big double doors closed tight, blocking out the sun's heat. There's a jacket pooled at the bottom of the stairs. I hang it back on the bannister. It's soft denim lined with fleece – it must have been cold wherever he flew in from. You'd roast wearing it here. As I hang it up I catch its scent: orange-ish, woody, manly.

'Mr Abbott?'

Through to the reception room, the dining hall, the ballroom, the living room. They're exactly as we left them when we prepared the villa for new guests. He's upstairs, then. We never go upstairs when guests are here, unless they ask us up to sort a blocked drain or whatever. Bedrooms are their private space.

I'm kind of relieved. I retreat back to the servant's staircase and lock the door behind me. The flat's just as it always is: cosy, cluttered, zero natural light. I sink into the pink velvet sofa and flick on the telly. Some French drama, too fast-paced for me to follow, but really I just want the noise. Maybe I should have asked Deb to stay. I hate this lost feeling I get when I'm left on my own. I turn the TV up.

I'll try meeting Mr Abbott again tomorrow. Not too early, though. He'll need to sleep off that hangover.

He wakes me the next day with the slam of his shutters. He can't get the hang of fixing them back, apparently. I snort, pulling the covers over my head. The mistral's strong – he'll smash a pane if he keeps letting everything slam in the wind like that.

He's talking to himself in the kitchen. I can't quite catch the words through the ceiling, but I can tell from the up-and-down of his voice that he's reciting something.

I check my phone. It's eight in the morning – too early for me to go up and introduce myself. The strange lost feeling that gripped me last night has gone, and I'm glad of the extra space in the double bed. Deb's such an irritating person to share a bed with. The other night she started sleep-talking about Tory politicians.

I lie back and listen to our solo guest rattling about the house. I wonder what he looks like. I've not got much to go on – the waist down, basically, and the voice. I'm guessing dark curls and brown eyes; stubble, maybe; a loose-collared shirt. An heirloom on a chain around his neck.

He sings a few lines of something – a pop song I half remember. I grin up at the ceiling. He's *totally* tuneless.

By the time I get out of bed it's half nine and he's on the terrace with his coffee. I heard the machine whirring away and his footfall on the walkway outside before I mustered the energy to roll out from under the covers. I overthink my outfit – shorts, skirt, dress? In the end, irritated with myself, I grab a tank top and yesterday's shorts off the floor and yank them on, pulling my hair up into a bun and tying it there with one of my bracelets.

Mr Abbott's nowhere to be seen when I get to the terrace. No coffee mug, so wherever he's wandered off to, he's taken it with him. I scan the dry, dusty lawns and flowerbeds that Victor the gardener sweats over every Thursday, but there's nobody in sight in the villa grounds. Maybe I misheard? I head to the kitchen, tugging my hair out of the bun again.

It's tidier today. There's a note.

Hello, phantom caretaker. Ever so sorry about the mess last night, I got rather carried away. Off out to explore now, but perhaps you could look at the shutters in my bedroom while I'm out. I can't fathom how you're supposed to stop them slamming shut incessantly. The noise is driving me mad.

Dylan Abbott

The noise is driving *him* mad, is it? I roll my eyes and screw up the note, shoving it in my back pocket. There's no trick to the bloody shutters. If he looked at them for ten seconds he'd figure out where they latch to the wall to stay open. All the same, I head up to his bedroom to check. I know which one he's in. I'm pretty good at telling which doors are opening and closing, now. Bathrooms three and four are tricky, and I sometimes get the eighth and sixth bedrooms muddled up, but the rest I've nailed.

He's chosen the best room in the house, the suite where Deb and I stargazed on the balcony the day before yesterday. It has a four-poster bed lined with heavy blue damask and enormous windows that look out over the vines. The bed's unmade and his clothes are tangled at the door to the bathroom, as if he stepped out of them before heading for the shower. The room smells the same as the jacket did: orangey, musky, male.

I open a window. The shutters are fine, obviously, no surprise there. I pin them back for him and consider writing a reply to his note, but what am I meant to say? Look at the shutters, and do that, next time? I imagine myself doing it, signing it off *the phantom caretaker*, but no. Summer Addie isn't *phantom* anything. Instead, on a whim, I breathe a cloud on the window and sign my name there in the fog. *Adeline*. No kiss.

He doesn't come back for so long I risk a swim in the meantime – Cherry's mum says we can if the guests aren't around. I'm back in the flat and wringing out my hair in the sink when there's a knock on the door.

I look down at myself. *Eep*. Wet bikini, that's it. I rush through to the bedroom and scrabble around in the wardrobe, which is pointless, because all the good clothes are on the floor or in the wash. Another knock. Shit. I grab a crumpled ball of orange fabric – a swing dress, no obvious stains, it'll do – and pull it on as I dash back to the door.

I open it, and there he is. The man upstairs. I'd imagined him all wrong. His eyes are the first thing I notice: they're pale green, almost yellow, kind of sleepy-looking. His lashes are way longer than you'd usually see on a guy, and his hair is floppy and sun-kissed brown. The only thing I got right was the shirt: it's pale cheesecloth, crumpled and unbuttoned way too far down.

No heirloom around the neck, but a gold signet ring on his little finger. Behind him I can see the trail of my wet footprints, leading from the pool to the front door of the flat.

'Oh,' he says, double taking with a flick of his hair. 'Hullo.'

'Hi.' I swallow the *Mr Abbott* at the end of the sentence. It feels weird to call a guy my own age *mister*. My wet hair drips down my back, and I'm grateful for it cooling me down – I'm flustered. All that dashing around.

He gives a slow, small smile. 'I had you down as a wrinkled old man, phantom caretaker.'

I laugh. 'Why?'

He shrugs. The flustered feeling isn't easing – I think it's him, maybe, the green eyes, the unbuttoned shirt.

'Caretaker. It just sounds . . . wrinkly.'

'Well, you're not what I expected either.' I stand a little straighter. '"The Abbott family". It just sounds . . . oh, I don't know . . . like more than one person?'

He pulls a face. 'Yes. That. The rest of them bailed, I'm afraid, so you've just got me. Thank you for fixing my shutters, by the way. You're a miracle worker.'

'They just . . .' I trail off. 'You're welcome.'

We look at one another. I'm very aware of myself: how I'm holding my shoulders, the wet bikini soaking through my dress. He's watching me steadily. A slow, confident stare, the sort that snares you across a bar as you wait for a drink. It's a little bit too practised, a little too deliberate. Like he's seen someone else do it but never actually given it a go himself.

'What can I help you with?'

I adjust my dress. It clings to my bikini.

'Well. For starters, I lost my key.'

That slow stare shifts for a moment, turning boyish. Much better. He's cute, in a scruffy, hapless kind of way. Like a Yorkshire Terrier puppy. Or a member of an X Factor boy band before they've made it big.

'I can't be trusted with keys,' he says.

'I can sort that, sure.'

'Thank you. You're very kind. And . . .' He pauses, looking at me, as if making his mind up. 'I'm looking for someone,' he says.

'You're . . . what do you mean?'

'I'm trying to find somebody, and I think you might be able to help?'

I tilt my head, curious. My pulse flutters a bit faster. Maybe he's *very* cute, actually. His eyes flicker to the wet patches on my dress, and then up to my face again. All very quick, like he didn't mean to look and he's worried I've noticed. I press my lips together to hide a smile. I wonder if he's smoother when he's sober or if he's always like this.

'Do you have a car?' he says.

I nod.

'Do you think you could drive me somewhere?'

Dylan

She's like a water sprite, with her dark, wet hair and her river-blue eyes. Finding her here in this little flat, buried underneath the house . . . It's as if I've *unearthed* her, as if she's been waiting for me and at last I've come to free her from her windowless existence.

It's possible I've drunk a little too much. I hope she can't tell. I'm trying to do the good kind of staring, not the leering kind, but I've had three quarters of a bottle of wine while reading Philip Sidney's *Astrophil and Stella* in the hills above the villa with lunch, and I have to confess I don't entirely trust my judgement.

As I climb into the passenger seat of the blue-eyed caretaker's rental car, I try to sober up and listen to what she's saying – something about the shutters – but my mind is busy stuttering over a new idea, something about *quick little hands with bitten-down nails.*

As we pull out of the villa's gates, I cast another look at her profile: a delicate, turned-up nose, a hint of freckles on her cheekbones like fine droplets of water on sand. There's a quickening in my stomach, half fear, half excitement, or maybe just desire. I knew this summer was going to be magnificent, and here, now, with the wind tearing in my ears and the sun's heat pressed to my cheek, with a dark-haired beauty beside me, her pale thighs bare against the leather seat, her—

'You're going to break the fridge door, by the way,' she says.

I startle. 'Hmm?'

'The fridge door. You keep yanking it from the bottom of the handle. Try pulling from the top, would you – otherwise Deb and I will have to sort someone to fix it and all the tradesmen around here think we're morons. We'll end up having to try and do it ourselves.'

I deflate a bit.

'How can you tell?' I ask, rallying. 'Have you been watching me, little phantom caretaker?'

She looks at me, her blue eyes sharp. She has a mole on the top of her lip, just left of where her Cupid's bow mouth rises in soft peaks.

'Don't call me little. It's patronising.'

I waver. The feeling of grandeur, of magnificence, it slips. Am I playing this all wrong? She *is* little, in my defence: fine-boned and fragile, her collarbone pressing against her skin like a root, her wrists so narrow I could circle them both with one hand. She turns back to the road, smiling slightly; I think she saw me waver.

'And I wasn't watching you,' she continues. 'Just listening. All the pots on the top of the fridge rattle when you yank it that way.'

'Listening?' Hmm. I have spent much of the last two days loudly reciting lines from *The Faerie Queene* – my primary inspiration for the poetry collection I'm working on, a sort of homage to Spenser. And yesterday I sang the whole of Taylor Swift's '22' to myself on the terrace with a bottle of wine as a microphone.

'You have a lovely singing voice,' she says, biting her bottom lip. I watch her white teeth pull at the soft pink skin and for a hot, bold second I imagine those teeth digging into my bare shoulder.

'Really?'

She glances at me incredulously. 'No. Of course not. You're rubbish. You can't possibly not know that?'

I swallow again. Rallying is getting somewhat harder. 'You're a little rude; did anyone ever tell you that, phantom caretaker?'

'My name is Addie,' she said. 'And I'm not rude. I'm . . . blunt. It's charming.'

She says it as if she's just figuring it out herself, then flashes me a smile that zips right through me. The line of poetry I'd been playing with is lost as my mind sharpens in on the curve of her lip, the way that dress clings to her breasts. The unsettling way she keeps setting me back. I'm reassessing: she's like a water sprite, yes, but a fierce little one with teeth and claws, half sweetness, half wild. Marcus would love her.

It's odd being here without Marcus. He and I have been travelling together all summer – I'd intended to take three weeks out from our trip for a family holiday here at Cherry's villa, but my relatives all cancelled after a classic rerun of an Abbott family favourite, the perennial 'everyone is a disappointment' dispute. This old gem invariably ends with my father screaming spittle and invectives at us all, and my brother and I promptly spending reckless amounts of cash to spite him. This year I have gone easy on him: I've merely robbed him of the opportunity to get his money back by attending this holiday solo.

Mum is still leaving me voicemails three times a day. They're all the same: *Dylan, my darling, your father is very sorry, please do call us back.*

Funny how my father never phones me himself, given how terribly sorry he is.

My long summer in Europe was his idea. Like the classic English gentleman, I should go and sow my wild oats on the Continent before returning to the duties of real life. I have resolutely rejected this idea all summer, of course – I'm here looking for Grace.

But Grace is proving very hard to find. And here's Addie, tiny and beautiful, living fairylike beneath my feet.

'So who was it who saw your friend in La Roque-Alric?' Addie asks, as we wind our way through the vineyards. There's nobody on the road but the two of us, and even through the wind you can hear the crickets rattling out their strange song from the dry undergrowth bordering the tarmac.

'Just a friend of a friend.' I wave an arm vaguely. The truth is, the lead came from Instagram-stalking people who had liked Grace's last post; I'd rather not share this with Addie. I'm sobering up a little – perhaps it's the fresh mountain air – and without the edge of the wine, I'm beginning to feel somewhat out of my league here. Addie is sharp and self-possessed and has really quite phenomenal legs and I don't think I put any product in my hair this morning. I surreptitiously check – no, nothing, *damn*.

'Is she missing, or what?' Addie asks.

I think for a moment. 'She's whimsical,' I say eventually. 'She likes to keep people guessing.'

Addie raises her eyebrows. 'She sounds tedious.'

I frown. 'She's wonderful.'

'If you say so.'

Grace was with Marcus for most of third year, though neither of them ever gave their relationship any sort of label. She'd flirted with me outrageously after a tutors' dinner in Trinity term, and Marcus had laughed. *Why not?* he'd said, when Grace had climbed into my lap and I'd looked at him, drunk, a little lost. *We share everything else.* So Grace and I became . . . whatever-we-were just before the summer, and then she disappeared. *Off to travel, boys*, her note had read. *Come catch me. G*

It was exciting for a while, and it's given a shape to mine and Marcus's aimless wanderings around Europe, but we still haven't found her, and the clues she's been leaving us – odd texts, late-night voicemails, messages passed on by youth-hostel owners – are becoming briefer and fewer. I've been getting rather worried about her losing interest in the both of us and the trail running cold;

once that happens, I'll have no choice but to answer the question of what the hell I'm doing with my life, a question I am at great pains to avoid.

Ahead of us, the road winds its way up the hillside into dark woodland, then opens out again to reveal parched, chalky fields scored with vines. I don't mean to be critical but Addie is driving *far* too slowly – these tailback roads are meant for speeding on, but she's crawling up the hill and braking for every corner like an old lady in a Škoda.

'You strike me as a man who gets driven more than he drives,' Addie says. 'But I can *feel* you back-seat driving.'

'My *father* gets driven,' I say. 'I drive.'

'Well, look at you.' Addie laughs. 'Aren't you just a regular guy!'

I frown, irritated – with her, for a second, and then with myself – but before I can think of a suitable response we round a bend and above us is a village cut into the rockface, so beautiful it distracts me altogether. The rough stone of the cliff is dotted with houses in the same shade of pale, sandy yellow, their higgledy roofs slanting this way and that between cypress and olive trees. A castle sits atop the hill, the slitted windows of its turret turned our way like narrowed eyes.

I whistle between my teeth. 'This place belongs in a fairy tale.'

'It's my sister's least favourite place around here,' Addie says. 'She hates heights.'

'You have a rather negative outlook on the world,' I tell her, as we wind our way up towards the village. Fields of olive trees give way to dense hedges and stone walls cut into the side of the hill, with scrubby bleached grass clinging doggedly to the crevices.

Addie looks surprised. 'Me?'

'The fairy-tale castle is too high up, my whimsical friend is tedious, my singing voice is not to your liking . . .'

She pauses and purses her lips in thought. That mole shifts. Suddenly looking at her lips is too much for me: I'm gone, thinking about kissing her, thinking about her mouth against my skin. She catches my eye and her gaze seems somehow molten.

I swallow. She turns back to the road, shifting into a passing place as a rattling open-backed truck comes barrelling down the hill.

'I don't think of myself as negative. Practical, maybe.'

I make a face accidentally – still tipsy, then – and she catches it and laughs.

'What?'

'Just . . . ah. Practical. It's the sort of thing you say about someone matronly and stout. An aunt with a knack for darning socks.'

'Oh, *thanks*,' Addie says dryly, pulling her sunglasses down from the top of her head as the road twists again, bringing us head-on with the low, fierce sun.

'It was you who said practical,' I point out. 'I'd call you . . . feisty.'

'Not if you didn't want booting out of the car, you wouldn't.'

'No?'

I admit, I knew that would get a rise out of her.

'How about bolshy? Sassy?'

She cottons on and a smile tugs at the corner of her lips. 'You're trying to wind me up, aren't you?'

She likes to be teased, then. I file that away.

'I'm showing you how enlightened I am. After making the mistake with *little*.'

'And the judging of my driving.'

'And that.'

I'm getting somewhere – her tone has warmed. We're in the village now, and between the houses the view is breathtaking: distant, hazy blue hills behind tumbling fields of olive trees and grapevines. There's something mythic about it all. It feels like a setting, rather than a place, as if stories are meant to be made here, and the sense of grandeur resettles on my shoulders as I breathe in the husky scent of olive trees on the air.

Addie parallel parks outside a little café. It has plastic tables underneath a bamboo awning; a group of Frenchmen sitting by the door watch us with mild interest as we make our way inside.

I ask the woman behind the till whether she's seen a tall, hippy-ish young woman with pink hair down to her waist, gold piercings in her nose and a tattoo of an English rose on her shoulder. No, the woman says, so I try purple hair, or blue – Grace goes through hair dye the way Marcus goes through pretty first-year girls who've yet to be informed of his terrible reputation.

Oh, yes, the one with blue hair – she was here a week or so ago with a man, the woman at the till tells me. An older man with a big belly and a pocket watch. She sat in his lap and fed him cubes of Gruyère. No, she didn't leave a message.

I narrow my eyes. As much as I'd like to say this doesn't sound like Grace, there's really nothing that sounds *unlike* Grace – she is wholly unpredictable. That's what Marcus likes about her, I think.

'Your French is good,' Addie says as we make our way to one of the outside tables with an Orangina each.

'It gets me through. How's yours?' I'm suddenly wondering how much of that exchange she followed.

'Oh, pretty crap, really. But I understand enough to know she said there was a bloke with your friend,' Addie says, looking sidelong at me. She stretches her legs out; I can feel the Frenchmen glancing her way, their eyes following her movement. 'Does that bother you?'

'Not especially, no.' I run a hand through my horribly unstyled hair and try not to stare at Addie's legs.

She quirks her eyebrow at me, that teasing smile returning. 'Seems like you're making an awful lot of effort for a woman who can't even be arsed to send you a postcard.'

'It's not like that with Grace,' I say, because I don't want her seeing me that way, like a man chasing after a woman who doesn't want to be found.

Addie takes that in with a tilt of her head. 'How come your family aren't here, then?' she asks. I wonder if she's nervous. If she is, she hides it very well; her delicate, elfin features are hard to read, smoothed out like a fresh page in a notebook.

'Familial dispute. Nothing special.'

'Where are the rest of them? At home? They've just skipped out on three weeks at Villa Cerise?' She pauses as I shrug *yes*, and her eyes widen. 'Who *does* that? The place is amazing.'

It is. I feel rather proud of myself for coming, now, and I say something vague about appreciating the privilege which makes Addie's eyes soften. Her gaze holds mine for a moment too long; my pulse beats hot under my skin.

'How have you been entertaining yourself, then, while you've been here?' I ask.

She gives me a shrewd look that says she knows what the question really means.

'Sex with guests,' she deadpans. 'Non-stop, really. Shagging all over the place.'

I watch her sip her Orangina through a straw. Just hearing her say *shagging* is embarrassingly titillating. I want her. I haven't had sex for two months, and suddenly I can't fathom doing anything else; I feel almost faint with the desire to lean forward and kiss her.

'Really?'

'No, obviously not. That would be disgustingly unprofessional.'

Oh, right. I pull up short, eyes flicking away from her lips.

She laughs. 'I'm just messing with you.'

Now I'm thoroughly bewildered. Has she been shagging all over the place or not? Is sleeping with guests off the cards? God, I hope not. If it is, maybe I can just move to a nearby hotel, though that would look a little . . . desperate.

Addie's eyes are mischievous; I sip my drink and try to collect my thoughts.

'Most of the guests are – what would you say? – *wrinkly.* Dads and granddads and rich guys with hot girlfriends permanently attached to their arms.'

'Ah?' I manage. 'So . . .'

'So I've spent the last two months doing my job.'

'Right. Of course.'

'And getting wasted on the wine they leave behind. And tanning. And stargazing on my back in that insane infinity pool.'

I think this means I'm all right to look at her legs again.

She watches my gaze shift over her and her lip quirks. 'Penny for your thoughts?'

My heart beats faster. 'They're . . . not suitable for public discussion.'

'No?' Her eyebrows lift; that smile grows, and my nerves settle a little. She shifts so her bare foot touches my leg – she's kicked off her sandals under the table. 'Maybe we should find somewhere more private, then.'

'How long is the drive back to the villa?' I ask. It comes out rather more quickly than I intended.

She slides the car keys across the table. 'Depends who's driving, I'd say.'

'I bet you a hundred euros I can knock fifteen minutes off your time here.'

Her eyes widen. 'Done,' she says. 'But be warned. I'm not beneath dirty tactics.'

My imagination goes haywire. I take the straw out of my drink and down the rest in one while Addie laughs. I know what this beautiful village is for, now: it was built all those hundreds of years ago for this moment, the moment when Addie slips her sandals on and walks ahead of me to the car, hips swaying with promise.

I defy anyone to drive better than me in these conditions.

Addie slips her dress down one shoulder, then the other. I would say my eyes are on the road approximately twenty per cent of the time, and I've just remembered about all the wine I drank at lunch-time, but – oh, no, I've forgotten about it again because Addie has dropped her dress to her waist and I'm *fixated* at the sight of all that creamy pale skin. Her bikini is dark orange, two minuscule triangles, a few strings tied at the back of her neck, and her eyes are wicked and wide, mouth open in a laughing smile.

My throat is extremely dry; for a fleeting moment I wish Marcus could see this, a girl stripping in the passenger seat as I speed down a narrow French road with the sun in my eyes, then she touches my leg and I forget Marcus altogether. I am driving extremely dangerously, but quite frankly this would be the best possible way to go.

By the time we pull into the entrance to Villa Cerise I am so turned on I'm shaking. I turn to Addie and meet the heat of her gaze square-on, and there's that teasing edge there, like a challenge, but there's a little vulnerability too. Her creamy skin has goosebumped in the cool breeze of the air con; I can see her nipples beneath the thin fabric of her bikini top. My breath is coming fast. I hardly know where to start. Her eyes move to my lips – then, at a sound outside the car, she glances to the window.

I'm just mustering the courage to place a hand on the bare skin of her thigh when she says,

'That's not Deb's car.'

I pause with my hand over the gearstick and follow her gaze to the rental car now parked under the plane trees outside the villa. I stare at it blankly. It's not registering. Car, yes, I see that, but why could it *possibly* matter more than kissing Addie right this very moment?

'Are you expecting someone?' she asks.

I let out an involuntary little moan of despair as she reaches to pull her dress back up, then try to disguise it as a manly clearing of the throat.

'Uh, no.' Reluctantly I return my gaze to the other car and try to slow my breathing. Is it – my stomach drops, blood pounding – but no, it's not my father. I recognise the jacket slung over the back of the bench at the front of the house, facing out towards the fountains and the valley beyond. It's brown leather, Gucci, and my uncle Terence has worn it almost every day for all twenty-two years of my life.

'For fuck's sake.' I kill the engine and press my forehead against the steering wheel.

'What?'

'Uncle Terry.'

'Your *uncle* is here?'

'He was supposed to come. Before the familial dispute.'

I straighten up, close my eyes for a moment, and then open the car door.

'Dylan, my boy!' roars a voice from the terrace. 'I was beginning to think you'd absconded! O-ho, who's this beautiful young lady? Where did you find *her*?'

Well, that's done the trick. There is no greater turn-off in this world than my uncle Terence.

'Hello, Terry,' I say wearily. 'This is Addie. She works at Villa Cerise.'

'Hi,' Addie says, waving up at Terry. 'Anything I can get you, sir?'

I look askance at her. She's wearing a new expression, a strange, plastic smile. This is her speaking-to-clients face – I'm pleased to see how different it is from the slow, wicked grin she gave me within moments of us meeting.

'Dinner! Do you do dinner?' Terry asks.

I cringe. 'Addie isn't . . .'

'Absolutely,' Addie says smoothly. She adjusts her dress a little higher at the neck. 'I can request a chef for you – there are some fantastic local ones, I'll fetch you the list.'

I watch her go. Her hips aren't swaying now. I am *desperate* with longing.

'Pretty, that one,' Terry calls down to me. 'But I expect you're still smitten with the blonde from Atlanta?'

I cringe again as Addie pauses in the doorway to the kitchen for a moment, one hand on the stone wall. Terry is out of date in all senses – that jacket of his hasn't looked good since the nineties, and Michele from Atlanta hasn't been on the scene since Michaelmas term of third year, for Christ's sake.

'What are you doing here, Uncle Terry?'

'I heard on the grapevine that you'd decided to go ahead with the family holiday!' He grins down at me. 'Three weeks of sun and wine with my favourite nephew? And none of the rest of the rabble? How could I pass that up? Come on up here, boy, let's open a bottle to celebrate.'

I drag my feet up the steps and across to the terrace. The pool lies at one edge, glinting pale blue; beyond the water, the vineyards look hyper-real under the sun's glare.

Terry slaps me on the back. His receding hairline has retreated so far now that he just sports a small patch above the forehead and one of those around-the-ears styles that monks used to favour in medieval times.

'Good to see you, Dylan.'

I grit my teeth. 'You too, Terry.'

My family. They're like a bad cold I can't shake, a dreadful pop song I can't stop singing. How do I get rid of them?

And, more immediately: how do I get rid of Uncle Terry?

NOW

Addie

The sun's properly up now, starbursting on the windscreen, making me squint even with my sunglasses on. The road ahead looks kind of dusty through it, like everything needs a wipe.

Dylan hasn't said a word for over half an hour. We are three hundred miles away from Ettrick and having him in this car is making it hard to breathe. He still wears the same aftershave. Light and woody, a hint of orange.

'I'm actually a very modern man, thank you very much,' Marcus is telling Deb. She just called him a caveman. He said something sexist that I didn't catch, which is probably for the best.

'Oh, yes?'

'You know what I did the other day?'

'What?'

'I *moisturised.*'

I have to bite back a smile. I forgot this about Marcus. How charming he is, when he wants to be.

'And do you know what Dylan's talked me into?'

'What has Dylan talked you into?' Rodney says, when Deb doesn't answer. She's on her phone – that'll be annoying Marcus. He likes undivided attention.

'He's got me going to his *therapist*,' Marcus says, in a scandalised whisper.

I blink, processing. Marcus is in therapy? *Dylan's* in therapy? That's so weird. Like one of them taking up knitting or something. I bet their therapist is having a field day with these boys, though. Years of material.

'How have you found therapy?' I ask Dylan, trying to keep my voice light.

I look at him for just long enough to catch the bob of his Adam's apple as he swallows. 'Good, thanks,' he says.

Right. Well then. We drive on in silence for a while. I'm dying to ask why he went. When did he start? Was it because of me? But that's *so* self-absorbed.

'I realised I was a little, uh . . . That some of the relationships in my life weren't entirely healthy.' He swallows again.

Everyone in the back of the car is very, very quiet.

'I thought I could do with some help sorting that. You know. From a professional.'

My cheeks are hot again. That'll teach me for being self-absorbed.

'Let's play a game,' says Marcus. 'I'm bored.'

'Only boring people get bored,' Deb says.

'Only boring people say *that*,' Marcus corrects her. 'Five questions. I'll go first. Ask me anything. Go on.'

'What's the worst thing you've ever done?' Deb asks promptly.

Marcus snorts. 'Which particular social construct would you like me to measure "worst" by? I don't really subscribe to a standard system of morality.'

'How very exciting of you,' Deb says flatly.

Marcus looks put out. 'I caught and cooked one of our neighbour's pet ducks, once,' he says after a moment. 'Will that do?'

There is a collective gasp.

'That's – that's awful!' exclaims Rodney. 'Why?'

Marcus shrugs. 'No food in, shops were closed.'

'You *ate* it?' Rodney says, and I can hear him shrinking back into his seat.

'With hoisin sauce. Next question?'

'Have you ever been in love?' Deb asks. 'Or does that not fit into your non-standard system of morality?'

The silence stretches too tight. I don't look at Dylan.

'I fall in love a hundred times a month, darling,' Marcus says lightly.

The next song is playing: Taylor Swift, 'I Did Something Bad'.

'Nobody falls in love a hundred times,' I say, before I can stop myself. 'You couldn't. It would kill you.'

Marcus snorts so quietly I almost don't catch it. I feel myself flush.

'The only time I've ever fallen in love was when the midwife handed me my son,' Deb says.

I shoot her a grateful look for the change of subject. I can feel Marcus's gaze on the back of my neck. He'd look away if I met his eyes in the mirror, I know he would, but I don't quite have the nerve.

'He's the only man I've ever met who's struck me as worth the effort, frankly,' Deb continues, with a quick smile for me. 'Next question for Marcus?'

'What's the nicest thing you've ever done for someone else?' Rodney asks.

We all look at him, surprised.

'Is that OK?' he asks, cringing.

'Christ, man, you're a walking apology, aren't you?' Marcus says.

'What – I . . .'

'He's polite, Marcus,' I say. 'It's a good thing. Most people appreciate it.'

Marcus waggles his eyebrows and I catch something in his expression in the mirror. A challenge, maybe.

'Ooh. Dylan, watch out. You've got some competition,' he says.

'Shut up, Marcus,' I snap. 'You know it's not like that.'

'Come on, guys,' Dylan says, reaching to turn the radio up. 'Leave it, please.'

'Not like that?' Marcus says. 'Well. Heard that before, haven't we?'

The anger rises all at once and I feel my cheeks flare red. I hate him. I hate him, I hate him, and God, I'm *still* not brave enough to tell him to fuck right off like I want to.

'Marcus.' Dylan's voice turns sharp. 'Don't say something you're going to regret.'

The car feels like it's shrinking, its grimy windows leaning in.

'What I'll regret is sitting here while you pine for her all over again and I say nothing. That woman broke you, Dylan. I thought you'd realised that now. You'd be better off jumping out of this car into the fast lane than you are letting her work her way under your skin again.'

What the *hell*? I'm hot, heart pounding, I'm *raging*. I open my mouth to yell at him but Deb's already there.

'Where do you get off talking about Addie like you know a thing about my sister, you—'

'Oh, I know about your sister.'

'Marcus, shut the *fuck up*,' Dylan shouts, and I jump. I'm holding the steering wheel so tight it hurts.

'I will not shut up! I'm sick of you treating me like some fucking basket case you need to fix when—'

'Umm, Addie?' Rodney interrupts in a small voice.

'You're lucky to have Dylan,' Deb tells Marcus. 'You're lucky to have anyone, frankly.'

'And what's *your* problem?' Marcus yells at her.

'Addie,' says Rodney, with rising urgency. '*Addie* . . .'

'I know. I know,' I gasp. 'Oh my God . . .'

'What's *my* problem?' Deb snaps, as Dylan says,

'Marcus, you *said* you'd *try*, you *said*—'

And Rodney keeps saying my name, louder and louder, and—

'Everyone, *shut up*,' I scream.

The car is drifting. I thought it was me at first – my head's all over the place – but it's definitely the car. What does it mean if the car's pulling left? My first thought is *ice*, and something about steering into the swerve, but it's hot enough that the sun is shimmering above the tarmac. It's definitely not ice.

I move into the left lane. I'm swerving, pulling the wheel too far right to compensate, crossing the white lines. I try to slow down. For a mad second I think my foot is on the wrong pedal. The car doesn't react properly when I brake. It feels like trying to shout but not getting any sound out. I push down harder and the car slows a bit, still dragging me left and I let out a sound, a frustrated, frightened *guhh*—

'There's a hard shoulder, Addie, get on it,' says Deb behind me. Everyone else is quiet. I can hear them breathing.

I work my way down the gears: third, second, first. I hope this hard shoulder isn't going to end. There's a ringing in my ears like the world's muffled. My neck still hurts from the whiplash, I notice absently. From the last time we crashed.

'Hold on,' I say grimly.

We're not going faster than ten miles an hour, now, but as I ease the parking brake on everyone still jolts forward. The car groans. We sit in silence, and then, very slowly, I lower my forehead against the steering wheel.

As I wait for my heart to stop trying to claw its way up my throat, Dylan slowly reaches across and hits the button to put our hazards on. We all unfreeze.

'Fuck,' Marcus says behind me.

'Goodness me,' says Rodney.

'Everyone all right?' Deb asks.

I twist, forehead still on the steering wheel, and look at Dylan. His face is slack with shock. For a sharp second it reminds me of his expression when he stood in the doorway to our flat as I beat his chest with my fists and told him no, he couldn't leave me.

Marcus gives a shrill laugh from the back seat. 'Fuck me, Addie Gilbert, you just saved our lives.'

My breathing still isn't slowing. I wonder if near-death experiences get more or less scary each time. Like, should I be calmer because I've already had one car crash today? Or panicking more, because I've still got all that leftover terror in my system?

There is a knock at the car window, passenger side. I shriek. My hand flies to my chest. Behind me, everyone screams. But Dylan's reaction is the most surprising – he throws an arm out in front of me, as though we're still moving and we're about to hit something.

'Hello? You all right in there?'

I squint. The sun's behind the man at the window – I can only just make him out. He's big and tough-looking, in his fifties maybe. He has peppery stubble across his sagging jaw. Beneath the white vest he's wearing I can just see half the text of a tattoo: *unconditio—*

'Do you need help?' he asks.

Dylan drops his arm and winds down the window.

'Hi,' he says, clearing his throat. 'We've broken down. I suppose you gathered that much.'

The man makes a sympathetic sort of grimace. 'I saw you,' he says, gesturing upwards. We've stopped just shy of a big concrete bridge running over the motorway. There's a set of steps running down the bank to our left. He must have come down when he saw us. What a nice man. Assuming he's not an opportunistic murderer.

'Do we need to, you know . . . call the AA?' Rodney asks.

'We should get out. Right?' I direct this at the stocky Good Samaritan currently eyeing us through the car window.

'Oh, yeah,' he says, nodding. 'Yeah, but get out this way.' He points behind him.

Dylan clambers out first, then Deb, Rodney and Marcus. I climb out last, over the gearstick, which is a pretty technical manoeuvre.

By the time I emerge from the car our burly Good Samaritan's eyes have settled on Deb and widened with delight.

'Hello, gorgeous,' he says.

Deb gives him a cursory look and I suppress the urge to eye-roll. We don't have time for this shit.

'I need to call our breakdown cover,' I say, looking down at my phone. 'Can someone walk to the nearest one of those post-thingies that tells them where we are?'

'I'll go,' Dylan says. He clears his throat, embarrassed – his voice came out all squeaky.

Deb already has the car bonnet open and is rummaging around in there. Rodney sidles over to the Good Samaritan.

'So,' he says to him, in the bright tone of someone who does not have a natural gift for small talk. 'What do you do?'

I close my eyes. This is *not* how this weekend was meant to go. Why aren't I speeding down the motorway singing Dolly Parton at the top of my voice, with Deb eating Minstrels in the passenger seat? That was the plan. And that sounds *so good* right now.

Dylan calls the number out to me as he walks back to the car. His T-shirt billows in the breeze and his hands are tucked in his jean pockets. He looks too good – it hurts. I turn away, staring out at the traffic as I ring our breakdown cover.

This is dangerous. Not the car troubles, I mean, but Dylan. For a split second there, as I watched him strolling across the tarmac with his hair blowing in the wind, I didn't mind missing out on Dolly Parton and Minstrels with my sister. I wanted to be here. With him.

*

Two hours. Two *hours*.

'My breakdown cover guarantees roadside attendance within thirty minutes,' Marcus says as we spread a blanket out on the verge.

God, I hate him. And he still unsettles me. If anyone else had said what he said before the car broke down – that shit about how I *broke* Dylan – I would have left them on the side of the road. But with Marcus, even now, I have to fight not to slip into old Addie. Little Addie, forgettable Addie, Addie who's always second place. He brings out the worst in me in pretty much every way.

'Yes, well,' I say, trying to keep my voice steady. 'I bet my breakdown cover is a lot more affordable than yours.'

'That'll be your mistake,' he says. 'You get what you pay for.'

He's still not quite meeting my gaze, I notice. Dylan, Rodney and Deb have all set off in different directions for a wee, and right now, stuck setting up the picnic with Marcus, I wish I had a weaker bladder.

I just have to rise above. Be an adult.

'Me and Dylan can put the past behind us for one day, Marcus. Maybe you should try and do the same?'

He snorts. 'You'd like that, wouldn't you?'

'I'll just . . .' the Good Samaritan says from behind me. 'I'll just be getting on, then, eh?'

'Oh, God, sorry.' I blush, swivelling to look at him. 'Thanks so much for your help.'

I just don't have the headspace to be polite to guests right now. Rodney's bad enough. He gives off this vibe of total ineptitude. As if he needs constant looking after, like a toddler, or my dad at a party.

'I didn't catch your name, sorry?' I say.

'Kevin,' the Good Samaritan says. The rush of traffic creates a constant wind. We're all raising our voices a bit, like we're in a noisy pub. 'I drive lorries.'

'Kevin who drives lorries,' Marcus says, 'you look like a man with stories to share – why don't you sit yourself down with us and tell us some tales?'

I double take. Somehow while I've been facing the other way Marcus has found my bag of top-up snacks. He's already snapped off half the fruit-and-nut bar, which he is now gnawing. I narrow my eyes and then look back at Kevin.

He isn't smiling, not technically, but he's kind of . . . smiling without smiling. Like how dogs do. Now that I'm calming and the sun's not behind him, I take a moment to look at him properly. He's short and stocky and weathered. I don't reckon Kevin spends much time on self-care. His body is dotted with tattoos: a Union Jack on the front of his leg, just above the knee; a date, 05.09.16, at the side of his neck; a small and surprisingly cute dog on his forearm, labelled *Cookie, RIP*.

Kevin's eyes drift to Deb as she walks back towards us. 'Why not? This job's only a favour for a friend. I'm not really on duty,' he says.

And so Kevin who drives lorries comes and joins us on the picnic blanket.

It's a fairly tight fit. We're in a circle around a mound of snacks. The sun is high enough to burn me, and I slather on sun cream while Deb lifts the bottom of her T-shirt to tan her stomach.

'We're almost two hours behind schedule,' Deb says, squinting as she checks her phone screen. 'We'll never make it in time to help set up for the barbecue now. We're still in . . . where are we?'

'Just past Banbury,' Kevin supplies, swigging from the large bottle of lemonade he and Deb have been passing back and forth.

'Bloody hell,' Deb says, lying back on the blanket again. 'We've barely got anywhere! Shouldn't someone call Cherry to give her a heads-up?'

Dylan and I exchange glances. Cherry is *not* going to be happy if we're late for the start of the wedding celebrations.

'Let's wait a bit,' I say. 'The breakdown recovery guys could be early. They said two hours at the worst. Plus we budgeted loads of time for stops, Deb.'

'What's your story then, all of you?' Kevin asks, eyes on Deb. 'Seems like a lot of people to fit in a Mini.'

Dylan coughs. A lorry shoots past in the left lane and Deb's hair flies up in response.

'Should I not ask?' Kevin says.

Marcus points at me. 'Addie broke Dylan's heart' – he turns to point to Dylan – 'about a year and a half ago and then totalled his car this morning. She feels guilty for ruining his life so she's giving us a lift because we're all going to the wedding of Cherry, the only person in the world who has ever liked both Dylan and Addie.'

My heart beats faster, the rage bubbling again. *Addie broke Dylan's heart*. Like he didn't fucking *eviscerate* mine. I fight to hold my tongue, because I shouldn't rise to it, I *mustn't*.

Deb sits up on her elbows. 'That's bullshit,' she says. 'Better version: Dylan walked out on Addie in December 2017. Biggest mistake of his life, obviously, and he knows it.'

Dylan looks down at the grass.

'Then Dylan drove into the back of our car and destroyed his. We said we'd give them a lift to Cherry's wedding like the very good people we are. And *I* liked both Dylan and Addie,' she adds. 'For a while.'

Kevin looks between us all. You can see the gears working.

'And him?' he asks, pointing to Rodney.

'Oh, Rodney's just along for the ride,' Deb says, lying back down again.

'Sorry,' says Rodney.

Marcus rolls his eyes. Dylan is still staring down at the grass. I wish I could see his face properly.

'Aren't you going to tell her?' Marcus demands, nodding to Deb. 'Dylan, Christ, have some balls. Tell her it wasn't like that.'

The motorway roars through the silence.

'Fuck's sake,' Marcus says, getting up and brushing down his jeans. 'Anyone getting flashbacks to 2017, or just me?'

'Marcus,' Dylan says quietly. 'Just leave it, OK?'

'Leave it? *Leave* it?'

'Marcus.' Sharper this time.

Rodney's head swivels back and forth between Marcus and Dylan as if he's watching table tennis. I clench my fists in my lap. I want to leave. My muscles are tensed, ready.

'What about *Etienne*, Dylan?'

My nails cut into my palm. My heart rate soars. I really didn't think Marcus would *say* it.

'Don't talk about what you don't understand,' Deb snaps.

Kevin looks between us all, forehead creased. 'Bloody hell. It's like an episode of Jeremy Kyle out here.'

'What's not to understand?' Marcus asks. He sounds genuinely exasperated, and I can't look at him. I can't sit here any longer. My body aches with tension.

I get up so abruptly I spill Rodney's little plastic cup of orange juice. He yelps and rights it, but the juice is already spreading across the blanket.

I walk away. Up the bank, towards the steps Kevin came down when he found us. My heart's pounding. I hear Deb call for me. I don't look back. It takes me a while to realise someone's following me, and another few seconds to clock that it's Dylan.

'Go back to the others,' I say, glancing over my shoulder at him.

'No,' he says.

'Dylan, just go.'

He says nothing this time, but I can still hear him above the rush of traffic. I walk faster and reach the road that crosses the motorway bridge. There's a path here, narrow enough for one person to walk along. To either side are fields separated from the road by grassy banks dotted with white flowers. If it wasn't for the roar of the cars beneath me, I'd feel like I'd stepped into the countryside.

'Addie, come on, slow down.' He jogs to catch me up. 'Are you OK?'

I stop and spin on my heels so fast he stumbles and almost collides with me.

'Am I OK? Marcus is so . . .' I look away. It's hard, standing this close to Dylan and meeting his gaze. 'He's such a dick.'

'I know. I'll talk to him.'

'No, don't. Just . . . give me a minute.'

'I know it's hard to do, but the best thing is just to ignore him.'

'Oh, and that's what you're doing, is it?'

This is so familiar. It's like slipping into an old pair of shoes. I'm angry because I'm ashamed, I know that, but I still say the words that'll hurt him.

'Because to me it looks like you're still his trusty sidekick. Following him around like a puppy.'

Dylan opens his mouth to snap back at me and then closes it again. He looks at the ground. My heart hurts. I remember this sense of self-loathing so well. Is this still who I am? Just because it's familiar, does that mean it's me?

Maybe those old shoes don't fit me any more. The anger's gone as quickly as it came.

'Sorry,' I say. 'Sorry. I didn't . . . I'm just upset.'

He looks up. 'It's not like that with Marcus,' he says. 'Not any more. He's changing.'

Ugh. No. I tear my gaze aside, turning to keep walking away from the motorway.

'He hasn't changed a *bit*. You can't change a man like Marcus.'

'I understand why you'd think that.' Dylan's voice is calm and level. 'But I do believe he's getting somewhere. He's different.'

Dylan's walking beside me now, on the roadside. His arm brushes mine, snagging a little against the sticky sun cream on my skin. For a moment I can smell him again. The scent makes me dizzy, as if the world's going warped, like when someone gets pulled back in time on the telly.

'Doesn't seem to be different when it comes to me.'

'You know he doesn't know the whole story,' Dylan says quietly.

'I know.' I take a road left into a new-build estate lined with parked cars and squint as the sun hits a window. 'He's still a dick, though.'

Dylan doesn't dispute it. We walk on for a while in silence. This feels weird, like we're suddenly improvising a scene we've run through a thousand times before. Dylan's expression is serious. I can't seem to recover that anger that went out of me when I saw how I'd hurt him. Suddenly all I want to do is make him smile. It's such a forceful sensation that I press a hand to my stomach to stem it.

'While we're here, just the two of us, I . . . I want to say I'm sorry for what I said about your decision to stop talking to me,' Dylan says into the silence. 'That was your choice.'

In fairness, he's always respected that choice. Even though I've ached so many times to take it back.

'I thought it would make it easier. To . . .' I trail off.

'Yeah. Did it?'

No. Nothing made it easier. I was unmade, when Dylan left me, and there was no simple way to rebuild myself. Only piece by piece.

'It's not been the easiest couple of years,' I say, in the end.

'No.' His arm brushes mine again – on purpose, I think. 'I wish I could've . . .'

'Don't do that.' It comes out strangled. 'Don't wish things.'

He stays quiet. 'Marcus *has* changed. Is changing. Just look out for it – please. For me.'

'Don't do that either. Don't say *for me* like . . .'

'I'm sorry. But I want you to know I wouldn't be in a car with Marcus if he was still the man you knew when we were together.'

I glance at him. He wouldn't have said something like that a year and a half ago. I play spot-the-difference again: the shorter hair, a little line between his eyebrows . . . and now when Marcus is being a prick to me, Dylan snaps at him. That's new too.

The frown, the hair, the snapping – it all adds up to make him seem kind of worldlier. A bit damaged, a bit stronger. More self-possessed.

'We should probably . . .' He sighs and looks behind him. 'We've left a very weird combination of people by the side of the motorway.'

I rub my face and laugh shakily into my hands. 'Oh, God. Kevin the trucker has probably killed them all.'

'Or Rodney. It's always the quiet ones.'

We smile at one another. I turn back first, my arm brushing his again.

'I was wrong,' I say on impulse. 'About the not-talking. It was worse. I – it – I wish I hadn't asked you to leave me alone.'

I watch the corners of his mouth turn up. There was a time when I would have done anything to make him smile like that.

'Thank you for telling me,' he says simply.

We walk back towards the Mini in silence. It's hard to know what to say after that. I'm walking slower than I should be. I like the feeling of him beside me.

We both stop as we reach the steps down to the motorway.

'Oh, Christ,' Dylan says. 'Can't leave them alone for five minutes, can we?'

Dylan

Beneath us, on the motorway verge, Rodney, Kevin and Marcus form a bizarre tableau – they seem to be conducting some sort of amateur Olympic Games.

Rodney has an empty bottle held like a javelin, his other arm sighting the throw (thankfully he is aiming *away* from the busy motorway). He is sporting an expression of comical concentration on his face. Meanwhile Marcus and Kevin are squatting down to lift two suitcases.

'It's all in the legs,' Marcus is saying as he grabs hold of my luggage. 'You don't *need* upper-arm strength.'

Addie's sister watches over proceedings from the picnic blanket, where – from my limited understanding of such things – she seems to be expressing breast milk into a hoover-like contraption attached to her chest.

Kevin hefts the suitcase with practised ease. 'Upper-arm strength helps, though.' He proceeds to bicep-curl the suitcase while Marcus – who's never had the patience or dedication required to regularly go to the gym, or in fact regularly do anything – attempts to lift the suitcase above his head like a weightlifting champion. He gets halfway and then sets it down again, looking rather red in the face.

'Just getting a good grip,' he says.

Kevin chortles, doing a few casual squats.

Addie sighs beside me. 'I do not like the way Deb is looking at that trucker.'

'*Kevin*? Really?'

'She's not had sex since having Riley. She said something about wanting to *get back in the saddle* this weekend.'

Her expression mirrors mine.

'Is Rodney actually taking part?' I ask, watching him practise the throw before going in for the real thing. He looks a little like an animated stick figure with his knobbly knees jutting and his feet turned out. The bottle sails up the bank, not quite reaching the line of trees at the top, and then topples gracelessly down again.

'Just joining in, I guess, in his own way,' Addie says, with something that sounds a lot like fondness. 'He doesn't seem to have fallen for Deb like the other two, does he?'

'Kevin's certainly smitten, but I would say Marcus is . . .' I pause carefully. 'Doing what Marcus does whenever there's a woman in proximity. Not that Deb would ever go anywhere near him, all things considered. Oh, bloody hell, there he goes,' I say as Marcus topples over below, suitcase thudding to the ground beside him. 'He had to pick *my* suitcase, didn't he?'

Kevin carefully sets Marcus's suitcase down. Rodney stretches a hand out; it takes Kevin a moment to realise he's asking for a high-five. Rodney's delighted expression when their palms clap suggests that Rodney is accustomed to people leaving him hanging.

'You lot are a right laugh,' Kevin says, bouncing on his toes, seemingly energised by all the bicep-curling.

'Really? Even Rodney?' Marcus says, brushing himself down as he stands. 'Kevin, you need to broaden your horizons. You know I once met a woman who could fellate her own toes? Now *she* was fun.'

'Gosh,' says Rodney, as Kevin roars with laughter and slaps Marcus on the back.

Deb spots us and waves, then removes her breast pump; it's only my extremely quick thinking that saves me from the sight of Addie's sister's nipple.

'If you lot want anything else to eat or drink, it's not a long walk to Tesco from here,' Kevin says, and there's a huskiness to his tone that makes me wonder if he might have seen rather more of Deb's breast than I did.

Deb pushes herself to standing. 'Why don't you show me?' she says briskly to Kevin.

'Called it,' Addie says.

'What? You don't mean – they're not going to have sex on the way to Tesco, are they?'

'You really have changed,' Addie says dryly, then her cheeks flare as she registers what she's said. She's right to blush – I'm *gone* the moment she says it, thinking of all the nights we couldn't wait until we got home, sex against walls, in the backs of cars, on the dry chalky soil of the vineyard next to Villa Cerise . . .

'Off to the shops!' Kevin says, with a cheery wave. His broad grin looks more like a grimace – I get the impression he's not especially accustomed to smiling. Looking at Kevin is proving very helpful with the sexual thoughts, so I watch him make his way up the bank and try to concentrate on his grisly balding head.

It doesn't work. All I can think about is Addie's soft, curved hip, Addie's bare thighs, Addie's long dark hair splayed across my chest as she presses her lips to the band of my boxers. It seems almost unbelievable now that holding her body against mine wasn't always a fantasy – that once upon a time I could reach out and touch her.

THEN

Addie

Can't the girl find us another bottle of vino? She'll have a naughty secret stash somewhere, I'll bet.

The girl. The girl. There's been plenty of knobbish visitors in the last six weeks at Villa Cerise, but Dylan's uncle Terry is getting under my skin like none of the others have. Him and Dylan have been up on the terrace ever since we got back from La Roque-Alric – I've been getting on with jobs down here and in the house, but I can still hear them. Terry's the 'fun guy' of the boys you'd see at a pub quiz machine. The one who never gets laid but talks like he's screwed every girl in the bar. That guy, but twenty years on. Still 'fun', still not getting any.

I frown at my reflection in the mirror on the living-room wall of the flat. That was bitchy. I'm better than that. I just . . . need to take a breather.

I examine myself more closely. The mirror's a bit convex – or maybe the other one, concave. Anyway, it makes my nose look tiny and my eyes buglike and huge. I turn my head a little to and fro, wondering what Dylan sees. Whether he'll still see it tomorrow.

I've always felt like I have a forgettable sort of face. Deb has these beautiful thick eyebrows that she's never plucked – they make her face look iconic, like she's a model. My eyebrows just look like . . . I don't know. I can't even think of anything to say about them.

Ugh. I look away from the mirror and reach for the bottle of wine I just fetched from mine and Deb's 'naughty secret stash' – because, as irritating as it is to prove Terry right, we totally have one. My heart thumps too fast as I make my way up to the terrace. It's ridiculous, the way my body reacts to Dylan. I've not fancied anyone like this for ages.

'Here you go!' I say as I approach them.

My mood improves a bit at Dylan's expression – that cool, practised stare he was doing earlier has gone, and he's sort of *gazing*, as if he's longing for me, as if he wants to undress me slowly. My stomach tightens. I kind of assumed that Terry arriving would put an end to the staring. Like having an extra onlooker would make Dylan realise, *Oh, she's not that special after all.*

'Good girl,' says Terry, reaching for the bottle. 'I knew I liked you.'

I give a tinkling laugh that sounds nothing like my real one. 'Anything else I can get you?'

'Won't you join us?' Terry asks, pointing to an empty chair. 'It must get lonely down there in the bowels of the building . . .'

Dylan frowns, shifting in his seat. He doesn't have to worry. I'm not about to sit through an evening of family banter with pervy Uncle Terry.

'I think I'll just go to bed, actually,' I say. 'Long day.'

They let me go with minimal protest, and when I close the door to the flat behind me, I lean against it, eyes closed. I remember that look of Dylan's. The longing look. My breath catches.

I try to go to bed – I've been so low on sleep all summer – but I'm too restless. It's so hot. I kick one leg out from under the sheet, then the other, then give up on it altogether and leave it crumpled in the bottom corner of the bed.

I'm lying there hoping for a knock on the door, if I'm honest. I've finally started to drift off when it comes, and for a moment I think I've dreamt it. But there it is again, a soft double-tap.

I sit up sharply in bed. My mouth tastes stale and my lips are dry. God knows what my hair looks like. I dash to the bathroom to run a toothbrush around my mouth and scrape my knotted hair up into a messy bun. It looks too 'done' – I redo it. By the time I get to the door, the sleepy eyes I'm blinking Dylan's way are totally fake. I'm wide awake now. The night air is still warm, and as Dylan steps inside the flat he brings the smell of sun-baked vines with him.

'I wasn't sure you'd wake,' he whispers as I click the door shut behind us. 'You strike me as a heavy sleeper.'

I am, actually. My ex always complained that I snore way too loudly for such a small person, but that doesn't feel like the sexiest of admissions, so I shake my head.

'I was . . . not exactly waiting, but . . .' I flush, already wishing I'd said something that sounded more assertive. More like Summer Addie.

A slow smile grows on his lips. His eyes turn cocky again. He's wearing that put-on confidence he had when he first turned up on my doorstep. He reaches one hand out and takes mine, tugging me gently towards him.

'I feel we left a few things unsaid,' he tells me, voice low.

I step close enough that I have to tilt my chin up to look at him. Just his hand in mine is enough to start my pulse racing again. His floppy brown hair is all styled now, falling artfully over his forehead. Somehow it makes him look even scruffier.

'Oh?' I breathe. 'Un*said*?'

'Perhaps I mean undone,' he says, dropping my hand to undo the buttons on the cami I wore in bed. His fingers move slowly, starting at the top, his knuckle brushing against my breast as he unbuttons. He doesn't shift the fabric until every button is done. I'm already breathing hard when he finally pushes the straps back over my shoulders and lets the cami pool to the floor behind me.

We're still in the kitchen – we've barely moved a few paces from the front door. For a moment he just looks down at me. His eyes are wide, lips parted. My breath hitches. Then he moves, backing me up, his hands shifting down to my waist, his lips closing in on mine. My back hits the door hard just as our tongues touch.

This kiss isn't a first kiss, it's foreplay. I lose track of time, of everything, drowsy with wanting, hearing myself moan, grabbing fistfuls of his shirt until he breaks away from me to yank it over his head. When my bare skin touches his we both gasp.

'Christ,' he says, pushing my hair back with one hand as he lowers his lips to mine. 'You're *killing* me already.'

I writhe against him, one leg lifting, pyjama shorts ruching. I'm unbuckling his belt when the knock comes at the door behind me.

I jump so much my teeth knock into Dylan's with a jolt. We stumble away from the door, tangled together. Dylan spins just in time to shield me from view as Uncle Terry pokes his head around the door.

For God's sake. Terry is absolutely the sort of man who knocks right at the same time as he turns the door handle, isn't he?

'Yoo-hoo!' he calls. 'Maddy? Oh, well, hello, you two!' He chuckles. 'Am I interrupting?'

I cringe back into Dylan, burying my face in his chest. His arms close around me. *Maddy*. I get called that one a lot, and Ali, and Annie.

'Go *away*, Terry,' Dylan says. 'Go outside until the lady's decent, for God's sake.'

'Whatever you say, Dylan!' Terry says, chortling, and I hear the door click shut again.

'Oh, God,' I say into Dylan's chest.

'Fuckity bollocking arsehole Uncle Terry,' he says, moving to fetch my camisole and his shirt off the kitchen floor. He's breathing so heavily his chest is heaving. I'm not much better.

'I can still hear you, my boy!' Terry calls.

'What are you *doing* knocking on her door at two in the morning!' Dylan yells so loudly I jump.

'What are *you* doing knocking on her door at two in the morning, that's what I'd like to know,' Terry calls back.

'I think it's pretty obvious what I was doing,' Dylan says, running an exasperated hand through his hair. 'And her name is *Addie*. Not Maddy.'

I snort with laughter. This is obviously horrifying and not at all funny but also . . . It is a *bit* funny. That *yoo-hoo* as Terry stuck his head around the door.

'I heard a commotion,' Terry says. 'When I came down for a snack. Thought I'd better check the lady was all right!'

'I'm fine, thanks, Mr Abbott,' I call, then cover my face with my hands. 'Oh God,' I whisper.

'I'm so sorry,' Dylan says beseechingly. His hair is sticking up all over the place and his lips are swollen. The bravado is gone. He's even sexier this way. A little lost-looking.

I stand on tiptoes to press a slow kiss against his neck. I feel his Adam's apple bob as he swallows back a groan.

'Another time,' I whisper. 'You know where to find me, now.'

Dylan

She's mesmerised me. I'm Odysseus at Circe's island, I'm Shakespeare's Romeo, I'm – I'm nursing an almost-permanent erection.

It's been four hours since Addie pressed that single, burning kiss to my throat in the clutter of her little kitchen, and I've barely slept an hour since. My brain is rammed with rushed, heated poems, borderline erotica; they look even worse when I write them down. In a moment of insanity at around six in the morning I decide to fold them and post them under her bedroom door, but thankfully I stop myself just as I head out of my room, realising that this will almost certainly make me look creepy, or – perhaps worse – desperate. Instead I return to my bed and imagine reading them to her here, naked, then I have to take a cold shower.

It's ten in the morning before I see her again. She arrives on the terrace where Terry and I are taking our coffees – she's fresh-faced, wearing a patterned little dress that flirts around her upper thighs with each step. In her hand is a paper bag dappled with buttery stains: fresh croissants from the nearby village. Her fingers graze mine as I take the pastries. Never has patisserie been so sexually charged.

'Thank you,' I murmur.

'You look a little peaky,' she says, and that mole on her upper lip shifts as she tries not to smile. 'Didn't sleep so well?'

'I owe you an apology, my nephew tells me!' Terry calls. 'I'm sorry for barging in, it was very ungentlemanly of me.'

When she turns from me to Terry I want her gaze back immediately. I want her all to myself.

'I've forgotten it all,' Terry says, waving his arm. 'Don't remember a thing. All right?'

Addie pauses for a beat. 'Thank you,' she says, with a small smile. 'I appreciate that.' Then she turns and walks away.

'Where are you going?' I blurt.

She looks over her shoulder at me. 'Jobs to do,' she says, smiling. 'You'll see me around.'

She returns while we take lunch on the terrace; she's wearing a red swimming costume and proceeds to clean the leaves out of the swimming pool. I think I am going to cry. The task involves an *excruciating* amount of bending over.

I get drunk mid-afternoon, thinking it might help, or at least make Uncle Terence seem more interesting. All it does is loosen my tongue.

'I think she might be the one,' I tell Terry, flopping back on the sofa. It's too hot to sit outside now – we've retreated to the cool of the enormous living room with its silk tapestries and endless cushions.

Terry chuckles. 'See if you still feel that way once you've . . .' He gives a crude gesture that makes me want to throw the bottle of wine at his head.

'It's not like that,' I insist, topping up my glass. 'She's so . . . *wonderful*. I've never fancied someone this hard.'

I meant to say *this much*, but what I've said is more accurate. I'm *pained* with wanting her.

'Ah, the impulsivity of youth,' Terry says benevolently. 'Wait until you've seen her gain twenty pounds and develop a fascination with the shopping channels.'

'Uncle Terry. Literally everything you say is totally unacceptable.'

'Your generation, so sensitive,' he says, sitting back and balancing his wine glass on his beer belly.

I knock back my drink. No day has ever passed as slowly as this day.

Terry invites Addie to have supper with us when we pass her in the hall, but she declines, her eyes on me. I'm not sure what it means: is she turning down more than just that invite, after a day to think? The idea that she might not want me to come to her flat tonight makes me positively light-headed with despair.

Over dinner Uncle Terry doesn't stop talking about Uncle Rupe and how poorly he invested his money in the 1990s. This could not be less interesting to me – I despise talking about money, it makes me uncomfortable – and all the ranting means Terry eats so slowly I want to reach across and stab the rest of his steak with my own fork to steal it off his plate. He's not quite finished mopping up the juices with his bread when I get up to clear away the plates, and he squawks as I whisk it out from under him.

'I know why you're so keen to get rid of me,' he says as I carry the plates through to the kitchen and leave them on the side. 'You want to sneak down to the servant's quarters, don't you?'

I grit my teeth. 'I want to see Addie, yeah.'

'She's already got you wrapped around her little finger, I see. Swanning around in swimwear and teasing you all day long.'

I walk back into the dining room as he shakes his head and laughs.

'You're going to have your hands full with that one.'

Terry is always obnoxious but hearing him talk about Addie like this is intolerable. I bunch my fists. He isn't as bad as Dad, at least. For a moment I imagine what it would have been like if the whole family had come on this holiday, as my father had intended. Uncle Rupe and his wilting American wife; the trio of sharp-nosed cousins from Notting Hill; my brother, Luke, without his partner, Javier, because Javier is never invited. Luke would endure the sly homophobia of my family in quiet, stifled agony, and I would want to punch somebody, and Dad would tell us how disappointing we are and Mum would spend the holiday desperately trying to fix everything, as she always does.

No, this holiday is a gift, despite Terry's presence. I slowly unclench my fists.

'Look,' I say. I must try not to sound desperate, though, of course, I absolutely am. 'If you can just spend tonight on your own, you and I can go on a tour of the local vineyards tomorrow. All day. Just us. I won't even drink, so I can drive you.'

Terry looks torn. Always the self-described 'life of the party', he is absolutely frantic about being left alone for even a moment. But wine tasting is one of his favourite occupations, and I know the promise of my undivided attention for a whole day will have some sway.

'All right,' he concedes. 'Perhaps I could . . . read. A book.'

He looks around in a lost sort of way.

'There's a TV in the living room,' I tell him. 'And they've got all the *Fast and Furious* films on DVD. All of them.'

He brightens somewhat. 'Well. Enjoy yourself, boy.' He winks. 'I'll sleep with ear plugs.'

I suppress a shudder. 'That's . . . Right. Thanks. Have a good night, Terry.'

Addie

Dylan's out of breath when he gets to the door of the flat. He must've sprinted down from the dining room. It's been adorable, watching his hangdog eyes following me all day. Yesterday he seemed sexy, interesting – today he seems sweet. Earlier I caught him writing in a leather-bound notebook by the pool and his tongue was sticking out between his front teeth.

'Hi,' he says breathlessly. 'I am here in the hope that even after a day of overhearing my uncle's objectionable views, you might still be interested in kissing me.'

I laugh, leaning on one hip. I'm wearing a pair of dungarees cut off above the knee, with my red swimsuit underneath. I always feel most me-ish in dungarees. I was annoyed with myself this morning for changing into that short dress for Dylan when I got back from the bakery. It had worked – his jaw had literally dropped – but it had felt a bit . . . cheap.

'How did you manage to get rid of him?'

Dylan's hands clench and unclench like he's itching to reach for me. The heat builds in my stomach.

'I promised him a whole day of undivided attention visiting

vineyards tomorrow.' Dylan brushes his hair out of his eyes. 'May I come in?'

I pause as if deliberating, but the tortured misery of his expression makes it too hard to keep up. I laugh, stepping aside. 'Go on then.'

'Oh, thank Christ for that,' he says, and then he closes the door behind him and, taking me gently but firmly by the shoulders, pushes me up against it. 'Where were we?'

'Round about here, I'd say.' I tug him closer. He's at least a foot taller than me, and I'm already standing on tiptoes and tilting my head to meet his gaze. His eyes are all smouldery.

'I think you're going to be the death of me, Addie. I've spent the last eighteen hours dizzy with wanting you.'

I've never met a man who speaks as well as Dylan. Not his accent, I don't mean that, but the actual words. Everything he says sounds like it ought to be written down.

'Nobody ever died of wanting,' I tell him, moulding my body to his. 'And maybe a little patience would be good for you.'

'In my experience, patience is awfully dull.'

He kisses me. He's a great kisser, but that's not why my body flames the moment his tongue touches mine. It's the intention behind the kiss that's done that. This kiss says, *This time, I'm here all night.*

Our first time is frantic. All shaking hands and gasping breath. We don't make it out of the kitchen, and when we untangle ourselves, weak-limbed and laughing, he turns me around and brushes away flakes of bread crust from the skin of my bum and thighs.

'God, you're stunning,' he says, voice hushed.

He's behind me, and he holds me in place when I move as if to turn. His hand is still brushing over my thighs, more deliberate now. Gentling. I glance over my shoulder. He's looking at my body like he's learning it, almost reverent. He meets my gaze and his eyes catch me up and I want him again, already. So much my pulse starts racing.

My legs are shaky; I stumble as we make our way to the bed. When I collapse face down on the mattress he's just seconds behind me, pulling my body flush against his. He traces soft kisses up the back of my neck and I feel that quiet heat unfurl in the pit of my stomach again.

'This,' he says throatily, pressing a single finger to the spot where my waist becomes my hip. 'This place might be the sexiest half an inch I've ever seen.'

'There?' I say, turning in his arms. 'Seriously?'

He shifts down the bed a little. 'Maybe here,' he says, and presses a string of hot, slow kisses to the skin of my throat. I tip my head back with a moan.

'Or here.' The slope of my breast. 'Here.' The dip of my hip bone. 'Here.' The soft, sensitive skin of my thigh.

He's like no one I've ever slept with. We take our time now. Minutes slip by in a haze, like I'm dreaming. He's fierce, then teasingly slow, then so gentle and sweet I'm shocked to find myself moved, eyes pricking as he leans his forehead against mine and shifts back and forth just a little, not enough, not yet, until I'm jellylike and wild with wanting him.

We fall asleep tangled and sweaty. I wake in the dark, totally disorientated. His chest hair is tickling my cheek. I sit up sharply and look down at the mess of clothes and bedsheets, the book I kicked off the nightstand at some point after midnight. Dylan's naked form, long and tanned, coming into focus as my eyes adjust to the dark.

I smile into the gloom, pressing my hands to my face. This feels like . . . more than a summer romance. It feels epic.

The sun's up when I wake again, and Terry is banging on the door to the flat.

I fell asleep with my head on Dylan's arm. It spasms abruptly as he wakes and I dodge, just about avoiding a sharp smack in the face.

'Oi!' I yelp.

'Hmm?' he says, turning absent eyes my way. He does a comedy double take, hair falling into his eyes. 'Oh, hullo.'

I can't help smiling. 'Hi. You nearly decked me.'

'Did I?' Dylan shuffles up to sit against the pillow, brushing his hair back. He rubs his cheeks like he's trying to bring his face back to life. 'Oh, Christ, sorry. I'm a flailer. So sorry. At least you're a snorer, so we're even.'

'Hello?' Terry calls from outside the flat. 'Dylan!'

I groan, turning my face into the pillow. We can't have got more than three hours' sleep. I'd like to stay in bed for another nine or so.

'Bloody Uncle Terry,' Dylan announces to the ceiling.

I laugh into the pillow. 'Are all your family this weird?'

'Oh, definitely. But different-weird. Varied.' He rolls over and plants a kiss on my shoulder. 'Morning,' he says, resting his forehead against me. 'Please stay exactly like this, in this attire, in this bed, until I return from booze-cruising with my uncle?'

'I'm not wearing any "attire",' I say, twisting to look at him.

'Precisely.'

'Dylan! We should be setting off!' Terry calls.

Dylan leans forward and kisses me gently on the lips. 'All right. You can dress, and move around, if *absolutely* necessary. But don't disappear. Please?'

'I'm here all summer,' I say. 'I'm not going anywhere.'

He smiles then. Laid back, a little dishevelled, hair already falling back into his eyes. 'Perfect,' he says. He kisses me softly. 'Last night was . . . unforgettable. You're extraordinary.'

I blush so fiercely he chuckles – I'm sure he can feel the heat radiating from my skin. I want to tell him he always says the perfect thing, but it feels too much. I don't want to give him that. I don't want him to know how completely he has me already. If he knows that, he has all the power. Then the joy of yesterday – his hangdog eyes following me around the pool – will be gone.

NOW

Dylan

The accidental breakdown cover men are here, fixing Deb's car. I really do try to listen to the explanation about what happened with the brakes and the steering but there's something about car talk that just makes me switch off entirely. A similar thing occurs whenever my father talks to me about rugby. I could learn the whole of *Twelfth Night* off by heart aged sixteen, but I am still unclear on what exactly they're all doing when they get in a scrum.

While Kevin launches into an in-depth chat with Deb about brake fluid, with Rodney at his shoulder, nodding eagerly, I watch Addie. And Marcus watches me.

'You keep staring at her like that, you're going to give her the creeps,' Marcus says, sidling over with his hands in his pockets.

We're still on the verge; I've already got so accustomed to the roar of traffic I don't hear it now, and the realisation makes me think of the crickets in France, how I'd tune out their endless chirrups and only know they'd been singing when they suddenly hushed.

The car guy laughs at something Addie says, and I feel a shock of almost-pain as I watch her smile back at him. He's handsome – Spanish, perhaps, with a short beard and striking eyes.

'I know you don't want to hear this,' Marcus says quietly as he follows me down the bank towards the others. 'I'm not trying to be a dick. I lost my head in the car, fine, but the point still stands, Dyl – I wouldn't be your friend if I didn't say it. You can't go back there. You need to move on. Christ, I would have thought you had already. It's been almost two years, hasn't it?'

I want to hit him. Maybe I could hit him, just once? I've wanted to so many times and I never have. Perhaps one punch would get it out of my system, and then I could go back to being a mature, supportive friend.

'Addie,' Deb calls, waving her phone. 'Addie . . . Cherry's ringing.'

Deb returned from her trip to Tesco looking very happy and dishevelled. When I asked the obvious questions – *Sorry, but how? As in, where?* – she announced with great glee that Kevin had a shipment of chairs in the back of his lorry, and that she'd been able to fulfil two of her favourite activities simultaneously: having sex and having a nice sit-down.

'Don't answer,' I call, just as Addie says,

'Don't pick up!'

Everyone watches the phone ringing out in Deb's hand.

'We're going to have to tell her eventually,' Deb says as the call goes to voicemail. 'We'll never make it there to set up for the barbecue now.'

She opens Maps on her phone.

'We've travelled one hundred and twenty miles in five and a half hours. There's still . . . three hundred miles to go.'

Addie throws her head back and groans up at the sky. '*How* has this gone so wrong?'

'Let's just drive faster,' Marcus says.

'It's five hours of solid driving,' Deb says. 'And it's . . . almost eleven right now.'

'What time did we say we'd be there?'

'Three o'clock,' Addie says, pulling a face. 'And I'm not speeding. I've already got three points on my licence.'

I stare at her, mouth open. She scrupulously avoids my gaze.

'Me neither,' Deb says. 'I have a son. I'm not allowed to die these days.'

'I'll text her,' Addie says, chewing her lip. 'That's . . . that'll be fine.'

Everyone makes supportive noises, as though this is an ingenious idea, when we all know it's a cop-out.

'Right – back in the car, everyone. Oh! Kevin,' Addie says, stopping short. 'Sorry. I forgot you weren't part of the gang.'

This seems to please Kevin. Then his grimace-smile wavers. 'You're going? Already?'

'Car's fixed,' Addie says, gesturing to the breakdown guys and shooting them a smile.

The Spanish one definitely just checked out her arse. I absolutely must *not* look like I mind. But I do, a lot. God, she's so beautiful.

I catch Marcus watching me again, his eyebrows raised, and I try to studiously look at something other than Addie.

'You don't want to stick around, have lunch? See the inside of the lorry cab? Eh?' Kevin says.

All of this is directed at Deb, who is busy packing food into plastic bags and seems to have written Kevin out of her reality altogether. Since their return from Tesco she's regarded him with the same absent-minded blankness with which Addie looks at Rodney. The Gilbert family's ability to focus on what matters to them and ignore everything else is truly remarkable.

'Well,' Kevin says, grimace-smile fading. He rubs his chin. 'Goodbye.'

'So long, Kevin,' Marcus says, climbing into the front seat of the car. His friendliness has ebbed since Deb went to Tesco with Kevin; Marcus doesn't like to lose, even if he didn't particularly care about winning.

The rest of us say our goodbyes, which just leaves Deb. She finishes tidying the litter and half-eaten food we've all discarded on the verge-side, touching her hand to her lower back as she straightens up.

'Oh. Bye, Kevin. Thanks,' she says, focusing on him at last.

'Perhaps we'll cross paths again!' Kevin tries.

'Seems unlikely,' Deb says, opening the car boot and chucking in the rubbish bag.

'Call me!' he yells as she slams the car door.

It takes a while for Deb to pull out into the slow lane – the traffic shoots by, gleaming bonnets catching the sun – and Kevin waits on the verge to wave us off. I watch him shrinking away in the mirror and feel Addie's leg pressed against mine in the back seat, and I wonder why we all find it so very hard to let the Gilbert women go.

We drive for an hour or so without any incident. Well, technically speaking, without incident – as far as I'm concerned, every slight shift of Addie's leg against mine is worth a whole poem.

Having her so close is making me dizzy. I've thought about seeing her again more times than I could possibly count, but it's nothing like I expected. In my mind she'd looked exactly as she had when I left her – tired, sad eyes and dark hair to her waist – but she's different now. She's warmer; less guarded, oddly enough; she knows herself better. The edges of her nails aren't bitten down raw, and there's a stillness to her that's completely new.

And then there's the hair, of course, and the glasses, both of which I'm finding impossibly sexy.

'So, Rodney,' Deb says over her shoulder, as she moves the car out into the fast lane. 'What's your story?'

'Oh, I don't have a story,' Rodney says.

Marcus huffs a laugh. He's been gazing out the window from the front seat, suspiciously quiet. It's too hot in the car; there's a nasty sort of stickiness to the air, like the stale fug of a room that's not been aired since somebody slept there.

'Everyone has a story,' Addie says.

She glances at me, but it brings our faces so close – a kiss away from one another – that she turns to the front again within half a second, a blush colouring her cheeks.

'Rodney?' she prompts.

Rodney squirms. 'Oh, really, nothing to tell!'

I look at him with a pang of pity, then realise – as Addie just did – how close our faces are now we're turned towards one another. I can see every pore on his nose.

'Come on, Rodney – what is it you do, for instance?' I say, quickly returning my gaze to the road ahead. The middle seat is unequivocally the worst. There's nowhere to put my feet, for starters, and my arms feel very inconvenient, like a couple of extra limbs I really should have had the decency to leave in the boot.

'I work with Cherry,' Rodney says. 'I'm in the sales team.'

I can tell without looking that Addie is as surprised as I am. I don't know why none of us had thought to ask how exactly Rodney knew Cherry, but this wasn't the answer I'd been expecting. Since moving to live with Krishna in Chichester, Cherry works for a luxury travel company, selling ten-thousand-pound holidays to people who are far too busy to organise them for themselves. Not one of those hideous package sites that's always shouting at you to book things before somebody else does, but a boutique travel agency with a cosy office and staff who are astonishingly nice to you. The niceness only applies to the right sort of person, of course. It's very exclusive.

Rodney doesn't exactly scream exclusivity.

I should say something – I've left it too long. 'That's great!' I say, much too enthusiastically. Addie shoots me an amused glance and I make a quick face, like, *What would you have done?* I feel rather than see her smile.

'What's the most embarrassing thing you've ever done, Rodney?' Marcus asks, without turning around.

'Marcus,' Addie begins.

'What? Five questions! *I* did it earlier, didn't I?' He turns then, and smiles. 'Come on, Rodney, it'll be fun. We're all friends here, aren't we?'

This is a wildly inaccurate statement.

Rodney clears his throat. 'Umm. Most embarrassing . . . Oh, let's see . . . I once wet myself in bed.'

There is a long silence.

'With a girl there,' he says.

'*What?*' everyone choruses.

'What, like, as an adult?'

'Well, yeah,' Rodney says. 'Haha!'

I cringe as Marcus laughs to himself. I suspect Rodney has not heard the end of this story and will sincerely regret sharing it.

'Next question?' Rodney says hopefully.

'Like, full-bladder-wet-yourself?' Deb asks, with curiosity. 'Or just a dribble?'

'Oh, gosh,' Rodney says. 'Haha! Let's not go into the details?'

'I think you're misunderstanding, Rodney,' Marcus says. 'The details are the only interesting part.'

Addie leans into me for a moment as she adjusts her seat belt. I wonder if she feels that heat between us too, if the left side of her body is blazing like the right side of mine, hypersensitive to touch.

'Let's allow Rodney to retain some dignity,' Addie says. 'When did you and Cherry become friends, Rodney?'

'What a waste of a question,' Marcus says.

'Christmas party, year before last,' Rodney says, with pride.

I remember Cherry telling me about that Christmas party. She always has excellent anecdotes, largely because she's so ridiculous – she's always in one scrape or another. For a while I used to hope for them, because when she needed rescuing it would usually be Addie who turned up to save her. Cherry always caved eventually and gave me the details of exactly how Addie was, what she was doing, whether she was dating, and all the other questions I would insist on torturing myself by asking.

That particular Christmas party had been one month before the night out with me in Chichester when Cherry had first met Krishna, her now fiancé. That Christmas she'd had one ill-fated sexual encounter with a man who had subsequently spent a year sending her very poorly written poems, a story that had always made me feel deeply uncomfortable (embarrassingly bad poets always hit a nerve); if I remember the tale correctly, she also bought shots for everybody in the business and kissed seven colleagues at that party. This was an entirely standard Cherry anecdote; I remember her telling it at the pub in a fit of giggles, and when Grace had said to her, *Darling, have you no shame?* Cherry had said, *What's shame good for, except keeping people down?*

'She's fun, isn't she, Cherry?' I ask Rodney.

He beams. 'She's brilliant. Helped me through all sorts.'

Ah – so he's a Cherry charity case. Cherry collects waifs and strays like a benevolent nineteenth-century widow: she once put up fifteen homeless teenagers in a large marquee in her parents' garden; she owns eight rescue animals, who have about six limbs remaining between them. Even Addie and Deb's stint as caretakers was a by-product of Cherry's boundless goodwill: Deb was between jobs, and Addie was planning on spending the summer working in her local old-man pub before Cherry swooped in and got them four months in Provence.

I swallow. Thinking of that summer brings an ache to the back of my throat. I can't cast my mind back to the heat and dust and sexual tension without feeling sure that I rolled the dice, then, and came up with the wrong numbers. We were both so unformed. So sure of ourselves and so utterly lost.

If we'd met now, as adults, would we have been able to make it work?

The music shifts. Taylor Swift, 'We Are Never Ever Getting Back Together'.

A timely reminder from the universe. Or Marcus, rather, who I now realise is manning the Spotify playlist.

Addie

Bloody hell, it's hot in this car. The air con can't contend with five adults and – I check my phone – thirty-degree heat. The forecast says it's going to be thirty-six by mid-afternoon. Wish I'd not bothered putting make-up on now. It'll probably be puddling on my chin by the time we get to Scotland.

Dylan shifts beside me. He's being a gentleman and not complaining about being in the middle seat, but his knees are jutting up towards his chest and he's pulling both elbows in. Kind of a T-rex pose. We'd save a lot of space if I sat in his lap.

I blink. That thought was . . . inappropriate. Dylan's body is pressed against the side of mine. He's radiating heat, and as Taylor Swift sings out from the speaker – Marcus is on a Taylor thing, probably trying to make some sort of point – I think about how easy it would be to put my hand on Dylan's knee. Instead I press both palms together between my legs and try to get a bloody grip on myself.

This is Dylan. He left me. I don't love him any more.

But God, that orange-wood scent of him. My body's forgotten the misery and the heartbreak and it only remembers my face pressed to the hot skin of his neck as he moves inside me. The gasps, the euphoria. The joy of falling asleep naked and hot in his arms.

'Flapjack, anyone?' says Rodney.

I swallow and press my legs closer together. My heart is beating a bit too fast. I feel as if Dylan can tell somehow. He's holding himself still, like he doesn't trust himself to move. The radio, playing something hot and pulsing – 'Lover', maybe – is not helping.

I've forgotten what it's like to want someone like this. Has anyone else ever made me feel this way? Will anyone else ever make me feel this way again? God, what an awful thought.

I lean forward so I can see Rodney past Dylan. He's holding a large Tupperware of homemade flapjack. No idea where he conjured that up from. As I examine the contents of the plastic container in Rodney's lap, I can feel Dylan's eyes moving over the bare skin of my shoulders. The hairs rise on the back of my neck. Sweat prickles between my shoulder blades. I want him to touch me. Run his finger down my spine.

I lean back quickly, looking straight ahead.

'I'm fine,' I say. 'Thanks.'

'Just me, then,' Rodney says cheerfully, tucking in.

Next time we stop I'm going to make sure I'm sat between Marcus and Rodney. That'll sort me out.

THEN

Dylan

I'm giddy with her. Intoxicated.

We've had a week of bare skin and syrupy heat, the sun setting behind the vines like an egg yolk dropping into a bowl. The nights are languid, long, ours. Terry has come to tolerate Addie being around for some of the day, but really I only have her once he's gone to bed – she's not herself when Terry's there, but once she's closed the door to the flat and kicked off her flip-flops, she's pure, undiluted Addie.

Tonight we've arranged to meet on the terrace once Terry's gone to sleep; she's dressed in her pyjamas, the silky peach-coloured ones with the little shorts, and her long dark hair is loose around her shoulders. She holds out a hand to stop me as I approach her, and she's smiling the sort of smile that promises new, delicious things.

She strips off slowly. Her pale skin looks almost silver in the starlight, and a line comes to me, *silver slip of a starlit girl*, but I shake it gone as she approaches the water and dives in, her slim white form a shooting star in the dark. She breaches the surface smoothly, barely a ripple.

The pool alarm sounds.

Christ, it's *so* loud. Addie yelps and covers her ears, wading over to hit the right buttons; I'd help if I weren't bent double laughing, but I'm hard, still hard, quite honestly *always* hard when Addie's around. We spin in unison as soon as the alarm ceases its roaring, and there it is: the tell-tale light on in Uncle Terry's window.

'Fuckity bollocking *Uncle Terry*,' I groan under my breath, still laughing.

Addie just lies back on the water, arms spread, star-shaped. 'He'll just think the wind set it off. Come on. Come in.'

I watch the light warily.

'All your talk about living every moment, finding meaning and seeking "pure, undiluted joy" and you won't join your naked lover in the pool?'

Lover. The word has made its way into the poems I've scrawled in my notebook after leaving her bed, and already it's begun to shift, losing its languid *R*, fast becoming *love*.

I have no doubt about whether this feeling is really love – how can it be anything else? It's excruciating, euphoric, so big I can't seem to write it down.

After a moment's indecision I strip off and jump in the pool.

'A very elegant dive,' Addie tells me, smiling, swimming over and pulling my body against hers. She's cold, her skin pimpling, miniature diamond droplets catching on the tips of her eyelashes.

The villa door creaks open. We freeze. Addie puts a finger to my lips.

'Hello?' Terry calls.

Addie presses her face against my neck, trying not to laugh. There are no lights out here, just the stars, but if he comes on to the terrace, Terry will see the shape of us, pale against the dark blue water.

The door closes again. He's gone back inside.

'See?' Addie says. 'Told you.'

We circle in the water, holding each other, unhurried. A few days ago I couldn't have managed this – I'd have hitched her up on to the edge of the pool and begun kissing my way up the inside of her thighs. But seven long nights of holding her like this, naked against me, and I can just about manage the luxury of savouring her.

'Addie,' I whisper.

'Mm?'

'You're amazing. Do you know that?'

She presses wet lips to my collarbone. I shiver. *Savour*, I remind myself, though it's becoming a less tempting option by the moment.

'Here I am . . .' I tell her, then steal a quick, deep kiss. 'Spending my summer flopping like a fish, shape-shifting, trying to figure myself out . . .'

I swallow. Even talking about it brings that shuddering panic back to my throat, the weight like a heavy hand pushing at my chest, my father's voice in my ears; I concentrate on Addie, her slicked-back hair glossy in the dark. Addie, my answer to everything.

'And here *you* are,' I say. 'Already perfect.'

She huffs, a little laugh against my neck.

'That's nonsense. Nobody's perfect. Definitely not me. Don't do that.'

'Do what?'

'Make me your manic pixie dream girl.'

I drift back so I can see her face, indistinct in the darkness.

'What's that?'

'You know, in films? The girl who's there to help the hero find himself? She never has her own story.'

I frown. She often does this, turning a compliment into something uncomfortable.

'I didn't mean anything like that.'

'Just because I know what I want to be, and where I want to live, and all that, it doesn't mean I'm . . . done. I'm figuring things out too. I mean, God knows if I'm going to survive Teaching Direct when the summer ends.'

I shake my head, pulling her in again, no longer treading water. 'You'll be brilliant. You'll be a wonderful teacher. A natural.' I dip my head to kiss her. 'You're always teaching *me* new things.'

She smiles reluctantly, and I move closer, shifting her up so her legs wrap around my waist.

'I worry nobody will take me seriously.'

'Why wouldn't they?'

She chews her bottom lip, stroking my wet hair back from my face. 'I don't know. People just don't.'

There's that rare, raw vulnerability in her eyes again; she's watching me closely, and I have a creeping sense that this is some sort of test.

'Maybe I give off a vibe. A low-potential vibe.'

'Low potential?' I pull back, genuinely aghast. 'You?'

She laughs, low and throaty, and turns her gaze aside. 'I'm just . . . I've always been kind of *middle*ish. Middle sets in school. Average grades. The only thing about me that isn't average is my height.'

She *is* pint-sized. I love it, how I can almost span her back with one hand, how she has to tilt her head right back to kiss me.

'Addie Gilbert,' I say, in a serious voice. 'This is very important.'

'What is?'

I lean forward so our lips are barely a centimetre apart. 'You. Are. Extraordinary,' I whisper.

'Oh, shush,' she says, breaking away from me and swimming backwards.

I lunge for her. 'No, no,' I say, as imperiously as I can manage. 'Enough of this absurdity. You're going to *take* this compliment if it kills you.'

She's laughing now. 'No, God, don't start,' she says, as she eludes me again, ripples slipping between my fingers.

'You're absolutely extraordinary. Do you know what people would do to be as *together* as you are, aged twenty-one? You don't take shit from anybody, not even me, and I'm *very* charming.' I lunge again, catching her ankle until she kicks away, giggling and spluttering. 'You care about people – don't think I haven't noticed you trying to curb Uncle Terry's excessive drinking, and helping Victor with the weeding since he hurt his back.'

'Oh, please,' Addie says, treading water in the deep end. 'You'd have to be an idiot not to see Terry's a liver problem waiting to happen. And I ought to have helped Victor with the weeding *before* he hurt his back. That would've been the above-average thing to do.'

I roll my eyes. 'You care about doing your job properly. Even though it's just me and Terry here, you're still on top of everything, noticing every detail.'

'So I got you a fresh towel this morning and sorted the dodgy fridge door. Big whoop.' Addie ducks under the water to dart away from me, dolphin-style.

'Addie,' I say, getting exasperated. 'It's not about that on-paper nonsense, not really. It's about *all* this. You're just good at life. All of the important bits. I mean, you say I'm always talking about finding joy and meaning and living in the moment, and I *am* – we all bloody well are—'

'Well,' Addie says, 'those of us who have the luxury of time for musing on life's meaning.'

'Right, right, but I mean . . . you're just so good at taking life as it *is*. *Nobody* I know does that.'

'Everyone you know goes to Oxford University,' Addie points out. 'And, by definition, thinks too hard.'

'Are you ever going to accept a single nice thing I say about you?'

She swims towards me, at last. 'You can tell me I look beautiful tonight.'

'You look beautiful tonight.'

'Ah, now you're just saying that . . .'

I grab her and tickle her as best I can in the water – she flails and splashes and laughs, her head thrown back, eyes shining with glee.

I chase her to the end of the swimming pool. As she twists, she spreads her arms against the pool's edge, dreamlike in the darkness, and locks her legs around me again. We slow, chests heaving, then still. She rakes her fingers through my hair again, a little harder this time.

'I like you, Dylan,' she whispers. 'More than I ought to.'

My pulse quickens. 'There's no ought.'

'Course there is. Give it a few months, you'll be off chasing the next blonde from Atlanta. You with your romantic notions and your beautiful speeches and your notebook full of poetry . . .' She leans her head back and looks up at the stars. 'You're going to break my heart, Dylan Abbott. I can feel it.'

I frown and reach to tilt her chin downwards again. 'No. That's – I was – we're not like that. We're different, me and you. I'll never break your heart, Addie.'

She smiles wryly. 'And so said every gentleman to the girl who lived in the servant's quarters, eh?'

Addie

All right, I'm freaking out.

We're moving way too fast. Anyone can see that. It's only been eight days. Of course he still looks at me like I'm a queen – we're sleeping together every night and he doesn't actually know me well enough to have anything to dislike.

I wish I hadn't said all that stuff about being middleish last night. I should be playing it cool, keeping him chasing. That's what Deb would do, and men *never* fall out of love with her. She actually finds it quite annoying.

The problem is, Dylan's just so sweet. His sleepy green-yellow eyes. The way he seems to *see* me. It's all making me fall in love with him, and that is absolutely the stupidest thing any woman can do after one week of sleeping with a bloke on holiday.

I spend the morning away from the villa. We needed some food in, and I take way longer than I have to in the Intermarché. Afterwards I drive into the village and chat to the café owner in broken French while I munch my way through a huge pain au chocolat. I make him laugh and stand up a little straighter. I don't need Dylan. This was my summer before he came, and look, it's beautiful.

I mean to head straight to the flat when I get back, but Dylan's sat reading poetry aloud on the stone balustrade around the terrace. He's thirty feet up from me down here in the courtyard. His legs are dangling over and he says something to himself about *silver slips of starlight*. I can't resist stopping to look up at him, holding my forearm up to block the sun. The feeling hits me in the chest, a huge gust of it.

'Oh, good,' he calls down. 'Someone to serenade. Ever so embarrassing to be serenading without an object.'

'An object!'

'Purely a figure of grammar,' he says hastily, and I laugh. 'Subject-verb-object and all that.'

'Is it one of your poems?' I ask. He never shows me his own work, though he's always happy reading me bits of sixteenth-century stuff. It doesn't make sense to me. Where Dylan hears something incredibly profound, I just hear something you could say in way fewer words.

'It was, but only because I'd got distracted. I'm reading Philip Sidney,' Dylan says, waving a battered paperback down at me. '*Sir* Philip Sidney, actually. Courtier, diplomat, poet.'

'Old guy?' I guess.

He smiles. 'Yeah. Died 1586.'

'*Very* old guy.'

Dylan's battered brown Havaianas dangle from his feet over the edge of the balustrade.

'Read me something,' I call. I want to get it, the poetry thing. It's just so foreign to me.

'*My true love hath my heart*,' he begins, '*and I have his.*'

'His?'

'It's a woman speaking, not Philip himself,' Dylan says. 'He's not saying he's in love with a man. He was almost certainly a homophobic bigot, what with being a rich chap in the sixteenth century. Come up here, would you? I want to hold you.'

I grin despite myself. 'Philip!' I say, making my way towards the steps up to the terrace. 'First-name terms, are you?'

'Phil. Phil-man. Philster,' Dylan says, poker-faced.

I'm giggling now. 'Go on. Your true love's got your heart, you've got his?' I climb up beside him on the balustrade and he wraps an arm around my waist, tucking me in close. I snag his beer and take a swig.

'*My true love hath my heart and I have his. By just exchange one to the other given. I hold his dear and mine he cannot miss. There never was a better bargain driven.*'

I kind of get that, actually. I think. Love as a bargain. Like, giving up your heart is scary, but doable if the other person does it at the exact same moment, like two soldiers lowering their weapons.

The rest of the poem is a muddle of words in the wrong order – *For as from me on him his hurt did light* and that sort of stuff. When he finishes reading I swap him his beer for the book.

'Yeah?' Dylan says. He looks so excited as I take the book. It's adorable, but it kind of scares me too, because of all the times he's read me something and I've not got it.

'If I like this one,' I say, 'will you show me one of yours?'

He pulls a face. 'Oh, God, it'd be like showing you my teenage journal. Or . . .'

'Your internet search history?'

Dylan grins. 'Why, what's in yours?'

'Is that what you need?' I ask, arching one eyebrow. 'Tit for tat?'

'You're calling my poetry tat, are you?' Dylan says, then feigns thoughtfulness. 'Though, tit would be a . . .'

'Shut up. You know what I meant. You need me to tell you something embarrassing too?'

'It'd help, certainly.' Dylan sips his beer, and I can tell he's trying not to grin.

I hesitate for a moment and then swing my legs around, leaving the book on the ledge. The morning away from the villa has made me feel in control again. There's no harm in giving him a little more of myself, is there?

'Come on.'

I lead him back to the flat, through to the cupboard where me and Deb are storing our suitcases. Dylan leans on the door frame and watches as I pull out my suitcase and unzip it.

He laughs when he sees what's inside and my cheeks instantly flush. I'm already clumsily re-zipping the case by the time his arms close around me from behind.

'No, no, don't. I *love* this. Please tell me you build model trains for fun.'

I squirm in his arms. Why did I do this?

'I love it, Addie,' he says, more gently. 'I wasn't laughing at you. It was – it was a delighted laugh. A surprised one.'

He presses a kiss to my cheek. After a long, painful moment I lift out the Flying Scotsman. It's tucked at the base of the suitcase where it won't get squashed. There's a wheel missing but otherwise it survived the journey to France pretty well.

'It's my dad's thing,' I say. Dylan tries to turn me in his arms but I stay put. It's easier this way, not looking at him. 'He's always loved it. We used to do it together, with Deb, when I was a kid. She went through this phase where she was train mad, and that's how it started, and then Dad just never stopped. I usually do a project with him whenever I go home. This is the one we did before I came to France.'

'It must take *ages*,' Dylan says. 'May I?'

I let him take it and step away. I glance up from under my eyelashes. He's not laughing now. He's examining the model train like it's totally fascinating.

It's like he's just dropped the last coin into the slots machine. It all comes rushing down and I'm falling in love with him, I am, I can't stop myself.

'It's amazing,' he says, inspecting the joins. 'Is it hard?'

I shake my head. I'm feeling so much I'm sure he must be able to see it all radiating off me.

'It just takes patience,' I manage.

'Ah, I'd be dreadful at it.'

I laugh. 'Yeah, you'd be crap.'

He kisses me on the cheek again. They're still burning hot.

'So? Where's my tat?' I say, moving away. It's that or burrow into his chest. The emotions are getting too big.

'Really?' He grimaces, rubbing one hand up and down his arm. 'Do I have to?'

'I showed you my train!'

'Your train is adorable. My poems are . . . pompous self-indulgence.'

'I bet they're brilliant.'

He shakes his head. 'Nope. Drivel. Really, Addie, they're tripe.'

'Come on. I know you've got your notebook in your pocket.'

'That? I'm just pleased to see you.'

I lunge for him. He runs, darting through into the kitchen, down to the courtyard, through to the gardens. I catch up with him on the lawn and tackle him. He shrieks as we go barrelling into a rosemary bush.

'Christ!' he says, laughing, breathless. 'Are you secretly a rugby player, too?'

'Built for it,' I say, fumbling for the pocket of his jeans. 'Are you going to let me steal the whole book, or read me one?'

'Read you one, read you one,' he says, rolling out of the bush and brushing himself down. He holds out a hand to help me up, then pulls me over to the bench set on the edge of the lawn. The view's amazing from here. The vines are so perfectly spaced on the hills, like green pinstripes.

Dylan leafs through his notebook. I set my legs across his lap and nestle close.

'A short one?' he says in a small voice.

'OK. A short one.'

He clears his throat and begins.

Before I Heard Her Name

All that time – poised
In the dark, waiting,
Questless, undone, unmade –
And it wasn't a guiding star at all.
It was a heart, mine.
She had it even then,
Before I heard her name.

My eyes prick. I don't get what it means, not really, but I don't think that matters. I know he wrote it for me.

'Addie? Ads?'

I swallow. I hide my face in his neck. 'I love it,' I whisper. 'I love it.'

Dylan

For the first time, we spend the night in my suite instead of Addie's flat. The grand house makes her look smaller than ever, her fine-boned hands trailing up the oak bannister, her tiny shoes left at the bottom of the stairs; she seems a little skittish, dancing out of my grip and treading so lightly you can hardly hear she's there at all. Once we're in bed, though, she's herself again: fierce and beautiful, heavy-eyed, plaintive when I make her wait.

Tonight, I plan to tell her I love her. It's risky, certainly – there's a very real chance I'll scare her away. She's always retreating then returning, disappearing to the village for hours and then curling up catlike beside me when she comes back; unzipping that suitcase and then trying to zip it closed again like she wishes she'd never given me that glimpse of herself. She ebbs and flows, my river sprite.

Addie lies with her head on my chest, her legs tangled in the dark blue coverlets, her hair spilling across my arm. I stare at her, *aching* with it, loving her, loving every freckle that leaves its tiny kiss on her cheek, and I have to tell her, I have to, it's burning on my tongue.

'Addie, I—'

'Holy *shit*.'

She moves so fast she's up and flattened against the bedroom wall before I've even processed what she's said.

'Addie? What? What is it?'

'There! Out there! A face!'

'Outside? We're two floors up!'

My heart starts to beat faster. I'm not good at this sort of thing. I'm not the man who slips out of bed in the night to investigate the noise downstairs, I'm the one who says, *It's probably nothing*, and stays under the covers, quietly quivering.

'I one hundred per cent saw a face,' Addie says. She's very pale. 'It was right up against the glass for a second, then it was gone.'

I edge off the bed and reach for my boxers, tossing Addie her dress. She slips it on with shaking hands.

'I swear I saw it,' she says.

'I believe you.' I don't *want* to believe her, particularly, but any hope that she's joking evaporates as soon as I see her terrified expression. 'Maybe it's Terry joshing around?'

'It wasn't Terry.' Addie rubs her arms. 'Where's the key?'

'What?'

'The key to the doors,' she says impatiently. 'To the balcony.'

'Oh, good God, no, you're not going out there,' I say. 'Absolutely not. What if there's a murderer out there?'

She stares at me blankly. 'What's your plan, wait for him in here?'

'Yes! No, I mean, it's safe in here! There are walls and locked doors between us and the murderers!'

Addie half laughs at that. Her jaw is set now and she lifts her chin. 'I'm not waiting, trapped in here. That's way worse. Dylan, sweetie, come on – give me the key.'

She's never called me *sweetie* before, and I'm not sure I like it – it feels like something she would say to a friend, or maybe to a rather frightened child. I straighten up and pull back my shoulders.

'I'll go. See who's out there.'

Addie raises her eyebrows slightly. 'Yeah? You sure?'

I'm surprised to discover that I am indeed sure. It's a humbling realisation: this is love, then. That explains a great deal about many irrational acts throughout history – every man who ever went to war must have *really* fancied somebody.

I take the key from the bedside table and walk to the balcony doors, trying very hard to remember to breathe.

Just as I fiddle around with the lock there's a thump on the glass. Two hands thrown flat against the windows. A chalky pale face. Eyes wide, the whites showing. Teeth bared.

I jump so much I trip on the rug and go tumbling backwards, falling with a thud that sends a dull shock of pain up my back. Addie's screaming, a truly guttural, terrified scream, and for a horrifying moment I really think I might wet myself. The slam, the eyes, the teeth. I looked away when I fell; for an endless second I can't bear to look back.

When I do, the face is still there, grinning, shaking the handles of the doors. It takes another moment – teetering, ice-cold – to meet its gaze and realise exactly who is standing on my balcony.

'Oh, Jesus Christ . . . Addie. Don't worry. It's Marcus.'

I stand gingerly. Marcus is still cackling and slamming his hands on the balcony doors, and I shake my head as I try to unlock them.

'Stop messing with the handles,' I tell him. 'You're making it worse.'

'You *know* that man?' Addie asks.

I glance back at her. She's clutching at the neck of her dress, pale, her eyes wide and round; she reminds me of something wild, a tarsier, an owl. Her hair is ruffled and tangled from the night in bed, and for a strange second or two the adrenaline shifts to something more like desire, and I want her again, Marcus on the balcony forgotten.

'Well, hello,' Marcus says, pressing his face to the glass, his eyes on Addie. 'Where did he find you? You're like a little doll, aren't you?'

'Excuse me?' Addie says, moving to stand beside me. 'Who is this guy, Dylan?'

As I finally manage to unlock the doors and Marcus barges his way into the room, I feel absurdly proud of Addie. *Try not to get too bored without me*, Marcus had said when I flew to Avignon, and now here I am with Addie, with her fierce blue eyes and her liquid dark hair, and I found her all on my own.

Marcus stretches out a hand to her and gives her his most charming, leonine smile. He smells of booze, an acrid scent like rotting fruit. 'Forgiven?' he says.

Addie raises her eyebrow. 'On what grounds?'

'Hey?'

'Forgiveness is earned, typically,' she says, reaching for her underwear at the foot of the bed and balling it up in the pocket of her dress. 'That balcony thing . . . it wasn't funny.' She heads for the door.

'Hey, hey,' I say, rushing to her side. 'Hey, don't go. I thought you were going to sleep here.' The day has slipped away, ripples through my fingers, and I still haven't said the words hanging heavy in the air. I want to say them now, *Don't go, I love you*, but—

'I need some time to calm down,' she says.

Now I'm closer, I can see fine tremors running up and down her limbs; the flush on her cheek is too lurid.

'Are you OK?'

She gives me a short smile. 'Fine.' She looks at Marcus. 'Nice to meet you,' she says, with some irony if I'm not mistaken, and then she walks out the door.

'I want her.'

This is the first thing Marcus says to me.

'You . . .' I'm still looking at the door, a little lost. Addie left so fast, and . . .

'That one. I want her. She looks interesting.'

Suddenly that protective instinct that was so lacking when we heard the noise on the balcony kicks in full-throttle: *You can't have her*, I want to say. There comes a rush of what must be aggression, or maybe adrenaline – something deep and instinctual, some distant relation of the impulse that sets my heart racing when Addie touches her lips to mine.

Marcus looks at me appraisingly. He tucks a curl behind his ear and pouts.

'Oh, you *like* her,' he says. 'I figured you were just fucking her.'

I recoil. Marcus laughs.

'Oh, you *really* like her. You won't even let me *talk* about fucking her.'

'Just . . .' *Stop saying that, stop saying it, stop saying it.*

'So is that girl the reason you didn't tell me your family hadn't turned up? We could have spent a fortnight here already!' Marcus says, spinning on the spot, arms outstretched. He's dressed in a loose white shirt and shorts that would look absurdly short on me, but somehow work on him; his hair is long enough to be pulled back in a ponytail at the nape of his neck now, and even *that* looks good.

'I'm here with my uncle Terry,' I say. 'I didn't think you'd want to come.'

Marcus raises his eyebrows, clearly not buying the lie. 'You knew I'd take her off you, that's why,' he says, leaning forward to punch me on the arm.

It hurts. I turn aside, half laughing so he can't tell it's made my eyes prick. My whole body aches to go after Addie – I should be downstairs with her, not here with Marcus.

He reaches into his pocket and pulls out a little plastic bag with a round plug of weed inside. He waggles it at me.

'Here, or outside?' he says.

I haven't smoked since getting here. It's been a pleasant change to have a clear head, and I consider saying no, but even as I have the thought, I know I won't do it.

'Outside,' I say, thinking of Addie having to clean the smell out of the curtains and bedsheets. 'Come on. I'll take you down to the pool.'

As we talk about Marcus's week down on the terrace, our feet trailing in the water, I think of Addie and Deb. From what Addie's told me, she and her sister are just the same as me and Marcus: joined at the hip, always a pair. I wonder if sometimes Addie resents it, always being Deb's little sister, her partner in crime.

'You *sure* I can't have that pretty one with the blue eyes?' Marcus says abruptly, kicking up a splash with one foot.

It takes me a moment to realise he's talking about Addie. 'You're such a caveman.'

'What! I'm asking. I'm being polite.' He stretches his hands out, like, *Look at me, aren't I evolved?*

'You can't have her.' I'm surprised to hear how steady my voice sounds. It's not often I say no to Marcus – not often anyone does.

'Oh, she's yours, is she? My, aren't we getting territorial! Now who's the caveman?'

'She's . . .'

Addie is bigger than that sort of talk. She is wild and clever, sharp and bright, always twisting out of my reach. She isn't mine. I'm hers.

'She's different,' I settle for. 'Addie's different.'

Addie

It takes me ages to calm down. What a wanker. Who does that? Who arrives at someone else's house and climbs up on to the balcony and tries to break in instead of just knocking on the bloody door?

I throw laundry into the washing machine. Is this Dylan's life away from here? People like his uncle Terry and that prick who called me a *little doll*? It's midnight – not my usual laundry hour, but I can't sleep and I want to *do* something.

I wish Deb was here to make me laugh about it all. It wouldn't seem like a big deal to her – Marcus is clearly a bit of a dick, but yeah, that's all there is to it. Whereas to me, it seems like . . . the bubble bursting. I should have known things with Dylan were too good to be true.

The next morning I stick to the routine and head down to the village to fetch us all croissants. When I get back Terry and Marcus are lying on either side of Dylan on the terrace. They're quiet, sunglasses on. The stone is already hot under my bare feet.

'Ooh, for me?' Marcus says, raising his sunglasses as I approach.

Dylan gets up quickly, meeting me halfway.

'Hey,' he breathes. For a moment as our fingers touch it feels like it's just the two of us in the heat.

'Come on, Dylan. Have you forgotten how to share?' Marcus calls.

I let go of the bag. 'There's plenty of croissants in there,' I say, already backing away. 'I bought enough.'

I stay away for the rest of the day. Marcus puts me on edge. He's built like a Topshop model, skinny and pale and cool with this half-styled shock of curly hair. So yeah, he's attractive, in an I-sing-in-a-band kind of way. But he's kind of cold behind the eyes, somehow.

Dylan knocks on my door at midnight. I smile up at the ceiling. I'm in bed, but I'd hoped he'd come. I like that he gave me space today, but I like it even more that he's come to see me once everyone's gone to bed.

I answer the door in my pyjamas – cropped T-shirt, cotton shorts. It's not Dylan. It's Marcus.

'Evening,' he says. 'I think we got off on the wrong foot.' He half smiles at me, head tilted. 'Want to come have a drink on the terrace? Make peace? For Dylan's sake?'

He's all chilled and casual, but he holds my gaze just a little bit too steadily. It makes everything feel off. Like there's another conversation going on under this one, but I can't quite translate it.

'Where *is* Dylan?' I ask.

'Oh, don't blame him for not being here,' Marcus says. 'I insisted on seeing you alone. I wanted to apologise.'

Well, he hasn't, has he? He's not actually said sorry.

'Come on,' he says, leaning on the door frame. His T-shirt rides up, showing a white triangle of toned, bare midriff. 'Let's get wasted and see if you like me by the morning. It usually works, I find.'

Dylan is sat waiting for us on the terrace, feet dangling in the pool. He beams when he sees me, pushing his hair out of his eyes and patting the stone beside him. I'm almost by Dylan's side when Marcus dive-bombs into the water. I stumble back, surprised and – bloody hell – half drenched.

Dylan laughs. 'Christ, Marcus, you're such a child.' His tone is fond.

Marcus surfaces, his curls flattened to his head. 'Let's get pissed, shall we?' he says, lunging for the bottle of red beside Dylan.

As Marcus swims off with the wine, Dylan looks at me. He's worried. Good – he should be.

'You OK?' he whispers, passing me his glass.

'Mm,' I say. I take a long gulp of wine. 'Thought it would be you knocking on the door, that's all.'

Dylan bites his lip. 'Oh, no, was that wrong? Should I have come around first? I didn't know whether to – Marcus was sure you'd want him to apologise himself, and that did seem . . .'

'Can you get up on the roof?' Marcus asks. He's lying on his back now, open bottle bobbing in his hand. He's carefully keeping it upright, I notice.

Dylan and I turn to look at the villa.

'There's a loft,' I say after a moment. 'You can get to it from the bedroom next to Dylan's. But I don't think there's a way on to the actual roof.'

Marcus swims to the edge and heaves himself up out of the pool. The water sluices from him, plastering his T-shirt to his skin. He doesn't bother drying off, just heads straight for the house, leaving a small river behind him.

'Let me guess,' I say. 'We're going on to the roof?'

'What Marcus wants . . .' Dylan spreads his hands. 'He tends to get.'

There's a trapdoor from the loft to the roof. I don't know how I never spotted it. I guess it never occurred to me to climb on to the slanted roof of a three-storey villa.

By the time we've explored the whole upstairs, located the trapdoor, found a ladder and got the trapdoor wedged open, we're all drunk. I'm dizzy as I climb up the rungs, but aware enough to know this is massively dangerous. Marcus is already up there. I can hear him scrabbling around on the tiles. I look down at Dylan. He looks different from this angle, sort of younger.

'Dylan? You coming up?' Marcus calls from the roof.

I take another step, my head and shoulders emerging above the trapdoor. It's hard to read Marcus's expression in the darkness as he looks over and sees me instead of his best friend.

'Are you going to help me out?' I say eventually.

He stretches out a hand. The roof is only gently sloped here, and Marcus has his feet lodged in the guttering so he can't slide off, but still, it's mad, this. We could really die.

I take his hand and let him help me up. His skin's cool. He smells of the pool, and an aftershave a bit like Dylan's, but sharper. I shuffle on my bum, carefully twisting so I can lie back and look at the night sky.

'Wow.' There are so many stars, more than I've ever seen before. They're everywhere, stretching out all around us, sliding into the edges of my vision. *The sky is so big*, I think. I've drunk too much wine too fast – I'd never normally have a thought like that.

'Sublime, isn't it?' Marcus says. 'In the Edmund Burke sense.'

I've no idea what that means. If it were Dylan, I'd ask, but there's no way I'm asking Marcus.

Dylan coughs from beneath us. 'Shit, Terry's up!' he hisses. 'Let me go fob him off, hang on.'

Marcus laughs lightly. It's so dark, just the light from the loft bulb shining up through the trapdoor. Marcus's hand brushes the back of mine for a moment as he shifts on the tiles.

'He's scared to come up,' Marcus says.

'Who, Dylan?'

'He doesn't like heights. But he tends to forget until he gets there.'

I can hear the smile in Marcus's voice. I can hardly look at all the stars above us, like my brain just won't take it all in.

'You weren't scared,' Marcus says.

'I was.'

'But you're up here anyway.'

'Sure.'

'Are you the sort of woman who always does the dangerous thing?'

I smile at that. 'Not at all. I'm not that exciting.'

'I think you are,' Marcus says. He shifts. I think he's turned to look at me, though it's hard to be sure in the darkness. 'And I'm excellent at reading people.'

'Right,' I say, humouring him. 'Sure you are.'

'Your school reports always said you had *lots of potential*. You've worn those bracelets on your wrist since you were thirteen, maybe earlier – you feel naked without them. You love to dance, and you love to be seen, and you hate to be forgotten. And when you stand at the edge of a sheer drop with somebody else . . . you think for just a moment about pushing them off.'

My foot slips a little and I gasp. Marcus chuckles.

'Am I right?'

'You're a cliché,' I tell him, resettling, pulse slowing. 'You're even trying to mansplain *me* to *myself*.'

'Ah, but I'm right, though.'

I shake my head, but I've found as the evening's gone on that it's hard to be pissed off with Marcus. You get the sense he doesn't take a single thing seriously. Telling him off would be like trying to discipline a cat.

'I do love dancing,' I concede. 'I'll give you that.'

'I'd dance with you now if the roof were a little flatter,' Marcus says.

I frown. He's flirting. I don't really know what to do about it, and the silence stretches, awkward, until he laughs into the dark.

'You really like Dylan, don't you?' he says.

'Yeah, I really like him.'

'He told you about Grace?'

'The woman he was looking for when he got here? Yeah, he told me.' We've not talked about her much. Just enough to make me feel pretty confident he's not actually that bothered.

'So he told you she was with me when they started sleeping together?'

'I . . .' *What?*

'Oh, he didn't betray me, or anything as prosaic as that. I can feel the judgement coming off you in waves. I knew, he knew, that's just how we roll.'

I can hear Dylan coming back into the loft below us. 'Is it very high?' he calls up at us. 'I mean, of course it is, but . . . Is it *very* high? You know, does it *feel* high?'

Marcus laughs. 'He's kidding himself if he thinks he'll really do it,' he says, and this time when his hand brushes mine I can't write it off as an accident.

'He'll do it,' I say sharply, and shift away. 'You can't even tell there's a drop!' I call down. 'It's too dark! It's just stars and stars and stars. Come on. It's amazing, you'll love it. Just climb up the ladder and stick your head out so you can see.'

Dylan emerges eventually, lit from below. His face is frozen in an expression I've not seen before. I can't help smiling. He looks absolutely adorable, his sleepy green eyes almost clenched shut, his hair all mussed.

'Look up,' I tell him. 'Just look up.'

He tilts his head back. I hear him breathe out. Marcus is silent behind me.

'Good God,' Dylan says. 'It's like . . .' He trails off.

'There's not much that leaves Dylan unable to find a simile,' Marcus says wryly.

Dylan looks back towards us. His eyes aren't clenched quite so tightly now, but I can't tell who he's looking at, me or Marcus.

'Well?' Marcus says, as the moment stretches out. 'Are you in or out, my friend? Up or down?'

Dylan takes a tentative step up the ladder and pauses again. 'Oh, God,' he says in a strangled voice.

I shuffle closer. 'You don't have to,' I say. 'You can see it fine from there.'

His mouth takes on this fixed look, like he's gritting his teeth, and he takes another step up the ladder, then crawls himself up on to the roof. His chest is heaving by the time he's next to me, but he lies back beside me without a word. I reach for his hand and squeeze it tight.

'Dylan Abbott,' Marcus says, sounding mildly impressed. 'Aren't you just full of surprises?'

NOW

Dylan

Deb is driving, Dolly Parton is playing, and Marcus is hungry; the result of these three things in combination is almost certain to be bad, so I am very much on edge.

'You just have to wait,' Deb tells Marcus, voice raised over Dolly.

Addie's still sitting next to me, still so distracting I have to close my eyes whenever she moves. Thank goodness for Rodney, squashed to the other side of me, intermittently singing along to 'Here You Come Again' with infuriatingly incorrect lyrics.

'There!' Marcus yells, so suddenly everyone jumps. 'Burger van! Pull over!'

'Fucking hell!' Deb says. 'Stop shouting at me!'

'Pull in, then!' Marcus says urgently. 'I need food.'

I lean forward. 'He is much easier to manage when he has been fed, just to flag.'

Deb makes a noise somewhere between a growl and a *fuck-sake* and pulls over just in time, braking so hard we're all thrown forward. Addie rubs the back of her neck, wincing.

'Are you OK?' I ask her, as Deb parks up by the burger van.

For a second I want Addie to say no so that I can do something, check her shoulder, her neck, just *touch* her. It's such a bizarre, torturous thing to be pressed up against the one person whose body I know almost as well as my own, to have my thigh sliding against hers, and not even be able to place my hand on her arm.

'Fine, yeah, just the whiplash from earlier,' she says. She turns her face away from me, examining the sun-streaked trees through the window as her fingers test at the muscles of her neck; my hands twitch with the urge to cover her fingers with mine.

'Bacon butties!' Marcus says, climbing out of the front passenger seat and slamming his door.

Addie opens her door and I climb out behind her; my legs are so stiff that when I stand, I make that *oof* sound men like my uncle Terry do when they sit down on a sofa.

'We weren't meant to stop for lunch until we got to Stoke-on-Trent,' Deb grumbles, dropping into step with us.

'You're the one who had to fit in a quickie with a trucker,' Marcus says over his shoulder.

There's a couple of blokes in sweat-dampened T-shirts eating bacon sandwiches at their cars, squinting against the fierce sun, but there's no queue, and Marcus all but runs to the van.

'Was Marcus being judgemental there, d'you think?' Deb asks, turning to me and Addie. 'Do I need to bollock him?'

'Definitely,' Addie says, just as I say,

'Definitely not.'

They both turn to me and, in perfect unison, raise their eyebrows.

'Marcus doesn't really do judgement, honestly,' I say, spreading my hands. The twin gazes of the Gilbert sisters are somewhat terrifying, and my heart skips a little. 'I just mean, there's almost no life choice that Marcus would find unacceptable.'

'I give no shits for whether he likes my life choices,' Deb says. 'I personally couldn't be happier with them, trucker-quickie included.

But if he has opinions on my decisions, I'd like to inform him that he should keep them to himself.'

This is one thing that does not seem to have changed about Deb. She may now be a mother – something I never thought I'd say about Deb Gilbert – but she still has that unbelievable ability to *genuinely* not care what other people think. I've never met anyone else with that skill; plenty of people who feign it, or aspire to it, but none who embody it quite like Deb.

'I can still hear you,' Marcus calls, having placed his order at the van. 'And can confirm that I have absolutely no opinions about your life decisions. I myself am very partial to a quickie with a randomer.'

He walks back to us, taking a large bite from his bacon butty, as behind him Rodney places his order.

'Bacon butty with egg, mushroom and burger sauce, please, sir!' he says.

'His life choices, on the other hand,' Marcus says, pointing to Rodney, 'those I have opinions about.'

'What would you like?' I say to Addie as Marcus and Deb start squabbling again.

'Oh, I'll get mine,' she says quickly, reaching for the pocket of her dungarees.

This is just the sort of moment that would once have made me freeze up: any conversation about money with Addie felt like a trap, because I *never* handled it right. I'd insist on paying, which was wrong; I'd make a big fuss of letting her pay, also wrong; I'd say something stupid like *Why does it even matter who gets this, it's only a fiver*. When Addie used to say I was weird about money, I found it infuriating, but I get it now. These days I am well acquainted with the stomach-writhing terror of a declined card, the genuine joy of finding something you want for dinner in the reduced section at the supermarket. I've had a friend insist on paying for me many times, now, and I know precisely what that feels like.

'Sure,' I say, stepping aside slightly so Addie can order first. Easy and casual is what I'm aiming for, and I think I come pretty close, or at least, as close as one can get when making a huge effort to make no effort at all.

Addie double takes before giving her order. It's just a tiny blink-blink and a turn of the head, but I love it, I love that I've surprised her. *See, I've changed!* I want to shout. *I'm different, I'm better, you were right, I was a tit about* all *those things, but look how much less of a tit I have become!*

'Bacon and egg butty, please,' I say instead, to the woman inside the van. 'No sauce.'

Addie

'Dylan *didn't* try to stop me paying for something just now,' I hiss to Deb.

She's leaning against the car, working her way through a hot dog. Deb eats at serious speed. She claims it's all about focus, but I'm pretty sure she just doesn't chew.

'What, he didn't even go all blustery and awkward and drop something first?' Deb asks, mouth full.

I shush her, glancing at Dylan. He's stood with Marcus and Rodney, looking painfully sexy, even while eating a bacon and egg butty, which is very hard to do attractively.

'He was just totally normal about it.'

'Astonishing. Do you think now he's . . . Addie? Ads?'

There's something in my throat.

I cough but it stays there, and it's hard to breathe, I can feel it sitting there right in the top of my throat. Whatever it is feels enormous, like a golf ball, and my breath's coming too fast. I'm starting to panic.

Someone hits me on the back, right between my shoulder blades. *Hard.* A small lump goes flying out of my mouth and I can breathe again. I double over, gasping for air. I retch and taste acid in my throat. My neck hurts again, a nasty hot pain like when you twist it the wrong way too fast.

'All right now?'

I straighten slowly and turn. It's Marcus. He's looking at me properly, as if he's actually trying to see me – so far today he's looked at me like he's really trying *not* to.

It was him who slapped me on the back. I don't know how he got over here so fast. Dylan and Rodney are coming but they're still a good few seconds behind him.

'Fine,' I croak.

Marcus is frowning. His eyes move over my face. The feel of his gaze on me is suddenly so familiar, and I flush, remembering how he used to look at me, once.

'Addie, are you all right?' Dylan says, appearing behind Marcus with Rodney in tow.

I swallow and wipe my eyes. I can still feel where it was, that lump in my throat.

'All fine, just a bit of bacon rind.'

Marcus has backed off now, but I know his eyes are tracking me. I look at Dylan – he's glancing at Marcus, but he turns back when he feels my gaze, and as he meets my eyes his expression is so tender. It makes my heart ache. He shouldn't be looking at me like that, not now.

The sun beats down. Marcus watches me, I watch Dylan, Dylan keeps his eyes on both of us.

There's a plop, and suddenly everyone's gaze turns down, following the sound. Rodney has just dropped the whole fried egg out of the end of his butty. It lies there, flaccid and pale, right next to the lump of bacon rind I just spat out.

'I'd imagined this road trip being a bit more glamorous than it's turning out to be,' Deb says to me after a moment. 'Hadn't you?'

'Careful, Rodders,' Marcus says, nodding to Rodney's butty. 'You're about to lose the bacon, too.'

THEN

Dylan

I wake the next morning to a crushing headache and a tall blonde straddling me, one hand firmly gripping my face. If it weren't for the headache and the fact that the blonde is extremely familiar, I would assume this were a particularly exciting dream, but alas, it's just Cherry.

'*Oof*,' I say, pushing her off me. 'What are you *doing*, woman?'

'Just finishing up!' she says. 'There!'

She has a pen in her other hand – an ominous sign. I wipe the back of my hand across my face and it remains clean, which is even more alarming, since it indicates permanent marker.

'What have you done to me? And why are you even here?'

'Everyone's here!' Cherry says, hopping off me.

'What do you mean, everyone?' I sit up, rubbing my eyes.

Cherry, true to form, is bounding about my suite like a puppy exploring new terrain, which feels particularly ridiculous given that this villa not only belongs to her parents but is in fact named in her honour.

'Marcus messaged yesterday saying you were holed up here on your own with my Addie!' Cherry says, blonde ponytail flicking as she disappears into the bathroom. 'Why didn't you tell me! I am *such* a fan of you and her as a couple, I predict huge things, *huge* – wow, that's a lot of condoms, Dyl! Ambitious much?'

I shove back the covers and climb out of bed, following Cherry into the bathroom and steering her away from where she's rifling through my toiletries.

'Boundaries,' I say. 'Remember we talked about those?'

The door to my bedroom bursts open before she can respond. In they all tumble: my brother, Luke; his boyfriend, Javier, with Marcus riding piggyback on his back; plus Marta and Connie, two of the girls from our third-year house at university. And Grace.

I'm only wearing my boxers, but that doesn't stop them all piling into me; I manage to stagger back so that when we fall, we land on a chaise longue in a tangle of limbs. Connie kisses one of my eyes – I think she's aiming for my forehead; Luke ruffles my hair like Dad used to do when he was in a good mood; Marcus grins down at me, his face no more than an inch from mine. Cherry has given him the artistic treatment too: one of his eyes has been covered with a drawn-on eyepatch, like a pirate, and he is sporting a very detailed goatee.

'Morning,' he says. 'I thought things were getting boring. Didn't you?'

'We're going hiking, Dyl,' Cherry calls, disappearing out of the bedroom door. 'I'm getting Addie!'

'Wait!' I yell, but she's already gone, and there are far too many exuberant bodies piled above for me to follow her. 'Shit,' I say. 'Marcus . . .'

'You didn't think to tell me you were going on the family holiday solo?' my brother says, heaving himself off me and settling on the floor, arms loosely braced on his knees. He lifts his eyebrows enquiringly as Javier collapses down beside him, his waist-length hair falling across Luke's arm as he tips his head on to my brother's shoulder.

'Luke is sulking,' Javier informs me.

'Connie, stop it,' I say, swatting at her.

She's picking something out of my hair; she shows me what's in her hand, and it's a large dead bug. I make a face. I'm not entirely sure what we all got up to last night.

'Luke, I'm sorry, I just . . .' *Wanted to do my own thing for a while. Wanted some time to be me. Wanted Addie.* 'I don't know, really,' I finish weakly.

Luke's eyebrows stay high, but Javier tugs on his arm, and he lets it go with a sigh. My brother has my dad's looks: he's all broad and stern, his hair a tone lighter than mine and cropped short.

'Dad's furious about this, you know,' Luke says.

'So that's some consolation,' I say, and his grin matches mine.

'And you.' I turn on Grace. 'Where have *you* been?'

She throws her head back to laugh. Her hair is dyed blue, and she's dressed like she's stepped right out of the 1960s: psychedelically patterned dress, white sandals that tie up the leg, and one of those headbands that instantly makes you look slightly stoned. It's a testament to how beautiful she is that she does not look utterly ridiculous. Instead, as always, she's iconic; Grace has this air of drama to her, all long languid limbs and glamour, like a starlet on the brink of her big break.

'Ah, sweet Dylan,' she says, offering a hand to help me out of the human pile-up beneath which I am currently attempting to handle this hangover. 'Marc told me you got bored of chasing me.' She flashes me a wicked smile. 'I simply *had* to see this other woman for myself.'

'Here she is!' Cherry shouts from the doorway.

They all turn at once to look at Addie. She's wearing a cropped sports top and shorts, ready for the hike Cherry has promised; her dark hair is pulled back, showing off the delicate curves of her cheekbones, and beside Cherry she looks tinier than ever. I watch her shrink under the force of the combined attention of Luke, Javier, Marcus, Grace, Connie and Marta.

Grace moves first. She reaches out and takes both of Addie's hands, spreading their arms wide, holding Addie back so she can look at her properly.

'Grace,' she says. '*Enchantée*. I can see *precisely* why you've got my boys all a-flutter – you're absolutely *fascinating*; I can tell just by looking at you. Would you mind ever so if I wrote you down?'

I close my eyes for a moment.

'Pardon?' Addie says in a small voice.

'Oh, I'm writing a book,' Grace says expansively. 'It's all about this time in our lives, when we're just *swirling* through life, finding ourselves, getting lost, getting high . . . It's *terribly* pretentious, as all coming-of-age stories are, really, but I can't seem to help myself.' She throws her head back for another long, leisurely laugh. 'That ought to be the title: *I Can't Seem to Help Myself*, by Grace Percy.'

'Grace,' Marcus says, and he hooks a finger through the belt loop on her dress and tugs her back towards the rest of us. 'You're terrifying her.'

'Oh, am I?' she says earnestly to Addie. 'I'm sorry. I just can't ever be bothered with small talk – we're clearly going to be friends, I thought we might as well launch in. *Did* I terrify you? Do tell me, Connie says I need to be told or I'll never improve, don't you, Connie, darling?'

Addie pulls herself up, half laughing – it's hard not to laugh when Grace is in full flow. 'You didn't terrify me at all,' she says. 'It's lovely to meet you. All of you.'

'Dylan?'

It's Uncle Terry. He marches into the room in his swim shorts, hairy belly overhanging the elasticated waist, then comes to a sudden stop. He looks at everyone in turn, finally settling his gaze on me.

'Dylan, my boy,' he says, 'are you aware that you have a rather large penis drawn on your forehead?'

Addie

OK. OK. I've got this.

I'm shaking a little. I'm sure Marcus clocks it as I help Marta pour out the first round of the champagne one of them turned up here with.

Meeting Dylan's brother, his brother's partner, Dylan's housemates, and *Grace*, all at once? It's a lot.

I've texted Deb asking her to come back. I need back-up. Thank God Cherry is here, at least. She shoots me a reassuring smile across the kitchen and I feel a little better.

'Here, let me help you take those outside,' says Luke.

You have to look hard to see the resemblance between Dylan and his brother. Luke is bulkier and looks like the sort of guy who'd play rugby and call it 'ruggers'. But when he smiles his face changes completely. He falls into step beside me as we each take two glasses through to the lunch table set up on the terrace. I thought I'd have to go to the Intermarché again to stock up, but it turns out Grace went on her way here. The table's now laden with cheeses and olives and fresh bread.

Grace isn't at all what I expected. She seems very genuine to me, which is kind of surprising in a woman who dyes her hair blue and says *enchantée* without irony. She's currently sunning by the pool and looking totally gorgeous beside the pasty form of Uncle Terry. I should feel threatened, probably, but Grace just . . . hasn't really let me.

'You doing OK?' Luke says, looking at me sideways.

'Yes! Yeah,' I say, swallowing. 'Just . . .'

'It's a lot,' he says. 'This is classic Marcus. Of course he didn't bother warning you and Dyl that he'd invited us all.' He rolls his eyes affectionately as we set the glasses down. 'He's acting out – he's probably pissed Dylan's preoccupied with someone other than him, for once. I've never seen Dylan look at any woman the way he looks at you. I think you're going to be really good for him, you know. He needs someone to ground him. Like I ground Javier.'

I smile at his expression when he mentions his boyfriend. 'Javier seems great,' I say, straightening the knives and forks. Habit, I guess. It's a bit weird being here as Dylan's . . . whatever-I-am, as well as the villa's caretaker.

'He is. I want that for Dyl. And for Marcus,' he adds. 'Of course.'

'Dylan said you and him were friends with Marcus when you were kids?'

'Mm. We sort of adopted Marcus, really. Or he adopted us, maybe. Never been big on functional families, this group,' he says, indicating the collection of beautiful people sprawled around Terry, by the pool, 'and me, Dyl and Marcus are no different. You make your own family, don't you?'

I think of my family. My dad, solid and reliable. My mum, always quietly one step ahead. Deb, whose last text to me read *You need me, I'm there*.

'Stop hogging the new girl, Luke!' Marcus calls across the terrace at us. 'Addie, come on, I want to show you something.'

I hesitate for a moment. Marcus is stood on the steps down to the courtyard. His hair is pulled back in a ponytail now, and with the drawn-on eyepatch and goatee he should look ridiculous, but it's actually all quite . . . I don't know, villainous.

'He's not all bad, you know,' Luke says beside me. 'There's a good guy in there somewhere. He's just got a bit lost.'

I make a dubious face. Luke laughs.

'Though by all means, tell him no. He doesn't hear it very often. Might be good for him.'

After another moment's pause, I roll my eyes slightly. 'Oh, go on, I'll humour him.'

I leave Luke at the table and head over towards Marcus. He trots off before I've caught him up, leading me down the lawn to the scrubby area near the villa's boundary. He stops so suddenly I nearly pile into him, and have to put a hand on his shoulder to steady myself.

'Shh,' he says, beckoning me to stand next to him. 'Look.'

I follow his gaze down to the shaded grass. It takes a moment for me to see what he sees: a snake. I breathe in sharply as I meet its slitted gaze. I've not seen a single snake all summer, but this one's enormous. Coiled, all muscle. Its scales are almost-black and pale yellow.

I crouch down. I don't know why; it just feels like the right thing to do. Marcus kneels beside me, and for a while we just stay like that. Watching it watch us.

'It's beautiful.'

'Pure power,' Marcus says.

'Is it poisonous? Or venomous, or whatever?' I ask in a whisper.

'No idea.'

That should probably scare me, but it doesn't. The snake isn't moving, just waiting.

'He loves you, you know,' Marcus says.

For a weird second I think he means the snake.

'Dylan's easily hurt,' Marcus goes on. His voice is level. 'By the people he loves.'

'I'm not going to hurt him,' I say.

'Course you are,' Marcus says, tone still light, eyes still on the snake. 'You're too complicated for someone like Dylan. Far too interesting.' He turns his head to look at me then. 'This summer's when you wake up, isn't it, and you're only just getting started. You're just beginning to play around, and he's nearly ready to give up and settle down and say, *This is who I am, I'm done*.'

There's something indecent about his gaze. It feels hot. I keep my eyes on the snake, but I know my cheeks are starting to blush pink. I should have stayed up with Luke on the terrace. Nice Luke, who said I'd be good for Dylan.

'I'm not playing around,' I say. 'I don't know where you got that idea from.'

His gaze burns. 'Maybe you should be.'

This conversation feels like it's sliding away from me.

'You act like you know me. You don't know anything about me.' I try to keep my voice as steady as his.

'I told you, I'm an excellent judge of character. I like the look of the dark, messy parts of you, the fun parts. But Dylan wants a good girl.'

I frown, heart thudding. That's *so* inappropriate. I don't want to be here. As I move to stand, the snake recoils and slithers away from us.

'I'm not Grace,' I say shortly, brushing down my knees. 'You don't get a part of me just because I'm Dylan's.'

He stands and I almost step back when I see his expression. His eyes are dark and angry. It's disorientating how quickly he's changed, or maybe he looked like that before, but I couldn't hear it in his voice.

'Well, you might be all Dylan's,' he says as I turn to walk away from him. 'But he's not all yours.'

Dylan

Getting this lot off on a hike is akin to herding cats, but if I let them all lounge around the pool as they're requesting then I will have an under-exercised and petulant Cherry to deal with, which on balance will likely be worse.

Marcus is in a foul mood, which isn't helping matters, and Addie is . . . I don't know quite where Addie is. Never with me, that's where. At least Marcus has lost interest in her now, predictably – no woman has ever retained his genuine attention for more than a day or two, and it seems the danger time has passed, thank God.

'Come *on*, Dyl!' Cherry wheedles, bouncing on the spot. 'You said wait until it cools down, and it's cooler now, so can we just *go*?'

'Marta! Connie!' I yell. 'Trainers on!'

'All right, *Dad*,' says Marta, pouting; Connie laughs as I scowl at the pair of them.

'Where's Addie?' I ask. 'Marcus, are you wearing those shoes?'

'Evidently,' Marcus says, shoving past me on his way to the kitchen.

'Grace, are you ready?'

'Not at all,' she says, lying back on a sun lounger.

'Could you *try*?' I snap.

Grace's charm is a lot less charming now that I'm not interested in sleeping with her, I must say. She lowers her sunglasses and gives me a look that says she knows precisely what I'm thinking. I redden; she smiles slowly.

'Isn't it a good thing that I'm not the sensitive type?' she says. 'I'll be ready before Marta and you know it, darling. Go take your frustration out elsewhere, please, you're in my light – or better yet, go and find the beautiful woman we've all *rudely* ripped from your arms. That's really what's got you so grumpy, isn't it? That we've ruined your romantic tryst by arriving *en masse*, as if we're all in a terribly comical scene from *The Marriage of Figaro*?'

Damn Grace – I always forget how perceptive she is behind the glamour and indolence and allusions. She gives me another beautiful smile and pushes her sunglasses up her nose again as I stomp off the terrace and down the steps to the courtyard.

There's a new car parked rather haphazardly behind Grace's rental car; I step a little further, and there's Addie, in the shade of a plane tree, speaking to a woman who I immediately realise must be Deb. She has black, wavy hair and light brown skin, and she's standing on the edges of her feet, tipping them in and out as she talks, her T-shirt sliding off her shoulder. There's an air of careless confidence to her even from here, as if she is in possession of the genuine no-fucks-given attitude the rest of us are feigning when we pose for Instagram.

I catch sight of Addie's expression as I approach them and pause, watching, because *oh*, this is my Addie. Wide, open smile, no tension, easy laughter. That glint of sharp humour in her eyes, like she's poised to surprise us all.

'The one with the bald patch?' Deb's saying. She's peering towards the terrace; I'm hidden here, I realise, behind the bulk of Grace's car.

'What? No, you mongoose, that's his uncle, Terry,' Addie says, laughing.

'*Oh*, yeah, the one with the ponytail and the eyepatch?'

'No,' Addie says, more sharply this time. 'That's Marcus. Dylan's mate.'

I step forward; staying here any longer feels like lurking. Addie's face lights up when she sees me and something explosive happens in my chest, a chain reaction, a Catherine wheel sent spinning.

'Here's Dylan,' she says, coming towards me. 'Dyl, meet my sister.'

Deb turns and looks me up and down so openly I almost laugh. She looks nothing like Addie, but there's an Addie-ness to her all the same – the way she tilts her head, the sharp narrowing of her eyes as she takes me in.

'Interesting,' she says eventually. 'You went for the one with the cock on his face?'

NOW

Addie

It is so hot and everyone in this car is *so annoying.*

I'm driving, with Dylan beside me. We're somewhere outside Stoke-on-Trent. That's about two hundred miles south of where we should be right now.

'Is there anything to eat?' Marcus asks. 'I'm hungry again.'

I don't need to check my mirror to know that Rodney has just offered him a flapjack.

'Not that,' Marcus says. 'There's only so much glorified porridge one man can take. No offence, Rodney.' He twists to look in the boot.

'For God's sake,' Deb says. 'Would you boys please watch your extremities? Addie, I need to break soon to pump again.'

'That boob contraption you were using when we broke down? You have to do it again? Why?' Marcus asks. I glance at him in the mirror. He's managed to get some Fruit Pastilles from the back of the car and is staring at Deb's chest while he tries to open the sweets with absolutely no elbow room.

'I lactate,' Deb says, deadpan.

'Next services in twenty-one miles,' I say, nodding to the sign on the roadside. 'That OK, Deb?'

'It would have been if someone hadn't poked me in the nipple.'

'Did I?' Marcus says. 'What a waste, I didn't even notice.'

'I can probably pump in the car,' Deb says. 'Rodney, can you reach that bag?'

There is a short spell of what looks like Twister in the back of the car. Rodney eventually produces the bag with Deb's breast pump in it. Deb fiddles around with her top. Rodney contorts himself so that he is facing the other way, closing his eyes and covering his face with his hands. I stifle a grin. Meanwhile Marcus opens the Fruit Pastilles and scatters them absolutely everywhere. One hits me in the ear.

'Fuck's sake,' he says. 'Pass that red one over there, would you, Rodders? I've never been with a woman who's breastfeeding. What happens when you have sex, Deb?'

'Marcus!' Dylan snaps.

'No? I can't ask that? Christ! Being well behaved is exhausting.'

I hear the whir of the battery-powered breast pump starting up. It sounds a bit like there's a washing machine in the back of the car.

'All right. Five questions for Dylan,' Marcus says after a while.

He sounds more subdued now. Hmm. Worrying. At least when he's pissing around he's not up to anything evil.

'I'll start,' Marcus says. 'Why haven't you tried to get your poems published yet?'

I dial down the volume on the music and glance at Dylan. I want to hear the answer to this one.

'I don't think they're ready,' Dylan says eventually.

Interesting. It's the only answer I'd accept, and one he never gave when we were together. It was always, *Oh, they're just drivel*, or, *Nobody wants to read that.*

'Well, all right,' Marcus says. He shifts in his seat. 'When will they be ready?'

'Is that another question from my five?'

'Yes, it's another question,' Marcus says testily.

'They'll be ready when . . . I . . . I don't know. When I can read them without wincing.'

I frown. 'What if they're meant to make you wince?'

'Hey?'

'I don't know a lot about this stuff – you know I don't – but your best poems were always the ones you let me read last.'

Quiet descends again. The music's a whisper now, and I can feel sweat trickling down the inside of my upper arms.

'You never told me that,' Dylan says.

'Didn't I?'

'No. I could never tell when you liked a poem.'

This genuinely surprises me. 'I always liked them.'

'Next question,' says Marcus. 'Why did you suggest we drive to the wedding together?'

I look at Dylan and catch his reaction. He's startled.

'I guess I thought – we were ready for that,' he says.

'Why? You cut me out for almost a year, and then, what, I did something good? What was it? I'm jumping through hoops in the dark, here, Dyl.'

Dylan cut Marcus out for *almost a year*? I shoot him another look, but he's turned his face towards the window.

'It was Luke, actually,' Dylan says. 'He told me about your . . . apology thing.'

Another long silence, just the sound of Deb's breast pump, the low music and the wheels on the road. The traffic is beginning to slow again. Cars close in around us.

'I suppose I thought I'd give you an opportunity to get around to apologising to me, too.'

I keep glancing in the mirror. Marcus catches me looking at him and I quickly turn my eyes back to the road.

'I assume it was your therapist's suggestion,' Dylan goes on. 'And that there was a reason you'd managed to apologise to Luke, Javier,

Marta, your stepmother, your father, and *my* mother for your various indiscretions and misbehaviours, but not yet got around to me.'

His voice is rising – he's hurt, maybe, or angry, but he's keeping it in check. I know that tone well.

I catch Deb's eye in the mirror. I widen my eyes, like, *Don't ask me what all this is about.*

'Whenever you're ready, Marcus,' Dylan says lightly. 'I'm listening.'

Dylan

A phone rings in the long, stifling silence; Deb fumbles around and swears as she tries to find her mobile without letting go of the breast pump.

'Saved by the bell,' Marcus says under his breath, just loud enough that I can hear him. My heart is thudding unsteadily; I really thought we were getting somewhere there, but of course Marcus wouldn't perform his apology on cue – I'll likely never get one now I've asked for it. And besides, he hardly knows the depth of what he ought to be apologising for; no wonder he feels like he's jumping through hoops in the dark. I clench my fists in my lap. *He's trying*, I remind myself, and I think of what Luke said when we last spoke: *Write Marcus off if you want to, I won't judge, believe me – but don't pretend you're giving him a chance when you're clearly just not.*

'Hello? Is Riley OK?' Deb says.

Addie's on alert immediately – her eyes dart towards Deb in the mirror as the traffic crawls around us, hunched cars inching along like beetles, sunlight glinting on their backs.

'OK. Oh, yeah, of course, now's good,' Deb says, and Addie relaxes.

They've always had that bond, the Gilbert sisters; I've envied Deb more than once for the way she slots in with Addie so instinctively, as if the two of them were made to come as a pair.

'Is it Dad?' Addie cocks her head, listening, then gives a quick grin. 'Put him on speaker, Deb.'

The voice of Addie's father cuts through the stuffy heat of the car, and it's like catching the scent of Addie's shampoo in the street, like hearing the rattle of beaded bracelets. It's like stepping back for half a second into the life where she was mine.

'. . . told your mother it wasn't meant to be that colour, but she says it's perfectly fine, and not to mention it to you,' he's saying. 'Oh, bugger, probably shouldn't have told you that. But it was *so* yellow. I'm sure babies didn't poo yellow in my day.'

'What shade of yellow?' Deb asks.

I look back; Marcus is gazing out the window moodily, but he pulls a disgusted face at that. I find myself smiling. Losing Addie was so all-eclipsing I rarely thought of the other people I lost with her, but hearing Neil's voice makes me miss him in a way I can honestly say I have never missed my own father.

'I'd go for . . . mustard? English mustard, that is, the powdered kind.'

'Ooh,' says Rodney, 'that is *quite* yellow.'

'Oh, hello,' Neil says cheerfully. 'Who's that, then?'

'We've got company,' Deb says. 'That's Rodney, and . . .' She trails off.

Addie is furiously shaking her head at her. The joy at hearing Neil again seeps away, because of course Addie doesn't want her father to know I'm here in the car with them. I walked out on his daughter: he must despise me.

'And . . . Rodney made flapjack,' Deb finishes. She pulls a face at Addie.

'Flapjack!' Neil says, sounding genuinely enthused. 'Lovely!'

'Dad, the yellow poo,' Deb says, with the air of a woman getting back down to business. 'Talk to me about texture. Loose? Firm? Peanut butter?'

'Your dad's such a nice guy,' I say into the silence that follows once Neil finally hangs up.

'He's all right,' Deb says, with unmistakable fondness. 'Why, what's yours like?' She pauses. 'Oh, sorry, he's a bit of a shit, isn't he?'

Marcus laughs at that. He seems to be cheering up a little, and frankly it would have been impossible to stay angry for the duration of Neil's very serious, very earnest discussion of Riley's faecal matter.

Deb's finished pumping, and there's a lengthy pause while she rummages around for the cool bag to store the bottle of milk. Rodney, who is ostensibly trying to help, seems to have more limbs than an octopus – Addie winces as one of his knees shoves into the back of the driver's seat.

'Yeah, my dad's . . . difficult,' I say, when the commotion has died down. 'I can't blame him entirely for that, though. I have consistently disappointed him – I've made something of an art of it, actually.'

I feel Addie glance at me but keep my eyes on the road ahead. The heat is hovering on the tarmac, blurring the car in front and turning it into an oil painting, perhaps, or a live stream on poor WiFi. This whole day has an air of surrealness to it, and the blur, the heat, the fierce sun, they make it feel even stranger.

'We've reached an understanding,' I say. 'He keeps out of my life, and I keep out of his. We've not spoken since December 2017.'

Addie startles as I say the date. I look down at my hands in my lap. For a wild second I imagine reaching across and covering her hand on the steering wheel with mine.

'I found out something rather unpleasant,' I say. 'About my father. Or, more precisely, about my father's girlfriend, who, it turns out, lives a very nice life in a townhouse in Little Venice that he pays for out of the family business.'

In the long, shocked silence, Rodney unclicks his Tupperware of flapjack again.

'And you found that out in December of two years ago?' Addie says slowly.

I nod, still looking down at my hands.

'No,' Marcus says. 'That day?'

I glance up at Addie, anxious. The colour rises slowly up her chest, her neck, to dapple her cheeks.

'That's what you'd been talking to Luke about when I texted you?' Marcus says.

'Mm. He'd been home.'

'Confronting your dad?'

'Talking to my mother,' I correct him. 'Confronting my dad would be . . . Ah.'

That's something Luke and I have never had the courage to do, not even for this.

'You know your dad's going to be at Cherry's wedding, right?' Marcus says, and I can hear his expression: eyebrows raised in incredulity.

I take a slow, wobbly breath, because there it is again, the moment I think about seeing my father – a weight against my chest like the heel of a hand pushed against my ribs. *The power he has is mine/given, and now I choose/to take it back.* It's my most popular poem on Instagram, just three lines long, titled 'Simple'. It's one of my least favourite poems now – I wrote it in the months after I'd lost Addie and cut off contact with Dad, and now its oversimplicity seems faintly pathetic. As though freezing out my father would flick the switch, and here I'd be, perfectly healed and happy, my own master.

'Dyl?' Marcus prompts. 'You know your mum and dad are invited, right?'

'Yes,' I say. 'I know.'

'And you've not seen your dad for over a year and a half?'

'No. I've not.'

'And you're just going to . . . see him at the wedding?'

'Yes.'

There's a long silence.

'Is there a game plan beyond that point?' Marcus asks dryly.

Addie keeps glancing at me, her gaze like sunshine on my cheek.

'Not yet,' I say rather helplessly. 'I'm hoping I'll know what to say when I get there. Luke will be there too. It'll be all right with Luke there.'

'OK!' Marcus says, and I hear him stretch, and Deb say *oof* as he presumably elbows her somewhere. 'Well, luckily we've got about two hundred or so miles to work on *that* shitshow of a strategy.'

THEN

Addie

Marcus changes completely after our trip to see the snake. No more flirting, no charm – he pretty much ignores me. But I sometimes feel his gaze on me when I'm not looking. It takes me a couple of days to notice that when Marcus is watching me, Grace is watching Marcus.

'You're looking at him again,' I tease her as we wash up the breakfast things side by side. She's washing, I'm drying and surreptitiously picking off the bits of scrambled egg she's missed.

'Who, Marc?' She's been idly staring at Marcus on the terrace, through the window above the kitchen sink. 'Oh, I'm a lost cause, aren't I? I just find him so *fascinating.*'

We get on well, me and Grace. She can be a little much sometimes, but I've lived with Cherry: I have pretty good tolerance for intense posh people. Plus she's incredibly smart, and like Dylan she's not patronising about it. And, crucially, she's never looked at Dylan the way she's always staring at Marcus.

'If you find him so fascinating, then why . . .' *did you sleep with his best friend, too?*

Grace laughs, getting the subtext. 'Darling, I'm the *queen* of self-sabotage, don't ask me why I do anything. Besides, Marc isn't the sort of guy you go steady with, is he? If we'd been exclusive, he would have lost interest even more quickly than he did. He wanted free-spirit Grace, sexual-adventurer Grace, always-out-of-reach Grace. He wants games and scandal.'

'You deserve someone who wants you for who you really are,' I tell her. 'And doesn't try to turn you into somebody else.'

She laughs, throwing her head back. 'I've yet to find a man like that,' she says.

I wince, and she clocks it straight away. She presses one soapy hand to mine, stilling it for a moment to catch my eye.

'I'm sorry,' she says. 'That wasn't about Dylan. He's not a bad man, nothing like that, he and I just weren't . . . Oh, it wasn't *real*.'

'Was it a game? To Dylan?' I force myself to ask. 'The whole thing with you?'

Grace sobers, pressing her lips together. 'Yes,' she says. 'I'm sorry, darling, I know you'll probably find that terribly distasteful, but I don't think he ever liked me, and honestly, I didn't like him that way either. Marc was losing interest, and . . . sleeping with Dylan, it got Marc's attention in a way I never could with any other man. And I think Dylan liked having something that was Marc's for once.'

I flinch at that. Grace sends me a sympathetic glance but keeps going.

'Leaving for Europe was a master stroke on my part, frankly, because if those boys need one thing, it's a sense of purpose, and so they chased me *far* longer than they would've if we'd all stayed in Oxford. I think they liked the idea of sleeping with the same woman more than they ever liked me.'

My teeth are gritted tight. 'I'm sorry,' I manage. 'That's horrible.'

'Oh, I gave as good as I got, darling,' Grace says, passing me a plate. 'And I've done *plenty* worse to others. If you run with this lot' – she nods to the figures draped around the pool – 'things are always going to get a little messy. The difference is, with Marc . . .' She sighs. 'I can't seem to *shake* him the way I've always shaken everybody else.'

'I get it,' I say, stacking the plate.

Grace smiles slowly at me. 'Dylan's really got under your skin, hey?'

I blush. Grace smiles.

'Well. May he prove to be a man who deserves you,' she says, handing me another plate with a flourish.

They break stuff: a lamp in the ballroom, a door on the second floor. Connie's finger, which means she spends a night in a French emergency room with Uncle Terry, who was the only person sober enough to drive her, since his hangovers are worse than everyone else's and he can't keep up.

They drink and laugh and get high and the days turn blurry under the sun.

Meanwhile I fix everything. Except the finger – that's outside my expertise.

In fairness to them all, they do treat me and Deb like part of the gang. Not like the caretakers. It's just when something goes wrong and they yell for me or my sister that I'm reminded we're not quite on a level here. I'm not really one of them.

'They're like overgrown children,' Deb observes one day, looking down at them all on the lawn. Connie has her head on Marta's stomach, Grace is sitting up against Marcus's legs, Luke and Javier are intertwined. Dylan's off with Uncle Terry somewhere, I think, trying to keep him amused. Deb and I have been clearing insects out of the pool – Marta swam right into a giant hornet earlier and nobody's heard the end of it.

'Do you like them?' I ask Deb.

'Oh, how can you not?' she says, leaning on the terrace balustrade. 'But I'd keep them at a bit of a distance, personally. I don't see how you can get in the middle of *that*' – she points to the tangle of limbs below – 'and not end up in a mess.'

I tilt my head to her shoulder, not quite letting it touch. I'm so grateful she's here, my sister. Sometimes this week I've felt like I'm getting kind of lost. Or maybe losing the confidence to be Summer Addie. But with Deb, I'm always myself. The proper Addie, the real one.

'I love you,' I tell her. 'Thanks for coming back when they arrived.'

'Of course,' she says, surprised. 'You only ever have to ask, and I'm here. Always. Isn't that how this sister thing works?'

Dylan's a bit different with his friends. He laughs more and says less. His poetry isn't something he gushes about, it's the punchline to someone else's joke. He's still charming and lost-boyish. But he's . . . quieter. Sometimes even I lose track of where he is in the crowd.

At night, though, he's mine. We've given Deb the bed in the flat and once the partying is over for the evening, I collapse beside him in that enormous four-poster. We have sex a *lot*, but we talk a lot too. All night, on our last night. Nose to nose, hands linked.

'The sound of teeth against a spoon when someone's eating soup, insects that scuttle, people who don't listen,' he whispers. It's five in the morning, and his voice is hoarse. We're talking about pet peeves – I've no idea how we got here. 'And yours?'

'Yes to people who don't listen,' I say, and press a light kiss to his lips. 'That's a good one. And rats. I hate those too. And it drives me nuts when your uncle Terry says *women!* Like he can instantly win a debate with that. You know, when one of us has said something he doesn't agree with?'

'Oh, Uncle Terry is a pet peeve all on his own,' Dylan says, grimacing, and I laugh. 'I'm sorry. He's awful.'

'He's . . .' Hmm, what am I allowed to say here? He *is* Dylan's uncle, after all. I change tack. 'Is your dad like him? Terry's his brother, right?'

There's a long, still silence.

'No, Dad's different,' Dylan says eventually, and his tone has changed. 'He's . . . tougher than Terry.'

I frown. 'What does tougher mean?'

'He's just not much fun,' Dylan says. 'What's your dad like?'

That was quick. Given that we just spent forty-five minutes talking about Pokémon and Ninja Turtles, I really thought Dylan's dad would take more than ten seconds to discuss. I try to make out Dylan's expression in the darkness.

'You guys don't get along?' I ask quietly.

'Let's just say he's one of those people who doesn't listen,' Dylan says.

He leans in and kisses me then, slowly. I feel the kiss moving through me like I've swallowed something hot. He's trying to distract me. It works.

'So? What about you, what's your dad like?' Dylan asks again, resettling his head against the pillow.

'He's just Dad, really, I've never thought about what he's *like*,' I say, but I can feel myself starting to smile just at the thought of him. My heart aches for home, and I tighten my fingers around Dylan's. 'I'm as close to him as I am to my mum. He's really good at advice, and he's funny, but you know, Dad-funny.'

Dylan chuckles at that. I can feel him relaxing again.

'Do you miss them?' he asks. 'Your parents?'

'Yeah, I do.' That feels like a bit of an embarrassing thing to say when you're twenty-one, and I blush in the dark. 'At uni I always went home loads midterm, so this is the longest I've ever not seen them, actually. But I've got Deb. And it's been amazing, this summer.'

'Amazing, hey?' Dylan whispers.

I swallow. My heart rate picks up. 'I don't want it to end,' I say.

My voice is so quiet Dylan shifts even closer to hear me. I can feel his breath on my lips like a feather.

'Who said anything about ending?' he whispers. He's shadowy in the dark, but I can see his eyes flicking back and forth as he looks at me.

I sort of knew. I didn't think he'd say he was leaving the villa and that was it, summer romance done. But even so, my heart is thundering now. I want this conversation so much it scares me. I shift away a little, turning my face into the pillow. Dylan runs his hand up my back, making me shiver.

'Can I tell you something?' he says quietly.

I wriggle, pushing the sheet down away from my face, suddenly breathless. I think he's going to say it and once he has, that's it, like he's putting a timestamp on our lives. Creating a before and after. I feel it coming like I'm speeding towards something, and for one panicked moment I think I ought to slam on the brakes.

'I love you,' he says. 'I love you, Addie.'

It sends a shock zinging through me. Like someone pressed refresh. My heart beats in my ears. I think of that poem, about how scary it is handing over your heart, like a soldier lowering his weapon.

But I do love Dylan. I love him when his friends are taking the piss out of his poetry, and I love him when he's just woken up, sleepy-eyed and grumbling. I love him so much I sometimes genuinely find it hard to have a conversation with anyone else, because all I'm thinking about is him. Us.

'I love you too,' I whisper.

I've never said it before. When my ex tried to bring up the love thing I would usually find a reason to slip away: an empty drink, a friend across the room, a passing spider. And before him, there was nobody serious. I wonder whether Dylan's ever said it before.

'I sense some thoughts are occurring,' Dylan says, nuzzling into my neck. 'Are you about to head off to the Intermarché?'

I laugh at that, though I hadn't realised he noticed me slipping off when things felt too intense.

'No supermarket necessary,' I say. 'I guess it's just . . . I mean, you're going travelling now, so . . . What does this even mean?'

I kiss him then, because I can hear the need in my voice. I don't like it. I don't want to think about how much I'll miss him.

'It means we'll talk all the time on the phone, and on Skype. I'll send you poems on postcards. I'll come find you the moment I'm back in England,' Dylan says. He smooths back my hair. 'But . . . I could stay here for the rest of the summer instead? Should I stay?' He pulls back slightly.

I could say yes. *Miss out on your summer plans, don't go to Thailand and Vietnam, stay here with me.* I could tell him what to do. He'd do it – if there's one thing I've seen this week, it's that Dylan is easily led.

For a moment the temptation tugs at me. It would be such a small thing to do it. Like a foot slipping, the brush of a hand.

'No,' I say, pressing my lips to his. 'You go. Don't let me mess up your plans. This summer's about figuring out what *you* want, right? So go figure. And then come find me when you're done.'

Dylan

For the rest of the summer, we travel, Marcus and I. My shoulders become accustomed to the stinging ache of the backpack's weight; I lose count of the number of wonders I try to comprehend, beaches so white they look like snow, jungles so lush the path you took yesterday has to be recut with a machete the next day. Boat rides and cramped trains and the yells of marketplaces, bartering and sweating and drinking and wondering what the hell I'm doing with my life and always, always missing Addie.

I should be having the summer of my life, but wherever we are, I'm lost. With Addie, for those beautiful, sun-soaked weeks in Provence, I felt myself take shape – falling in love with Addie took the whole of me, and for once I felt completely happy with where and who I was.

I thought I'd leave France and take that with me, but I left it there with her. Some days, once again, to my disgust, I struggle to even get out of bed; I'm as formless and fretful as ever, always one line away from a finished poem, always a step behind Marcus. Always disappointing my father.

He rings me when I'm at Phnom Penh airport. Addie will be going home to Chichester in three days; Marcus has gone off somewhere in search of bottled water, and I'm staring at the departures board. We're due to leave for Preah Sihanouk for our last week before heading home, but . . . perhaps I could just leave now. Be waiting for Addie at the airport when she returns, see the joy on her face when she catches sight of me in the waiting crowd and sets off at a run to throw herself into my arms.

'You better be coming home,' Dad says, when I pick up.

It's late August. According to our original plan, we should have been home weeks ago – but what was the point of going back to the UK while Addie was still in France?

'Nice to hear from you, Dad,' I say. The tone is less sharp than I'd intended – I cop out at the last minute and end up sounding quite pleasant.

'Enough nonsense. This trip to Europe has escalated ridiculously.'

I scowl. 'I only stayed a few extra weeks.'

'You've missed all the deadlines for graduate schemes. What are you *doing*, Dylan? When are you going to grow up?'

I lift my gaze to the ceiling. The criss-crossed strip lights leave a garish tartan pattern on the inside of my eyelids. There's no need for me to say anything – Dad will say what he wants to say, irrespective of my responses, or lack thereof.

'You're planning on living at home, I presume. As much as you're planning anything. Your mother says it's no use buying you a flat in London yet, and I'm inclined to agree with her. You haven't earned it, frankly.'

Mum wants me to decide for myself if London is where I want to be. In some ways, her quiet faith that I'll figure my life out is almost worse than my father's absolute conviction that I won't.

'We'll talk it all through properly once you're back, but I'm sure I'll be able to find you something in the business – though you'll have to commute to London, which won't be easy.'

I feel the life eking out of me as the call goes on. I'm a toy version of a man, flopped in my seat, waiting for someone to lift my strings and jerk me into life.

Marcus ambles back to me with two water bottles; his hair is longer than ever, dry and sun-streaked, and his clothes badly need washing. He grins at me and throws me a bottle from too far away – I can't catch it with the phone to my ear, and it hits me in the stomach.

I do know, on some level, that this problem of mine is not real. I have a whole world of opportunities in front of me. I can do anything I want, more so than almost any other being on this planet, probably.

But the dread doesn't seem to know it. The dread just knows that the future is enormous, and awful, because, inevitably, no matter what I do, I'll fail at it.

'I'm actually going to stay out here a while longer,' I say, when there's a break in my father's monologue.

I sit through the silence. It's a relief, like the moment when you scratch at a scab. From the second I saw Dad's name on my phone screen, I knew this silence was coming; everything leading up to this has just been a horrible means of building suspense. Once it's done – once I've let him down – it's perversely easy.

'I don't know why I bother,' Dad says, voice already rising into a shout. 'This is useless. *You're* useless.'

And so begins the usual diatribe: *waste of space* features heavily, as does the question of what he ever did to deserve such disappointing sons, which I have heard enough times not to attempt to answer, tempting as it might be. I stay quiet, that miserable dreadful weight sitting heavy on my chest. Marcus taps his watch and nods at the departures board – the flight to Sihanouk International Airport is boarding.

Dad hangs up when he's run out of unpleasantness to shout at me. The sharp beep makes my eyes prick. As I follow Marcus to the gate, I think suddenly of holding Addie, my hands splayed against the tight muscle of her back, and I physically falter, half stumbling for a step, as if my feet are trying to tell me I'm walking the wrong way.

Marcus turns and looks at me, eyes measured.

'Come on, man,' he says. 'Fuck your dad, fuck all of them. Let's forget the real world for a few more days.'

Addie

'Where is he, then, this Dylan?' my mum asks, settling down on the sofa beside Deb.

We're in the living room at my parents' house. At last. I hadn't realised how much I missed home until Deb and I walked through that door and I breathed it in. I'm still in the clothes I travelled in – it's weird to think that the dust stuck to the sun cream on my shins has come back with me all the way from Provence.

'He's not home from travelling yet,' I say, sipping my tea. Proper, English tea, with chalky water from a kettle that needs descaling.

'You'll like him, Mum,' Deb says as she tugs her socks off. Deb only really feels at home when she is no longer wearing her socks. 'He's sweet. And *obsessed* with Addie. Which is good because she is completely obsessed with him.'

I flush. 'No, I'm not,' I say automatically.

Deb rolls her eyes. 'Please. You pined after him all summer.'

'I did not *pine*! I just missed him, that's all.'

'Yeah, well, I miss being able to eat what I like without getting fat, but you don't see me crying about it,' Deb says. She grins at me as I pull a face.

'Deb helped loads with the heartbreak,' I tell Mum. 'Really understanding.'

'I was excellent,' Deb says placidly, crossing her ankles on the coffee table. 'I kept her fed and watered and didn't use the WiFi when she was Skyping Dylan. I was *saintly*.'

My mum smiles at us both over her mug, eyes crinkling at the corners. I've missed her so much – it hits me right in the gut.

'And when will I be meeting this boy?' she asks.

'Soon,' I promise. 'I'm not sure when he's home, but he says it'll be soon.'

'Hey, I can hear you!'

'Hello? Can you hear me?'

'Yep! Yep! Hi? Hello?' I wave at the laptop screen. My grin is becoming more and more fixed.

'Hey!' Dylan's face breaks into a smile. He's in a dark corner somewhere. All I can see is brown panelled walls and the fan in the ceiling. I think he might be in Cambodia, but it could be Vietnam. I'm a bit embarrassed to have lost track.

'How are you doing?' Dylan and I say at the same time.

We laugh.

'You go.' Both of us, again.

'OK, I'll start,' I say, because this is going to stop being cute soon. 'I'm nervous.'

'Yes, you are!' Dylan says. 'You are going to be brilliant.'

That doesn't make . . . total sense, but I reckon he got the gist.

'These training days have just been a lot,' I say. My face stares back at me on Skype: I look so young. Way too young to be teaching teenagers anything.

'Teaching Direct is famously tough, but so are you,' Dylan says.

I smile reluctantly. 'I wish you were here.'

He beams. 'You do?'

'Of course I do.'

'Well, you never say it,' he says.

'Yes, I do! I totally do.' Don't I? I feel like I must, right?

'Nope. Never.'

'Well, I thought you'd be home by now. When *are* you coming home?'

His face goes sort of dark, like he's had a bad thought. 'I don't know. I need to figure out what I want to do before I come home, you know? That's the deal we made, right?'

'Right,' I say, and in the back of my head I'm thinking, *What, you can just travel for ever if you want to? Are you not going to run out of money?*

'My dad has these plans for me, and I'm not sure how I'm going to . . .' He chews his lip, staring off at something in the distance. 'I need to be able to present a different plan to him if I'm going to get out of living at home and working for the family business.'

'Oh, OK.' I know enough to know Dylan doesn't want to work for his dad, but I'm not really sure what he *does* want to do, other than write poetry, which he obviously can't make a living from right now. 'So what are you thinking? In terms of your different plan?'

His face is falling and falling. He looks morose, almost sulking. I frown slightly.

'Dylan?' I prompt.

'I don't know,' he says, brushing his hair out of his eyes irritably. 'I don't know. That's why I'm still here.'

'You think you have to be, like, in Thailand to figure that out? Wouldn't it help to just come home and be looking at job ads and stuff?'

'Don't *push*, Addie,' he says, and I pull back from the screen, startled. 'God, sorry,' he says immediately. 'I'm so sorry. I'm just worrying about all this a lot and feeling like a bit of a waste of space and just generally getting all up in my own head about it, and Dad's ringing me almost every day, threatening all sorts, and I just want to escape the world for a bit longer, you know? When I'm out here, I can press pause on everything. I can't mess anything up.'

I'm not sure that's true, to be honest. But I can at least see the logic.

'Well, take the time you need,' I say. 'Of course.'

His face lightens a bit then. 'Thanks. I knew you'd get it.'

I push down the vague sense of unease. I don't get it, honestly. I'm pretending because I don't want to be that mean girlfriend who cramps his style.

'So tell me all about what you've been up to this week,' Dylan says, settling back in. 'I want to hear it all, every single detail. I've been . . .' But then he goes pixelated and his voice turns into a *tut-tut-tut* and he's gone.

I slam the laptop closed in frustration. This is crap, this virtual relationship thing. It's not *real*. I want him holding me. I want him back.

Starting my first term at Barwood School is totally brutal.

I'm so lucky to have got a place on this scheme. If I didn't know that, I'd quit a hundred times over. Kids are *evil*.

By the first half-term I've almost managed to salvage my Year Eights' respect after a catastrophic start. (I got them to make rockets out of papier-mâché and they *all* made cocks. I cried, someone broke their toe. It was all very bad.) Years Nine, Ten and Eleven have been all right from the beginning, and the Year Sevens are mostly quite cute. But Year Eight is filled with pre-teen demons. Winning them over is up there as one of the most difficult things I've ever done, but hands-down the most rewarding.

And Dylan's still not here. We still Skype at least once a week and we message all the time, but I'm freaking out. How could I not be? He seems different. So distant. When I ask when he's coming home he says, *Soon!* And I try to understand, and not be pushy or needy or whatever, but no matter how sweet he is to me, he's not here. He can say he loves me, but he's not really *showing* it, is he?

We've had months apart now, and why? Because he's, what, finding himself? If it was anyone else I'd be scornful. It's only because it's lovely, lost-boy Dylan that I'm trying really hard to see that he's clearly not in a good place, and he seems to think coming home will make things worse. But God. It's not exactly complimentary, is it, your boyfriend staying away for months for no good reason?

He's forgotten you, says the little voice in my head. Middling, middle-of-the-road, nothing-special Addie. Did I really think I'd be able to keep a guy like Dylan interested beyond one hot summer?

It's Fireworks Night. Deb and I have big plans.

She's been my rock these last few months. We're both living at home while we save up for our own places. Deb listens to all my tearful rants about work. She makes me tea every morning, bringing it in as I do my make-up and kissing me briskly on the top of the head. When I think about writing Dylan an angry email – *Why won't you just come home?* – she confiscates my phone and reminds me Gilbert women don't beg.

So Fireworks Night is going to be a celebration of sisterhood. I've booked us a table at a fancy bar in town, for their Fireworks Extravaganza, which is a regular night out but more expensive, basically. We dress up: five-inch heels, short dresses, no tights. After months of making myself look as dowdy as possible for school, I want to feel sexy. And maybe after all this time waiting for Dylan to come home . . . I kind of want someone to notice me.

To my surprise, it doesn't take long.

'No, don't tell me. I'm going to guess your name,' says the guy next to me in the scrum for the bar. He has to raise his voice over the music. He has a rugged sort of sexiness to him. Old acne scars on his cheeks, bright blue eyes, a short beard.

'Give it a pop,' I say. 'You'll be here a while.'

He nods at the queue ahead of us. 'Conveniently, I'm not going anywhere. Hannah.'

'Way off.'

'By which I mean, Ella. No, nope, sorry, meant to say Bethan. Emily. Cindy?'

'Are you even trying?' I ask.

'Well, hmm. What would you say if I told you this was a shameless gimmick to get you talking to me?'

'I'd say I was shocked and appalled.'

He grins. 'Will you let me buy your drink, Emma?'

'Much too soon to say. It'll be twenty minutes before we get to the bar.'

'Hoping for a better offer in the meantime, Cassie?' the blue-eyed guy says, looking around with his eyes narrowed comically, like he's scouting for the competition.

Actually, I'm deciding. Is it crossing a line if I let him buy me a drink? Do I *want* to cross a line? Have I already crossed one, back when I wriggled into this dress that I used to wear when I wanted to pull on a uni night out?

'Addie!' Deb yells from behind me.

I turn.

'Aha!' says the blue-eyed guy. 'Addie. My next guess.'

'I got us a bottle for our table,' Deb shouts.

Around me, the crowd groans with envy.

'How?' I mouth, already pushing my way back to her.

'See you later, Addie?' the blue-eyed guy calls, but I've made my mind up, and I don't look back.

Dylan

She's talking to some guy at the bar when I arrive. It's *searing*, the jealousy, a hot lick up the back of my neck, a cold hand on my nape, and suddenly I am sickeningly aware of what I really did as I wasted all those days lying on my back on interchangeable beaches and failing to write, failing to think, failing to anything. I left her, here, looking like this: astonishingly beautiful, fay-like, perfection in miniature.

Her dress shows every curve. The desire hits me a few seconds after the envy, and as I watch her laugh, the lights catching the sheen of make-up on her cheekbones, I feel *devastatingly* out of her league. What kind of moron dosses around in Bali when he could be here with a woman like that? How could I be so stupid? Whatever misery has been gripping me over the past few months – the thick black dread, waiting for me every morning when I woke – feels more ridiculous than ever now that it's cleared and I'm here, watching her. What was I *doing*?

'I did warn you,' Deb says, at my shoulder.

I messaged Deb last week to say I wanted to surprise Addie on Fireworks Night – she'd mentioned that she and Deb were excited for a night out. *Well, it'll definitely surprise her*, Deb said. *I think she's pretty much given up on you ever coming home, to be honest.*

'I'm such a tit,' I say, rubbing my face. 'I thought . . .'

'She'd wait for you for ever?'

'She's still waiting, right?' I say, watching worriedly. 'She's not . . . seeing someone else?'

We've never talked about being exclusive. We fast-forwarded past that, right through to *I love you* – I assumed it was unnecessary. Now I'm recapping every Skype call, scanning through every word I can remember for a male name, that hot lick of jealousy working its way down my spine.

'Of course she's not seeing someone else.' Deb folds her arms. 'What were you *doing*?'

Hiding. Running away. Sinking. Drowning.

'Trying to figure things out,' I say weakly. 'I thought . . . Addie said to come home to her when I knew what I wanted to do with my life. And then I kept staying, and kept not figuring it out, and coming home felt even, you know, even harder.'

Deb frowns. 'That wasn't very sensible.'

'Yeah. I'm getting that.'

The man beside Addie ducks his head to speak to her and I want to whimper.

'Can't we tell her I'm here now? Please?'

Deb looks at me in an evaluating sort of way.

'Do you really love her?'

'I really do.'

'Then why did you stay away for so long?'

I grind my teeth in frustration. I can't tell her about the dread, the lethargy, the terror, and even if I could bring myself to share the shame of that, deep down I don't believe it's an excuse. That thick dread has hit me before, once, when I was a teenager, and back then my father made it very clear that it was nothing but weakness.

'I don't know. OK? I don't know. Marcus kept saying I should stay, and my dad was on at me to come back and start work at his business, and Addie has this whole new life here and I wasn't sure ... how I'd fit in it.'

'So you opted out?'

'So I waited. Until I was, you know, the man she'd want.'

Deb looks me up and down. 'And you're that now?'

I sag. 'Well, not really, no.'

'No. You look pretty much the same, aside from the tan.'

'Please, Deb,' I beg, as Addie laughs again, lifting a hand to her hair to smooth it back. 'I messed up. Let me fix it.'

'All right,' Deb says. 'Fine. But don't *keep* messing up, will you? You made her happy for a few days in France, I'll give you that – but since then you've made her bloody miserable. Now go hide and I'll lure her back to our table with alcohol so you can surprise her. If you're going to do this, you had better do it properly. I want to see my sister smiling again.'

Addie

'Addie,' he says.

We're at the table, pouring out cava from the bottle Deb conjured up from somewhere. I look at my sister before I turn around. She grins at me. She knew he was coming.

'I missed that happy face, Ads,' she says, as I turn in my seat, already beaming, and look at Dylan.

He's swept me up out of my chair before I can say anything.

'Christ,' he says, 'Addie Gilbert, do you have *any* idea how much I've missed you?'

I mean, I don't, really. He said *I miss you* plenty on Skype, but he always sounded so flat. If he missed me, why didn't he come back? But the thought evaporates the moment he presses his lips to mine. *This* is my Dylan. A flop of brown hair, startling green eyes. Ridiculous as it sounds, he seems to smell of sunshine and vineyards even here in this sticky club. We kiss for so long everything melts away, music pounding around us. We break apart eventually, and he laughs, smoothing his thumbs across my cheekbones.

'I'm so sorry I took so long to come home. I'm a fool. Forgive me?'

He apologises so easily. I don't know any other guys who do that.

It's like he's not got that male ego thing, the pride that's always getting wounded. I love that about him. But . . . I'm not sure it fixes things. Can you get rid of a mistake with one easy apology like that?

'Oh, God, Addie, please,' he says, pressing his lips to mine again. 'Don't be angry with me. I can't stand it.'

'Where's Marcus?' I ask.

Dylan looks surprised by the question – it surprised me a bit too. 'Home,' he says. 'In Hampshire. I told him I wanted to come straight here to see you, so he went back to stay with his dad.'

I nuzzle into Dylan's chest as my mind whirs. As the months have gone by, I've wondered about Marcus. Whether he's the reason Dylan didn't come home sooner. I can't imagine he was in any rush to get Dylan back to me.

'And . . . you're here now?' I ask him.

'I'm here now. For good. In full knowledge that I should never have left your side.'

'I'm drinking your cava!' Deb yells at me. 'You look busy.'

I laugh and give her a thumbs up, then drag Dylan to the dance floor as Deb knocks back my drink. Me and Dylan dance, pressed so close together every inch of us is touching. The strobes flash. My head's spinning. I'm giddy with having him back.

'You know,' Dylan says, close to my ear so I can hear him over the music, 'I'm beginning to think my life thus far has been one long string of poorly made decisions and very foolish mistakes, except for the day I knocked on your door.' He presses his lips to my hair and I hide my smile against his chest. 'I'm not leaving your side now.'

'That's going to be a bit tricky,' I say, pulling on his hands to get him dancing again. He's pretty good. I'm not sure why I assumed Dylan would be a bad dancer but this is a nice surprise.

'Tricky?'

'Your family live two hours away, don't they?'

He doesn't catch it. I repeat the words, my lips against his ear.

'I'm not moving home,' he says. He sounds triumphant. 'I'm moving here.'

'Here?' *That's* the grand plan he's spent months coming up with? 'Here, like, Chichester? What are you going to do for work?'

'I'll figure it out,' he says, and there's that shadow on his face again. 'If Chichester will have me.'

The lights paint his hair yellow, green, yellow. The music's so loud it's more buzz than noise.

'What, you're going to rent a flat here?'

'Or buy one. Dad's always on at me to get on the property ladder.'

I gawp at him for so long he laughs a bit uneasily, pulling me closer again.

'Or not, whatever. I just want to be here. I should have been here all along.'

Someone bashes into me, throwing me hard against his chest. I stay there, wrapping my arms around his waist. I've always believed everyone should get a second chance. And he's sorry, and was it that bad, anyway, him staying away a bit longer than he said he would while he figured stuff out?

And . . . I still love him. So there's that, too.

I sneak him into my room. The moment we click my bedroom door closed we're breathless, literally clawing each other's clothes off. Dylan tears the neckline of my dress and pauses, seeming surprised at himself, which makes me laugh so much I have to cover my mouth with a hand to keep quiet.

His body is the same but different. The tan lines are clearer, the muscles a little firmer maybe, but it's *him*, Dylan, home, and the feel of him against me is enough to send me quivering. We kiss hungrily, open-mouthed. I'm desperate. Aching. I'm so frantic I mess up the condom, and Dylan laughs, breathless, stilling my hands with his own.

'We have time,' he says, voice hoarse. 'I'm not going anywhere.'

He lays me down on the bed, moving on top of me. His arms bracket me. I lift my chin, demanding a kiss, and he presses his lips to mine, slow, soft. By the time he reaches for a second condom I've begged, literally *begged* him, and when at last he moves inside me we both cry out.

I sort of go through tiredness and out the other side. The alcohol probably helps with that. Dylan's body clock is a mess anyway with all the travelling. So at eight a.m., after zero hours of sleep, sated and giddy and probably still drunk, I bring him downstairs to make bacon and egg sandwiches for breakfast.

My mum arrives a few minutes after we put the rashers under the grill. She pauses in the doorway to the kitchen in her favourite dressing gown. It was purple originally, but it's a mushy sort of grey now.

'Well,' she says. 'I don't know what I'm more surprised to see. A young man in my kitchen or my daughter making a fried breakfast at eight o'clock in the morning.'

'Dylan,' Dylan says, wiping his hands on the apron he insisted on wearing and stretching one out for Mum to shake. 'Pleasure to meet you.'

'Oh! *Dylan!*'

Mum gives me one of those significant looks that only parents do. As if, as soon as you have a kid, you lose the power of subtlety.

'Yes, Mum, this is Dylan,' I say, turning back to buttering bread and trying not to smile.

'And he's back now, is he?'

'Absolutely,' Dylan says. 'And not going anywhere. Ever again. Ever.'

My smile widens.

'Well. I'm pleased to hear that, Dylan,' Mum says, and I can hear that she's smiling too. 'Now, brace yourself. If your father smells bacon he'll be out of bed like a—'

'Who's cooking bacon?' Dad yells down the stairs. 'Is it for me?'

NOW

Dylan

Charnock Richard Service Station, highlight of the M6, is resolutely grimy and grey beneath a deep blue sky. We all squeeze ourselves out of the Mini like a bad joke in reverse.

Marcus stretches expansively, fists clenched, and with his hair blowing into his eyes he looks like the scrappy little boy he once was, swamped in a Winchester College blazer, small enough that the older kids thought he'd be easy to pick on, smart enough that he owned them all by the end of autumn term. He had two teachers he didn't like fired; he somehow got Peter Wu kicked off the cricket team so he could play in his place; he soon had a reputation as a young man who made things happen.

I remember the day when a sixth former had thrown Luke into a wall and called him a *dick-sucker*. Marcus was a head shorter than Daniel Withers and half as broad, but as he approached the older boy there was an energy to Marcus, a wildness, like he was vicious and held on a very thin leash. *I won't fight you*, Marcus told Daniel, as I cradled Luke's bruised head against my shoulder. *But I'll end you. Slowly, piece by piece, until you're nothing but a punchline to people around here. You know I can.*

'So are we going to try one of these aberrations, then?' Marcus says, pointing to the sign advertising Greggs vegan sausage rolls.

'I thought they went against your philosophy,' I say, falling into step beside him.

He grins at me. 'You ought to know I never stick to one philosophy for long.' His smile drops as we enter the service station doors. 'Dyl . . .'

He glances behind him; the others are still crossing the car park, Addie's glasses glinting in the sun. She's unfastened the top of her dungarees to cool off, so the top part hangs down, flapping at her waist; underneath she's wearing a tight white crop top that clings to her skin and the ruched fabric of her bra.

'You know your dad offered me a job?'

I turn back to Marcus, faltering mid step. '*My* dad?'

I watch him resist the urge to say something facetious – I can see the words on the tip of his tongue, then the thought that swallows them back.

'Doing what?' I ask.

'Copy-writing for the company's new site. It's just a six-month thing, but, ah . . .'

It's a job my father has offered me countless times: *the best I can do for an English graduate who's got no work experience*. I'm sure offering it to Marcus is intended as a jab for me – why else would my father care to offer one of my friends a lifeline?

'I really need it, Dyl. I've got no money coming in from Dad still, and a criminal record,' Marcus says, pulling a face. Even Marcus – the man who makes things happen – could not get the police to drop the charges when he drunkenly smashed up the front of an estate agent's office.

'Well, then take it.'

'I didn't realise you two weren't *speaking*.'

'Luke has cut him out too. When he and Javier told Mum and

Dad about their engagement, Dad said he wouldn't come to their wedding. So . . .'

Marcus winces. 'Fuck. I . . . I didn't know. Luke must be . . .'

'Yeah. It's been tough. But he deserves more than half-recognition from his father. For what it's worth, I think cutting Dad off has been much healthier for Luke than seeing him and never being able to bring Javier home.'

'I should call Luke. I've been – I need to call him.'

We walk on in silence. Luke forgave Marcus long before me, but then, it's easier to forgive when it wasn't your life that was ruined – and living thousands of miles away in the States can't hurt, either.

'If . . . if you don't want me to take the job . . .' Marcus's eyes are pleading.

For a swift moment I'm tempted to say, *No, don't take it*, and see how much his loyalty to me will stretch, but I don't. I'm not that man. And I suspect he may well have already accepted.

'Of course you should take it. It's a good opportunity.'

We've wandered into Waitrose, drawn by the cool blast of the fridges; Marcus opens the door to the milk and makes a show of trying to climb in, and despite myself, I laugh.

'Remember when you made me down four pints of milk after a night out at Wahoo?' he says, rubbing his back against the cool glass like a bear against a tree.

Wahoo was one of the Oxford nightclubs – actually a sports bar that transformed itself for students at night. It always smelled of sweetcorn and inexplicably played the shopping channel on its TV screens while the DJ blasted out something by Flo Rida.

'I did *not* make you down four pints of milk,' I say, glancing at the tills. A young woman in a Waitrose uniform gives us an uncertain look; she is presumably trying to work out which rule Marcus is breaking by attempting to insert himself into the milk fridge.

'You definitely did,' Marcus says. 'Why else would I have done it?' He flashes me a grin that says he knows what I'm going to tell him.

'Because you're a senseless hedonist,' I say, and his grin widens. 'Come on, get out of there, the woman behind the till is trying to work out if she needs to section you.'

I flinch at my choice of words, but Marcus doesn't clock it; he throws the woman at the till a look.

'Eh, she's harmless,' he says. 'Wouldn't call security even if I pinched a two-pinter. Which I won't,' he says, rolling his eyes as my smile drops. 'Christ, what will it take to convince you I don't do that sort of thing any more?'

Addie, Rodney and Deb come into the shop and pause as they catch sight of Marcus trying to pull the fridge door closed with him inside. I give him a pointed look as he registers their expressions.

'Well, if you were hoping for a full personality transplant, you might as well give up on me now,' he says, and he's not grinning any longer. 'But I'm hoping you'll meet me halfway.'

'Excuse me,' says the lady at the till. 'Can I help you?'

'Oh, would you?' Marcus calls back. 'I just need a foot up and a few milk cartons shifted and I reckon I can wriggle into the second shelf.'

'I'm not . . . I don't think you're meant to be doing that,' she says, perplexed.

To my surprise, I can hear Deb and Addie laughing. I glance at them and the sight of Addie hiding her giggle behind a hand, her bracelets sliding down her arm, sets off something warm deep in my stomach, like the moment hot water hits tea. That laugh sounds like comfort, easy pleasure, the delight of somebody you love loving you back. I'd forgotten the way her eyes narrow when she laughs.

Marcus is right, I think – I'm pushing him too hard, expecting too much, or perhaps expecting the wrong thing altogether. He's *Marcus*. That's not going to change. And, quite honestly, as I watch him reason with the bemused shop assistant, I realise I don't want it to.

THEN

Addie

From the moment Dylan gets home, he barely leaves my side. Even on Christmas Day he drops around in the evening, making the drive all the way from his parents' place in Wiltshire just to hand-deliver our presents and join us for microwaved mulled wine in front of *Elf*.

Once term restarts in January, he's actually a really great support about work too, now he's around to listen. He always seems to get things from the kids' point of view. He was a delinquent at secondary school, apparently. Almost kicked out of the super-posh private school his parents chose for him. Though he claims that was mostly Marcus's fault.

I come home from work one night in January and find Dylan sprawled on the sofa, watching Dad's latest documentary. He's staying in an Airbnb while he flat-hunts, but he's here most nights. Already smiling, I kick my shoes off in the hall.

'You must come and try fly-fishing at ours,' Dylan is saying as I come into the room. He sips from one of our most chipped mugs – clearly Mum doesn't see him as a guest any more. 'My family has fishing rights for a stretch of the Avon, and they go to waste. My brother and I proved disappointingly poor sportsmen. Luke could never be doing with it and I didn't have the patience,' he says ruefully, scratching the back of his head.

My dad blinks a few times. 'Right,' he says. 'Golly. Thanks.'

I catch my mum's eye. She's tidying up around the living room – my mum is always bending down to pick up an errant sock or a used glass – and I watch as her lip twitches in amusement. *He's so posh,* she mouths at me. I pull a face.

'Don't pretend you don't love the idea of owning half a river one day,' she whispers to me as she passes me to the kitchen.

I laugh and follow her. 'You like him though? Right?'

'Why do you keep asking me that?' she says, loading the dishwasher.

I move to help her. She bats me away for putting a cereal bowl in the bottom instead of the top.

'I just . . . I want you to like him.'

'Well, I do.' She looks at me shrewdly. 'Do you want me to say he can stay here until he finds his own place, instead of hopping around all those short-term rentals?'

I blink, startled. 'Whoa.'

'He's here all the time anyway, sweets,' she says, straightening up and wiping her hands on the back of her jeans. They're 'mom jeans', made of thick old denim and turned up at the bottoms. 'Your dad and I talked about it last night.'

I say nothing. My heart flutters. Do I want that? Dylan living here? It feels . . . big.

'Ads?' Mum tilts her head. 'No? You two are so inseparable, and you seem so settled together . . .'

I lean against the counter, scraping at the skin on the edge of my thumbnail. 'Yeah. No, we are.'

She lowers her voice. 'But you're not feeling sure about him?'

'No, I am, I am, it's just . . . that time when he was away, I sort of started thinking . . . he didn't actually like me much. Or he would have come home.'

'He did come home, didn't he?'

'Yeah, but . . . not for ages. And I was starting work, and I kind of needed him here.'

'Did you tell him you needed him?'

'I wanted him to just . . . *know*,' I say, wincing at myself.

Mum waves me out of the way so she can wipe the surface behind me. 'You should talk to him about it and clear the air, sweetie.'

I chew my lip. Trouble is, I really raised the bar for myself in those weeks in Provence. Three weeks was just enough time to be sexy and interesting and a bit mysterious. Now Dylan's here, on our second-hand sofa, and I'm back late from work in my worn black trousers and dowdy blouse . . . I do worry that this just isn't very *Dylan*, all this. All my real-life stuff. He fell in love with Summer Addie. I'm definitely not the girl I was *before* the summer, but I'm not exactly Summer Addie now either, am I?

'How do you do it?' I ask impulsively, watching my mum tuck her hair behind her ear as she scrubs at the surfaces. 'With Dad? I mean . . . you've been together for . . .'

'Twenty-five years,' Mum says, glancing over her shoulder with a smile. 'And it's all about compromise, I'd say.'

'Like how you always let Dad watch the telly after dinner and you tidy up?' I say, raising my eyebrows.

'Exactly. He cooks!'

'But you do all the thinking about what to make,' I point out. 'And the shop.'

She frowns. 'We each do our fair share.'

There is no point talking to my mother about mental load. For her, Dad is the ultimate modern man because he irons his own shirts.

'Will you at least let me wash up?' I ask.

'Of course!' Mum says, passing me the rubber gloves. 'You really are a changed woman these days. Gone is the layabout student, in comes the responsible young lady who notices the pile of dirty pans by the sink.'

I stick my tongue out at her. 'Urgh, I don't know,' I say, turning on the hot tap. 'I don't know why I'm holding back. I'll ask him about moving in for a bit.'

'Only if you're absolutely sure, sweets – you've got a whole life ahead of you, there's no need to rush things. Oh, Addie, careful with that plate, it was your grandmother's . . .'

I let her step in and wash up the plate I am not qualified for.

'But I don't think you need to worry about him not being as interested as you are,' Mum continues. 'He hardly leaves your side.'

'Can I help?' Dylan says from the doorway.

Mum gives me a significant look, as if Dylan coming in to help with the dishes is a sign he can't bear to be parted from me.

'I'm home!' Deb yells through the house, slamming the front door. 'Is the Addie shadow here? Oh, good, hi, Dylan. I need your help with a job application. Can you read it through for me and make it sound, you know . . .' She chucks her bag down in the corner of the kitchen. 'More clever?'

'The Addie shadow?' Dylan repeats, half laughing.

Deb waves that off, tsking as she finds no clean glasses in the cupboard. She heads for the dishwasher. 'Damn, is that running?'

'You're welcome,' Mum says mildly.

'Addie's shadow, like . . . I follow her around in a sinister fashion?' Dylan asks.

'No, just like you're attached to her ankle,' Deb says. 'I'll have to use a mug – Dad! Dad! Have you got my French bulldog mug through there?'

'No,' Dad roars from the living room.

'You left it under your desk,' Mum says. 'I cleared it up this morning. It's in the dishwasher.'

'*Under* the desk?' I ask.

'Attached to her ankle?' Dylan repeats, his brow furrowing.

'When's Cherry arriving?' Deb asks.

'Tomorrow,' Dad calls, in a loaded sort of way. Dad's sulking because when Cherry stays he has to clear out of his 'study', the box room at the front of the house that he's filled with crap. Parts of train and aeroplane models, old issues of *The Beano*, laptops that died but for some reason must not be thrown away. Dad hates guests coming. It gives Mum the perfect excuse to tell him to clear out the junk.

'Do *you* think I'm clinging to your ankles?' Dylan asks me, with a very sweet frown.

My heart seems to open up for a moment, and everything suddenly feels simple. I loop my arms around his neck and kiss him on the lips.

'I think you should cancel the Airbnb.'

He pulls back. 'What do you mean?'

'Mum says you can stay here while you wait to buy a flat.'

'Ooh,' says Deb, shoving past us. 'Dylan's moving in!'

My cheeks go red. 'Not moving *in*,' I say, already regretting it a bit. 'He stays over most nights anyway.'

Dylan blinks his long eyelashes at me. Just as the worry starts to bloom in my belly he wraps me up and presses kisses to my cheeks, my forehead, my neck. I laugh, wriggling in his arms.

'Thank you,' he says, lifting his head to speak to my mum. 'That's so kind of you and Neil.' He lowers his mouth to mine again, then presses his lips to my ear. 'And thank *you*,' he whispers.

'Wait until you've stayed a few weeks,' I say, pulling away, but smiling. 'You'll be so sick of Dad's snoring through the wall and Deb banging around the kitchen at five in the morning, you'll be out the door like a shot.'

Dylan collects Cherry from the station. I have no idea where he magicked the car up from. One day he just . . . had one. Brand new and smelling of that flowery air-freshener made by people who have clearly only heard about roses and lilies second-hand.

Cherry turns up on my parents' doorstep looking like the perfect public-school princess, as usual. Her hair is in a simple high ponytail and she looks like she isn't wearing any make-up, but I know how much time and effort – and how many products – go into giving that impression. Cherry and I shared a room in second year at uni. There isn't much we don't know about each other. Boundaries were blurred. Lines were crossed. Knickers were borrowed.

She throws herself towards me over the threshold. As we hug, we do that squealing thing girls do in American high-school films. That was a joke, once, but we definitely ditched the sense of irony a while back.

'Addie! God, I've missed you!'

'Come in,' I say, tugging her inside. 'Dad's decluttered your room again.'

Cherry's often here. Her parents are even more eccentric than she is: if she's home for more than a week or two they usually rope her into doing something totally bizarre, like knitting a mile-long scarf for charity or helping to rehome a load of nuns.

'I hope Neil left me a model aeroplane to do again,' Cherry says, heading for the study. She sits and bounces on the bed, looking around happily. 'Home!' she says. 'Well. One of them. One of my favourite ones. Oh! Mr and Mrs Gilbert!'

'Welcome back, sweet,' Mum says as Cherry bounds towards them for hugs.

My parents love Cherry. Everyone loves Cherry. Not loving Cherry is like hating puppies.

'I'll put the kettle on, shall I?' Cherry says, shoving Dylan out of her way with her hip. 'We have *so much* to talk about.'

She's already on her way through to the kitchen. We all follow in her wake.

'I am such a good matchmaker,' Cherry tells Mum as she fills the kettle. 'Didn't I tell you I'd find Addie someone?'

I frown. 'I didn't need—'

'And it's a good job you spent your summer in France,' she says, waggling a finger at me, 'because *teaching*? There's no men in teaching.'

'There are!' I say, laughing. 'Our head teacher is a man.'

Cherry rolls her eyes, flicking on the kettle. 'Oh, of course the *head* is a man. I bet he's old and dull.'

'He's young and interesting, actually,' I tell her, pointing her to the mug cupboard. 'And hot.'

'Ooh! Set me up?' Cherry says, digging around. 'Where's Deb's bulldog mug? Has she locked it away?'

'Are you always this loud?' Deb asks, appearing in the kitchen doorway. 'I don't remember you being this loud.'

'Deb!' Cherry runs in for a hug and then stops short, socks skidding on the lino. 'No hug! I remember. Hi! You look so pretty!'

Deb smiles. 'Hey, Cherry. You can have my mug. It's in the bottom drawer, inside the spare washing-up bowl.'

Cherry spins on her heels with a quiet *yes* and a fist-pump and heads for the drawer.

'What?' Deb says, as we all stare at her. 'You try saying no to that woman.'

Dylan

Young and interesting and *hot*?

I take the tea Cherry offers me and she scans my face for a moment, turning serious; she knows me too well.

'OK?' she mouths.

I smile, forcing the fear back to wherever it reared up from, dark and grasping. 'Of course.'

She looks unconvinced, but then Deb starts complaining about the fact that Addie's mother now insists on the purchase of skimmed milk, rather than their usual semi-skimmed, and a debate begins about whether full fat is green top or blue top, and Cherry is lost to me again.

I swallow, cupping the tea between my palms, watching Addie. She's wearing her favourite dungarees, and her dark hair is still in the lopsided bun she slept in; she's all unkempt and wild and at-home. It's perhaps the Addie-est she has ever looked, here with her family clattering around her, and I feel terrifyingly sure that every man in the world must be in love with her.

Young and interesting and hot, she said. I've never even heard her mention the head teacher before. I do recall her saying that the senior staff were very supportive, but I think I had assumed they were all middle-aged women.

My phone buzzes in my pocket and I wince – it will be my father. I ignored his last phone call, letting it ring and ring in my hand, watching his name bobbing on the screen like a fishing lure on the water.

'No way!' Cherry is saying. 'The lady across the road? The one with all the ear piercings?'

'Yes! That one!' Addie says, doubling over, laughing so hard her cheeks are turning rose-pink.

'And what about the cat?' Cherry says, eyes wide.

'Shipped off to her mum's,' Addie's mother says, laughing. 'Haven't seen it since!'

They all crack up – even Addie's dad is chortling, and I've only ever seen him laughing when sportspeople fall over on the television. I wish I caught the beginning of the story instead of spending the last five minutes inside the tortured labyrinth of my own brain.

I ease my phone out of my back pocket and check it.

> Call me. You can't be serious about this Chichester nonsense. You need to come home and start doing something with your life, for God's sake.

I swallow.

'You OK?' Addie asks, glancing down at my phone.

I switch it off quickly, turning the screen black. 'Fine,' I say. 'Just my dad, on at me to view another property.'

Addie laughs. 'Listen to you. *Property*. You're such a grown-up.'

Me, the grown-up? Every day she comes home from work and kicks off her shoes with a groan, pulling her hair out of its bun, and then she tells me all about the kids who refused to hand over the cigarettes they rolled on their lunch hour, and I try to say something helpful and supportive, but truly I feel like a fraud. Addie's in the real world.

I don't even know what the real world is. The dread is tugging at me again, and in its way the fear of it is almost as bad as the dread itself.

My phone buzzes again: Marcus this time.

Hello?? You still out there? I've forgotten what you look like, my friend.

I feel an unmistakable twinge of guilt – since getting back to the UK, I've not seen Marcus as often as I should.

Come over tonight? I have something really cool to show you and it would be nice to actually spend some time?

'What d'you think?' Addie asks me.

'Hey? Sorry,' I say, shaking my hair out of my eyes. 'I missed that.'

Addie huffs through her nose. 'Are you writing a poem in there?' she asks, pointing at my forehead.

'Something like that.'

'Give me the line and I'll find you a rhyme, Dyl!' Cherry yells across the kitchen, popping the toaster down.

I have tried many times to explain to Cherry that poems do not always have to rhyme, but she is not to be persuaded.

'Thanks, but I'm good, Cherry.'

'Cherry! Berry! Very!' Cherry chants, ducking under Deb's arm to get the margarine out of the fridge. 'Derry! Kerry! Merry!'

'Does she have a volume switch?' Addie's dad asks her mum.

'She winds down eventually,' Addie's mum says fondly. 'She's just excited.'

'Could we take her for a walk, or something?' Addie's dad suggests, with some desperation.

'We were talking about what we're going to do tonight,' Addie tells me, voice raised over the noise. 'Wine, a film? Cherry bingo – we drink every time she exclaims something?'

I want to. I don't want to let Addie out of my sight even for a moment; I know on some level that I'm still paying for that time away, or perhaps not paying for it but earning it back. But there's that text from Marcus. *It would be nice to actually spend some time?*

'I'm seeing Marcus this evening,' I say. 'I'm really sorry.'

An expression flickers on Addie's face. Not quite irritation, but perhaps something related to it – disappointment? Churlishness? She turns away so fast I can't tell.

'Cool, no worries,' she says, heading out of the kitchen, slipping away.

Joel, Marcus's dad, played for Arsenal in his youth, earning over fifty thousand pounds a week, and the house he built himself is designed to demonstrate that fact in every possible way. The mansion has an aura of forced glamour, of blaring, teeth-gritted, garish extravagance. The taps are made of gold – not just gold-coloured, but built from real, solid gold – and the bannisters are wrought iron, twisted into the repeated symbol of the Arsenal badge.

I've been to Marcus's house so many times that I've stopped noticing how absurd it all is – the gigantic walk-in wardrobe in every bedroom, the cinema in the basement, the theme-park-style slide in the back garden. I have to consciously stop and take a moment to appreciate the sheer and disgusting decadence of it all.

'You're late,' Marcus says, making his way down the grand staircase. 'You missed dinner. India dropped around tacos.'

India is Marcus's stepmother. She's half Joel's age and a former backing singer for Miley Cyrus; she built an empire on selling vegan dog treats, and her Instagram following is over two million. Marcus's mother died when he was five, and India arrived on the scene a mere six months later. There are hundreds of reasons why Marcus would despise her, but once you meet India, you quickly realise why he loves her so much. Or rather, why he did, once.

India is loud, kind and straightforward to the point of rudeness. When Marcus was a teenager they would have screaming matches, veins popping in their foreheads, arguments so loud and vicious you'd never think they could reach any sort of resolution, and then somehow, miraculously, India would get an apology out of Marcus for whatever he'd done, and they'd be playing golf together again. This is how Marcus's family worked, until, in our first year of university, India left Joel for Joel's brother.

I've never seen Marcus so broken. He went *wild*. Endless parties, orgies, ten-thousand-pound trips to ski resorts and run-ins with the police. The night I found him alone on the college chapel roof with a bottle of absinthe was the tipping point: Joel told Marcus he'd send him to rehab if he didn't clean up. I remember the phone call, how Marcus's eyes flicked to mine and widened for a moment, and I thought, *At last, something's got to him*. I should have thought of rehab myself: Marcus hates nothing more than the feeling of being abandoned somewhere, alone.

He never cleaned up, exactly, but he managed to rein himself in a little after that. Or rather, he's still managing.

To my surprise, India didn't check out when she left Joel. She still visits Joel's house to see Marcus; she still rings him and messages him. She's still his stepmum, she says, but he's never really seen her that way again, and now the screaming matches just end with Marcus slamming out of the house and calling me.

It's no wonder, really, that he was so keen to keep travelling. And when I couldn't muster the energy to get out of bed, Marcus understood – he never said it, but I knew the dread had come for him before too.

'What was it you wanted to show me?' I ask Marcus as he joins me downstairs. His shoes are muddy; they leave a trail on the floor, cartoonish, pale brown footprints on the pristine marble.

Marcus jerks his head for me to follow him and heads for the garden. 'You'll love it.' He grins at me over his shoulder. 'Come on.'

I smile back despite myself. Marcus's good moods come and go like rain showers, but when you catch one, it's a joy.

We step out into the grey evening light. The back porch – about the size of a squash court – is lit by soft pink lights embedded between the flagstones; they give Marcus a faintly ghoulish air, as if he's a character in a horror film, uplit in pale red. Beyond, the lawns stretch down to the man-made lake in which Marcus celebrated his twenty-first birthday. Everyone had protested when he insisted on bikinis and swim shorts – it was a lake in Britain, for God's sake – until the first brave person dive-bombed in and discovered that the lake was fully heated.

We traipse all the way down the lawn. Marcus jumps between the stepping stones India had laid when he was a child. As the pinkish light from the porch recedes, he flips on the torch on his phone, sending its beam scattering this way and that as he leaps from flagstone to flagstone.

There's a small jetty on the lake – this is where India and Joel got married. I must have been about eight. Joel and my mother met at a gala in London; our families have been friends ever since. I'd stood beside Marcus during the ceremony; he was dressed in a pale blue suit and waistcoat, and there was a wreath of flowers in his curls, skewed, looping over one ear. He cried when they said *I do*, just tears down his cheeks, no shoulders shaking, no gulps for air. Until then, I'd known that Marcus was sad to have lost his mother, but I'd never *felt* it before. I'd held his hand tight; across from me, down the aisle, my brother had reached to hold his other.

'Where are you taking me?' I call.

Marcus is getting ahead of me now, almost at the jetty. His torchlight catches the surface of the water and sends reflections shuddering; I catch sight of a boat bobbing uneasily on the lake.

Marcus stands aside, lighting the boat so I can get in first. It's a small wooden thing with two paddles and planks to sit on. I eye it with suspicion.

'Get in, wet-arse,' Marcus says, giving me an affectionate shove. 'As if you didn't spend half your childhood fishing.'

'On a bank,' I point out. 'Fishing on a bank.'

Marcus gives me another shove, enough to make me think he'll help me into the boat if I don't get on with it. I leap in, landing unsteadily, grabbing at a plank to keep myself from falling completely. Marcus laughs behind me, and the beam of his phone torch skitters around us, lighting the distant trees, the dark lake, the jetty, as he jumps in beside me. It's cold enough to see my breath when the torch beam swings my way.

'Where are we going?' I ask.

'All in good time, my friend! Grab an oar, would you?'

We row erratically across the water. For all his dabbling in every sport imaginable at university – and with a sportsman's genes – you'd think Marcus would be good at this sort of thing, but he's useless. For a while we go around in circles, splashing each other, swearing, laughing, until we get the hang of it.

I'm warming up now, and with the warmth comes a fizz of excitement at being out adventuring. It's often like this with Marcus – he brings out the bravery in me. With Marcus by my side, I'm *somebody*, the sort of man who throws caution to the wind, who defies his father, who chooses poetry when he ought to know better.

There's no jetty at the other end of the lake, just a bank to scrabble up – we're both soaked through by the time we make it to dry land, and as Marcus ties the boat messily to a wooden pole near the water, I come to the conclusion that his dad must have turned off the lake-heating over the winter. The water is eating its way through my jeans, gnawing cold at my fingers.

'This way,' is all Marcus says as he leads me towards the trees. I fumble for my own phone, checking it's still dry, and hit the icon to turn my torch on – Marcus's light isn't enough any more. The trees close around us, their roots snagging under my feet. There's a path here – it looks like a vehicle came this way, leaving two thick ditches, holding the dregs of the day's rainwater like old tea. My shoes are wrecked. I'm in trainers – I should be wearing wellies. You never know what you'll need when Marcus summons you of an evening.

Just as I open my mouth to ask him – again – where he's taking me, the trees open out, and Marcus's phone lights up a building.

It's a cabin. The whole thing seems to be built of wood, though it's hard to see in the bland yellow light of our phones. There's a porch, raised above the muddy forest floor, and the front is mostly glass – there are windows right up to the pointed tip of its roof. Marcus steps forward to press something, and suddenly the edges of the roof, the porch railings and the door are lit up in small, twinkling fairy lights.

'This is . . . Has this always been here?' I ask, moving forward, flashing my torch up at the beautiful wooden beams above the porch.

'Nope. Dad's been working on it this last year. Come on – wait 'til you see inside.'

He races up the steps, and I follow him in, tugging my soaked, filthy trainers off at the door. It's deliciously warm inside. The walls are wooden and the floor is carpeted in thick, shaggy rugs. It's deceptively big – there's room in the living area for two sofas, and I can see a kitchen, and a toilet tucked away under the staircase.

'This is incredible,' I say, poking my head up the stairs. There's another bathroom and two bedrooms up there, wood lined, with plush grey carpet and double beds.

'It's ours,' Marcus says. 'Mine and yours.'

I pause on my way back down the stairs. He looks up at me, waiting at the bottom, grinning.

'What?'

'Dad had it made for us. It's like a . . . granny annexe, but for grads. A graddy annexe.'

He's off, heading for the kitchen, pulling us each a cold beer from the fridge. I follow him slowly, feeling the soft rugs beneath my socked feet, and try to process.

Mine and yours.

'Your dad built us a *house*?'

'Why not?' Marcus says, shrugging and passing me a beer. 'We've got this land.'

'I didn't even know you owned this bit past the lake,' I say, circling, looking at the pictures on the walls.

Marcus laughs. 'Of course we do. We own right up to the road. Dad's had a tarmac track put in between here and there, so we can drive straight in – parking's out the back. I just took you the scenic way across the lake for maximum impact,' he says with a wink. 'Girls will love it.'

'I can't . . . live here,' I manage. 'If that's actually what you mean?'

Marcus swigs his beer, throwing himself back on the sofa. 'You absolutely can live here. Look.' He wipes his mouth. 'We both know London and your dad's company isn't the right move for you, and fuck knows you don't want to go live at home in Wiltshire. Where else are you going to write your life's opus?'

'I'm moving to Chichester,' I say. 'I told you. I'm going to get a job there. Live with Addie's parents until I find a place I like.'

Marcus snorts. 'Shut *up*, you pillock,' he says. 'You're not actually doing that. You can't move in with the parents of some girl you screwed this summer. In *Chichester*.'

I recoil. The cold beer sweats in my palm.

'She's not just some girl. It's Addie.'

Marcus turns his face away for a moment. He's almost finished his beer already; he bounces up, heading to the fridge for the next one.

'How long have you known Addie?'

'You know how long.'

'Just answer me.'

'I met her in early July.'

'And?'

'It's January. So I've known her . . . six months.'

'And how many days have you *spent* with Addie?' Marcus's bottle of beer hisses as he flicks its lid off.

'That doesn't matter.'

'Except it does, clearly. Otherwise we'd still be marrying girls we met one time at a country dance like people did in the olden days. We've evolved past that, Dylan. Nowadays we date. We shop around. If we really like someone, we spend more time with them, then we move in with them a few years down the line. Then . . . maybe, if we've lost the will to live or whatever it is that compels people to settle down, we marry them. We don't rearrange our lives because of a good shag.'

I put my beer down, then pick it up again and reach for a coaster. My heart is thudding against my ribs.

'She's *not* just a good shag. I love her.' My voice sounds strangled. I push my hair out of my eyes; it sticks damply to my forehead.

Marcus growls under his breath and throws his hands in the air, then sucks at his beer as it begins to froth over.

'Dyl, I get it. She's gorgeous, she's smart, she doesn't take shit from you. I get it, believe me. But Addie . . . she's not right for you.' He runs a hand through his hair. His movements are even more frantic and erratic than usual; I wonder if he's taken something. 'She's not right.'

I gulp down three cold mouthfuls of beer. My head is spinning. 'She *is*,' I say. 'She's perfect.'

'*Stop* that,' Marcus shouts, and I jump, beer running down the back of my hand. 'Don't you see what you're doing? You're turning her into something she's not. You don't understand her. She's not your beautiful muse, Dylan, she's messy and dark and raw. She's a disaster waiting to happen. She's got power and she doesn't even know it yet, you know? She's like . . . she's *untapped.*'

I stare at him. He's pacing now, tugging at his curls.

'She's not right for you,' he says. 'OK?'

'Well, I think she is,' I say, a little helpless. He's definitely high – I don't know how I didn't clock it earlier. He hasn't even seen Addie since France, and we hardly even talk about her – I can't fathom when he could have got around to deciding she's so catastrophic for me.

I watch him try to gather himself, pausing mid step and pivoting on his toes to look at me.

'Role reversal,' he says. 'What if it was me doing this? With her? What would you say if I was changing my whole life and being a different person and *idolising* this girl? You and India would be teaming up for a full-scale intervention and you know it.'

I pause. That's actually true, to be quite honest. But I'm not Marcus. He falls in and out of love with women the way he falls in and out of love with everything: rapidly, thoughtlessly, with flair. Whereas I . . . I've never felt this way before.

'I know this maybe looks – fast – or a bit spontaneous, but I might as well be in Chichester as anywhere while I figure out what I want to do, and . . .'

Marcus stretches his arms out. 'Fine. You can do the whole buying-a-flat-in-Chichester thing if you must. But crash here while you're looking. Don't tell me squeezing into Addie's parents' house is better than this.'

For a split second I imagine myself here, wandering down to the lake on a morning with my notebook tucked into my coat pocket and a pen behind my ear, giving myself the space and permission I need to write. But no. I *want* to squeeze into Addie's parents' house.

I want to stand with her in the kitchen as they clatter around her making jokes about cats and semi-skimmed milk; I want to know how her bun slips sideways in the night, how her voice is low and throaty when she wakes, how she blinks and squirms when I open her bedroom curtains.

'I can't just live at the end of your dad's garden. That's – it's so good of him to have said I can join you here, but . . .'

'Dad built it for the two of us,' Marcus says abruptly. 'There was no "joining me here" about it. This is ours. A monument to friendship.' He raises his beer to me, but his eyes are stony.

'That's amazing. It's amazing,' I say, floundering. 'I just need a minute to think about all this. It's quite a change of plan.'

I look around. There's an enormous TV, flat screen, fixed to the wall above a wood-burning stove. The cushions on the sofa are pristine white fur.

'All right. Let's just get drunk and enjoy it,' Marcus says, downing the rest of his beer, shoulders suddenly relaxing; you can see his mood shift. 'And I'll give you another talking-to in the morning, by which time you will hopefully have seen sense.' He grins, up off the sofa again, heading to the fridge. 'Come on, Dylan, my man – I'm in the mood for mischief. Let's see if we can revive the Dylan who completed every Jameson Society assignment in record time in first year.'

Marcus slams a bottle of tequila down on the table, making me jump again.

'Alexa?' he yells. 'Play Zara Larsson, "Lush Life".'

I jump again as speakers blare. Marcus is already up, already dancing. He's the sort of man who can dance alone and not look like a tit, a quality I've always coveted.

'They'll be here soon,' he says, glancing up at the clock hanging above the doorway. He dances his way to the wine rack set beneath one of the kitchen cabinets. 'Let's get some wine chilling, now, shall we?'

'Who's coming?' I down the rest of my beer; I'm suddenly desperate to get drunk.

Marcus shrugs. 'A few people from uni, a few from around here . . . Everyone you'd want at a housewarming.'

'Let me invite Cherry and Addie and Deb,' I say, reaching for my phone.

Marcus snatches it out of my hand. One moment he's stacking wine bottles in the fridge, the next he's dancing away with my iPhone in the air.

'Hey!'

'*One* night without the ball and chain,' Marcus calls over his shoulder, disappearing out the kitchen door into the woods outside.

'Hey, wait,' I call, following.

The door kicks back in my face. I push it open again, and the cold hits me like an upended bucket of water. My breath clouds. The fairy lights twinkle, turning Marcus gold as he runs into the trees.

'Oi! Give me my phone back!'

'Tomorrow morning,' Marcus yells, laughing. 'For tonight, you're solo Dylan, not Addie-plus-Dylan, all right? You'll thank me, I promise! You're so whipped these days.' This is said to my face – he's back, without my phone, bounding up the steps and smiling at me like we're both in on the joke.

'Have you just left it in the woods? What if it rains? And my phone gets wet?'

Marcus rolls his eyes as he pushes the kitchen door open again. 'Then you'll buy another one,' he says. 'Come on. I want my Dylan back.'

'I've not *changed*,' I say, frustrated. 'I've not gone anywhere.'

Marcus claps a hand on my shoulder. Back in the warm of the cabin, my hands begin to thaw again. I can feel the slight buzz of that beer already.

'The fact that you're even saying that tells me you need help,' he says. 'And I consider it my sacred duty to save my best friend. All right? Now have another drink, and have a smoke, and try to remember how to have fun.'

The night passes in flashes. The weed is stronger than anything I've ever smoked before. My heart races; I'm quite sure that I'm *just* about to die. It gives everything an awful immediacy: this is my last dance, my last drink, the last person I'll ever speak to.

The women arrive in packs, shedding their fur coats on the backs of sofas and strewing them across beds. The cabin is a mass of bare shoulders and legs and the perfume is stifling in the heat. I spend at least half an hour trying to work out how to turn the heating down, buffeting my way through the crowds to squint at dials on walls and boxes in cupboards, but to no avail. My shirt sticks to my back. Every breath seems to come too short, and the only thing that helps is dancing. When I'm moving it's like I can outrun the fear, as if I'm spinning out of its grasp, and if I ever stand still Marcus is there with another drink, a pill, a woman with skeletal cheekbones and plump, hungry lips. So it feels best to keep moving.

I forget myself for a while, and it's bliss. The next thing I know I'm sitting on a bed with two women – one very tall, one very short. The tall woman has her hand on my knee; her face looms in my vision, black-rimmed eyes, eyelashes impossibly long.

'Are you and Marcus a thing?' she asks me. 'I've always wondered.'

I stand and the hand drops away.

'He's so *pretty*,' the tall woman says, as though she never touched my knee at all. 'If he's straight, I'm calling dibs.'

'I need to . . . go outside,' I manage. The door handle won't turn. My heart is beating so fast I worry it'll come loose somehow. I rattle at the handle, throw my shoulder against the door. Behind me, the women laugh.

I turn the handle the other way and the door comes easily – I fall through into the hall outside. A man I've never seen before is kissing a girl who's sitting on the bannister, her bum hanging over, her legs wrapped around his waist. If he lets go, she'll fall. I edge past, terrified to touch them, terrified to send her dropping.

The door to the woods outside is open to let out the heat; I stagger through. The porch is full too, more bare limbs, more writhing bodies. I run until the music is quiet enough for me to hear the sound of my shaking breathing. The woods are pitch-black. Something touches my face. I scream. It's a branch, heavy with night-time dew, and it leaves a wet handprint on my cheek.

I curl up somewhere, my back to the bark of a tree. The moisture creeps into my jeans, my boxers, so cold that soon I can't feel the ground underneath me at all. I hug my knees. I think of Addie, how she makes me feel the very opposite of this bleakness, how effortlessly she fills the grasping, hopeless hole in my chest. She's never felt so far away from me, not even in those months we spent apart. The music thrums behind the darkness like the night is growling.

'Dylan?'

I scream when something touches me again. This time a hand.

'Come on, you're freezing.'

He takes me back to the cabin. The music gets louder and louder and louder. The beat is too fast – I want it to slow down. I ask Marcus and he laughs and squeezes my arm.

'You're OK, Dyl. Let's just get you warmed up. You've forgotten where your limits are, that's all.'

He takes me upstairs and kicks a drunk man out of the bath so he can run it for me. When I ask about the music again he shouts down the stairs and it changes: something eerie and slow that I like even less.

I cry when I get into the water. It hurts. It feels like someone has bitten off the tips of my fingers. Marcus holds my hand tight.

'You're OK,' he keeps saying. 'You're all right.'

'I don't know what I'm doing,' I say, and my shoulders shake. 'I don't know – I don't know what I'm meant to do. I'm losing myself again, aren't I?'

I remember suddenly that my phone is out there in the woods somewhere, with all those messages from my father waiting for me in the dark, and I shudder so hard I splash Marcus with water. He swears quietly, letting go of my hand for a moment to brush the drops off his T-shirt, but his hand is back in mine before I have time to be afraid.

'Nobody knows what they're doing,' Marcus tells me. 'Lie back. Go on. You need to get your whole body in the water. You should stop thinking so hard, Dylan. You're your own worst enemy.'

'Dad wants me to work for his business.'

There's a fine crack running down the centre of the ceiling. I trace it with my eyes, tipping my head back, letting the water touch the crown of my head.

'Fuck your dad. He's been controlling your life for ever. Make your own choice.'

'I did. I have.'

'It's not making your own choice if it's for a girl.'

I flex my hands. My fingers still hurt. I look down – my toes are yellow-white.

'How do I know I'm making my own choice, then?'

'You go with your gut.'

'I *am* going with my gut.'

'You're going with your dick. And working for your dad, that'd be going with your head. I'm talking *gut*. The thing that you know deep down makes the most sense. The thing that's truest to who you are.'

To be true to yourself, you have to have a sense of self to work with.

'I've always had your back, haven't I?' Marcus lowers our joined hands into the water.

I hiss as the pain takes hold.

'Yeah,' I say. 'Yeah, I know, I just . . .'

'I'm giving you the chance to do what you want to do. You can write here. Isn't that what you've always wanted?'

'Poetry isn't – it's not a job.'

'It is if you're good enough.'

'I'm not,' I say automatically. The line on the ceiling is shifting a little to and fro in my vision, blurring.

'That's not your gut talking.'

I let the heat creep into my bones and stare at the crack above me and I know Marcus is right. If I really thought I wasn't good enough, I'd stop writing. Deep down, I love what I write, and I think other people might too, one day.

'Do you trust me?' Marcus asks.

Marcus and I applied for Oxford together. English, because Marcus said that was easy to get into, and if I wanted to be a poet that would be a good place to start. The same college, because why would we do anything else?

Luke grew up and fell in love and went to the States for his undergrad – or, really, to escape Dad – but Marcus has never left my side. And I've never left his, the small boy with the curly hair and the flower wreath hanging wonkily over his ear.

'Of course. Of course I trust you.'

'Then listen to me when I say this is what you want.' He loosens his grip on my hand. 'I'll kick everyone out. Don't get out the bath until I come back. I think standing might be a little beyond you for the time being. And also, don't drown.'

I hear the door click shut. At some point, without me really noticing, the urgent knowledge that I'm about to die has eased away. In its place is the familiar, clutching confusion that dogged me all last summer, beneath the dread – the sense that I'm doing something very important, and that I'm doing it entirely wrong.

NOW

Addie

Every time I check Google Maps, Scotland gets further away.

'How is this even possible?' I say as Google turns a little more of my journey from blue to red. 'We're driving towards Scotland, but every time I check, Scotland takes longer to get to?'

Deb and I are back in the front seats. This feels like the right order of things, if I'm honest. I am too grumpy to be crammed in the back with an assortment of men I did not want on my road trip.

'Someone's got to tell Cherry how late we are,' I say, rubbing my eyes. 'She's going to cry, isn't she?'

Something happened to Cherry when she started planning her wedding. The carefree Cherry who had cheerfully scrubbed her one-night-stand's vomit out of our bedroom carpet at uni had transformed into a woman who could not stand the thought of her wedding bouquet containing fewer than sixteen dark red roses. Everyone says people change when they're planning a wedding, but I'd assumed that only happened to crap people, ones who deep down had always been a bit ridiculous and had just hidden it well. But no. The wedding mania had even got to Cherry.

'She's not going to cry,' Dylan says firmly.

There's a long pause. I wait. He waits. I am totally confident Dylan will crack first. He may have changed, but he's not changed *that* much.

'I'll call her,' Dylan says.

I smile.

'Don't be smug, now,' Dylan tells me, with the hint of a smile. 'Or I'll do it on speaker.'

Why is sitting in traffic so much worse than driving? I would rather drive for eight hours than sit in traffic for four. At least if you're going at sixty there's some sense of progress. As it is, I've been inspecting the back end of an Audi for actual for ever. There's roadworks, that's part of the problem – only two lanes instead of four.

It's half past four. We were meant to be in Scotland by now, at Cherry's pre-wedding barbecue, but appear to be . . . I squint at a road sign catching the sun. Bloody hell, we're not even at Preston. Cherry didn't cry on the phone, but she went dangerously high-pitched. We *really* need to crack on to Scotland now.

The last song ends and I flick through one of my favourite country playlists. So many of these songs make me think of Dylan. I swallow. My finger hovers over 'What If I Never Get Over You', Lady A, but I shouldn't. It'll probably make me cry hearing that with Dylan in the back seat.

I settle for 'We Were' by Keith Urban. As the riff starts up I sink back in the seat and take a deep breath. This journey with Dylan is just as hard as I thought it would be. Worse, even, because he's different. He was always quieter in a group, but that quietness doesn't feel like Dylan stepping into the background now. It reads more like . . . thoughtfulness.

'Give Rodney a bit more room, would you?' Dylan says behind me. I don't have to turn to know what he's talking about. Marcus will be sat with his legs so far apart he might as well be at the gynaecologist's.

'Rodney's fine,' Marcus says. 'If we must listen to this filth, can't we have a classic?'

'Dolly!' Deb says.

Marcus groans. 'Not Dolly Parton, *please*. Johnny Cash?'

'Your knee is halfway into his side of the car,' Dylan says, with a quiet firmness that makes me smile despite myself. 'Just sit up a bit.'

'All right, Mum, bloody hell,' Marcus says. 'How about it, Addie? A bit of Johnny Cash? Please?'

I raise my eyebrows in surprise. Marcus's tone is almost . . . polite. I'm suspicious, but when I turn in my seat to glance at him he's just looking out the window, expressionless. I watch him for a moment, wondering. I meant it when I said I don't believe a man like Marcus ever changes. And an occasional *please* isn't going to make me feel differently. But all the same, when I turn back to my phone, I hit play on Johnny Cash's 'I Walk the Line'.

Deb switches lanes at snail's pace in a vague attempt to get some forward momentum. Our windows are closed to give the air con its best shot at actually cooling someone down, but I'm dying for fresh air. The cars on either side of us are full of people yawning and bored. Feet up on dashboards and forearms leaning on steering wheels.

The car parallel to ours has three teenagers in the back, all squabbling over an iPad. From the outside, we probably look like a group of friends off on holiday together. The parents in that car are probably so jealous of us.

If only they bloody knew.

'Google says all routes are red,' Rodney pipes up. I turn and see him peering at his phone. His hair is slick with sweat and sticking to his forehead, and there's a triangular dark patch from the neck of his T-shirt down his chest. God. Rodney's having a shit day. Imagine thinking you'd found a nice, cheap transport option to a wedding, and ending up trapped in a sauna-car with us lot.

'How long's it saying it'll take us to get to Ettrick?' I ask Rodney.

'Umm. Seven hours.'

'*Seven hours?*' everybody choruses.

Deb gently leans her head forward against the steering wheel. 'I can't go on,' she says. 'And I'm bloody *desperate* for a wee.'

'We could finish this bottle of water?' Rodney suggests.

'Rodney, are you familiar with how women pee?' Deb says.

'Not . . . very familiar, no,' Rodney replies.

Marcus sniggers.

'Well. I'll draw you a picture when we get there,' Deb says.

'Oh, wow, thanks?' Rodney says.

'If we swap, you can hop out and nip behind the treeline,' I say, nodding towards the fields beside the motorway. 'Nobody's moving anyway. I can't *remember* the last time we moved forward.'

'Are you sure?' she says, glancing ahead at the stationary traffic.

'How badly do you need to pee?'

'Even my pelvic floor exercises will not help me soon, Ads.'

'What's a pelvic floor?' Rodney asks.

It's like having an actual child in the car.

'Ready?' I say to Deb.

She nods, and we each open our car doors. God, it's nice to breathe some fresh air. Even if that fresh air is nasty, smelly pollution. It's hotter out here than in the car – I can feel my skin burning in real time as I walk around the back and meet Deb halfway.

'I was right, wasn't I?' I say to her as she passes me. 'Giving Dylan and Marcus a lift?'

'Oh, yeah. Worst idea ever,' Deb says. 'What *were* we thinking?'

I watch her weave her way through the rows of cars and up on to the bank, disappearing into the scrubby trees. At first, when the cars start moving around me, I feel a bit seasick. Like when you're on a train and you think it's leaving the station because the train on the other platform is pulling away, and your brain gets all confused. Then the car behind us hoots. And the car behind that. I come to my senses.

'Shit.'

I yank open the driver-side door and climb in. Marcus is already laughing like a bloody hyena, and Rodney is going, *oh dear, oh dear*, like a flustered old lady having trouble with her nerves.

'Ah,' says Dylan. 'This is . . . a conundrum.'

There's a good three hundred yards between me and the Audi in front already. I glance in the wing mirror and catch sight of the cars behind us trying to inch into the other lane. There's no hard shoulder either, because of these roadworks – we're out of options.

'Fucking shitting fuckity shit,' I say, then blush, because I nicked that particular arrangement of expletives off Dylan, and I haven't used it for years. Apparently him being here has reminded me of one of the few gifts he gave me that I did not give back: the talent of swearing like a true toff.

'We can't stay here. She can't run into the traffic to get to us anyway, and someone's going to go into the back of us. Shit.' I start up, going as slowly as I can get away with. 'Can you see her? Did she take her phone?' I glance down at the car door – nope, there's the phone. 'Bloody bollocking fuckity fuck,' I hiss between my teeth. 'What do I do?!'

'First things first, you probably need to drive faster than ten miles per hour,' Dylan says apologetically. 'Or we might all die.'

'Right, right,' I say, accelerating. 'Oh, God, can you see her?'

Dylan strains to look out the window, but he's on the wrong side. 'Marcus?' he says.

'Can't see her,' Marcus says. 'This is priceless.'

'Oh dear, poor Deb!' says Rodney.

'Yes, thank you, everyone,' I say, trying not to hyperventilate.

'Shall I come off at the next junction? Where will she expect to meet us? What do we do?'

'Breathe, Ads – it's Deb. She could handle being dumped alone in the Sahara. She'll just find this funny. Or mildly annoying,' Dylan says, and I jump slightly as I feel his hand on my shoulder. He withdraws it quickly. I wish I hadn't jumped.

'Oh, God,' I say, letting out a strangled laugh. We're going at thirty now, which is about the same speed as everyone else as the motorway starts to get moving again. This would usually feel annoyingly slow but right now, while Deb's spot on the verge slips away in my left mirror, it feels *way* too fast. 'I need to get into the left lane. Marcus, would you please stop fucking cackling back there? It's not helpful.'

Dylan snorts with laughter. I catch his eye for a moment in the internal mirror. He pulls a face.

'Sorry,' he says. 'It's just . . . It is . . . a bit . . .'

I swallow down a laugh, but it comes back, and before I know it my shoulders are shaking too. 'Shit,' I say, lifting a hand to my mouth. 'Why am I laughing?'

'Pissing behind a tree!' Marcus snorts, voice shaking with laughter. 'Imagine her face when she comes back and we're gone!'

'Oh, no, oh, gosh,' Rodney says, and I can hear that he's stifling his laughter too.

We're coming up to the next junction. I indicate, still giggling, kind of also crying, generally just feeling totally unhinged. Why the hell did I let Deb get out the car for a wee?

'The traffic just hadn't moved in so long!' I say.

'It was always going to move as soon as Deb got out,' Dylan says. 'It's sod's law.'

'I'm an idiot,' I say, still laugh-crying. 'This was a *terrible* idea.'

'You're not an idiot,' Dylan says, sobering. 'You gambled and lost, that's all. Or, you know, Deb did. Hey, there's a Budget Travel Hotel – pull into their car park, maybe?'

I make a last-minute indicate and follow his direction. As I pull into a space in the car park and turn the key in the ignition, I realise I'm shaking.

Things don't seem so funny, suddenly.

'How will she know to find us here? Should we go looking for her?'

'Let's just try to think like Deb,' Dylan says, as I twist around in my seat to look at the three of them.

Marcus is grinning into his fist, shaking his head. Rodney has his arms around himself in a sort of protective hug, like a kid on their first day of school. And Dylan is chewing thoughtfully at his lip. The sun catches across his face like the beam of a spotlight, turning his eyes pale lemon-lime, and more than anything I want to kick Rodney and Marcus out of this car and crawl into his lap.

It's weird. Dylan was never the person I would turn to when I was upset. So it's not a habit thing. Back when we were together, he was the last person I'd choose to cry on – mostly because when I was crying, it was because of him, and he'd not have a clue I was even upset. That was how we worked. We were so close but we barely told each other anything.

'Think like Deb,' I repeat. 'OK. Well, she's always practical. She'll swear a bit, then she'll go, what now?'

'Maybe she'll try and hitchhike?' Rodney suggests. 'Hail someone down?'

'Maybe,' I say slowly. 'Or she might try and walk. I think she'll assume we came off the motorway as soon as we could, right? How long would it take her to walk from where we dropped her to here? Rodney?'

Rodney busies himself clicking away on his phone.

'We were driving for, what, a few minutes? It can't be that long a walk?'

'An hour,' Rodney says. 'It's an hour's walk, unless she cuts across the fields, which would save her some time.'

'An *hour's* walk?' Marcus says, leaning forward to look at the phone over Rodney's shoulder. 'Are you sure your phone isn't broken? All you do is tell us everything takes fucking for ever.'

'Sorry,' Rodney says, stretching the phone out for Marcus to look. 'It's just . . . what it says . . .'

Marcus rolls his eyes. 'Well, I'm getting out,' he says. 'Deb isn't the only one who needed a piss. Do you think that place has toilets?'

'The Budget Travel? Yes, I think it probably does have toilets, Marcus,' I say.

'Excellent.' He climbs out the car, shaking his damp T-shirt with two fingers, unsticking it from his body. 'Ugh,' he says, as he slams the door behind him.

'Thoughts on driving off now?' I say.

'Deb, though,' Dylan says.

'Yeah. Damn,' I say, watching Marcus amble his way towards the hotel entrance.

'I am *really* sorry about him,' Dylan says quietly.

Rodney unclicks his seat belt and shifts up into Marcus's seat so he and Dylan have more room. They each sigh with relief.

'Yeah, well. Marcus is Marcus,' I say, still watching him go.

'Do you two not like him?' Rodney asks.

'I don't like him, no,' I say flatly.

'I don't like him most of the time, either,' Dylan says.

I glance at him, surprised.

'He . . . he's a complicated man. But he's family, really. I'm holding out hope that one day he'll turn things around and change. It's just . . . When do you give up on a person, you know?'

'When they're bad for you,' I say, before I can stop myself. 'It's like any relationship, romantic or friendship or family or whatever. If it's toxic, you should walk away.'

'I think . . .' Dylan pauses, choosing his words carefully. 'I think you step *back* when it's toxic, certainly. But I'm not sure I would want to give up. Not if I thought there was good in someone, and that I might be able to help them find that good. Not once I'd recognised how the relationship was hurting me, and hardened myself to that.'

I look at him. I don't agree with him – I don't think you can *harden yourself* against the hurt someone like Marcus inflicts on people. But if I've learned anything over the last year or two, it's that there's no one way of dealing with pain.

'Someone should stay here, in case Deb figures out where we've gone,' I say after a moment. 'But I think the rest of us should split up and go looking for her. If we all take our phones, there's no harm in that, right?'

'Marcus should stay here,' Dylan says immediately. 'He'll definitely wander off if we leave him to it, then we'll have two wedding guests to track down.'

I snort. 'OK, fine. You tell him, would you? I'm going to go over the fields. I feel like I need to . . . do something.'

Dylan nods. 'Are you happy to leave Marcus with the car keys?'

I pause for a moment. 'Umm.'

'Yeah,' Dylan says.

'He's an adult,' I say. 'He wouldn't drive off without us.'

We all think about it.

'Maybe you should stay with him,' I say. 'Just in case.'

Dylan

The first emergency phone call comes from Rodney, approximately forty minutes after he and Addie have left in search of Deb.

'Oh, hi? Dylan?'

'Yes?' I say patiently, watching Marcus pacing the perimeter of the car park, kicking an empty Coke can as he goes. He's antsy, which is concerning: if he doesn't find entertainment soon, he's going to create some. A line of poetry takes root as the sun beats down on my neck – *Heavy-handed heat/Drumbeat, a Coke can skits between his feet* . . .

'Oh, hi, it's Rodney. Umm? I think I've, I think I've found something. Was Deb wearing white trainers?'

I squint against the sunshine. Marcus is doing keepy-uppies now, very poorly.

'Yeah? Maybe? I can't really remember.' I take a swig of water. The kind lady on the Budget Travel desk let me refill our bottles, and said she wouldn't charge us for parking, in the circumstances. That might have had something to do with Marcus flashing her one of his oh-so-charming smiles, usually guaranteed to get him his way.

'Because I'm in the river,' Rodney begins, 'and I think I've found one of Deb's shoes. Is it possible she may have drowned?'

I spit out the water.

'What?'

'Well, in films, when you find someone's shoe on a riverbank, it's usually because they're dead?'

'Bloody hell, Rodney. Hang on. Are you sure it's her shoe?'

'It's a white trainer,' Rodney says. 'Wasn't she wearing those?'

'I don't . . . can you send me a picture? Maybe she just kicked them off and went for a dip to cool off.'

'Where's the other shoe, then?' Rodney asks helpfully.

On her corpse obviously, according to my overactive imagination. No, that's clearly ridiculous – Rodney is, after all, a completely ridiculous person.

'Send me a picture of the shoe, maybe. I'm sure it's fine, Rodney.'

'OK. Thanks, Dylan! Speak soon!' He rings off, casual as you like. I blink down at my phone.

'Any news of our runaway?' Marcus calls, kicking the Coke can at someone's four-by-four. I flinch as the can catches the bumper.

'She didn't run away, technically,' I point out. 'We ran away from her. And no, Rodney's just being weird, he thinks he's found her . . . shoe . . .' I finish, looking down at the photo Rodney has just sent over to me. 'Oh, for Christ's sake.'

I hit dial.

'Hello, Rodney speaking! How can I help?'

'What? Rodney, it's Dylan. That shoe. It's a man's shoe. Obviously. What size does it say on the bottom?'

There's a pause.

'Eleven,' he says. 'Oh! Does Deb have very big feet?'

'No,' I say, as patiently as I can manage. 'No, Rodney, she doesn't.'

'Great! It's someone else who must've drowned, then,' Rodney says, sounding cheered. 'I'll get out the river, in that case.'

'You're . . . *in* the river? Actually in it?'

Marcus perks up at this and sidles nearer.

'I'm trawling! For bodies!'

'You're . . .'

'No need now though, if it isn't Deb.'

Rodney's absolute conviction that there is a dead body in the river is really throwing me.

'OK. Thanks, Rodney. Keep at it.'

I pull a face at Marcus as I hang up. He laughs.

'That man is truly pathetic,' he says. 'A wet flannel in human form.'

'Leave him be,' I tell him. 'He doesn't mean any harm. Would you stop kicking that? You'll scratch their paintwork.'

'You're your father's son,' Marcus says, quirking his eyebrow and giving the can another kick. He sees my expression and relents, dribbling the can away again across the car park. It's so hot we're both sweating through our T-shirts, and I glance enviously towards the cool, air-conditioned lobby of the Budget Travel Hotel.

'Come on, let's sit in there,' Marcus says, already heading inside. 'Maggie at reception will be delighted for some company. Maggie, my darling Maggie,' he coos as we step through the doors. 'We're *melting*.'

'Oh! You poor loves. Won't you come in? Sit in the lobby. Can I get you boys a drink?'

Maggie the receptionist has already fluttered off in a cloud of cheap perfume and the clatter of beaded necklaces. Marcus and I sit down on the plastic seats in the carpeted lobby of the hotel, and we stretch our legs out in unison with a groan; given all we've done all day is sit down in a car, I feel astonishingly exhausted.

'How do you do it?' Marcus asks, wiping his forehead with the back of his hand. 'With Addie?'

'Do what?'

'You don't even seem angry. After what she did to you. I just can't understand it.'

I press my lips together and watch Maggie flit back and forth in the doorway behind the front desk, carrying various bits and pieces – glasses, ice-cube trays, and, at one point, a bottle of hairspray.

'It's complicated,' I say. 'Just leave it, Marcus.'

'She cheated on you.'

I wince. 'She . . .'

'You know she did. I showed you the fucking photograph, Dylan.'

'I know you did,' I snap, before I can stop myself. 'And have we talked about why *you* were there? Why you cared so much what she was up to?'

He goes still. After a long moment his hands shift, and he begins to tug at the thin loop of black leather he wears around his wrist, but he doesn't lift his gaze towards me.

'I've always had your back,' he says eventually. His voice is quiet.

'Yes, well. I think that rather went beyond the call of duty, didn't it?'

Maggie descends with water glasses.

'Oh, Maggie, you're an angel. An *angel*,' Marcus says, and it's like the conversation we've just had never happened. I once wrote about that, the way that Marcus's mood would shift lightning-like. *A cloud ripped, gone/and the sun's back/exposed, raw as joy/until the wind blows.*

'Thank you,' I say, taking the glass of water from Maggie.

She hovers in front of us, all flushed cheeks and sensible shoes, blossoming under Marcus's gaze. I'm saved from any more flirtation by my phone ringing. I pull it out of the pocket of my shorts: Addie calling.

'Hey,' she says. 'Don't freak out. But I'm in A&E.'

THEN

Addie

It's February 14th – a school day, annoyingly, but Dylan and I have Valentine's Day plans for the evening. All he'll say is *wear warm socks,* which has got me totally intrigued. Deb reckons we're going on a hike. I hope she's wrong – I've been on my feet all day, and am hoping for the sitting-down sort of romantic.

I get a text from Dylan just as I'm leaving the car park.

> Don't panic, Ads, but I'm in A&E. Getting ready for our date (stringing fairy lights for a picnic at Dell Quay! It was going to be beautiful) and fell off a ladder. Just getting a little head scan to make sure I've not got something worse than mild concussion (I'm sure I haven't!) xxx

I stare at the text. Completely frozen.

'See you tomorrow, Addie!' Moira calls as she makes her way to her car, and it takes me way too long to answer her. Stood there in the rain next to my car, I imagine what it would be like to lose Dylan. It is awful. *Awful.* It would be unsurvivable.

I turn up at the A&E as fast as is legally possible. A bit faster on the stretches of the motorway where I know there aren't any speed cameras.

Marcus and I get to the doors of the emergency department at the same moment. At first I don't realise it's him. I've not seen him since France – a weirdly long time not to see your boyfriend's best mate, but Dylan's always had an excuse ready for him, and frankly I've not minded that he's clearly avoiding me.

We pause just inside the doors, in front of the reception desk. He turns to me slowly. Like he's dreading meeting my gaze, maybe. Or savouring it.

He looks just the same. A scribble of dark curls, sharp cheekbones, clever, intense eyes. 'Addie,' he says.

'Hello,' I say.

A nurse moves past us, his trainers squeaking on the floor. Someone's talking to the receptionist. We're still not saying anything. I just don't know what to say.

Marcus smiles slightly as he takes me in. 'You've changed,' he says, tilting his head slightly.

'My hair,' I say, lifting a hand to touch it. It's curled today – I wanted to look nice for my date with Dylan.

'No,' he says, and he's looking at me in that way he did in France. Steady and unapologetic. 'I mean, you're tougher.'

'What?'

I'm so over his I-can-read-people thing. He clearly hasn't changed a bit. He smiles slightly at my irritation but doesn't answer, just keeps looking at me. I press my cold hand to my cheek to cool it down.

'You're here for Dylan?' I say.

'Of course. And you?'

'Obviously.'

We stand for another moment. Marcus's eyes are still moving over me, assessing.

'He hasn't settled,' I say abruptly.

'Hmm?'

'You said he'd settle down. He hasn't. He still doesn't know what he wants to do, and . . . he still gets sad, sometimes.'

Dylan thinks I don't notice. We never talk about it. But I know him well enough to tell when he goes inward and gets lost.

'You could tell him what you want him to do, you know. That's what he's trying to figure out, really,' Marcus says.

I glance towards reception. The person at the desk is nearly finished, you can tell by their body language.

'He's figuring out what *he* wants,' I say.

Marcus smiles slightly. 'No, he's not,' he says, and his tone's almost mocking. 'That's not how Dylan works. He needs to be led.'

'Nobody needs to be led,' I say sharply, as I turn to make my way to the desk. 'And he's perfectly capable of finding his own way.'

'I thought he'd soften you,' Marcus says as we reach the desk. 'But you're all spiky now. I like it, it suits you.'

'Excuse me,' I say to the receptionist, still trying to cool my cheeks with my cold hands. 'Can I go in to see my boyfriend? He's in the waiting room.'

'Miss? Miss? Miss? Miss? Miss?'

Ugh. I really wish Tyson Grey had an off button. My hangover is horrendous and Year Eights are not what I need right now.

It's been a week since I saw Marcus in A&E – Dylan was fine, no concussion – and there Marcus was again last night, at Cherry's birthday drinks. I guess he's decided he can bear to be in a room with me now. It was weird and loaded and awkward between us and I drank too much and now my head hurts. Dylan kept asking if I was OK and I didn't know what to say. *No, I'm not OK, I really don't like your best friend.*

This morning Marcus posted a video on his Instagram stories of us all dancing together. Me, Grace, Cherry, Luke, Javier, Marcus, Dylan, and Connie and Marta, the Oxford girls from the villa. Marcus and I end up side by side and we're moving perfectly in sync while the rest of them have missed the beat completely, just drunkenly staggering. Over the video he's written *Dancing on the rooftop under the stars.*

I've watched it five times and it's only eleven o'clock. When I go to the loo in morning break I find myself opening it again, trying to understand it. I can't help feeling like it's about that night in France, but what's it supposed to mean? Now my head aches *and* I'm confused. Tyson Grey is like a bloody mechanical drill, *Miss Miss Miss*-ing at me.

I spin around as the classroom door opens. My first thought is that Tyson's walked out because I've been ignoring him. Once, when the mood took him and I was helping another student with their writing, he climbed out the window. But it's not Tyson – Etienne's just walked in.

He gives me a quick smile and scans the classroom. Everyone straightens up a little. Despite his age, Etienne's a pretty old-school head teacher. Technically the assistant head is responsible for behaviour, but Etienne is the one everyone gets dragged to see if they need a bollocking. Even the toughest kids hate being told to go to his office. It's the trump card in my back pocket and I've totally overused it. Etienne definitely thinks so too. This term I'm determined to do my own bollockings.

I continue the lesson. My voice has gone a bit squeaky, though by now I should be used to other teachers in the classroom – I'm always getting observed, it's part of the training.

'Tyson!' Etienne barks suddenly.

I jump, then try to style it out, stepping smoothly to reach for something from my desk. Crap. *I* was supposed to notice whatever Etienne just noticed.

'With me. Bring that.' Etienne points at a piece of paper on Tyson's desk. 'Miss Gilbert, Tyson will be with me for the rest of the lesson.'

'Of course,' I say, trying to look stern. 'Thank you.'

Thank you? Is that a bit pathetic? Oh well, too late now. Etienne walks behind Tyson, shooting me a weary look as he pulls the door closed behind them.

I head off in search of Tyson as soon as the lesson's done and I've turfed the rest of the class out for their lunch break. He's just walking out of the head teacher's office when I get there. Etienne's stood in the doorway, watching him go. He catches sight of me.

'There you are, Tyson, now's your opportunity,' he calls.

'Sorry, Miss Gilbert,' Tyson mumbles in the general direction of my shoes.

'Thank you, Tyson,' I say. Then, when he's moved by, I mouth at Etienne: 'What did he do?'

Etienne gestures me into his office and closes the door.

'Ah, you may want to brace yourself for this one,' he says. He has the faintest French accent – I can hear it in that *ah*, but then it's gone. 'Tyson was indulging his artistic side.'

I look down at the sheet of paper torn from an exercise book, lying on Etienne's desk.

It's not bad, to be honest. I can tell right from the off that it's meant to be me. Well, I can tell by the face. The rest is . . . much less accurate.

'Wow,' I say. My cheeks are getting warm. I keep my eyes on the picture. 'That's . . .'

'Yes, quite,' Etienne says. 'I'm sorry you had to see that. Teenage boys . . .' He spreads his hands, as if to say, *Don't you just despair?*

In the drawing I'm naked, in the classic comic-book woman pose: facing away, but twisting to look over one shoulder, just to make sure you can see breasts *and* arse. I'm very . . . buxom. And my waist is about the same width as my wrist.

'I hope you don't mind me taking this one off your hands. I didn't want you to feel uncomfortable.'

I smile. 'Thank you. No, I . . . It would have been an awkward one.' I chew my lip, looking at the drawing.

'Tyson will be in after-school detention for the rest of the month. He and I had a lengthy chat about the objectification of women, too,' Etienne says, leaning back in his chair, linking his hands behind his head. 'I'd say less than one per cent of that went into his skull, but you never know.'

'At least he apologised.'

'Mm,' Etienne says, sounding unimpressed.

'Well, thanks for trying, anyway. I appreciate that.'

I turn the drawing over idly. *Miss Gilbert the Seducter*, it says on the back. I laugh, shifting the paper so Etienne can see. He leans forward to read it, and his lips twitch.

'Oh, Jesus wept,' he says, suddenly sounding very English.

'At least it's gender-neutral,' I point out. 'I think I'd prefer to be a "seducter" than a seductress.'

Etienne glances up at me, that smile still playing on his lips. He's handsome in an obvious, symmetrical kind of way. Brown hair, brown eyes, the sort of white skin that tans easily.

'It's a good thing, your sense of humour, Addie,' he says. 'And your . . . realism.'

'Cynicism, you mean?' I say, before I can stop myself. It feels a bit like answering back to the head teacher, and I stiffen. But Etienne just shrugs, leaning back again.

'The world's full of dreamers,' he says. 'Practicality is underrated. You take these kids as they are. That's what'll make you a great teacher.'

I note the use of the future tense. Mainly because I did a lesson on it yesterday. But still, it's the first time I've had real praise out of Etienne. He's good at disguising criticism in a feedback sandwich, but I've always known the 'positives' he's pulling out are a stretch.

This is the first time I've felt like he's seen something in me that I wanted him to see.

'Thank you,' I say.

Etienne nods. It's a clear dismissal, and I head for the door as Etienne folds Tyson's drawing and tucks it carefully in a drawer.

Dylan

My parents' house was very grand, once. It still retains some of its magnificence, like an old woman who used to be a Hollywood star. The whole west wing is closed off now – it's too expensive to heat – and it shows the worst signs of wear from outside: there are several cracked windows, and the paint has peeled off almost entirely on the side that's exposed to the winds.

Dad resists every money-making enterprise available: he'd never let us host weddings or sell to the National Trust and move somewhere less remote and ramshackle. This is his family home. But no matter how well his business does on the stock exchange, there's never enough money to keep this place. The problem is a particularly dissolute great uncle – he squandered most of the family fortune playing poker, which makes him a charming romantic hero, but a very irritating ancestor. All he left when he died was the land and the house.

I stand on the doorstep and flinch at the sudden sound of gunshot. Shooting is the one enterprise Dad will allow on our lands, mainly because it's something his father did before him. Grouse and pheasants are a permanent feature of life at home – I once went into the downstairs bathroom and found a pheasant sitting in the sink. She'd got in the window, which jammed some time ago and still won't close, letting in a steady arctic draught that always seems to be directed precisely towards the toilet.

If Dad is out shooting, that at least means he'll come back in a good mood. I push the front door – it needs paring again, it's harder than ever to lever open – and step into the hall, the most done-up part of the house. There are freshly cut flowers on the pedestal at the bottom of the staircase and the tiled floor has been recently polished.

'Dylan?'

I smile. 'Mum?'

'In here!' she calls.

I roll my eyes. Mum has never grown accustomed to living in a house so big that 'in here' is not sufficient direction. She grew up in a two-up, two-down in Cardiff, and even thirty years of marriage to my father hasn't quite knocked that out of her. Their marriage was rather scandalous at the time, hard as it is to imagine my father ever having done anything remotely frowned-upon.

'The kitchen?' I yell.

'The front room!'

I follow the sound into the only living room we keep open, the grand front room that would have been intended for receiving guests when this house was built. The view from the tall windows is stunning – breeze-ruffled green fields, the dark thatch of woodland, not a person or building in sight.

Mum cups my face in her cold hands. She's wearing jodhpurs and a jumper that's lumpy because of all the layers she has on underneath; her cropped hair looks a little whiter than when I last saw her, but then, it has been almost six months.

'My darling boy,' she says, her hands tightening on my cheeks. 'Have you been trying to give your father a heart attack?'

I shift out of her grip and give her a hug. I can feel the dread creeping in already, slow fingers tiptoeing up my spine, dark fog collecting at my ankles. This house is full of it; here, I'm boy-Dylan, the kid who never took to sports, who could never get his head around numbers, who simply wouldn't toughen up.

'I don't know what Dad's so upset about,' I say, as I step away and fling myself down on the other sofa. It creaks ominously. It's Victorian, stuffed full of spiky horsehair that springs up immediately to pinprick the back of my legs. 'I'm here with a plan, anyway.'

The relief on Mum's face makes my gut twist. 'Wonderful! Have you applied for a job?'

I swallow. 'Not . . . exactly. But I've worked out what I want to do. I'm going to do a Masters in English Literature. I want to be an academic.'

She freezes, hands twisted in her lap as if she's wringing something out between them.

'Oh, Dylan . . .'

'What?' I almost yell it; I was poised and ready for this, defences up the moment I stepped through that great creaking door. 'Why not?'

'It's not . . . Your father wants you to choose something financially stable, Dylan . . . You know how things are here,' she says, stretching her hands out helplessly to indicate the ratty, moth-eaten edges of the curtains and the damp quietly seeping down the wall from the bathroom above. 'When you inherit . . .'

'*Luke* inherits,' I say, turning my face away from my mother and staring up at the ceiling. It sags a little, looming down, as if the house is ready to flatten me.

'Dylan,' Mum says quietly.

Dad wrote Luke out of the will when he came out as gay. I was ten, Luke was twelve. *Twelve.*

I ball my fists. I know I should feel more sympathy for my mother – being married to my father must be unspeakably difficult, even if she does love him. But I can't forgive her for failing to change Dad's mind about Luke. Dad acknowledges him, has him to visit, advises him on his business ventures – but he refuses to meet Javier, and he won't let his gay son inherit his estate.

'Just take the job your father's set aside for you at the firm,' Mum says gently. 'Dylan, you have a responsibility.'

'Elinor?'

My dad's voice. I stiffen immediately.

'In the front room! Dylan's here,' Mum calls, resettling her hands in her lap and straightening up.

There's a moment of silence, then Dad comes tramping down the hall, still in his hunting boots, heavy with mud.

He stands in the doorway and looks at me for a while. I hold his gaze and the rage-fear thunders and the dread flexes its claws and here it is, the reason my mother hasn't seen me for six months.

'Glad you've seen sense and come home,' my father says, already turning away. 'Help your mother with dinner. And then we're going to have a serious chat about your future.'

NOW

Addie

It's just a sprained wrist at worst. But Felicity, the passing Good Samaritan, insisted on taking me to A&E, so now I'm here instead of looking for Deb.

I've had it up to here with passing Good Samaritans, to be honest. Kevin was plenty.

'All right, love?' Felicity says, smoothing my hair with a hand. Felicity is a real toucher. Deb would hate her. Wherever Deb is.

Accident and Emergency at Royal Preston Hospital is pretty busy right now. Someone just got rushed by with blood painted down the front of their summer dress like an extra in a horror film, and there's a man sat across from me who seems to be holding his nose on to his face. I'm trying not to think about what'll happen if he lets go.

I've yet to see a member of staff move at anything less than a run. I'm just another person wasting their time. I make a second attempt to get Felicity to let me discharge myself, but she's having none of it.

'Not until your friends get here,' she says firmly, rubbing my good hand between her own. 'Ooh, your fingers are like ice! How *have* you managed to have cold hands in this weather!'

Felicity is in her sixties, I'd say, and she radiates maternal instinct.

She's wearing the sort of beige T-shirt you'd find in a charity shop and a pair of jeans with little flowers embroidered at the pockets. Her shiny black hair is pulled back in a neat plait.

She saw me trip on the motorway verge. I admit, it looked bad. I tumbled down towards the hard shoulder and fell on the tarmac, hands outstretched. But I was still *miles* from the cars, and the hard shoulder was all fenced off because of the roadworks. And yes, I tore the skin of my knees and got blood on my dungarees, and my wrist hurts like hell when I try to clench my fist or move my hand, but I'm *fine*.

'Please, Felicity,' I say. 'It's a mild sprain, I don't need an X-ray, I don't need to be here. I'm wasting everybody's time.'

Felicity pats my knee. 'Shush, love,' is all she says, craning her neck to follow the path of a passing nurse. 'Isn't it a long wait! Shocking! You'd think they'd keep things moving faster, wouldn't you?'

I bite my lip and hope no NHS staff are within hearing. I check my phone again: no notifications. Surely they'd message if they'd found Deb, which means she's still roaming around the fields of Lancashire trying to get back to us. Or hitchhiking to Scotland on her own. Or getting murdered by a trucker.

'Addie?'

My heart leaps. Dylan trips his way through the bags and kids and people between us and then he's crouching down in front of me, touching my shoulder, eyes searching my face.

'You're OK?'

'I'm absolutely fine,' I say. 'A bit of a sprained wrist, that's all. Will you please tell Felicity to let me go now? She won't listen to me.'

'Dylan,' he says, stretching a hand out to shake Felicity's. 'Thank you *so* much for looking after Addie.'

'You're very welcome,' Felicity says, smiling. 'She's a sweet little thing.'

I catch Dylan's lip quirk.

'A common misconception,' I say, and the quirk grows into a quick smile.

I notice Marcus then. He's hanging back, hands in pockets, watching us from near the door. For a split second before he clocks I've seen him, his expression is strange. Like he's trying to work out the answer to a puzzle. He meets my eyes and his face softens into something that might actually be concern.

'You OK?' he mouths.

I blink, surprised, and give a little nod. He smiles slightly and turns away towards the exit.

'Are you sure you don't just want someone to check you out?' Dylan says, brow furrowing again as he takes in the bloodstains on the knees of my dungarees.

'I'm sure. I want to go.'

Dylan shrugs helplessly at Felicity. 'Sounds like we're off, Felicity. Thank you again.'

Felicity clucks her tongue against her teeth. 'Come, now! She needs to see a doctor!'

Dylan smiles. 'If you can't persuade her of that, Felicity, I don't think I've much chance. When Addie makes her mind up . . . that's that. She doesn't change it.'

I pick at the dried blood on my dungarees and wonder what Dylan would think if he saw all the emails to him in my drafts folder. The countless times I almost changed my mind. But that's the thing about *almost*: you can be ninety-nine per cent there, you can be an inch away from doing it, but if you stop yourself from stepping over that line, nobody will ever know how close you were.

It turns out that asking to be discharged is the quickest way to get a doctor over in A&E. The exhausted young woman gets me to sign that I take full responsibility if I keel over now as a result of discharging myself. She even manages a quick smile before she dashes off again.

The sun is still blazing even now, so bright I have to scrunch up my eyes. It makes it harder to read Marcus's expression as we approach him at the car. By the time we're close enough, his face is blank.

'All right?' he asks me, as if he'd never come in to check on me.

'Yes, fine, thanks.'

Dylan opens the car door for me and I move to climb into the back seat, careful not to jar my wrist.

'Hang on,' I say, pausing, 'I should drive. You're not insured.'

'It's fine,' Dylan says. 'I can just . . .'

But I'm climbing out again. Marcus is already in the front passenger seat. I glance sidelong at him as I settle behind the wheel. He's slumped down in the seat like a bored kid, but when I wince as I try to let off the handbrake he flinches and his hand is over mine in half a second.

'Let me,' he says.

Behind me I hear Dylan shift in his seat.

'Thanks,' I say to Marcus, pulling my injured hand back into my lap.

Driving with a sprained wrist proves to be . . . challenging. Tears stand out in my eyes as I change gear. Marcus doesn't flinch again, just stares out the window.

'Is that my phone?' I say suddenly.

We're speeding down the motorway now. I wince as I feel around behind me on the seat with my good hand, holding the steering wheel carefully with the other. My phone is in the back pocket of my dungarees.

'Do you . . .' Marcus begins, seeing the problem, reaching to help me as I try to tug the phone out.

'I've got it,' Dylan says, leaning forward between the seats. His hand settles over mine and I goosebump. The hairs stand up on my neck as he slides my phone from my back pocket.

'Hello?'

I wait, tensed.

'Deb's fine,' Dylan says to me, and I flop back in my seat.

'Thank God,' I mutter.

Dylan rings off. 'Unbelievably, Rodney found her,' he says.

'Where was she?'

'Guess,' Dylan says.

'Umm . . . at the Budget Travel already?'

'No.'

'Walking up the motorway?'

'Nope.'

'Hitchhiking?'

'Incorrect again. You're underestimating your sister's knack for seeking out the absurd.'

'I give up,' I say. 'Where was she?'

'She was having a pint with Kevin the lorry driver.'

Kevin had written his number on the back of her hand, apparently. In the lobby of the Budget Travel, Deb tells us cheerfully that it was a damn good job she hadn't sweated it off. The first person she passed on her trails across Lancashire lent her their phone, and she called him right away to rescue her. The only hold-up was that he was in Lancaster and there was a lot of stationary traffic around the area. Obviously.

'Are you all right?' I ask, giving her arm a quick squeeze. 'I've been *beside* myself.'

'Oh, I'm fine,' she says.

'How did Kevin get as far as *Lancaster*?' is my second question. 'We left the picnic at the same time as him! And we only got to bloody Preston!'

Deb shrugs placidly. 'Kevin is a talented man.'

'And where's Kevin now?' I ask, looking between her and Rodney.

They both look terrible. Deb has her other breast pump – the non-battery-powered one – plugged into the wall and chugging away at her chest, but there are milk stains on the front of her dress, plus a long streak of what I hope is mud down the front of her shin. The sole of one of her shoes has come off. Meanwhile Rodney has actual pondweed tangled in his belt. His jeans are sodden. They're starting to dry from the top down, creating a sort of tie-dye effect. He totally reeks. God knows what everyone thought when he stumbled into the pub where Kevin and Deb were having their pint.

'Back on his way to Glasgow, with his chairs,' Deb says. 'He did offer to take me to the wedding, but I thought I should wait for all of you, really,' she says graciously.

'Oh, thanks.' I check the time on my phone and swear. This is just my standard reaction to checking the time now. 'It's eight. How is it already eight? Where is the time going?'

'Well, you went to A&E,' Rodney begins, 'and it took Kevin a little while to . . .' He trails off under my glare. 'A rhetorical one?' he says.

'Yes, Rodney, a rhetorical one. We need to get back on the move as soon as Deb's done.'

'But I'm *starving*,' Marcus whines. He's lying on his back on the carpet, arms and legs outstretched like a star. Gone is the subdued man in the car, the strange new Marcus who cared when my wrist hurt. He's disappeared as suddenly as he came.

'We haven't eaten in a really long time,' Deb points out. 'Shouldn't we get some food, at least? There's a Harvester right next door to this place.'

'A what?' Marcus and Dylan chorus.

I laugh. 'A Harvester. Come on. You'll love it.'

Marcus sits up. 'If it's food,' he says, 'I'm delighted with it.'

This mentality lasts until we're settled in a booth at the Harvester's and he's looking at the menu.

'What the fuck?' he says.

I hide my grin behind my menu. 'What?'

'What is this place? Pizza and cooked breakfasts?' He looks genuinely nonplussed. 'Is it, like, fusion?'

Deb snorts with laughter. 'It's food,' she says.

'And what, you go and get meat from there?' he says, pointing in the direction of the roast laid out in trays in the centre of the restaurant. 'This is monstrous. This is wonderful. Can I have as many Yorkshire puddings as I like?'

Forty minutes later and Marcus sits back with a groan, rubbing his stomach.

'That should keep him quiet for a while, at least,' Dylan mutters to me. 'How's the traffic looking, Rodney?'

I'm not sure at what point Rodney became chief of travel news, but it's stuck. He loves having a job to do. He's already whipping his phone out to check Google Maps.

'Ooh,' he says, pulling a face. 'Umm . . .'

'Not good?' I say.

'The M6 north is closed.'

'That sounds . . . bad . . .'

'It's not great,' Rodney says apologetically. 'Google's redirecting us through the North Pennines.'

'What's it saying time-wise?' I say. It's nearly nine now, and the light is fading through the windows of the Harvester.

'Six hours.'

I lay my head down on the table. '*Gnnh.*'

'There's no point getting there at three in the morning, Ads,' Deb says. 'Let's just see if there's rooms at the Budget Travel and set off early tomorrow. The roads will have cleared up and we'll actually have some sleep before the wedding.'

'No! We have to keep going!' I say, without lifting my head.

'Hey? Couldn't hear you there over the sound of your unrealistic expectations,' Deb says, sliding the menu out from under my face, forcing me to move.

'I *hate* giving up,' I groan. 'And I don't want to have to pay for a night in a bloody Budget Travel! We paid for that Airbnb in Ettrick, and . . .'

It dawns on me that I'm talking about money in front of Dylan. My face flushes.

'Don't offer to pay, either of you,' I say quickly, in Marcus and Dylan's direction.

'Nothing was further from my mind,' says Marcus. 'And Dylan's a truly penniless poet these days, anyway, so don't look to him for a handout.'

'Oh, right, I . . .' I'm all distracted now. I guess I should have figured Dylan would have stopped taking his parents' money if he wasn't speaking to his dad any more. 'Can't we just drive through the night?'

'You've got a sprained wrist and I have what I believe may be actual dog shit on my leg, Addie. I just tried to teach myself to hand-express breast milk in a copse on the edge of a field. I need to shower, and I need to chill the breast milk bottles and cool bag. And we all need to rest, or one of us will kill someone.'

'It's true,' Marcus says. 'I'm *this* close to murdering Rodney. If he cracks his knuckles again . . .'

Rodney pauses mid-knuckle-crack. 'Sorry sorry sorry . . .'

'Or apologises.'

'Sor . . .' Rodney cringes. 'Whoops.'

I sigh. 'All right. Fine. Let's see if the Budget Travel have rooms.' I raise a finger as Marcus opens his mouth to speak. 'No, we cannot see if there is somewhere five-star where we could stay instead. If you want more glamorous accommodation, you have to find it yourself, and I am not driving you there, and neither is Deb.'

'It's true,' Deb says. 'I'm not.'

Marcus meets my eyes for a moment. I'm actually pretty proud of myself for that little raised-finger rant. Standing up to Marcus isn't easy, even if it's just about hotel rooms.

'I wasn't going to say that. Whatever you choose to believe about me, I can cope without room service for a night. I was going to say, let me ask Maggie about rooms.' His trademark grin looks a bit more exhausted than usual. 'She'll probably upgrade us all to VIP.'

'This. Is bloody ridiculous.'

Deb and I exchange a glance over the double bed and then look away quickly. It's too hard not to laugh.

'Where am I sleeping? In the fucking cot?' Marcus says. He looks genuinely mystified.

I'll admit, the Budget Travel family room isn't designed for five adults. But it was good of Maggie to let us have the room at all – the hotel is full tonight, with a wedding going on somewhere nearby.

There's one double bed, two singles separated by a short corridor, and a cot.

Deb presses a hand to her stomach. 'Oh,' she says in a small voice, looking at the cot. God, it was so not worth her leaving her son at home for this disaster of a road trip.

'If anyone's got to go in the cot,' Marcus says, 'it should be Addie. She's basically child-sized.'

I examine the cot. It's a largish cot. But it's still a cot.

'I'm having the double bed,' I say. 'With Deb,' I clarify quickly as everybody immediately looks at Dylan. 'You three can sort the rest amongst yourselves.'

Deb's on her phone now, flicking through the latest pictures Mum has sent of Riley on the family WhatsApp. I can't see the phone screen, but I don't need to. Deb's eyes have gone soft and wistful.

'Come on,' Dylan says, tugging at Marcus's arm. 'Let's give Deb and Addie some space. Rodney, you too – let's get the rest of the bags from the car and decide who's sleeping on the floor.'

I catch his eye as he ushers them out of the room, grabbing the car keys as he goes. *Thank you*, I mouth, and he smiles.

'Oh, dear,' Deb says, putting down her phone as the door clicks shut.

'What?'

'That,' Deb says, pointing at my face. 'That *thank you*.'

'Was polite?'

'Was something you would not have said twelve hours ago. Which tells me . . . something has changed?'

I sit down on the bed and cradle my injured wrist in my lap. The swelling has got a little better, but it's still tender and the skin feels too tight.

'Nothing's changed. Well, I guess we've spent more time together, so . . . I've figured out how to be civil. Out of necessity. That's it, though.'

'No feelings?'

'Many, many feelings,' I say, lying back so my feet are dangling over the edge of the bed. 'Too many to figure out.'

Deb lies down beside me.

'You should really wash before you get anywhere near this bed,' I tell her.

She ignores that. 'Tell me.'

'You sure you don't want to talk about missing Riley?'

'Absolutely certain. That will not help. Tell me all the Dylan feelings.'

'All right, well . . . he seems different.'

'Does he?'

'More grounded. Less tolerant of Marcus. More mature. More self-aware.'

'Those are all excellent things.'

'I know. I know.' I rub my eyes with my good hand. 'But maybe I'm just seeing what I want to see.'

'You still love him?'

Trust Deb not to beat around the bush. I swallow and stare up at the ceiling.

'I hate when people say shit like *I think I'll always love you* when they're breaking up with someone, because, like . . . in that case, why aren't you still together? But with Dylan . . .'

'You think you might always love him?'

'Well, let's put it this way: I don't think I've stopped yet.'

'Not even when you wanted to burn his effigy at Bonfire Night that time?'

I smile. 'Especially not then. That was a blatant attempt to kick-start hating him. Fake it 'til you make it.'

'What about when you were seeing that guy from the school?'

My smile fades. 'I . . . He made Dylan disappear for a while. But he didn't make him go away.'

And then, more quietly, Deb asks, 'What about when he left you?'

The window's cracked open to let some cool air in, and you can hear the roar of the motorway.

'I've never let myself . . . I . . .' My throat seems to be closing up.

Deb waits patiently.

'I've never said it out loud, before, Deb,' I manage.

'That's OK,' she says. 'You can say it now, though.'

'I understand why he left.' I breathe out.

The cars roar on.

'He was wrong to leave you,' Deb says.

'But I understand why he did. Even then, I understood. That's why I was so angry. Because I knew – I felt – he was right to go.'

Deb turns her head to look at me. 'You once said to me you'd never forgive him for walking away.'

'I know. Forgiving him felt weak. And I wanted to feel strong.'

'"Forgiveness is the attribute of the strong",' Deb says. 'That was Gandhi, that was.'

A tear has worked its way from the corner of my eye towards my ear. I close my eyes, and another two go tumbling, wetting my hair.

'Do you think I should have forgiven him back then? Like he forgave me?'

'Addie . . .'

'No, it's OK, I can talk about it. I can say it.'

'You're crying.'

I laugh through the tears. 'Sometimes crying's good. Sometimes you need to cry.'

'Addie, your phone,' Deb says, rolling on to her side to reach my phone where I left it on the bedside table. 'It's Cherry.'

'Shit.' I sit up, then let out a gasp of pain as I accidentally move my hand. 'Pass it, would you? We need to tell her we won't be there until tomorrow. I should have called already.'

I wipe my face and answer the call.

'Hey Cherry,' I say. 'I'm sorry, but it's bad news.'

'No!' comes Cherry's tinny voice down the phone. 'No! No! No! You are five minutes away! You are!'

'We're not,' I say, grimacing. 'We're *really* not.'

'Krish's aunt and uncle are held up too, coming from London. This is *so bad*, Ads.'

'It's not, it's fine! There's just some bad traffic today, that's all. It'll have cleared up tomorrow and everyone will be there in plenty of time for the wedding.'

'Everyone was meant to be here today! We had to have our family barbecue without you!'

I smile, wiping my wet cheeks. 'I'm not technically your family, you know.'

'Shut up! What! Oh, God, Krish is beckoning me over – probably some new crisis – they're out of gypsophila at the florist, have you ever heard of such absolute rubbish? *Out* of it? It's the bread and butter of the floral world, Addie. The kidney bean in the chilli. Do you understand?'

'Not exactly, but I understand that things are seeming a little overwhelming right now,' I say, in the most calming voice I can manage. 'But you have Krish. That's all that matters. And even if the florist runs out of every bean in the chilli, or whatever, Krish will still be your husband by the end of tomorrow.'

'Yes. Yes.' I hear Cherry take a deep breath. 'That's what matters. Except . . . the other stuff does *also* matter. Not as much, you know, but still quite a lot?'

I laugh. 'Yeah, I hear you. Look, we'll be there as early as we possibly can tomorrow, and I'll give you the biggest hug, and then I'll run around pilfering all the gypsophila from the other florists of Ettrick if you want me to. Or I'll just stay with you saying calming things. Whatever you need.'

'I love you, Addie,' she says. 'I really do. Is it OK, the journey? God, sorry, I haven't even asked – you've spent the whole day with Dylan! Are you all right?'

'I'm OK. I've got Deb.'

'Thank God for Deb,' Cherry says. 'I wish *I* had Deb.'

'Sorry. We'll all be there tomorrow late morning, OK?'

'OK,' she says, in a little, very un-Cherry-ish voice.

'Oh, I can't remember if Dylan told you Rodney is with us as well, so he's going to be late too. And Marcus, but I guess you figured that out. And also don't care.'

'Yeah, Marcus *must* know he was a pity invite,' Cherry says. 'Who did you say was with you?'

'Rodney? He needed a lift from the Chichester area, so we picked him up. Poor man. He had no idea what he was letting himself in for.'

'Rodney?' Cherry says.

'Yeah?'

'Rodney who?'

'What? Err.' I glance at Deb. 'I can't remember. Rodney . . . Wilson, maybe? Or Rodney White?'

'Rodney Wiley?'

'Yeah, that sounds about right. Why? Is that a problem?'

'Ads . . . Addie . . .'

'What?'

Deb's unpacking – she looks over at me, catching my tone.

'Rodney Wiley is not invited to my wedding.'

'What?'

'Jesus, Addie, have you – is he actually with you? Is he with you now?' Cherry's voice rises.

'No, he's downstairs – what's wrong? Who is he?'

'He's the guy. The guy from that Christmas party.'

'Oh my God. The weird guy you slept with who wrote you love poems?!'

'Yes!'

'No!' I say, hand over my mouth. 'No! His name was not Rodney!'

'Yes, it was!'

'I would have remembered!'

'Well, I don't know what to tell you, Addie, because *you didn't*! Oh my God. Why is he coming to my wedding?' Cherry shrieks. 'You have to get rid of him!'

'What the hell is going on?' Deb asks.

'Is he like . . . dangerous?' I ask, eyes widening.

'Maybe!' Cherry says. 'I mean, well. Not really, no, but he's really bloody annoying. And he seems to have invited himself to my wedding which is *so weird*. How did he even get hold of you to ask for a lift?!'

'He was in the wedding Facebook group! Only people with the invite knew about it, so I just figured . . .'

'What's going on?' Deb asks again.

I wave an impatient hand her way.

'What do we do?' I ask Cherry. 'What do you want us to do? Is he still in love with you?'

'It's certainly looking that way, isn't it!' Cherry says, sounding almost hysterical. 'I doubt he's coming to the wedding to give us his best wishes.'

'You think he wants to try and stop the wedding?'

'Who are you *talking* about? *Rodney?*' Deb asks, coming closer. I switch the phone to loudspeaker.

'Cherry? What do you want us to do?' I ask.

'I don't know,' Cherry says, on the brink of tears. 'I don't know, just don't let him get here. Just get rid of him.'

Deb and I look at each other.

'You can do that, can't you? You'll get rid of him?'

'Yeah, of course,' I say. 'There will be no Rodney Wiley at your wedding.'

'OK. OK. Oh my God, I wonder what he was planning.' Cherry sounds like she's speaking through her hands. 'I have to go, guys, Krish is beckoning with both hands now, and he's really frowny – but you'll sort it, won't you? I can't *believe* you gave my stalker a lift *to my wedding*, God! Krish, hang *on*, would you – I've got to go, ladies, but do what you've got to do, all right?'

'We're not going to kill him, if that's what you mean,' Deb says.

'What! Deb! No! Just, you know . . . waylay him. Tie him up somewhere. Maybe give him a bit of a scare.'

'Cherry!' I say, starting to laugh.

'These are desperate times, Addie! I'm counting on you!'

She hangs up. Deb and I stare at each other.

'Huh,' I say.

'Well,' says Deb.

'I feel like . . . we maybe need to come up with some sort of . . . plan?'

'Like a dastardly plan?'

'No? Just like a normal, sensible plan.'

'Cherry said tie him up.'

'Cherry's wedding has driven her insane. We're not doing that.'

'The man needs to be stopped, Addie.'

'Yes, I know, but – we need to be clever about this. We don't want him to know we know. Then he'll realise Cherry's on to him. He might try another way to get there.'

Deb looks thoughtful at that. 'True. If we get rid of him now, he's still got a whole day to find his way to Ettrick.'

'Right.' I chew my lip. 'So as much as I do not want Cherry's stalker in our car . . .'

'Or sleeping in the same room as us . . .'

'I think maybe our best bet is to keep him close until the last possible moment, then, umm. Do something. *Not* tie him up,' I say, raising a finger.

'OK. Well, that's our dastardly plan then,' Deb says, with satisfaction. 'Keep our enemy close.'

There's a knock on the door. We both jump.

'Hello?' I say, a bit more nervously than I'd like.

'Hey, it's us,' Dylan says.

I glance at Deb. 'Come in.'

Dylan blinks at us as he and Marcus head inside.

'Are you guys all right?' he says.

'Where's Rodney?' Deb asks them.

Marcus starts emptying his pockets on to the side table – change, phone, wallet.

'He took the car and drove to get a sleeping bag from a shop nearby,' he says.

'He *what*?' Deb and I shriek.

Marcus stares at us. 'He drove to a shop. What's the matter with you two?'

'Rodney has the car?' I ask.

'What's wrong, Addie?' Dylan says.

'Oh, is this about the insurance?' Marcus says, rolling his eyes and kicking off his shoes. 'It's a ten-minute drive, Addie.'

'You're telling me that Rodney has driven off. In our car. Alone.'

'Yeah, pretty much. Why? Is that a problem?'

THEN

Dylan

When the sun first breaks through in April, Luke and Javier have a week in the UK, so we take a trip to West Wittering Beach – me, Addie, Marcus, Grace, Cherry, Luke and Javier. Things with Addie have been different lately. Ever since I told her I was going to stay with Marcus at the log cabin instead of moving in with her family, she's been distant, staying at work late, shrugging away sometimes when I move to touch her. I wish I could take the decision back.

Marcus is in a bad place again – now we're living together I see the evidence of his drinking, and every time Addie comes to the cabin, he's surly and childish, acting out. I hardly know how to navigate it all, and behind the drama at the log cabin is the drama with my father, whose position on my career plans has – unsurprisingly – not shifted in the slightest.

So it feels glorious to escape for a while and lie on the salt-scented sand with Addie beside me. She's deep in conversation with Grace, who's busy lathering Cherry in sun cream; Grace has to keep snagging Cherry by the arm and saying, *No, I'm not done yet, darling*, because Cherry has the sea in her sights and is clearly struggling not to immediately jump into it.

I try not to find Addie's friendship with Grace unnerving. I'm not proud of how I behaved with Grace; I was a different person then, and sleeping with the same woman as my best friend had seemed edgy and interesting, when in reality it was quite disturbing and probably not healthy for any of us. Whenever I think of that time I feel ashamed, so naturally I try to think of it as little as possible.

'Ads? You coming?' Cherry says, once Grace lets her go. She's bouncing on her toes; I squint as she sends a shower of sand in the direction of my face. The beach is packed with sunseekers who all seem to have an extraordinary level of kit: there are lobster-patterned windbreakers, innumerable sand buckets, carefully arranged deck-chairs, parasols impaled lopsidedly in the sand.

Addie sits up on her elbows. 'Dylan?' she asks.

'I'm reading,' I say, pointing to my copy of Byron's *Complete Works*. 'Maybe in a bit?'

Cherry drags Addie up. 'Forget Dylan, he's boring. *You're* not boring,' she says to Addie, who's resisting. 'Come! Swim! Swim!'

Addie caves and they stumble towards the water. I watch Addie, her dark ponytail bouncing, the neat lines of her beautiful body framed against the sea.

'You're an idiot,' Marcus says from beside me. He has his hat over his face to block the sun and his voice is muffled. He's already drinking, but Luke, Javier and Grace are too, so I try not to worry about it.

'Oh?' I say, turning my head to look at him.

He doesn't move the hat. 'Do you know how easy it would be for someone else to take her off you right now?'

'What?'

I glance back to Addie in the water. She's riding on Cherry's shoulders, arms waving as she tries to keep steady. Beside me Grace shifts on to her side, towards Marcus, listening, probably after more material for that book of hers. Javier and Luke are making out behind her, wrapped in Javier's towel; they roll over and gently knock Luke's beer over, letting it glug into the sand.

'*Oh, you go have fun without me, Addie,*' Marcus says, in a mocking voice. '*I will just sit here and be boring with my book on the first nice day we have had together in several months.*'

Something curdles quietly in my chest as the bad thoughts settle.

'I thought you would have *wanted* me to screw this up,' I say, and I try to keep my tone light, but I'm angry, I think, and surprised at myself. I'm not often angry. 'I thought you said she was all wrong for me.'

Marcus throws his hat aside as he sits up. 'Sometimes,' he says, 'it is really, really hard to be a good friend to you. I have been a *paragon* of restraint and you haven't a bloody clue, have you? Well, fuck it.'

He heads for the water, shucking off his T-shirt as he goes, and I watch as he dives in, swimming up to Cherry and Addie. They shriek when he lunges for Cherry's legs, and then they're all in the water, seawater flying up and catching golden in the sun, and I watch Addie swipe her hair out of her eyes, laughing.

Beside me Grace lies back with a yawn.

'Is it just me,' I ask, 'or did nothing he just say make any sense?'

Grace reaches across to pat me amiably on the arm. Her ribs are showing through the fabric of her designer swimsuit, and I frown – she's getting thinner, too thin maybe. She's got a modelling job now, and her hair is an uncharacteristically sensible brown: more commercial, apparently. She spends much of her time at coke-fuelled parties in either London or LA; her Instagram grid is full of photos of her draped around billionaires or sunning herself on yachts. She's not posted about her book on there for a while. I should check in with her more, but Grace is one of those people who I never think to worry about; she's always been the adult in the group.

'Marc doesn't understand himself, let alone you and Addie,' she says. 'Ignore him, darling. You're doing just fine.'

But I can't shake off the melancholy for the rest of the day. Marcus's words go around and around in my mind, like wasps circling something sticky and sweet, and I feel it again, the sense of wrongness, as if an object in the scene has been moved between takes.

Do you know how easy it would be for someone else to take her off you right now?

'If you keep insisting on this, Dylan, you won't see another penny from us,' Dad says.

This is the very last horror looming ahead, the final expression of my father's disapproval. Even Luke still gets a monthly stipend, and he now runs a string of gay clubs in New York.

I square my shoulders. We're standing in my uncle Terry's flat in Poole, staring at the roiling grey sea through the floor-to-ceiling windows. I've managed to avoid going home since the awful visit at the end of January, but I couldn't dodge Terry's fiftieth birthday party. Terry personally hounded me for an RSVP. In the end I accepted, having discovered that Addie would be away on a hen do – I know she has to meet my family eventually, but Christ, not like this. Everyone here thinks poor people aren't trying hard enough; there's an enormous swan-shaped ice sculpture in one corner and a string quartet in the other, and I am fairly confident the musicians have been hired because Terry is hoping the violinist will have sex with him.

'Do you hear me, Dylan? Going back to university isn't an option.'

If my father stops sending me money, I'll have to pull out of the flat purchase I'm midway through; I'll have to fund myself through the Masters degree. It means . . . I'm not even sure I know what it means. As much as it pains me to admit it, I've never not had money coming in from my parents.

It's the last step to freedom, letting go of that money, but I know too that my father's money *is* freedom, and by giving it up, I'm signing up to some of the toughest years of my life.

'Cut me off, then,' I say, watching the waves crash. 'I'll earn my way.'

The next weekend Addie and I meet for a walk in the Bishop's Palace Garden beneath a dusting of Maytime drizzle. Addie's wearing a grey cap and Lycra – she ran here from her parents' house, and her cheeks are still dappled pink from the exercise, and I love her so much I suddenly feel desperate with it.

'Move in with me,' I say.

She's a few steps ahead of me – we've stepped into single file to allow a man with a buggy past. She turns slowly on her heels to stare at me.

'You don't mean . . .' Her eyes flick uncertainly from my face to a couple passing by us, hand in hand. 'You mean at the log cabin? With Marcus?'

'No, no,' I say, moving towards her, taking her hands. 'Our own place.'

Her eyebrows draw together in confusion. 'Not the flat? Are you not buying that flat any more?'

I haven't told Addie about the money yet; the one time we talked about financials ended in an enormous and very uncomfortable argument, and these days when I mention my parents her face turns shuttered, so I've stopped bringing them up.

'It was a stupid idea, investing in a flat. I'm only twenty-two, for God's sake. Let's rent somewhere. Somewhere that's mine *and* yours. Near the school, so you don't have such a long journey on the bus . . . and near the university.'

Her smile grows slowly, and as she squeezes my hands and beams at me I feel as though I'm *better*, as if I've been in pain and it's lifted at last.

'You're serious?'

'I'm serious.'

'You're going to do the Masters?'

'I've decided to do it part-time, and work. Maybe bar work, I was thinking, or tutoring.'

Her smile gets even broader. 'Really? You're going to work?'

I feel a twinge of something like shame. 'Yeah, of course – no more dicking around on my eternal gap yah.'

She laughs. 'Dylan . . . are you sure?'

'I'm sure.'

She hugs me tight and I spin her around.

'Is this what you wanted?' I ask her, pressing my lips to her cap. 'Why didn't you say?'

'It's not what I wanted,' she says, burrowing her face into my coat. 'I mean, it's not like I had an idea of what I wanted in my head, I just want you to do what's right for you. But I'm happy, yeah. I'm happy I'm in your plan.'

You are my plan, I want to say.

'Shall we find a café? Get on Rightmove?' I ask instead, bundling her in beside me as we start walking again.

She nods, still smiling.

'Have you told Marcus?' she asks.

The glow of happiness dims a little at that. 'Not yet. But I will, soon. He's not – he's not *totally* on board with the idea, so . . .'

I trail off. Addie says nothing.

'He'll come around,' I say.

Addie still says nothing.

'You OK?'

'Yeah,' she says. 'Just . . . I got excited for a minute there.'

'And then . . . unexcited again?'

'Well, if you've not told Marcus yet, it's not – I'm just not sure you've totally made your mind up.'

'What do you mean?'

'Don't be mad. It's just usually when you say yes to something before you've chatted to Marcus about it, you end up changing your mind.'

I slow. 'Do I?'

'It's fine – I just won't start planning moving out quite yet,' Addie says, looking up at me with an effort at a smile. 'Sorry. Have I upset you?'

'No, no,' I say, though I'm not sure. 'And you know Marcus is only . . . he just has my best interests at heart.'

'Of course he does,' Addie says. Her tone is strange.

'Addie?' I slow again, shifting my arm from around her so I can see her face. 'Addie, are you annoyed with Marcus about something?'

'No, no! It's fine.'

'You said that already, and it's even less convincing this time.'

'It's *fine*, Dylan. How about that café? Dad says they do really good carrot cake.'

'Addie.'

She presses her hands to her face and lets out a little noise, half-growl, half-groan. 'Please don't, Dylan, I don't want to talk about this.'

'What's *this*? What are we even talking about? Marcus? Has he done something to upset you?'

'Has he . . .' She comes to a standstill and pulls away from my arm. 'Have you honestly not noticed?'

'Noticed what?' I'm going cold now; it feels like the moment in the horror film when you know something is about to jump out, and you're just waiting for that sickening jolt in your stomach.

'He has some kind of . . . problem with me,' she says. 'He ignores me, half the time. He hardly ever even looks at me, actually. And lately he always makes these little comments when we're all together. Things about how I'm bad for you, and stuff like that.'

I swallow, remembering the night when Marcus had told me

Addie was *messy*, *raw*, pacing back and forth with that foaming beer in his hand.

'And he was so desperate to get you to go and live with him in that weird cabin in the woods at the bottom of his parents' garden . . .'

'That was incredibly kind of him,' I say, frowning. 'Offering me somewhere to live.'

'I know, I know, but it was *also* – oh, never mind,' she says, walking again. 'I wish I'd never brought it up.'

'Don't do that, hey,' I say, jogging to catch up and snagging her arm. 'Hey, slow down, Addie! If you're upset, we should talk about it.'

'But how does it sound? It sounds *awful*. It sounds like I'm trying to get in between you and your best friend, and – and that's probably exactly what he *wants* you to think I'm trying to do, and now I'm playing right into his hands, and . . .'

'Ads, you're not making any sense. He's not playing anything. This is *Marcus*. I've known him since I was a kid. He's like a brother to me. He's . . . he's Marcus,' I finish weakly. We're at the café now, standing outside, looking in.

'Are you telling me you honestly thought he approved of me? I'm not buying it, Dyl. I bet he's always on at you to break up with me.' Her face is flushed again, this time with emotion.

'I . . .' I look away from her. 'He's had some concerns about us in the past, yes, but I thought – sometimes the two of you seem to get on really well. I thought you might be getting used to one another.'

She snorts. 'Yeah, I think that from time to time too. Then he's a dick again.'

'I know he can be a lot, but . . .'

'He's your Marcus. I know. I get it now, believe me,' she says. 'He's part of the package.'

I almost snap at her. If I didn't like Deb, would I ever make that awkward for her, the way she's making this difficult for me?

Her expression changes, just a flicker, and I have the strange sensation that she knew what I was so close to saying.

'I'm going to head home,' she says, 'I need to shower.'

'What about carrot cake?' I say, looking towards the café.

'Another time,' she says. She's already running.

I stand there and watch her go, that grey cap bobbing as she weaves between passers-by, and I feel as if something's stretching, a bungee rope, some kind of cord that holds us together. Does she want to live with me? Or not?

I slouch down on the sofa, the furry white cushions tickling at the back of my neck. They're somewhat less white than they used to be after five months of Marcus and me living in the log cabin.

'And then she literally ran off. How are we meant to move forward when she always *does* that?' I say, picking at the label on my beer bottle. 'Lately every time I try to get closer she pulls away.'

There's a loud bang from the kitchen; Marcus is cooking, which usually involves an extraordinarily complicated recipe, a trip out to a large number of supermarkets for ingredients such as lemon basil and tamarind paste, hours of intense focus in the kitchen and an eventual Deliveroo.

'She said I have a problem with her?' he says.

'Hmm? Yeah. Something like that.'

I wait, but there's no response, just more banging and clattering.

'You've not said anything to her, have you? Like . . . the things you said to me, you know, that night before I moved in here?'

'I avoid her wherever possible,' Marcus says grimly.

'Not all the time,' I point out. 'The other night you guys watched a film together while I was working on the Masters application.'

'Yeah, well,' Marcus says, and I hear him crack open a new bottle of wine. 'There's been the odd lapse. It's not easy being consistent.'

I roll my eyes. 'If you don't like her, why would you watch a film on the sofa with her?' I ask patiently.

'Good question, my friend. And if you do like her, why do you spend so much time sitting on that very sofa complaining about her?'

'I don't,' I say, frowning.

'You do. Half the time you're in agonies over what she's thinking. She's always keeping you on the edge, playing games.'

'She's not playing games.'

Marcus appears in the kitchen doorway, his eyebrows drawn together. 'You're too busy lusting after her to notice. But don't you think everyone gets that vibe off her?'

'What – what vibe?'

'The dark, sexual energy thing she's got going on. I hate to break it to you, Dyl, but that's not just for you. She gives it out in spades.'

'I have no idea what you're saying.' But my heart is suddenly beating sickly and hard, because in truth I do know what he means. There's this total honesty to Addie, an openness, a rawness; she's so *sexy*. I suddenly remember how she looked in that bar when I came home, how effortlessly that tight dress had clung to her, how she'd known it. I think of all the times we've walked into a pub and I've caught a man's gaze drawn her way like she's something magnetic.

'She's going to hurt you, Dyl.'

The frustration hits me quite suddenly; it's unusual that Marcus manages to get a rise out of me, but that tips me over the edge.

'You just don't want me to move out,' I snap. 'You want to keep me here.'

He recoils slightly, and I watch as the hurt registers in his eyes.

'I'm trying to look out for you. That's all I'm doing.' He's keeping his voice carefully steady, but the hand on his wine glass is white at the knuckles.

My phone beeps in my pocket; I fumble to check it so quickly I drop it, and I hear Marcus snort with derisive laughter as he heads back into the kitchen. It's a WhatsApp message from Addie.

Let's talk again tomorrow? Sorry things got heated – I shouldn't have bitched about Marcus to you. I'd love to move in with you ☺ xxx

Thank God. The worries melt away, the anger extinguished like a gas flame flicked off at the switch; I'm going to live with Addie, and find a job, and make my own way until I'm Professor Abbott, scholar and poet and lover of Addie Gilbert. Marcus's protective instincts will ease eventually; he'll grow to trust Addie, and she'll start to understand him better. Everyone will come around.

Addie

It's early summer, June time, and I'm still getting used to the pure joy of sharing a flat with Dylan.

Well, maybe not *pure* joy. We fight a fair bit now we live together. Teething problems, I think – and Marcus. He's always a good source of arguments. This morning me and Dylan yelled at each other for half an hour because Dylan spent two hundred quid on a television stand we don't need, but really we were arguing because yesterday Marcus accused me of *manipulating the situation* during a game of Charades at Cherry's house and Dylan once again failed to clock Marcus being a dick to me. And I couldn't exactly say, *Marcus was mean about my charades technique and you didn't stand up for me*, so instead I said, *We can't afford this*. Money's such an easy thing to argue about. Especially with Dylan.

As I pull into the school car park, Etienne is climbing out of his BMW. He raises his hand to me in greeting and I wave back, yanking the handbrake on and trying to remember if I pencilled both eyebrows or just the one. Can't recall for the life of me. It's been one of those days. Already.

'Ready for the summer to start?' Etienne calls as I lock the car and jog over. He smiles. We've relaxed around each other over the last few months. I don't think about every word before I say it any more, and my heart doesn't beat quite so hard when he comes into my classroom unannounced.

'Nah,' I say, wrinkling up my nose. 'Thought I'd stick around and help out at the summer school.'

He laughs, and I glow.

'You've done well this term, Addie,' he says. 'I've been really impressed.'

The glow brightens. 'Oh, thank you. I'm really grateful to you and to Moira for everything you've done to help me, and all your patience as I found my feet.'

'I have a good instinct when it comes to people,' Etienne says, holding the door open for me. 'I knew you'd make a great teacher. And I knew you'd be a good fit here with us.'

The outside door to the staffroom is stiff and heavy, and Etienne has his hands full of folders. To keep it open for me, he stands in front of it – I have to pass close to him to step through. I give him a brief smile as I brush past, then I breathe in sharply. His gaze is on my face, and there's a heat there. It's hard to define, but there's no mistaking it. It's wanting.

'Even Tyson's dad has come around to you,' Etienne continues as we head for the coffee machine, side by side now.

His tone is light and casual. There's no trace of that look. I avoid his gaze as we make coffee in the staffroom. We talk. Just chit-chat. Already I'm rewriting the scene: he didn't look at me strangely at all, he was just polite and held the door for me.

But then he touches my hand as we both reach for the fridge door. My heart skips. He catches my eye and there it is again, with a secret smile.

'Sorry,' I say, retreating, cheeks burning. 'You go. I'll wait.'

'No worries, Addie,' he says, still holding my gaze. And then – gone again.

I swallow and take my coffee straight to my classroom. I wish Etienne wasn't so handsome. I wish me and Dylan hadn't fought this morning. I wish I hadn't blushed.

I glance at the clock – only a couple of minutes until the kids start filing in. I've been stood here with my coffee, staring at my own blank whiteboard, doing nothing for almost ten minutes.

I pull my phone out and open my WhatsApp chat with Dylan.

I love you. Sorry for getting upset about a stupid TV stand xx

He's already typing.

Love you too. And it wasn't stupid. Or rather, it was stupid, because I spent too much money on it. I'll return it at the weekend.

I smile. Then he starts typing again.

But will you go for a drink with me and Marcus tomorrow night? I really want you guys to try and get along. Please? xx

I spend an hour trying to decide what to wear for the drinks with Marcus, getting more and more annoyed at myself with every outfit I chuck on the bed. It's a hot evening, still in the twenties after six o'clock. I toy with the loose cotton dresses I wore last summer in France, but they all look too short. I'm so used to wearing dresses that cover my knees for school now; a minidress looks kind of scandalous.

In the end I wear jeans, Converse and a threadbare white T-shirt that always slips off my shoulder. I'm going for carefree and cool with the shoulder-slip, but as soon as I leave the house I realise it's just an extra thing to think about. It keeps slipping too far and showing the top of my scratty strapless bra.

We head to a pub a few roads away from our flat. It has dark blue walls and pint glasses dangling from all the old beams on the ceiling, each with a little lightbulb inside. For a moment I see it as Marcus will see it: how try-hard it looks, compared to the cool London pubs he likes.

He's already there, at a table by the window. The street light streaming through the glass casts his face in triangles of light and shade. He's beautiful. I forget that, probably because he's usually being such an arse.

We hug hello. He holds me at a distance, hips away from mine, the way you hug a colleague or a distant cousin. He and Dylan talk for a while and I keep missing moments to get involved, opening and closing my mouth like a fish.

'So, Addie,' Marcus says, picking at a beer mat on the table. 'How's school?'

'It's good, actually. I've kind of figured out how to do this teaching thing, a bit,' I say, twisting my pint between my palms. 'Behaviour has been the toughest thing for me. Getting them to respect me.'

'Must be hard when you're not that much older than them yourself,' Marcus says.

'Yeah, and half of the Year Elevens are a foot taller than me already, too,' I say, pulling a face.

Dylan beams. It breaks my heart a little, how happy he is to see us getting on.

'And the hot head teacher?' Marcus asks. 'How's he?'

I feel my cheeks flush and it makes me blush even harder, because I know it looks like guilt.

'Etienne?' I say. 'He's fine. I imagine. Who told you he was hot?'

'Dylan's mentioned it,' Marcus says, shooting Dylan an amused glance. 'Once or twice.'

When Dylan's embarrassed, you can see it in his eyes – they go sort of tight at the corners.

Dylan has never once mentioned Etienne to me. Come to think of it, I don't think I've ever mentioned him to Dylan, either.

'Right,' I say, trying to sound like this is no big deal.

'He recruited you, did he, the hot head?'

'Yeah, him and Moira, the assistant head.'

Marcus gives Dylan a significant look.

'What?' I ask, looking between them.

'Marcus . . .' Dylan trails off.

'I have a theory,' Marcus says. 'If a man ever recruits a woman, on some level, he wants to sleep with her.'

'That's . . . that's horrible,' I say. 'And definitely not true?'

'So he doesn't want to sleep with you, then?' Marcus asks.

I blush again. Never have I hated my pale skin more.

'No, he doesn't want to sleep with me,' I say firmly. But I can feel Dylan's gaze on my cheeks. I can feel his uncertainty. 'It's not like that. Obviously.'

I want Dylan to say something. Isn't this where he should step in? Shouldn't he tell Marcus to shut up, back off, get lost? Marcus gives a little smirk and my blood boils.

'So anyway, I have some news,' Marcus says into the silence. 'I've got a new idea. An app.'

Marcus generally has a new idea on the go. All of them fizzle out or evaporate to make room for the next one.

'I figure, I can work on this anywhere, why not here?' he says, spreading his hands.

It takes me a moment to process. I'm still humming with embarrassment and anger. Still hot with it.

'You mean here, like, Chichester?'

'Yeah. I'm going to rent a place just outside town. Two-bed house with a jacuzzi,' Marcus says, leaning back. 'I'll throw a housewarming, obviously.'

'That's great,' Dylan says, but he's blinking too much – he's taken aback too. 'I thought you said nothing happened in Chichester, eh?'

'Well, I bring the party,' Marcus says with a grin. 'Chichester won't know what's hit it.' He slides out from his side of the table. 'Time for another drink. Same warm ale again, Addie?'

He doesn't meet my eyes. He hardly ever does, to be honest. Like I'm beneath him, not even worth looking at. I want to remind him, sometimes. How he looked at me at the start. He fancied me in France, I'm sure of it. He wasn't too good for me then, was he?

'Yeah, the same again, please,' I say. 'Thanks.'

Once Marcus has ambled away, I watch Dylan sip at the last of his lager and feel a rush of rage at his mildness. He always gives Marcus the credit. He's the same with me, too, and that's something I love, so it makes no sense for me to hate it. It's totally hypocritical. But I feel the anger all the same.

'Don't you think it's weird?' I say. I can't stop myself. 'Him moving to Chichester now, after making such a fuss about you coming here? And him bringing up Etienne being hot, like that? In front of me?'

'Why?' Dylan says, eyes flicking to mine. 'Is it awkward for you to talk about?'

It's the sharpest I've ever heard him speak to me. He yells sometimes, when we argue, but he's never quick and catty like that. I'm still staring at him when my phone buzzes into life on the table. It's Deb. I frown. Deb hardly ever rings me out of the blue, she usually messages first.

'Hang on,' I say to Dylan, sliding out of my seat. 'Back in a minute.'

I pass Marcus on my way out the door, already lifting the phone to my ear. His eyes lock with mine. It's so unusual, him looking me right in the eye, that it sends a jolt through me. His expression is hard to read, but it's soft, unlike himself.

'Leaving so soon? Was it something I said?' he asks. The corner of his mouth begins to lift. A slow, sardonic smile, and that softness is gone.

'Hello?' I say into the phone, moving past Marcus. I hear him breathe in sharply as I brush past. His shoulder collides with mine a touch too hard to be an accident, though I'm not sure if that's him or me.

'Addie?'

I step out into the cooling summer evening and press the phone to my ear. Deb sounds . . . strange.

'Are you OK?' I ask.

'Probably,' she says. 'Probably.'

'Are you *crying*?'

'Yes,' Deb says carefully. She sniffs. 'I'm having a bit of a crisis.'

'What can I do? What's wrong?'

'Well. Hmm. I think I may be pregnant.'

Deb is breathing hard, like she's preparing to leap off a diving board, or maybe in the very early stages of labour. Her expression's weird. Way too serious. I hate seeing my sister looking worried, it's like seeing Dad cry.

'It's just a stick,' I say. 'All you have to do is look at it, and then you'll know.'

'It's a *life-changing* stick,' Deb corrects me, looking down at the pregnancy test half hidden in her fist. 'And I'm finding looking at it totally impossible. *Because* then I'll know.'

'Yeah,' I say weakly. 'Yeah, that makes sense. I probably over-simplified, really.'

Deb pokes at her boobs with her free hand. 'They're not *that* sore,' she says. 'It's probably just a menstrual thing. I'm probably just about to start my period. My very overdue period.'

'Yes. It's probably that. So just take a little look at the stick and then . . .'

'Or I could be pregnant.'

'You *could* be pregnant.' I give the pregnancy test a significant look. 'If only there were some way to tell.'

'You're not being very supportive,' Deb tells me.

'I'm sorry, it's just the suspense is killing me. Please look at the test. I can't stand not knowing. We are basically one being, Deb. Your womb is my womb.'

Deb pauses in thought. 'That's very sweet of you to say,' she says. 'I think.'

There's a long silence. I shift a little on our parents' bathroom floor. It's carpeted, a worn dark-blue carpet that's always speckled with white flecks of toothpaste spittle and soap suds. I feel a sudden pang of homesickness. Everything's so easy here.

'If your womb is my womb,' Deb says, 'will you take this child, if there is one growing inside me?'

'Wow, err . . .'

'Oh,' Deb says in a small voice. She's shifted her hand and looked at the pregnancy test result.

I grab it off her. One line. Not pregnant.

'Thank God,' I say, clutching the pregnancy test to my chest, and then I remember that Deb just weed on it and chuck it across the floor.

I look at Deb. She's crying quietly with her lips pressed together.

'Oh, Deb, hey,' I say, nudging her shoulder with mine. 'Hey, it's OK. You're not pregnant, it's OK.'

'Yes,' she says, wiping her cheeks. 'Yes, it's OK. It's good. I'm just . . . Well. I'd imagined it, I suppose. That's all.'

'Imagined it? Like . . . imagined being pregnant?'

'Yeah.'

I wait, a bit lost.

'I'm never going to have a baby, am I?' Deb says.

'Do you . . . want to? I thought you didn't?'

'Me too. I don't know, now. I don't want a boyfriend. I don't want a husband. But I sort of wanted this baby for a minute. In the abstract. Which makes me think maybe one day I might actually want one in the concrete.'

'You don't need a husband for a baby!' I wave a hand towards the discarded pregnancy test. 'Look! You nearly just got one, all on your own!'

Deb laughs wetly. 'I guess. I've just always tried extremely hard not to. So it's a bit strange to think that maybe I want to have one after all. Don't I know myself at all?'

She looks genuinely perplexed.

'Sometimes you don't know what you want until you nearly have it,' I say.

'Well, that's a terrible system,' Deb says, scrubbing at her teary cheeks. 'Right. Life crisis over. No baby. Do you want a drink?'

I glance at the time on my phone. I ought to go back to the pub. Dylan will be hoping for that, and Marcus won't – all the more reason to go. But I want to stay here, at home, where everything smells of comfort and Mum's favourite washing powder. I want to stay with Deb, who always makes me feel like enough.

'Board game and wine?' I say.

'Perfect. Help me up, will you? My life crisis has made me weak.'

Dylan

Addie and I suit the summertime, I think – all the raw sunshine and long days, Pimms with strawberries and thick, velvet peach slices. As we adjust to living together, as we find new quiet patterns and learn who likes which mug best for their morning coffee, the thick dread feels far away from me, like someone I knew in another life.

We go up to London one weekend in Addie's holidays, to see a play – she was initially reluctant, claiming that everything I like is 'incomprehensible', but I talked her around with promises of famous actors and ice cream in the interval. It becomes clear within minutes that I have chosen very poorly: the website claims that this modern interpretation of Marlowe's *The Massacre at Paris* is 'as lurid and scintillating as an episode of *Love Island*', but it turns out no amount of neon swimwear could make this play accessible. I sit here, teeth gritted as the Queen of Navarre takes a full five minutes of groaning to die, and wonder what the hell I was thinking dragging Addie to London to watch this absolute car crash.

As Addie shifts beside me, bored, frustrated, I reach for her hand.

'Let's go,' I whisper in her ear.

'What?' She blinks at me in the half-darkness of the theatre.

'This is drivel,' I tell Addie, my lips against her ear. I feel her shiver at the contact and it makes me hot; I can never resist that shiver. 'It's dreadful, Addie. It's . . . what would Deb say? It's absolute toilet.'

Addie snorts with laughter and someone behind us shushes her; I tug on her hand and we make our way down the row with a chorus of *excuse me, so sorry, excuse me*. We fall out of the theatre, still hand in hand, and I do my best impression of the Queen of Navarre's lengthy death and it makes Addie laugh so much she cries splodgy droplets of grey mascara on the soft, freckled skin below her eyes.

'I need a pint,' she says, wiping her cheeks.

I resist the urge to google the best bar in the area, and instead let her pull me into the darkly lit, sticky-floored pub on the street corner; she manages to nab us a table with Deb-like proficiency, getting to the chair just before a suited banker type and his date.

We drink too much too quickly, giddy on our escape from the Queen of Navarre's clutches. I get up to go to the loo and everything shifts to the left a little; I have to put a hand out to steady myself on the table.

When I get back a guy is leaning over my seat, talking to Addie. He has a shaved head and a beard, and you can see the muscles clearly bunched beneath the fabric of his blue T-shirt. I can tell he fancies her. His body language says it all, and she looks so beautiful, dressed in cool grey silk with those gumball-bright bracelets working their way up her forearms.

'All right?' I say. I'm attempting to sound gruff; it comes out croaky. I'm drunker than I should be, and the sight of this man leaning over Addie, her dark hair falling over her shoulders like ink snaking through water . . . it kicks the fear back into gear with a suddenness that makes me wonder whether I ever truly relaxed.

'Dyl,' Addie says, smiling. 'Tamal here has already introduced me to his mother! What do you think of that, hmm?'

She's just teasing me. I think, on some level, I must know this. But as I register the elderly lady standing behind Tamal – he's asking if they can have our table so she can sit down – all I hear is the criticism. I'm angry, and again, on some level I do know that the anger is self-directed: I absolutely ought to have introduced Addie to my parents by now. But I haven't seen either of them since they cut me off, and I still haven't told Addie about that.

'Well, you'll be going home with Tamal, then, will you?' I say.

Everyone's shocked faces bring me back to reality. Christ, what a hideous thing to have said. I genuinely have no idea where it came from, and then a thought hits me like a punch in the gut: it's just the sort of thing my father would say.

Addie gets up quietly, with a smile for Tamal and his elderly mother, and walks away. I assume she'll wait for me outside the pub, but no, she's not there; maybe she'll be at the station; surely she'll meet me in Chichester so we can share a cab home. But she doesn't even come home. She goes back to her parents' house.

I'm beside myself; I go to Marcus's house at two in the morning, gambling that he'll be awake and alone and have the patience to listen to me talk about quite how profoundly I dislike myself. He answers the door in his boxers, and I notice how thin he's becoming – his ribs are pale shadows beneath his skin and there are indents at his hips like thumbprints.

'Have you left her?' he asks.

I think he was asleep; his voice is slurred, his eyes a little glazed.

'I fucked up,' I say, 'and she just walked away. I don't know if she's coming back.'

Marcus closes his eyes for a moment. 'Come in,' he says, stepping aside. The house smells stale and fuggy; the scent reminds me of those months when we lived together at the log cabin. The place has been exquisitely furnished, and I wonder if India had a hand in it, though Marcus hasn't spoken about his stepmother for months.

'What if she leaves me?' I say. I sound pitiful. 'What if I screw up so badly I drive her to someone else?'

'Then you'll know I was right,' Marcus says heavily, leaning back against the fridge, closing his eyes again. 'And you'll come here, and we'll get drunk, and things will go back to how they should be at last.'

Addie

We keep arguing. It's like we're either completely happy or fighting about something totally stupid. There's no middle ground with me and Dylan.

For our anniversary in July, Dylan takes me to the poshest restaurant in Chichester. He's got a job tutoring some super rich Russian kids – they give him hundreds of pounds as a birthday gift. I buy him a cafetière, which sits on our sideboard at home, looking a bit shit in comparison.

The restaurant is intimidatingly quiet. The food's tiny and every course seems to involve a foam.

'Mmm, delicious foam, said nobody ever,' I say, swirling my fork through a particularly large green bubble of it.

Dylan snorts into his glass of water. 'It's haute cuisine, darling,' he says, putting on his poshest voice. His natural voice, really. I hear it when he's on the phone to his mum. Who I have still not met. Another simmering not-yet-argument. My parents offered him the option of moving into their home back in January, that's how well they know him, and I've still not even *spoken* to his mum and dad.

'How's your, err, quaffled tripe?'

Dylan laughs so hard he nearly sprays me with water. I start giggling too, checking the other tables to make sure nobody's staring. The restaurant is full of sixty-year-old men with attractive women in their forties. So clichéd. I do a scan of the tables: affair, third marriage, affair, escort, that one's going to kill him in his sleep for the life insurance pay-out . . .

'It's griddled duck's liver,' Dylan corrects me, clearing his throat. His eyes flash with laughter. 'And you are a philistine.'

'Is that on the dessert menu?'

He smiles, a wicked slow smile that nobody gets to see but me. 'I hope so.'

His phone beeps. I raise my eyebrows. We said no phones.

'Sorry!' He wriggles it out of his trouser pocket. 'I'll turn it off.' He checks the screen and his face freezes.

'All OK?' I say.

'I . . .' He clicks through to read a full message.

I watch him, a forkful of grilled lettuce halfway to my mouth.

'Marcus is . . . he sounds like he's in trouble.'

My heart sinks. Marcus. Of course. He knows it's our anniversary. What else would he do but get himself into some sort of trouble?

'What's happened?' I ask, trying to keep my voice neutral.

Dylan's shoulders are tensed. 'He's been drinking too much.'

I know this. We've talked about it a lot. Since moving to that weird jacuzzi house on the edge of Chichester, Marcus has spiralled. More drugs, more alcohol, more blackouts. Even Cherry's worried about him, and Cherry is pretty relaxed when it comes to personal crises. She needs rescuing from drug-fuelled house parties now and then, but lately Marcus needs rescuing from roadside ditches.

'I think he's really drunk.'

I wait for Dylan to show me the message. He doesn't.

'OK? And you think he's in trouble?'

'It's hard to understand the message,' he says, frowning. Still not showing me.

My phone beeps. I wince. Clearly I've not put mine on silent either. But Dylan doesn't even notice.

I'mon to you xx

From Marcus. I go cold.

'What the hell is this?' I show Dylan the message, and as I hold it out, the phone buzzes again in my hand.

Dylan sees the next message before I do. As I turn the phone back towards me I feel him watching me, the way he sometimes does. A little warily. Like he thinks I'm someone else pretending to be Addie.

Ive seen you with him. don't think ii wont tell Dylan.

What the fuck?

'I have no idea what he's on about,' I say immediately, looking up at Dylan. 'But you're right. He's clearly drunk. This message is so . . . *creepy.*'

'I'm going to go and get him,' Dylan says, moving his napkin from his lap to the table.

'What? Now?'

He hasn't even finished his scrambled chicken entrails, or whatever.

'Yeah, now,' Dylan says shortly, already scraping back his chair. The beautiful women all look first. Alert to drama.

'But . . .'

'I'll see you back at home.'

I have to put the meal on my credit card. Dylan ordered some stupidly expensive bottle of wine and even though we didn't get as far as pudding, the bill is over a hundred and fifty pounds. Seeing the number makes my eyes sting with panicked tears. I can't stand to see the rest of Dylan's plateful going to waste, so I eat the scraps of his bullshit foamy dinner on my own and drink the wine. It's all totally humiliating.

When I get home, Dylan's on the sofa. He's slumped and soft-eyed but I'm raging.

'Sorry,' he begins.

'What for? The fact you ditched me at our anniversary dinner or that I just bankrupted myself to pay for it?'

'Oh, shit,' he says after a moment. 'I didn't think about . . .'

'Of course you didn't. Your precious Marcus was in trouble, wasn't he?' I move past as he tries to intercept me. 'No, no,' I say, and brush past him up the stairs.

'Addie, come on, let's talk,' he says, as he always does. But I know the best way to punish him, now. He hates my silence.

'I'm going to bed. Alone,' I say. 'You can sleep on the sofa. Or with Marcus. Whichever you prefer.'

When I come down in the morning he isn't on the sofa. He isn't anywhere. I sit down in the space where he was last night and try to remember to breathe. He's left me. He's gone, because I said that thing about sleeping with Marcus, or because I told him I wouldn't talk, or because I'm the sort of girlfriend who gets angry when he goes to help his friend.

But – ugh. What about all the other times I said it was fine? When we went for a weekend away in the Cotswolds and he left early for Marcus. When he didn't even make it to my sister's birthday party because Marcus passed out somewhere. When I asked for a cosy night in and he said, *Sorry, Marcus really wants some quality time.*

It's crossed my mind that Marcus might love Dylan. But he's only ever shown an interest in women, and there's nothing sexual in how he looks at Dyl. They're just . . . bonded in some way I can't understand.

The door clicks open and I sit up fast.

'Dylan?'

'Hey,' he says quietly. He drops his keys in the hall and takes his shoes off. The sounds are so familiar I can tell exactly what he's doing from the sofa.

'Where did you go?'

'I went to stay with Marcus.'

I swallow. 'Oh.'

'You said I could.'

'You don't need my permission, Dylan.'

'It doesn't feel that way, sometimes.'

He comes into the room. He's wearing one of Marcus's jumpers, a vintage one, patterned in olive-green diamonds. His hair is mussed and there are bags under his eyes.

'I'm sorry.' I hug myself. 'I hate that. I never want to make you feel like you can't do anything. I just . . . I think he calls on you a *lot.' And at very interesting times*, I want to say. *Like whenever you're doing something important with me.*

'That's what friends do, Ads. Come on. What would you do if it was Cherry? Or Deb?'

It wouldn't be Cherry or Deb. They would never expect this of me. And, frankly, if they sent a text like that to Dyl, I'd be pretty pissed off with them.

'I just think Marcus clearly doesn't like us being together,' I say, standing up, moving towards him.

It takes effort doing even that. I want to walk away, that's my instinct. I want to take the power back.

'And I sometimes feel like he's trying to sabotage things between us.'

Dylan shakes his head impatiently. 'Marcus said you'd say that.'

He takes a step back.

'He said it's not healthy, that you won't let me see my best friend.'

'I don't *not let* you see him,' I say. I'm stood still on the rug, Dylan out of reach again. 'In fact, I am always letting you see him. Name a time when I've said you can't.'

Dylan looks so lost. 'What do you want me to say, Addie? That I'll stop being friends with him?'

'No! No.' Although, actually, I wouldn't mind. 'I just want you to notice that he seems really set against me in a way that – that often causes these sorts of conversations. When we argue, it always seems to be about Marcus.'

'And that's his fault?'

'You think it's mine?'

Dylan sighs, looking up at the ceiling. 'I don't know. I feel totally confused. I can't seem to get my head straight. I love you both, and you're both telling me opposite things.'

He looks so distressed my heart melts. Taking those steps between us doesn't feel so hard, all of a sudden. I move towards him and pull him in for a hug, ignoring the fact that his hands stay in his pockets.

'I'll try harder,' I say. 'I'll try harder with Marcus, if that's what you want me to do.'

NOW

Dylan

'A traitor in our midst,' Marcus says. He's prowling around the Budget Travel family room, checking the windows as if we're in a le Carré novel.

'So we have no reason to believe Rodney is dangerous?' I ask. This feels like an important question which has yet to be taken seriously. Marcus loves intrigue; the Gilbert sisters take such news in their stride. I am the only person who would quite like to know if Cherry's stalker is going to kill anyone.

'Nah,' Deb says. She's freshly showered and looking significantly less bedraggled. 'Come on. It's Rodney.'

There's a knock at the door of our dysfunctional family room.

We all look at each other.

'Is that – what if that's him?' Addie whispers.

'That's a good thing,' Deb points out. 'We want him back. We need our car, for starters.'

'Hello?' calls a voice.

We all exchange glances again. The need for immediate action has rendered us all totally useless.

'Well? Is it him?' Marcus says, full volume.

Everyone hisses at him to shut up. The fact is, I'm not completely certain whether that's Rodney – I'm not sure I could identify him by voice alone, which is a little damning. Did any of us listen to Rodney at all during the last eighteen hours?

'Hi, guys? It's Rodney?'

'At least that clears that up,' says Deb, getting up to let him in.

We all sit up a bit straighter as Rodney enters – we're trying to look 'normal', I suppose, though judging by Rodney's puzzled expression we're not doing an especially good job of it.

'Everything all right?' he asks. He has a sleeping bag under his arm and the car keys in his other hand.

'Absolutely fine,' Addie says, rallying. 'Chuck me the car keys, would you, Rodney?'

Rodney obliges. It is such a poor throw Addie has to lunge across the bed to catch it with her good hand, and she grimaces in pain as the movement jolts her bad wrist. Marcus snorts with laughter at Rodney's shoddy throw, then seems to remember that Rodney is a potentially dangerous individual, and much more interesting than he'd first assumed, and stops snorting.

'So,' Rodney says, rubbing his hands together, 'Addie and Deb in the double, Marcus and Dylan on the singles, me on the floor?'

'That's right,' I say. 'We'll set you up at the bottom of our beds, Rodney.'

'There's more space here,' he says, pointing to the floor at the end of the double bed.

Addie shoots me a pleading look. There's something so beautiful about the silent conversation that follows – not for its subject, of course, but for its familiarity, the easy way we can slip back into each other's language. *Get him as far away from me as possible*, she's saying. *Already on it*, I reply.

'Let's give the ladies their privacy,' I say. 'If it's too much of a squeeze for you, I'll take the sleeping bag, and you can have the bed.'

Marcus looks at me as if he thinks I may have gone temporarily insane, but I'm relying on Rodney's gallantry here.

'Oh, of course, the ladies should have their space!' he says, horrified. 'Gosh, yes! And don't you be giving up the bed, Dylan.'

Marcus gives me an impressed nod, but it's Addie's tiny smile that makes my heart beat with something embarrassingly close to pride.

Deb yawns. 'Well, it's after ten, which is two hours later than my preferred bedtime these days, and I'm due a Skype with my baby early tomorrow, which is literally all I can think about right now . . . so you all need to get out of my bed.'

'We're going to bed at ten?' Marcus says, regarding me with bewilderment; I wonder when he last went to sleep before midnight.

I contemplate humouring him and going back to the bar, but frankly I don't want to.

'Yeah, we are,' I say, picking up my bag and heading down towards the other end of the room, where the single beds are set out with the cot. 'If you want to stay up, take a key.' And then, on reflection: 'And don't do anything stupid.'

There is a wounded silence.

'Mate. You've changed,' Marcus says.

I should bloody well hope so.

I lie on my side, the polyester duvet pulled up to my chin. I can just make out Marcus in the darkness; for all his protestations about our early night, he falls asleep with enviable ease. He is now breathing heavily a couple of feet away from me, grainy and grey in the dim light creeping between curtains that don't quite meet in the middle. Rodney is snoring in the way that my uncle Terry snores: very loudly, pig-like, almost grunting. It's quite reassuring. At least if he's snoring then I know he's asleep, instead of standing over me with a knife.

I can't believe the man who wrote Cherry all those terrible poems was *Rodney*. I hope my poems are better than his; I hope Addie didn't read them all and secretly think I was a total Rodney.

I turn over; I can't sleep. This is not an uncommon problem. I start to spiral, that's the issue. I have one thought – for instance, *I wonder what Addie thought when she read my poems* – and then I'm away, following the natural steps down that path, coming to the conclusion that oh, God, I still love her, I know I do. I feel like I never won't. Everyone says there's no such thing as The One and there's plenty of fish in the sea but every time I meet one of those fish, I just miss Addie more. I've given up on winning her back, and still that doesn't seem to be enough to forget her – you'd think the agony of unrequited love would be sufficient to put your brain off the whole affair, but it seems not.

I get up. There comes a point where lying in the darkness becomes unbearable, and very suddenly, that is precisely where I am. I tiptoe to the en suite, passing Deb and Addie in the double bed, two indistinct, quiet shapes. The Gilbert sisters, as inseparable as ever. I used to think Marcus and I were just like them.

There's not much to do once I've been to the loo – normally if I can't sleep then I wander about, maybe read something, even write. But there's nowhere to go here, except the car park outside, and I am one of the few members of my friendship group who is not quite eccentric enough to roam around a Budget Travel car park in my pyjamas.

Instead I look at myself in the mirror above the sink. There have been times, in the last year and a half, when even meeting my own gaze like this has been hard. Now I just see a sad, tired man who made bad choices, which is a step up from what I used to see.

I splash my face with cold water, letting it drip from the ends of my hair. I straighten up and let out a noise, then stop myself – the instinct to be quiet is still at the front of my mind. The door is opening; I forgot to lock it.

It's Addie. She jumps when she sees me, but she's quiet too, just letting out a little gasp, clutching a hand to her throat.

'Sorry,' we both whisper at the same time.

'I'll . . .' I start moving towards the door.

'No, I'll go,' she murmurs, hand on the doorknob. 'I don't even need a wee, I just needed . . .'

'Out?'

'Yeah.' She smiles ruefully. 'You're still a bad sleeper, then?'

Worse, now – I never slept so well as when she was in my bed.

'Rodney's not helping,' I say.

Addie clicks the door shut behind us, blocking out the sounds of three heavy sleepers.

'The snoring? Or the creepiness?' she asks.

'He's just so *tragic*,' I say. 'I read some of the poems he sent Cherry, you know.'

'The one about how her vagina was like a strawberry?'

'What? No?'

Addie covers her mouth with her hand. 'Oh.'

'In what way?'

'Hmm?'

'In what way was it like a strawberry? Because if it was the colour he was referring to, I'm not sure that's . . .'

I trail off and Addie starts laughing, hand still at her mouth to stifle the noise. She bends, shoulders shaking, one hand gripping the counter by the sink.

'Oh, God,' she says. 'We're all idiots, the lot of us.'

'And you think he'd go cherry rather than strawberry,' I muse, 'given her name.'

She laughs harder, and I feel myself grow taller. There's nothing lovelier than making Addie laugh.

'Dylan,' she says.

I don't know if she does it on purpose. She shifts her hand on the counter and suddenly it's on top of my hand, on the edge of the sink, and she's looking up at me, eyes bright with laughter. My heart is beating everywhere, right down to the fingertips beneath her hand. I can feel the joy growing, a great nuclear explosion from the centre of my chest, and gone is the idea that I ever stopped hoping she might love me again, because look, look how quickly it came back to me. It was never really gone.

She moves her hand. 'I'm sorry.'

'No, no,' I begin, clenching my fist to stop myself from reaching out for her.

She lifts that hand to her face, lying it flat against her cheek, her forehead.

'I shouldn't have done that,' she says. 'I'm so sorry. I've tried so – I've . . .'

'Addie?'

She's crying. I step forward tentatively, and she moves too, into my chest, and as my arms close around her we're two jigsaw pieces slotting into place. She fits perfectly; she belongs here.

'Addie, what's wrong?' I ask. It takes all my energy not to dip my head and press my lips to her hair, the way I would when she was sad, when she was mine.

'I'm sorry,' she says. 'I'm so sorry.'

'Shh. It's OK. You've nothing to be sorry for.'

Her fists clutch the fabric of my pyjama top; I can feel the wetness of her tears against my chest, and I hold her tighter.

'You make it look so easy,' she says, her voice muffled, vibrating against me.

'Make what look so easy?'

'Forgiving me,' she says, so quietly I almost don't catch it.

'Forgiving you?' I rub a hand up and down her back, slowly, carefully.

'I don't know if I can do that the way you can.'

'Addie . . . I don't expect you to forgive me. I understand how hard that is.'

'No,' she says, shaking her head into my chest. 'No, you don't . . . I don't mean I can't forgive you, Dylan – God, I forgave you months ago, right away, maybe, it's . . .'

She trails off, quivering in my arms, and I'm feeling too many things at once: hope, sadness, the loss of what we had—

The bathroom door clicks open. We freeze.

'Oh, fucking hell,' says Marcus. 'I should have bloody known.'

Addie

I flee the bathroom, shoving past Marcus. I can hardly see through the darkness and the tears. I wake Deb by kneeing her in the shin as I try to climb back into bed.

'Addie?' Deb whispers.

I burrow under the duvet.

'This is absolutely classic,' Marcus is saying in the bathroom. His voice is so loud. I bet Rodney is sitting up in his sleeping bag now, woken by all the noise. I clench my eyes tight shut and try to focus on my breathing, but it's coming too fast.

'We should have bloody well walked to that godforsaken bit of Scotland; I should never have let you get in the car with her!' Marcus's voice is rising.

'*He* was the one asking for the lift,' Deb says. She ducks under the duvet with me. 'Ignore him, Addie. You know he's hell-spawn.'

'Be quiet,' Dylan says to Marcus.

Deb and I both startle. It's a tone I've never heard Dylan use before. Not when we argued, not on the night when he left me.

'Just. Be. Quiet.'

We lie still. I can't see Deb, but I can feel her gaze.

'You don't know what you're talking about. And I won't have you speaking about Addie like that.'

'Are you *kidding* me?'

'What's going on?' Rodney says from the other end of the room.

'Why do you keep saying I don't know what I'm talking about?' Marcus is yelling now. 'Why does everyone keep saying shit like that when I am the *only* person who knows what I'm talking about around here? I took the fucking *picture*, Dylan. I saw her in his office letting him run his hand up her thigh like—'

There's a scuffle – Deb reaches across and grips my good hand tight, so tight it hurts, and inside me I feel the desperation again, rising up my gullet, and I tear my hand free from Deb's and throw myself out of the bed and through the bathroom door right into Marcus and Dylan who are locked together, roaring, fighting, and I push through the tangle of messy limbs and rage and get to the toilet just in time to vomit.

THEN

Dylan

I've never seen Marcus like this before. There's vomit in his hair, crusted to his curls, and his eyes are so vacant he looks like a zombie. The living room of his house is filled with takeaway boxes and every surface looks sticky, fetid; there's a circle of Fanta spreading slowly across the carpet. He must have freshly kicked it over on his way to answer the door.

'Marcus,' I begin, and then I catch him as he stumbles forward into me. I try not to turn my head aside at the smell of him. 'Marcus, what the hell happened?'

It's been three months since I left our anniversary dinner and found Marcus drunk in the middle of the road outside his house, staggering through suburban Chichester with a bottle in one hand and his phone in the other, a portrait of dissolution. Ever since then I've spent as much time as I can with him, but it isn't enough – he needs real help. Luke came to stay for a couple of weeks in September, and, actually, Grace has been here more than I would have expected – she's good with Marcus, too, he's calm with her – but neither of them can be on-call with him. Grace lives in Bristol now, trying to get herself away from the London modelling scene, and Luke's back in New York with Javier.

The days get shorter and darker and Marcus behaves more and more strangely. Last week I found him outside our flat – somewhere he's refused to come lately – trying to climb on top of our dustbin, and when I asked him why, he just kept tapping his nose. 'All in good time, my friend,' he said, a crisp packet from the bin flapping butterfly-like against his T-shirt. 'All in good time.'

Tonight I'm supposed to be taking Addie back to Wiltshire when she finishes at school, so she can finally meet my parents. I can hardly bear to think about the argument we'll have when I tell her we have to cancel again, but there's no way Marcus can be left alone.

'I knew you'd come,' he says, as I lever him upright and lead him towards the sofa. 'I knew it.'

'Yeah, I'm here,' I say wearily, setting him down on the sofa as best I can. 'Are you going to be sick again?'

'What? No! Fuck off. I'm not going – not going to be sick.'

As if there isn't already an acrid scent of vomit clinging to everything in here, including me, after helping him towards the sofa. I sit down in the chair opposite him and look at my feet. I feel bodily exhausted; a poem tugs at me, something about *the ache of giving* and *its quiet void*, but I'm too tired to humour the urge to follow its thread.

Starting the Masters has been intense – even part-time, it seems to take up every spare hour, and I'd forgotten how hard learning can be. I haven't exercised that muscle in far too long. All that time spent swanning around Cambodia reading modern novels and suddenly the texts I knew inside out for my finals – Chaucer, Middleton, Spenser – are foreign again, locking me out.

The evening bar work was manageable over the summer, when I was just spending my days at home with Addie, but the late nights are making it harder and harder to get up early and study. And every so often there comes a message from my mother, testing the water, seeing if I'm desperate enough to go begging to my parents yet.

My hope is that taking Addie home will be read as a peace offering; quietly, in the back of my mind, I never thought my parents would really cut me off for ever. They'd come around to the Chichester plan, I thought, and the gifts and monthly payments and credit-card pay-offs would resume. Realising this about myself is not pleasant, and besides, it's starting to look as though I was wrong.

'I'm going to save you, my friend,' Marcus says, waggling a finger at me. 'All this, all of it, it'll all make sense when you know. When you *know*.'

'What are you talking about?' I say sharply, more sharply than I should – he's barely able to form words, let alone make sense.

'I'm going to show you. How bad she is. How bad for you. Addie is. I mean, you think *I* need help, you think I need help, you . . .'

He rants at me about Addie all the time now, telling me to leave her, telling me to end it, telling me everything was better before she came into my life. I can only believe that this fixation on Addie is a symptom of his wider disease – alcoholism, I assume, maybe something else too – but it's awful, and as much as I try to shield Addie from it, she knows he despises her. I can't bear to hear him talk about her like this; I get up and head for the kitchen, stepping over a plastic container of Chinese food, noodles spilling out of its side like entrails. He needs water, if he can keep it down.

The kitchen is even worse than the living area – there are no clean glasses, and I wash two with hand soap because there's no washing-up liquid.

Marcus hasn't been this bad since India left Joel. I wake constantly in the night wondering what it is that's set him off so drastically, what's changed in him, what's made him so desperate he'd lose himself again. Marcus's dad has now cut him off, and India too, so he needs me more than ever – it's sickening, the things he's doing for rent and booze money. A few weeks ago, picking his phone out of a puddle of sticky hot sauce from the takeaway, I discovered his profile on an escort website.

'Drink this,' I say, passing Marcus the water. 'I'm going to go out and get you some proper food. Something nutritional.'

'Will you come back afterwards? And eat with me?' Marcus asks, looking up at me with glassy eyes.

'Yeah, I'll stay.'

He smiles. 'Good,' he says, flopping back on the sofa. 'Good.'

Addie

'Addie, calm down . . .'

I clutch the phone to my ear, sobbing. I'm sat in a cubicle in the staff toilets, doubled over with my hair in my face. I have to cry quietly. I can't risk another teacher hearing me. And I only have ten minutes before the bell rings and I have to go inspire a roomful of moody teenagers to write their own accounts of the bloody Battle of the Boyne.

'I can't do this any more, Deb,' I whisper. 'I feel like it's driving me insane. I'm someone I don't want to be. You know the other day I thought I saw Marcus going through our bins?'

'What?'

'But when I got downstairs there was just the guy from next door. And I felt fucking *mad*.'

'You're not mad. This whole thing with Marcus has just got very messy, somehow.'

'Do you think that he's trying to break up me and Dylan?'

There's silence on the other end of the line. I clench my eyes shut so tight I see little red dots when I open them again.

'Do *you* think that?' Deb asks eventually.

'I do. I really do. Clearly the guy has issues, like he drinks whisky for breakfast and stuff, and it's so sweet that Dylan is trying to help him, but I kind of feel like he's . . . evil. I think he's got it in for me. I think he's following me.'

'*Following* you?'

'Or maybe that's just like the bins, me being totally paranoid. I don't even know any more. But Dylan's there now, and there goes our trip to Wiltshire *again* . . .' My shoulders shake as I sob. I brush the tears off my skirt. At least it's black, so they won't show too much when I'm stood in front of the class again.

'That in itself is pretty suspicious,' Deb say. 'How many of those trips to Wiltshire have you missed because of Marcus?'

'Four,' I say, without pause. I know that number like it's engrained on the inside of my brain. I think about it *all* the time.

'Well. There's something solid you can't deny.'

'And Marcus never seems to have a meltdown unless I'm spending the evening with Dylan.' I glance at the time on my phone screen. 'Oh, God, I need to pull myself together.'

'Are we sure this is about Marcus, Ads? Not Dylan?'

I blow my nose. 'What do you mean?'

'He doesn't have to go and see Marcus. Does he?'

'He's a good friend,' I say, wiping my eyes. 'That's the whole bloody problem.'

'Right. Maybe.'

'Maybe?'

'Or maybe he uses Marcus as an excuse.'

I go still. 'Do you think so?'

'I really don't know. But it is pretty strange, this whole situation, and I find it hard to believe the whole mess is all Marcus's making. I know you think he's evil, but that does seem a bit simplistic, doesn't it?'

I know what she means. I'm putting all the problems of my

relationship on Marcus because it's easier than being disappointed in my boyfriend. I've thought that before. But then Marcus writes something barbed on his Instagram and I can't help thinking it's about me. Or he has a meltdown just when me and Dylan have got through an argument and things are better. Or Dylan comes home from seeing him and looks at me in that weird, wary way and won't touch me for a little while. And I'll think, *This is Marcus's doing.*

'I have to go, Deb,' I say, checking the time again. 'Thank you for talking me down.'

'Come over this evening, if you want to. We can play board games with Dad.'

I close my eyes at the thought of it. The comfort of home.

'Yeah. I'd love that. Thank you.'

When I walk out of the staff toilets, Etienne's there. I almost go right into him. My heart does a little hiccup as I look up at him.

'Are you all right?' he says.

It's the worst thing he could choose to say right now.

'Yes.' My lip is already quivering. 'Yes, I'm fine, thanks. Just heading to . . .'

He takes my arm. 'Addie,' he says.

His voice is deep and sympathetic, and it tips me over the edge. My shoulders start shaking again.

'Let's step into my office,' he says. 'I'll ask Jamie to see to your lot – 10B, is it, this afternoon?'

I nod, snuffling into my sleeve as he ushers me through into his office and closes the door gently behind me. I stand there in the middle of the rug and sob until he returns.

'All sorted. Please, sit down,' he says. 'Tell me what's wrong.'

'God, I'm so sorry,' I say, reaching for a tissue from the box on his desk and wiping my face frantically. I'm red with shame.

'Boyfriend?'

I nod, sitting down in the chair he's indicated.

Etienne shakes his head. 'Well. It's not my place to interfere. But nobody's boyfriend should make them cry in the toilets. It's what I'd say to a student. I'm sure it's what you'd say to a student, too.' He meets my eyes then. 'You deserve better, Addie.'

That makes me cry again. He moves around from behind the desk, rubbing my shoulder, ducking down to his haunches so he's at my level. My body reacts to his touch, something flaring shamefully in my belly.

'Take the afternoon off.'

'I can't – what about – Battle of the Boyne,' I manage.

He smiles. 'If necessary, I can step in, or Moira can. There'll be someone who can stick on a DVD of something vaguely educational.'

I'm still crying. He's still rubbing my arm, his hand warm and reassuring.

'If you ever need to talk, Addie, I'm here. Anytime. OK? You have my mobile number. Just call me.'

I don't go back to my parents' house, in the end. Instead I lie in the bed I share with Dylan and stare up at the ceiling and think of Etienne. My skin feels too hot, like my body is too big for it. I touch myself and imagine my hand is Etienne's, firm and steady. I feel sick afterwards. I can't seem to forgive myself, and I pace around the flat, scratching at my arms, wishing I could go back in time to last summer, when everything was perfect.

By ten o'clock, Dylan still isn't home. He's stayed with Marcus all day. I wonder for the first time if that's where he really is. What if Marcus is a cover-up? What if Dylan's met somebody else? Someone who's as perfect as he expects them to be. Someone clever and posh and poetic, someone who would never feel jealous of Dylan's sick best friend.

My phone buzzes in my hand. I've been staring at it vacantly, with no clear idea of what I want it to do.

'Hello?'

'Wow, hello,' Deb says. 'That was prompt. So, can I get your take on an ethical conundrum?'

'Sure?' I say.

I've forgotten to eat. I get up and head to the fridge, scanning it for something in-date.

'So if I know I want to have a baby, and I've thought of someone who is very willy-nilly with sperm distribution . . . Can I just have sex with him and get pregnant and then never tell him he's the father?'

I blink at the lump of cheddar I'm examining.

'Umm,' I say.

'It's Mike,' she supplies helpfully. 'That bouncer I went back with after your birthday night out.'

I try to compose my thoughts.

'He's not big on condoms, basically,' Deb says. 'Hello? Are you still there?'

'Yes, sorry,' I say, closing the fridge. 'Just absorbing.'

Deb waits patiently.

'I think that might be really wrong,' I say. 'Yes. I think that's one of the bad ones.'

'Oh,' Deb says, sounding crestfallen. 'But if I'd done it by accident, it would be fine.'

'Yeah, true. Only it wouldn't be by accident if you did it now.'

'Who's to know?'

'Well, me. You told me.'

'Damn it. Why did you have to pick up the phone?'

I sigh. 'Why don't you ask Mike if he minds?'

'He'd probably say he doesn't mind,' Deb says. 'But then there's the risk that when my child is seven or something and functioning really well in my lovely single-parent household he'll come sweeping in demanding rights.'

It's still so strange hearing Deb talk about having a child. I really thought she'd never come around. I should have known there'd be no grey area, no umming and ahhing. Deb is a yes-or-no sort of woman.

I wonder what she would do if she were me. Deb would never cry on the toilet over any man, and I feel a twinge of shame.

'Why don't you just get a donor? Aren't there private companies that do that sort of thing for you?' I ask.

'That sounds complicated. And much less fun than having sex with Mike.'

'Why Mike, just out of interest?'

'Hmm? Oh, I told you, he doesn't like condoms.'

I wait.

'And I suppose he's quite a good specimen. Tall, handsome, kind, funny, that sort of thing.'

'Sounds like a catch.'

'What? Irrelevant. I'm after a sperm donor, not a boyfriend.'

'Would it be such a bad thing to get one of those too?'

'You tell me,' Deb says dryly. 'You're not the best advertisement for relationships at the minute.'

I rummage in the cupboard for a loaf of bread. Stale, but it'll do for cheese on toast.

'I'd say being in a relationship with one person is great,' I tell her. 'The trouble is, at the moment I feel like I'm in a relationship with two people.'

'Dylan and Etienne?'

I freeze, holding a slice of bread hovering over the toaster.

'What?'

'No?' Deb says, sounding uncertain.

'Why did you say that?'

'Sorry, did I upset you? I thought you fancied him.'

'I meant I felt like I was in a relationship with Dylan and *Marcus*.'

'Oh, of course. Right.'

My heart is beating too fast. Deb knows me better than anyone. If she thinks I fancy Etienne . . .

I mean, don't I? A little bit? What have I just spent my evening thinking about? I rub my belly, feeling nauseous again. I love Dylan. I love *Dylan*.

'Sorry, Ads.'

I push down the toaster. I need to eat. It occurs to me as soon as I've done it that I should have put the bread under the grill, with the cheese.

'It's OK,' I manage. 'It's just . . . weird that you said that. I didn't realise I'd even talked about him.'

'You talk about him quite a bit, actually. But that's probably just me getting the wrong end of the stick.'

There's a long silence.

'Not . . . totally,' I say in a small voice.

'Oh. So you do fancy him?'

'Sometimes. I don't know. Oh, God, I'm an awful person. I'm a cheat.'

'Addie! Please. It's not cheating to fancy someone else a little bit. Do you like him more than Dylan?'

'What? No! Of course not! It's just . . . I guess things are so – so *fraught* with Dylan. So it's like an escapist thing.'

The sound of keys in the lock. I spin, guilty. The toaster pops and I jump.

'I've got to go. Love you, Deb.'

'What if Mike was the one who decided not to use a condom? Then it would be a known risk he was taking on his own.'

I close my eyes. 'Bye, Deb.'

'Oh, fine. Bye.'

Dylan looks exhausted. All the anger evaporates as I watch him stagger to the cupboard and pull out a glass, fill it with water, down it and pour another. I step towards him to hug him but he backs away.

'I stink of vomit,' he says. 'I need a shower. Sorry.'

My stomach twists. 'He was really bad?'

Dylan just nods. As he makes his way to the bathroom I stand there, sick with guilt and shame, because Marcus is unwell, and Dylan is helping him, and I am the most unreasonable girlfriend there has ever been.

The first text from Etienne comes ten days later, on a Saturday night.

> How are you doing, Addie? I mean, really. I know it can be hard to talk about at school. X

I leave it sitting in my pocket, determined not to reply. It isn't professional of him to text me about personal stuff outside school. But then I think, I wouldn't find it strange if it was Moira. Or even Jamie, and Jamie is a single guy my age too. It's me who's making this unprofessional. Etienne's just being a polite, supportive colleague and manager.

Dylan's looking after Marcus again. We've had a good week – we had a proper conversation about Marcus and how he's got this history of going off the rails. I promised to be more understanding.

> Doing much better, thanks. Really appreciate you stepping in to sort cover for me the other day. Addie

There's no reply. I begin to wonder if I've been too abrupt. But when I see Etienne on Monday he smiles at me, a supportive, I-know-you've-got-this smile, and I feel better.

It's like this for a month or two. The occasional text – nothing flirtatious or inappropriate. Just ever so slightly friendlier than we are in person. As Dylan's Masters begins to eat into his time even more, and as he takes more shifts at the bar, I'm alone a lot. Some nights I stay late at school. Etienne's often around, and we have quiet chats over evening cups of tea. Nothing more than that.

But I can't deny that it excites me. Nothing's happening. On paper, nothing's wrong. But I know otherwise.

I know Etienne wants me. Sometimes, I want him too.

It's two days before the Christmas holidays, and late – nine at night. Nobody else is around, not even the caretaker. Etienne has keys. He'll lock up.

'Addie?' he says, poking his head around the door to my classroom. I'm taking down a display that Tyson raked his fingernails through, Wolverine-style. 'Fancy a nightcap?'

It takes me a moment to realise he has a bottle in his hand. Red wine, by the looks of it.

'It's nearly the end of term, and we've both worked ourselves to the bone this year,' he says, waggling the bottle. 'We deserve a treat.'

I say yes to the nightcap. I follow him to his office. I fetch us glasses from the kitchen, and we drink the wine out of water tumblers. I'm wearing lipstick, and I leave a pink kiss on the edge of the glass.

We talk about work stuff, mostly. Laugh about the kids that do our heads in, complain about the ever-changing government guidelines, compare our least favourite parents. My cheeks are flushed pink and I'm drunk on half a bottle. Maybe a little more than half. I don't keep track of how often he tops up my glass and his.

It happens very naturally. His hand on my thigh. It takes me too long to realise it's strange.

I stand, move away. He follows me.

'Addie,' he says.

'I should go,' I say.

I turn towards the door.

He pushes it closed, over my shoulder, his body against my back.

'This has been such a long time coming,' he says in my ear. 'Hasn't it?'

There's a cold sort of dread in my stomach. He's right, I knew this was coming. What else had I expected? I feel like I'm slipping, or perhaps like I already slipped and now I'm falling, fingernails grasping for something to hold.

His lips are on my neck. I can feel desire, quiet and low, but above that I feel desperate disgust. At him? Myself?

I know when he pulls me back against him, against his hardness. I don't want this. Fuck. I can't do this, the thought makes me feel sick, the wetness of his mouth on my neck is like a tarantula across the skin.

'No,' I say.

I say no.

Dylan

Luke calls me around seven, and he tells me that my father is cheating on my mother.

I sit, slowly, on the edge of the sofa. For a long while I say nothing at all.

'Dyl?' Luke says. 'Dyl, I'm sorry. I can't tell you how much I've been dreading this phone call.'

I feel like my head is full of whiteness; I'm not exactly surprised, but it's horrifying, like being told you're not who you think you are at all.

'She knows?' I manage.

'I told her before I told you. I thought – I guess I thought she should know first. She was totally in denial. I couldn't convince her.'

I'm only half listening – a sudden rage is rising up my body, freezing hot, like ice burn. I'm so rarely angry that I hardly know how to hold the feeling: it seems to have found its way into my throat, my ears, the little capillaries spreading through my lungs.

'I don't think she'll ever leave him, you know,' Luke says. 'She just didn't want to hear it.'

A message comes through from Marcus; I check it abstractedly, hardly seeing it at first.

You need to come to Addie's school. She's there with Etienne, and . . . it doesn't look good.

The picture comes next. Through the window, the warm glow of the office inside, with the two of them sitting side by side, drinking wine out of tumblers, his hand resting on her upper thigh.

'Luke?' I say. My voice is strangled. 'I have to go.'

I press the off button to turn the screen black, then sit with the phone cradled between my hands, staring down, heart big and sick in my chest. The phrase *seeing red* has never meant anything to me before, but now I understand. I saw the image for less than a second but it's drawn on the inside of my eyelids like sparklers in the night.

Eventually, after those long, stifling seconds of stillness, I grab my coat and pull on my shoes – so slow, so mundane, as if my world isn't ending – and I run for the car.

Addie

He nips me with his teeth.

I turn in the cage of his arms. It's worse. He pushes up my skirt, hand running up my thigh, pulling my leg so that the muscle along the back of my thigh wrenches with a shot of pain, and I'm bunching my fists now, trying to turn my head aside, and I'm *clear*, I couldn't be clearer. I'm pushing his chest. I'm talking, I think – *Stop it, please* – and our teeth clatter, a dull thud inside my head as he keeps pushing his lips down on mine.

'I know you want this,' he tells me. 'Don't you?'

It's a sound outside that makes him turn his head aside for a moment. We can't see the window from here; he takes half a step back, then pauses, unsure. I remember something from long past. Self-defence classes in school, maybe. The fist that was pushing at his chest unravels and I grab his shoulder while he's unsteady and my skirt is already up around my thighs so I can bring my knee up hard between his legs and watch him fold over, letting out a noise like an animal and – finally, as I sob – letting me go.

I run. The door isn't locked. As I sprint down the corridor to the back exit, through the staffroom, I feel bone-cold with the fear that he's locked up the school, but he hasn't. He wasn't afraid I'd run. He knew I wanted it, he'd said.

I run all the way home. At least ten kilometres. My feet bleed. When I take my shoes off inside the flat I flinch when I see them. I'm shaking so hard I can't use my fingers properly. I sit on the floor and weep like I'll never stop crying. I claw at my skin. I dig my fingernails into my arms. I remember all the times I smiled at him when he smiled at me.

Dylan

I get there just as Etienne is coming out of the building; he turns, carefully locking up behind him.

'That's him,' Marcus says, suddenly at my shoulder. 'There. That's him.'

I know. I saw the photo. That split second of the image on the screen was more than enough for me to memorise every line of that bastard's face.

I run at him. Marcus calls to me – he sounds surprised. He's been drinking, and he isn't fast enough to catch me. My fist hits Etienne's jaw just as he turns. There's a hot pain in my knuckle, a jarring shock in my elbow. He doubles over.

'What the—'

'What the fuck were you doing with my girlfriend?' I say, realising with shame that I'm crying.

Etienne looks up at me, eyes wide. 'It's not what you think,' he says.

'No? Looked pretty cosy to me,' Marcus says.

Etienne looks at him quickly, eyes narrowing. He stays low, crouched. I keep my fists bunched at my sides and wish I wasn't sniffling and shaking like a child.

'She's . . . intense,' Etienne says. 'She's been coming on to me all term, finding reasons to spend time alone with me, staying late just to try and . . .'

'Shut up,' I say, wiping my face hard. 'Shut up, shut up, shut the *fuck up*.'

'No, go on,' Marcus says. He steps forward. 'Go on.'

'Look, I tried to be a good guy. But she's – I had a moment of weakness. She said how badly she wanted me and . . .'

He darts backwards as I move towards him again, but Marcus puts his hand out to stop me.

'I'm sorry,' Etienne says. 'I'm really sorry.'

'What happened?' Marcus asks. 'Where is she now?'

'I stopped her as soon as I realised what was happening,' Etienne says, eyes flicking between me and Marcus. 'She got mad and left. I didn't mean for anything to happen with her. She just . . . got in my head. I can't think straight around her.'

Marcus is nodding. 'Yeah,' he says. His voice slurs. 'Yeah. That sounds *just* like Addie.'

Addie

I call my sister. I will never be grateful enough for Deb. I barely have words to say it, but she never says, *I thought you fancied him.* She never says, *You wanted that.* She turns up at the flat and she undresses me like I'm made of something precious, then gets me in the shower. After I'm clean, she wraps me in my old threadbare dressing gown and holds me very tightly. It isn't a hug – she's holding me together.

The guilt sets in after the shock. It's all very predictable. When I'm no longer running from him, when the horror isn't right in front of me, I'm totally sure it's my fault. I fancied him. I drank his wine and I replied to his texts.

Deb says, 'What would you tell me? If I said those things?'

And I see the truth of it for a moment. I know what I would tell my sister. I know how fiercely I'd protest that consent is an ongoing process. That no means no whatever you've said before it. But then the clarity's gone again. There's just horror and shame.

Dylan

Marcus makes me go to the pub with him before I go back to the flat to see Addie.

'You need to clear your head,' he says, then he proceeds to buy me four pints, as if that will fucking help.

I cry into my drink. I don't tell Marcus what Luke told me because, quite honestly, I'm barely thinking about it. All I can think about is the pain in my chest, like it's cracking, like someone's pried my ribs apart and left them gaping.

'Don't get sad, get mad,' Marcus tells me, pushing another drink towards me. 'Addie's been screwing around with the teacher and God knows who else, pretending she's all sweetness and light. I *knew* there was something about her. Didn't I say? Didn't I say?'

Addie

Deb wants to stay. But I want Dylan. He'll be home soon. I need to wash again. I need to wash it all off and then I need to tell Dylan, because somehow that's almost more frightening than everything else.

But it turns out I don't need to tell him.

He's already been told.

Dylan

She looks different when I walk into the flat – her eyes are wide and frightened, kitten-like, and I know then that this is the first time she's betrayed me with another man. She wouldn't be able to hide this from me: it's written all over her face.

'I know what you did.'

That's what I say. And then I tell her I'm leaving, just like I practised it in the pub. I tell her there are some things I can't forgive, and I think to myself, *Yes, I'm right, and I'm strong for walking away. I won't be like my mother. I won't turn a blind eye. I'll be strong.*

At first she's very still. She looks so pale and small, like a little wild creature brought in from the cold, deciding whether to hide or fight.

The silence is horrifying; we're on the edge of something vast and empty. I'm dizzy from drink and sick with horror and I want to climb out of my own skin, be somebody else, *anyone* else.

'Aren't you even going to listen to my side of the story?' she says into the silence. Her voice sounds like a child's.

'Etienne told me everything. There's nothing you can say.'

The next few minutes are a blur. She throws herself at me, and

I think she's trying to hurt me, her little fists in my chest, her feet stamping, but it's almost as if she's trying to burrow into me, too, to get closer. She roars. It's grief, unmistakably. I think, quietly, *So she does love me, then. She doesn't want to lose me.* What a time to find out for sure.

Addie

There is no hurt like it. All the worst things have been confirmed. I'm as bad as I feared. I'm worse.

I tell nobody else, not even my mum.

Deb saves my life, I think. She makes all the calls. She takes me to the police station and never leaves my side. If she wasn't here, Etienne would have remained as the head teacher at Barwood School, and I'd have fallen apart.

Dylan

The doubt creeps in like damp. I wake up the next day in the log cabin at the end of Marcus's dad's garden, as if I've slipped back to that long dark winter before I stopped taking money from my parents. India picked us up from Chichester last night; Marcus must have rung her, I register, with a flicker of surprise that soon dulls again. I stare at the ceiling and touch – just for a moment – the thought of living without Addie, and it's enough to send me curling inwards like an insect, burying myself in the sheets.

I don't get up until the evening, and only then because my stomach gnaws with hunger.

'What if there was an explanation?' I say to Marcus, as we drink whisky on the floor of the cabin, in amongst the clutter of takeaway boxes. 'What if there was a reasonable explanation?'

'Like what?' Marcus is pale, almost gaunt, his eyes bruised with exhaustion. 'Just look at the photo, Dylan. Who she really is, right there in high definition.'

Addie

I know at least half of my suffering is the after-effects of what I've been through with Etienne. But all I can find is grief at losing Dylan.

I don't feel like he left me – I feel like he died.

He didn't even let me speak. The man I love would *always* let me speak. So who's Dylan?

Dylan

It's Deb who tells me the truth of it.

One week on from the night at the school, she turns up on the doorstep of Marcus's log cabin with her face twisted in disgust.

'You son of a bitch,' she says. 'You are an absolute piece of shit and I hope you burn in hell.'

She puts down a large box of my belongings and turns her back on me. 'The rest of it is at the end of the lane,' she says over her shoulder. 'You're lucky I didn't drop it in your fucking lake.'

'Hey,' I say. I dither in the doorway – I'm in just socks – and then chase her anyway. 'Hey! How *dare* you!'

She keeps walking.

'She cheated on me! *She* cheated on *me*! And you're here telling me *I'm* the one going to burn in hell?'

She spins on her heels then. 'Dylan. You're an *idiot*.'

She has never looked more like Addie, small and fierce and conceding nothing.

'What are you talking about?' I yell, but I'm starting to shiver now, a sense of wrongness settling on my shoulders through the drizzle. 'Marcus saw them. And Etienne told me everything.'

Perhaps the wrongness was there already. For the last few days I've drunk more than ever, because I've begun to see through the haze and remember my Addie, strong and honest, and it's impossible to assimilate that person with the Addie Etienne and Marcus showed me as I stood weeping outside the school.

'*Marcus* saw them, did he? And what was he doing there?'

This isn't the first time I've wondered about that. *Looking out for you*, is all Marcus said when I asked him. But he was right, wasn't he, and so following Addie didn't look like madness, it looked like foresight.

'And Etienne told you everything. *Etienne.* Do you know what it says about you that you believed the word of a man you don't know over the word of the woman you love?' Deb says.

The wet grass soaks up through my socks. My heart pounds.

'He forced her. Yeah, she drank some wine. She flirted a little, maybe. And then he tried to rape her.'

Raindrops snag in the loose strands of Deb's dark hair. She holds my gaze.

'But maybe you don't care,' she says. 'Maybe you still want her stoned in the village square, Dylan.'

I double over then and throw up on the grass.

Addie

He's sorry. Nobody has ever been sorrier. He's a mess of a person, he's awful, the worst, he's too easily led, he sees that now, he knows he has to sort himself out, he should never have assumed, he should never have left me, Deb told him everything, he knows now, please, please, he's sorry. He sits on my doorstep and weeps.

I don't open the door. I send him one message in response to the stream of gut-wrenching apologies that come that day.

Don't tell Marcus what really happened, I write.

I can't explain it, exactly. Perhaps I see something of Etienne in Marcus. Perhaps he makes me feel vulnerable. Perhaps it's that Marcus has always said he can see darkness in me, and my heart's never felt darker than it does now.

I just can't stand the thought of Marcus knowing.

Promise me that, I say. *And then, please. Don't send me any more messages. I know you're sorry. I understand why you did what you did. But please. Don't contact me again.*

NOW

Dylan

Marcus's nose is bleeding; a drop falls on the back of Addie's pyjamas as she bends over the toilet, retching, and it spreads on the fabric like red ink, its edges fuzzing. There isn't enough room in here for all of us. My head throbs where Marcus punched me in the temple.

'Addie, hey,' I say, pushing Marcus aside to kneel beside her.

He staggers back against the bath. Deb shoves through the bathroom door behind me and I glance up at her for a moment before looking back to Addie, who is clutching the toilet seat with shaking fingers. Her face is washed-out white, cream gone sour.

'Something she ate?' Marcus says.

Deb reaches out and flushes the toilet, ever practical.

'Come on. Come *on*. What am I missing?' Marcus says. 'Why's everyone acting like I'm the bad guy when she's the one who forced herself on a *guy who wasn't Dylan*?'

'*She* did not fucking force herself on anybody,' Deb says, and then closes her eyes for a moment. 'Sorry. Sorry, Ads, I – it wasn't my place.'

'Everything all right in there?' Rodney calls from outside the bathroom door.

'All fine, Rodney,' I say, keeping my voice steady. 'Just go back to bed.'

'Right,' he says uncertainly.

After a long moment Addie sits back, pulling the sleeves of her pyjamas over her hands, wincing as she jolts her injured wrist. She's not looking at me. Deb crouches on the other side of her, so all three of us are sitting on the bathroom floor, with Marcus standing over us, backed up against the bath. He's got a lump of loo roll held against his bleeding nose, and his eyes are already beginning to bruise, but even through all of that I can read his expression, and he looks afraid.

'What do you mean? What really happened that night?' he asks me. 'What didn't you tell me?'

'She asked me not to. That was her choice to make.'

I watch Marcus begin to understand. He turns, slowly, to look at Addie. 'Etienne? He . . .'

Addie doesn't look at Marcus. 'It never occurred to you that he might lie?' she says. Her voice is reedy and hoarse.

Marcus lets out a noise, half strangled, and sits down hard on the edge of the bath. He presses a hand to his forehead. The silence stretches on; behind us all, the tap drips.

'You let me think . . . Why did you let me think that?' Marcus says to Addie.

Deb passes him a fresh wad of toilet roll for his bleeding nose, and I am struck by the absurdity of all this, the four of us crammed into this mouldy bathroom, after all the years we spent circling one another, never close enough.

'You followed me,' Addie says to Marcus. 'Didn't you?'

Marcus turns his head aside. He's crying, I notice with a start; I catch Deb watching him with her eyes narrowed in thought. He brushes the tears away like he's just getting something off his cheek, a raindrop or a speck of dirt.

'Yes. Sometimes.'

He doesn't speak for a while, and the tap drips on. I think he's done, that's it, but then:

'It was like a – I can't explain,' he says, still staring off to the side. 'I was drinking way too much, I'd fucked up my life, India was mad at me, Dad wasn't talking to me – but I had this feeling that if I saved Dylan from screwing up *his* life . . . It was like, you know, that would save me, that would be a good thing I'd done, then I'd be OK. Dylan had always been there for me. I couldn't see him – I couldn't – I couldn't lose him too.'

Deb shakes her head. 'I'm not buying this. You had some – some *problem* with Addie. It can't have just been this messed up crap about protecting Dylan.'

Marcus looks up at the ceiling. My heart beats hard. I want to pull Addie against me, or just to touch her, smooth her hair back, press a kiss to her cheek.

'I don't know,' Marcus says. 'It was just a . . .' He gestured to his stomach. 'A gut-instinct thing. I felt like I just, I just *knew* she was bad news for Dylan, and then it sort of grew and she was always there, getting in Dylan's head, until all he thought about was her, until he was consumed by her, *mad* about her . . .'

'Oh my God,' Deb says. 'You loved her. You loved Addie.'

Everyone goes still.

It was my therapist who first suggested Marcus might have been in love with Addie; understanding that was the key to forgiving him, for me. I was Marcus's brother, his soulmate, his oldest friend. How he must have *loathed* himself for loving Addie; how easy it must have been for him to shift that loathing elsewhere, to hate her instead of hating himself.

But we've never spoken about it. Not once.

'You did, didn't you?' Deb goes on, insistent, and Marcus twists away suddenly, spinning so his feet are in the bath, hunching over with his hands to his face.

His shoulders shake. He's sobbing.

'Oh my God,' Deb says. 'That's why you were there at the school. That's why you cared so much if she was sleeping with Etienne. That's why you were always such a prick about her and Dylan.'

I look at Addie. Her eyes are huge, staring at Marcus's back as he hunches, trembling, on the edge of the cheap plastic bath, and I look at him too and think, *He's so small.* How can he have done so much damage?

'Marcus?' Addie says.

He slams a foot down in the bottom of the bath and we all jump at the sudden sound in the silence.

'Of course I fucking loved her. Of course I did. Fuck me, Dylan, you were dense as a brick back then, you were so stupid not to see it that I *hated* you sometimes' – his voice rises, fists bunched, shaking – 'because you would have made it so easy for me to take her. Always pushing the two of us together. Always so keen for us to get along. And I'm not the good guy, I'm not the guy who steps aside for his best friend. Do you know how hard it was? In the end I just wanted her *gone*, because it was torture, watching you with her, watching you fuck it up, watching you get it right—'

'You couldn't have taken me,' Addie says quietly. 'I would never have left Dylan for you, Marcus.'

'And I wasn't dense,' I say, without rancour. 'I was trusting. I trusted my best friend.'

'Addie, I didn't know, I swear,' Marcus croaks, face still in his hands. 'The teacher . . . I really thought . . . I went to the school sometimes. Saw you working late, with him. There's no curtains in that place, and with it all lit up . . .'

Addie is staring down at the bathroom floor. I want to tell her I love her, I love her, I love her, I'm sorry.

'I had to climb on to the skip to see you in the head teacher's office,' he says, voice dropping. 'I remember seeing his hand on your thigh, then you standing, putting your glass of wine down, him following you. Then you . . .' He swallows. 'Then you went out of view.'

I close my eyes for a moment.

'And I never saw you leave. Then Etienne came out and Dylan arrived and Etienne said . . .'

I cut him off. 'We all know what Etienne said.'

Addie lets out a little sound, a mew.

'Why didn't you say?' Marcus lifts his head a little, still facing away. His voice is thick. 'Why didn't someone *say* something?'

'I didn't want you to know,' Addie says, wiping her eyes. 'You . . . you were probably the very last person in the world that I wanted to know. You'd have said it was my fault. Wouldn't you?'

Marcus turns his head just enough that I can see his face from where I'm sitting. He drops his hands, removing the tissue; there are dried, bloody watermarks all down his mouth and chin. I've never seen him like this, so stark, so horrified. He looks very, very young.

'Of course I wouldn't. I wouldn't, Addie. God. I can't believe you could think that.'

Addie shakes her head, frustrated now. 'You thought the worst of me at *every* opportunity. You had it in for me. I couldn't *stand* the thought of you knowing.'

'Even if I was drunk and manic and whatever I was – please, Addie.' Marcus's voice cracks. 'You need to know that I truly thought you were cheating on Dylan. I thought there was something between you and the teacher.'

There is silence for a while. The bathroom tap drips faster and faster, and I wonder if it's been getting quicker like that all along. Addie shifts a little and lifts her gaze to mine.

She takes a deep breath. 'You weren't . . . I . . . I did . . . I had a crush on Etienne. For a moment I wondered – and I let him – and then I didn't want to, but he didn't stop, and . . .' She's sobbing now too, cradling her injured wrist in her lap, tracing her fingers across the swelling. 'Dyl, I feel like you stopped being angry with me because something bad happened to me, but that doesn't make me good. That doesn't erase the other stuff.'

That hurts my heart – a real, physical pain in my chest.

'Addie. No. Come on. Imagine it hadn't ended how it did. Imagine you'd just walked out of his office the moment you'd wanted to. Would you still have said you didn't deserve forgiving?'

She stays quiet. 'I don't know,' she says. 'I can't . . . untangle it.'

'There's no question, for me. You came close to betraying me, maybe, but you didn't. I don't care about almost. I care about what really happened. Everyone's got the potential to do the wrong thing – if we were measured that way, we'd all come up short. It's about what you *do*. And you told him to stop. You walked away. It was *me* who fucked up, Addie, and I hate myself for not letting you tell me what really happened when I came to the flat that night. I'd become the person I tried so hard not to be. I didn't listen. I failed you.'

She leans into me then, pressing her body against my chest, and I close my eyes and hold her close as she cries.

We sit in the bathroom for another five minutes, maybe. Addie's head is tucked beneath my chin, and I can feel Deb behind me, her leg against my spine, and there's Marcus with his back to us, hunched, broken.

Deb moves first. 'We should . . .' She nods towards Marcus. Addie and I shift, getting up slowly; Marcus remains motionless. We leave him there. Deb leads us all out of the bathroom, all shuffling in a line. In the street light that seeps between the crack in the curtains, I catch sight of Rodney. He's starfished in the middle of the double bed, mouth open, snoring.

Addie

As far as I'm aware, Marcus sleeps in the bathroom – or maybe just stays sitting there on the edge of the bath all night. I don't know. I'm not sure I care, either.

I don't know how to feel about it all. I'm not convinced it was *love*, what he felt for me, whatever Deb thinks, whatever Marcus says. I think Marcus just wanted what his best friend had. Even more so when he didn't get it.

Deb shoves Rodney over and makes do with a third of the double. I take Marcus's bed and lie on my side, watching Dylan sleep.

He looks so gorgeous in the darkness. The light from between the curtains catches on the tips of his eyelashes and leaves long shadows across his cheeks. Before I really clock what I'm doing, I push back the covers and cross the floor between us.

He wakes as I climb into the bed beside him, and for a split second – as he looks at me, eyes all sleepy and confused – I hesitate, feeling a pang of that old anxiety. For so long I thought Dylan wanted that sexy summer girl. A woman he could chase, the way he chased Grace. Someone out of reach. It's hard, even now, to come to *him* for once, be the first to lay my weapon down.

But then he smiles and pulls me into him, tucking his body behind mine.

'I'm sorry,' he whispers. 'I will always be so, so sorry.'

'Please don't,' I whisper back. 'We can't be sorry for ever. That's what forgiveness is for, isn't it?'

He pulls me in with the arm that's looped around me, the way it always was when we slept like this. The smell of him makes my throat tighten with emotion.

'I've got you,' he whispers, as he tucks me in. It's something he used to say, I can't even remember why. I know what it means, though: *I'm here. I've got your back. I'm yours.*

I lace the fingers of my good hand through his, pulling his arm into my chest. I used to just kiss his hand when he said it, maybe, or smile. But I've had a lot of time to think over the last year and a half and when I remember all the times he said he loved me and I didn't say it back, it makes me furious with myself. As if I was winning, somehow, by holding that back. As if there was some weakness in showing him I cared.

'I've got you,' I whisper. 'I've got you too.'

I'm woken by the buzz of my phone. It's in the pocket of my pyjamas. Dylan is still holding me, fast asleep. I smile. I start to second-guess – what was I doing, climbing into his bed like that – but shut myself up before I can really get going on it.

The message is from Deb.

Are you OK? Xx

I'm good. I'm in bed with Dylan xx

I hear her exclamation over the other side of the room and bury my smile in the pillow.

Well what does that mean?!

Haven't a clue. But . . . ☺

But smiley face, eh? Did you . . .

We just cuddled.

Disgusting.

Deb hates the word cuddle. I used to agree, until I didn't have anyone to cuddle me, and then I realised hating the word cuddle was a luxury of actually getting them.

'Are you messaging Deb?' Dylan whispers beside me.

There's a moment. I can *feel* the decision waiting to be made. Now that he's awake, should he let me go?

He shifts as if to pull away. I drop my phone and lace my fingers through his again, the way I did before. I can feel him smiling as he settles back into position.

'I said cuddle. She said disgusting,' I whisper back.

His laugh is so low it's almost inaudible, just a rumble against my hair. I feel almost panicked with happiness, and I tighten my grip on his hand so it doesn't slip away.

'Are you OK?' he whispers.

'I'm good. I'm really good.'

'I'm glad we talked. That wasn't *exactly* how I imagined that conversation would go, but . . .'

'Less vomiting?'

'Fewer bystanders.'

I smile.

'But I've wanted to say all of that to you for a really long time,' he says.

He tightens his arm against me for a moment in a brief hug. Obviously I've no idea what any of this means. It's just cuddling, and when we leave this bed, God knows where we go from here. Dylan and I had all kinds of problems aside from Etienne and Marcus. There's a hundred reasons why we . . .

'Stop,' Dylan whispers. 'It's OK. Relax.'

I loosen my shoulders. I hadn't even noticed I'd stiffened up.

'Let's just enjoy the last few minutes in this bed,' he says. 'And we can deal with the real world when we get out of it.'

'Dylan Abbott,' I whisper. 'Are you telling me to live in the now?'

Dylan

The morning is a flurry of activity – we plan to set off at seven, but Deb loses track of time Skyping her mum and Riley, and Marcus has locked himself in the bathroom and fallen asleep so none of us can get in to shower until he wakes up, and Addie can't find her glasses. Behind it all, I can hardly think straight for the joy of catching Addie's eye across the chaos and watching her smile. A poem begins to grow as we settle in the car and Rodney cheerfully hands around slabs of his flapjack for our impromptu breakfast. The new words come spooling: *the quiet blossoming, the rebloom/the hint of a wish of a chance*.

Addie, Rodney and I are in the back; Marcus is sitting up front, uncharacteristically quiet, his bruised face turned outwards towards the day that's just beginning through the window. If I was aware of Addie's skin against mine yesterday, today it *burns* me. I can hardly think of anything else, and I'm dangerously happy, so very hopeful, and then she reaches across and takes my hand and I really think I might cry with joy.

'Isn't that lovely!' Rodney says, beaming at our linked hands.

Addie laughs; her fingers lace more tightly through mine.

I mustn't get ahead of myself. We have so much to talk about. But – *the hint of a wish of a chance* – it's so much better than anything I've had for the last year and a half, and that great fissure in my chest is like a crack in dry soil, closing up at the first hint of rain.

The drive suddenly seems easy, as if the roads have heard the news – Addie and me, holding hands in the car – and agree that all should now be right in the world. It's only when we finally take an extreme-desperation break (Deb has banned comfort breaks and will only stop driving for 'anyone who will otherwise wet themselves') at a tiny services near Carlisle that I recall the other crisis currently occupying Deb's Mini.

'Someone go with Rodney!' Deb hisses at me and Marcus as we wander over to the service station shop. 'Don't leave the man alone!'

Oh, yes. Rodney the stalker. I remember.

'Not even to piss?' Marcus says.

'Especially not to piss! What if he escapes through the bathroom window?'

I'm not sure quite what Marcus and I are going to do about it if he does.

'Quite hard to have eyes-on when he's in the bathroom, Major,' Marcus says. His drawl is a little lacklustre today.

'What about urinals? Isn't that what they're for?'

Marcus and I exchange a puzzled glance.

'Just go! Go!' Deb says, shoving us towards the toilets.

'She's *really* not interested in me, is she?' Marcus says, turning to look at Deb again as she hurries off to rejoin Addie by the snacks.

'She'd rather have sex with Kevin the trucker than with you. So I think it's a no. And you're only chasing her out of habit, anyway.'

Marcus kicks a stone with his toe. 'Hmm. I preferred it when you always agreed with me. You know. Back before you got all independent-woman and friend-dumped me because your therapist told you to.'

'No, you don't. Back then our friendship was . . .' I trail off.

'Oh, I know,' Marcus says, still looking at his feet. And then, after a long moment, he says, 'Even before Addie. It wasn't healthy.'

I blink in surprise. 'Yeah. That's true.'

He shoots me a look. 'Don't sound so surprised. You're not the only one having therapy.'

'Sorry,' I say. 'I'm just glad to hear you say that. And it wasn't a friend-dumping, by the way, we weren't ever really . . .'

'Over?' he says, quirking an eyebrow.

That gets a reluctant laugh out of me. 'What can I say? I believe in second chances. Besides, you need someone who reminds you to be a human being when you're inclined to be an arsehole. And you're very lucky I am enough of an idiot to keep trying.'

The bathroom door swings shut behind us. Rodney is at the urinals, wide-eyed, as if we've caught him doing something X-rated.

'Oh, gosh, umm, hi,' he says, lifting one hand in a wave.

'Presumably I'm not allowed to flush his head down the toilet?' Marcus asks me.

'Correct. Well done.'

Marcus sighs. 'Reforming one's character is very tedious. Can't I just carry on being a dissolute reprobate?'

I smile slightly. 'No,' I say, looking at him carefully. The hollow cheeks, the hunched shoulders, the hunted, haunted eyes. 'No, I don't think you can.'

Addie

'I told you! We need a dastardly plan!'

'You know, we're saying dastardly a lot, but I'm not actually sure what it means?' I tell Deb. She's expressing again – the battery-powered one has run out, so she's plugged the other into a socket next to the storeroom. The two teenage boys behind the tills are staring at her like she's escaped from the zoo. 'Can't we just drive off without him? Or drop him somewhere?' I say.

'Like in a lake?'

'What? No! Why can I never tell whether you're joking?'

'It's the deadpan delivery,' Deb says, adjusting the poncho covering her top half. 'Don't blame yourself.'

'I was thinking we could just leave him somewhere, maybe, you know, take his phone . . .'

'I can't believe we're talking about this.'

I glance over towards the counter. Marcus and Dylan are trying to keep Rodney occupied while we come up with some sort of strategy. Marcus is doing a really shit job of pretending to be interested in whatever Rodney's saying.

'Maybe we can just talk to him? Reason with him?' I say.

Deb tilts her head, watching Rodney. 'He does seem ... pretty harmless.'

'Yeah. Yeah. I know Cherry was freaking out, but she's in crazy wedding mode. I'm sure if we just ask him not to come to the wedding, it'll be fine.' I feel a surge of relief at the thought. This is much more rational. It was the madness of that Budget Travel family room. We lost our heads.

'A sensible conversation,' I say. 'Yeah. I mean, he seems a bit odd, but he doesn't seem *dangerous.*'

Deb catches Dylan's attention and waves the boys back over.

'What, right now?' I say.

'Well, there's not a lot else I can do while attached to the wall,' Deb says. 'Might as well make use of the time. Hi, boys. Rodney. We just want to have a little chat with you about your plans regarding Cherry's wedding.'

Rodney's eyes widen. His body goes stiff. He looks frantically from me to Dylan to Deb to Marcus and back again. And then, very suddenly, he lunges towards Deb.

She lets out a squawk, recoiling. Dylan shouts, a sort of *hey*, and he's moving forward, arm outstretched to shove Rodney, but Rodney's too fast. He's snatched the car key from Deb's lap and he's already ducked past Dylan.

Marcus is the first to react when Rodney starts running. But Rodney's long, gangly legs are coming in useful – he's *fast*. Marcus only manages to snag the end of Rodney's T-shirt between his fingers before Rodney slips from his grasp, leaving Marcus staggering into a stack of bourbon biscuits.

I'm running before I've even thought about it. I can hear Deb swearing behind me as I push through the glass doors of the service station, and I'm with her, it *is* annoying to be plugged into a wall expressing breast milk when everyone else is chasing a potential criminal across a petrol station forecourt.

'Go on, get him!' she yells, like Delia Smith at a Norwich City match. 'Go on!'

Dylan is closest – my legs are too bloody short for this, and Marcus is tangled up somewhere back there in a heap of chocolate biscuits. I dodge a woman coming to pay for her petrol – 'Oi!' she yells – and duck between cars. Rodney's just metres from the Mini. Dylan is a few steps behind him, and he gets to him just as he opens the door, but Rodney turns as he gets in and shoves Dylan backwards, right into . . .

Me. We stumble backwards on to the bonnet of the car behind. The alarm goes off. The back of Dylan's head cracks into my collarbone with a dull, painful thud and my sprained wrist hurts so much I feel as if my hand must have fallen off. I roll free from under Dylan's body and I look up just in time to see Rodney driving off, in our car, with all our belongings.

'I knew it was a mistake to leave the dastardly planning to you ladies,' Marcus says from behind us. I can only just hear him over the alarm of the car we fell on. I turn to look at him. He's doubled over, bracing his hands on his thighs.

As I turn and watch the Mini's erratic path along the A7, the pain of my wrist comes rushing back. I let out a gasp and bend over, cradling my arm. Dylan's hand is on my back. By the time I've blinked away the tears and looked up again, Deb is here. Her outfit is once again stained with breast milk and her expression is thunderous.

'My cool bag was in that car,' she says, and somehow her voice cuts over the sound of the car alarm, no trouble. 'Now where the hell am I meant to store this?'

She waves a bottle of breast milk at us. We blink back at her.

'Next time,' she says, stalking back towards the petrol station, 'run *faster*.'

*

Everyone is grouchy. We don't talk for a while. Marcus pays for all the biscuits he crushed, and we just sit there next to the newspapers outside the shop, eating broken bourbons in the small patch of shade.

'At least we know where he's going,' Dylan points out, sipping his coffee. Thank God all of us had our phones and wallets in pockets. I think after Deb's experience yesterday nobody will ever leave their mobile in the car again.

'So what do we do now? Call the police?' I ask, pulling a face.

'That'll take for ever,' Deb says. 'Waiting for them, witness statements . . . I say we just catch him ourselves. Like Dylan says, it's not like we won't be able to find him.'

'But your car!' I say.

Deb waves a hand. 'We'll get it back. We just need to find a way to get to the wedding.'

'Can't we order a cab?' Marcus says.

'How far away are we?' I ask.

There is a long silence, until we all realise it was Rodney who used to do the directions. I pull up Google Maps on my phone and make a face.

'An hour and a half of driving. And it's a bank holiday weekend. That's going to cost a fortune, assuming we can even get a cab here within the next . . .' I check the time and whimper. 'Oh, God, we're going to miss the wedding if the cab takes longer than half an hour to get here.'

Deb calls as many local cab services as she can find. Nobody can get here sooner than an hour. We are not surprised by this. I'd say we're basically unsurprisable by now.

We sit in silence again. Every minute counts, obviously, but somehow all I have the energy to do is eat bourbons and cradle my sore wrist. I think I've felt a record number of emotions in the last twenty-four hours.

'There is *one* other option,' Deb says after a while. 'It's a long shot, though.'

'We're desperate,' I say. 'Long shots are all we're going to get.'

'Did anyone save Kevin the trucker's phone number?' Deb says. 'Because that man drives *fast*.'

Dylan

I'm not entirely convinced Kevin the trucker is a real person. I think he may be a special wedding-day sprite – no, hang on, goblin – who is sent to wedding guests in their time of need.

He was at the services within twenty-five minutes, and we are now somewhere between Carlisle and Ettrick, going at a speed that I am convinced should not be possible in a vehicle of this weight and size.

We have quickly learned that lorry cabs are not very spacious; Addie and I considered riding in the back with the chairs, but then realised once the doors shut, it would be pitch-black, and we might get impaled by a chair leg when Kevin went around a corner, and this would be an *extremely* bad time to die. So instead, all four of us are occupying the two passenger seats beside Kevin: Deb is sitting on Marcus's lap, and Addie is sitting on mine.

This is exquisite torture. Every time the lorry jolts, she bounces a little on my lap; I am trying to concentrate extremely hard on the presence of Marcus and Addie's sister beside me, but Addie is so close I can taste her perfume, I can hear the slight hitch in her breath when she feels my hardness under her, and—

'You try having a baby,' Deb tells Marcus. 'And see how heavy *you* get.'

'Never been much interested in babies, myself,' Marcus says, grimacing as Deb shifts on his thighs. 'Where did you even get yours from, anyway? You're single, clearly.'

He's trying to act normal, but I know him too well to buy it; his voice is reedy and he looks exhausted.

'Contrary to popular opinion, you can acquire a baby without also acquiring a life partner,' Deb says.

Marcus makes an *oh, really?* sound, an effort at interest. I stare at the fine threads of Addie's hair in front of my nose and try not to imagine how it'll feel between my fingers.

'I used a sperm bank,' Deb explains. 'I did think about asking a friend, but . . .' She shrugs. 'I didn't want it to get complicated.'

'Love a sperm bank,' says Marcus. 'Great way to get a little booze money once Dad and India cut me off. I was in and out of the Chichester one like a bloody boomerang. So, how far away are we?' he asks Kevin, while Deb absorbs that particularly terrifying piece of news. 'Could do with getting there before my legs go completely numb.'

'It's this turn-off,' Kevin says, checking his satnav. 'We're fifteen minutes away.'

Fifteen minutes. I can cope with another fifteen minutes.

We hit a pothole and I close my eyes, trying not to groan.

'You're our hero,' Addie tells Kevin as he pulls into the large car park. 'Thank you. Will you come and join the party?'

'D'you think I could?' Kevin says, breaking into one of his particularly alarming grimace-smiles.

I'm finding Kevin very useful right now; Addie has just climbed out of my lap and down to floor level, and before I move into a standing position I am going to need to spend the next few moments concentrating on Kevin's grimace.

'I'm sure Krish and Cherry wouldn't mind,' I say, immediately realising that they absolutely, definitely would.

'I warned Cherry about the situation, by the way,' Deb says, still perched in Marcus's lap.

'What!' Addie and I say in unison.

Deb turns bemused eyes our way. 'What?'

'Didn't she totally panic?'

'It was a text. Hard to tell,' she says, handing me her phone. 'You know what Cherry's like with the exclamation marks.'

Addie pulls a face as I climb down from the cab and show her the message. It starts with a string of emojis, followed by:

Call me as soon as you get here!!! And HURRY UP!!!!

'I think she might have panicked a smidgen,' Addie says.

'The Mini is in the car park,' Marcus says, pointing. 'Looks like Rodney's parked up and gone inside.'

Addie swears.

'What now?' I ask.

'Break into the Mini so we can change?' Marcus says, looking down at his clothes with distaste. 'I can't turn up at a wedding looking like this.'

Addie rolls her eyes. 'We need to get to the venue and find Rodney before he does any damage. If we're not already too late.'

'Gah,' Marcus says, but he follows us as we head out of the car park.

There are signs directing us to the wedding venue itself; they are all intricately hand-drawn with curling calligraphy and watercolour explosions of fireworks at their edges. It takes about a minute of following the trail to clear the towering pine trees around the car park, and as soon as we do, we let out a collective gasp.

Above us is an enormous, ornate castle. It's definitely not a genuine castle – or rather, it's a castle, but when it was built, nobody was thinking about defending this area from marauders – but it's so impressive it doesn't matter. There are turrets with flags flying, there's a thickly flowering vine climbing up almost as high as the battlements, and there's a moat complete with drawbridge.

We cross the water in stunned silence. We all knew Cherry and Krish were planning a large and fairly extravagant wedding, but this is something else.

There are guests already milling on the vivid green lawn at the front of the castle, a cacophony of colour: elaborate headpieces and hats, full-length ballgowns, saris and lehengas. Beside me, Addie looks down at herself, as if just remembering that she's still in the same white dress she put on this morning, with a shirt collar and a belt at the waist.

'Shit,' she mutters. 'It had to be white, didn't it?'

I scan the crowd for any sign of Rodney, but there are scores of people here already, perhaps hundreds, and I don't know what he'll be wearing. He could easily have changed into his suit, given that he had access to the entire contents of the Mini. Or he could be in Deb's pyjamas, come to that.

'Addie!' comes a voice from behind us.

We all spin. The synchrony is becoming uncanny. I think it must be the two days of poor air conditioning and endless country music: we are united now, as one, having breathed the same stale air for so many hours.

'Yeah?' Addie says, bewildered. Nobody nearby seems to be looking at us. We're near the building, right by a flowerbed overflowing with pink and purple flowers and . . . something . . . white.

'Addie,' I say, pointing to the offending patch of white fabric just visible behind a large bush.

'Addie! Get back here!' the voice hisses.

It's Cherry. She's in full wedding dress with her hair in pins; for a brief moment her face pokes out from behind the bush, eyes wide, cheeks rosy.

We all crowd in around her. Cherry scans us with the expression of a woman who does not have the mental energy to absorb anything that isn't immediately relevant to the crisis at hand – she barely even blinks as she registers the presence of the burly lorry driver beside Deb, and the large, technicolour bruising around Marcus's nose.

'Well? Where's Rodney?' she hisses. 'Is he here?'

'Happy wedding day,' I say, leaning to kiss her on the cheek and getting a faceful of leaves. 'How are you?'

'Insane,' she says. 'I'm insane. Don't ever get married, Dylan. It turns you into a monster.'

'OK, noted,' I say, trying very hard not to look at Addie. 'Listen, we haven't found Rodney *just* yet, but . . .'

Cherry groans, burying her face in her hands.

'Don't worry! We're on it!' I say, as Addie plucks a leaf out of Cherry's hair. 'Can you give us any clues as to what he might be planning? Given what you know about him?'

'I don't know him! I just slept with him! Once!'

'That hardly counts,' Deb says kindly.

'He likes romantic gestures, though, right? Hence the poems and stuff,' Addie says. 'Don't you think he'll try and find you before the ceremony? To change your mind?'

'Why do you think I'm in this fucking flowerbed?' Cherry says. 'This is Vivienne Westwood, you know. And *that's* bird poo,' she says, pointing to a leaf bobbing perilously close to her dress. Her hand is covered in beautiful, intricate henna art, ready for today's wedding ceremony.

'We need to lure him out,' says Marcus. 'And then pounce.'

He demonstrates pouncing. Cherry jumps.

'Where would he expect you to be?' Addie asks.

'I'm *meant* to be having my hair done in the bridal preparation chamber,' she says.

'That sounds unpleasant,' Deb says.

'Yeah, I think they went for "chamber" because of the castle vibe,' Cherry says, waving a vague hand at the battlements above us. 'But it's a bit unfortunate, isn't it, with all the torture associations?'

'So let's go there,' Marcus says. 'We'll hide, jump out on him . . .'

'And tie him up!' Deb finishes triumphantly.

Addie and I look at each other. The tying-up plan is sounding like quite a good one, presently, which I think shows how far we have all fallen. I have a feeling that if this journey had been any longer, it would have become progressively more *Lord of the Flies*, and Marcus probably would have eaten somebody.

'Addie? Dyl?' comes a voice from behind us.

Cherry squeals and ducks down again. 'Get him away from me! Get him away!'

'Cherry! It's just Krish,' Addie says, as we turn.

Krish lifts his hand in a slightly bemused wave. He's dressed in a traditional wedding sherwani, and looks magnificent in its golds and deep reds. 'Are you all all right?' He cranes his head. 'Is . . . Cherry? Is that you?'

'You can't see me! It's our wedding day!' she calls. 'Go away!'

Krish starts to laugh. 'What are you doing in a bush?'

'Last-minute crisis,' Deb says.

'Nothing for you to worry about,' Addie says, as Krish's grin drops. 'All under control.' She tucks a corner of Cherry's wedding dress behind her.

'You go mingle,' she says, waving a hand at Krish. 'We'll just . . . sort . . . things.'

Krish's expression turns suspicious. 'Is this very bad?' he says. 'I'm getting very bad vibes.' His eyes settle on Kevin and his frown deepens.

I straighten up and pat him on the arm. 'Absolutely not,' I say. 'You go and enjoy your special day.'

He is still looking unconvinced. I glance over his shoulder.

'Oh,' I say. 'Is that your grandparents? Talking to Mad Bob?'

Krish's eyes widen. Mad Bob makes Marcus look like the picture of restraint: he is known for compulsively undressing every time he has more than three drinks, and has been arrested so many times he couldn't get a job even if he needed to, which he doesn't, because he's just inherited half of Islington.

That gets rid of Krish. But it also draws my attention to something that, in all the excitement and stress and joy, I had genuinely forgotten I'd have to confront today.

My father is making his way towards us across the grass. Dressed in white tie, he looks as severe and sharp-cut as his top hat; there are new harsh lines on his face, scores on either side of his nose, blueish bags beneath his eyes. My mum's nowhere to be seen, which is unusual – she's generally by my father's side – and her absence makes my stomach turn. It's always safer if my mum's here too.

'Oh my God, is that . . .' Addie begins. 'Shall we go? Let you talk?'

I reach for her as she moves to walk away. 'No,' I say firmly, but my heart is racing. 'Stay with me – please. Deb, get Cherry back inside, and take Kevin, would you?'

'On it,' Deb says. 'Come on, Cherry, mind the bird shit.'

Marcus moves to stand beside me; he's on my right, Addie's on my left. I can feel Addie looking at me uncertainly; her sore wrist is cradled at her chest, and I slide my hand into her free one, locking our fingers together.

'Dylan,' my father says.

I'm holding Addie's hand too tightly, but I can't seem to loosen my grip. I've thought of this moment often; I've imagined telling my father, *Look how well I've done without you*; I've imagined saying, *You know, you could have been kind, just once*. I've imagined telling him that I'll never forgive him for the way he's always treated Luke.

But now that I'm here, I'm afraid. The truth is, I *haven't* done well without him – not in his terms, at least. I'm still a part-time Masters student with a small but significant debt on my account; I'm single but in love with a woman who I hope has it in her heart to give me another chance. To him, I look like I'm still on pause – the lost boy wandering the world, weak-willed and daydreaming and achieving nothing.

'Who's this?' Dad says, eyes settling on Addie.

'This is Addie,' I say. My voice comes out in a squeak, and I clear my throat.

Addie lets go of my hand for a moment to shake my father's; he looks her up and down, and his expression is so blatantly critical that I start to tremble with a familiar quiet rage.

'I remember hearing about you,' Dad says as he shakes Addie's hand. 'Taken him back, have you?' He shoots a grin at Marcus. 'Joel told me you two had fallen out – you've done the same, then? Taken my son back?'

'It wasn't quite like that, Miles,' Marcus says, voice pleasant.

My father's eyebrows rise. 'No?'

'No. It wasn't so much a falling-out as a—'

'Fisticuffs, eh?' my father interrupts, nodding to the bruises on Marcus's face. 'But no. Can't have been my Dylan who punched you, he doesn't have it in him.'

Addie slips her hand into mine again.

'Would you just shut up, actually,' Marcus says, 'and let me speak?'

There is a vast, shocked silence. I look at Marcus, expecting to see that his mood has shifted with its usual irrational speed, but it's not that, he's not angry: he's clearly trying hard not to cry.

'Your dad needs to know what sort of man you are, Dylan.'

Marcus is hardly ever serious, not *really* serious; there's always the suggestion he might just be taking the piss, or winding you up, or playing a part that'll slide away in less than a minute. On the rare occasions when he really cares about what he's saying, his voice is completely different – smoother and less drawling. It's like that now.

'I did things that Dylan hated – I ruined the best thing in his life – but he didn't give me up for good.' He's looking at my father, unblinking. 'He's always shown me that all I need to do to be worthy of his friendship is to try. And to say sorry.'

'Marcus . . .'

He looks at me and Addie.

'And I am. Sorry. I'm not good at saying it, but I'm trying with that too.'

'This is all rather dramatic,' my dad says with distaste, as I turn towards Marcus and meet his eyes. They're wet and frightened, and somehow very bare.

I reach with my free arm to hug him but he steps away, shaking his head, not done.

'Do you know what an achievement it is, to turn out that way growing up in your house?' Marcus says to my father, straightening up. He meets my dad's gaze like it's no effort at all, like he isn't even frightened. 'Do you know what it takes to be a good man when someone's *always* told you you're not good enough?'

My father stiffens. 'Marcus,' he says warningly.

I know that tone; it turns me cold.

'No, I know what you're about to say, and fuck your job,' Marcus says, swiping an arm across his face. 'I'll find something else. I'm not working for you when you're still looking at Dylan like that. When you still treat Luke like he's *less.* Christ. What a spineless, bigoted bully you are.'

My father's eyes flash and it makes my throat tighten instantly, like the air's thickened, clogging in the back of my mouth. He takes a step towards Marcus; Addie and I withdraw, and I hear her breathe in sharply, but Marcus doesn't even flinch. He laughs.

'Well,' he says. 'I'll leave you to get to know Addie.'

Marcus turns to meet Addie's eyes. He looks very tired, but that fire's still there even now, that quintessential Marcus energy that never quite runs dry.

'She's a better person than you or I could ever be,' he says, 'and Dylan's lucky to have her.'

Addie

I don't know what to do with myself. My eyes are pricking with tears. Dylan's holding my hand so tight it aches as we watch Marcus walk away, his shoulders hunched. *She's a better person than you or I could ever be.*

I've carried all that crap Marcus said about me for so long. How I wasn't good for Dylan. As if I had something bad in me, like I was holding a live grenade. It tainted me even before Etienne tried to break me.

Now I think he was right, in his way. I could have hurt Dylan a thousand ways, and sometimes I came close – sometimes my foot slipped. Back then, when we all met, I could have been that woman, and maybe that woman would have loved a man like Marcus. Maybe that woman would have kissed Etienne back.

But I know who I am, now. I'm the woman who holds Dylan's hand tight and looks up at the father he was always too afraid to introduce me to. The man whose contempt for the two of us is drawn on every grey inch of his face.

'Well,' I say to Miles Abbott. 'I don't expect we'll be seeing a lot of each other, unless you're going to take a leaf out of Marcus's book and ask for your son's forgiveness. But it's been a pleasure to see you. As in, it's been a pleasure to see you get totally demolished.' I flash him a grin, then turn to Dylan. 'Come on, Dyl. We've got a wedding crasher to catch.'

Dylan's shaking as we wind our way through the corridors in search of the bridal preparation chamber. He tries calling his brother, but Luke doesn't pick up, and that seems to make Dylan's shaking even worse.

'Hey, you're OK,' I say, pausing for a moment. Our hands are still linked. 'You did it. You saw him and walked away.'

He draws his free hand across his forehead, eyes drawn tight. 'I didn't even say anything.'

'You didn't have to. Staying quiet is powerful too, especially since he was *clearly* expecting you to come to him cap in hand.' I squeeze his fingers between mine. 'Marcus and I have your back. And maybe next time you will say something, if you want to – maybe you guys will figure it out, the way you and Marcus are doing.'

He leans back against the wall, and finally loosens his grip on my fingers, letting our palms slip apart. 'Does it bother you?' he asks quietly. 'That I . . . that I let Marcus back into my life after what he did?'

I think hard. It's too important a question to brush over, though that's my instinct at first.

'Maybe tell me how it happened. After . . .' I swallow. 'After Etienne.'

Dylan's eyes soften as I say his name. He reaches out to me. 'May I?' he says gently.

The corridor around us is huge, with a big arched ceiling and pink wallpapered walls, but the world suddenly feels small. Like it's just me and Dylan. I step towards him and he folds me in, hugging me close. I can feel his cheek resting on the top of my head. The happiness is seeping into me in every place we're touching – my crown, my chest, my stomach.

'After I left you, I couldn't get out of bed for a very long time.'

I pull back to look at him but he keeps me against his chest, so I relax again in his arms. My sore wrist hangs at my side, but the other arm is wrapped around him tightly.

'I was ... it was depression,' he says. 'When Marcus finally got me to the doctor, that's what they said.'

'You've suffered from that before,' I say into his chest. I hear his heartbeat quicken against my ear. 'Before we met. And when you were travelling. And sometimes ... it came for you, didn't it, when we were together?'

'I didn't – I thought ...'

'I knew when you got lost, Dylan. I know you. I was just too – too – I don't know. Too scared, I think, to talk to you about it.'

'Scared of what?' he whispers, cheek shifting against my hair.

'Showing you how much I cared, maybe. It freaked me out that there were parts of you I couldn't reach, but Marcus could.'

'He was there the first time, when I was a teenager,' Dylan says, voice low. 'He and Luke looked after me. My dad ...'

'Didn't.'

'No,' Dylan says ruefully. 'He didn't. That's caused me some issues, clearly.'

'So Marcus looked after you? When we broke up?'

'Not at first. I wouldn't let him in. I hated him, and I couldn't even tell him the truth about you, so he still thought you were – that you'd cheated on me, and ... I couldn't bear to be with him. I blamed him completely, at first, for me losing you. But in the end he just broke in. Dragged me out of bed, took me straight to the doctors and got me anti-depressants and CBT and therapy.' I feel him smile. 'I went to the counselling on the condition that he'd go see a therapist too. During that time, Marcus did some more stupid things – turned up on Grace's doorstep and yelled all sorts of nastiness at her, punched Javier—'

'Punched *Javier*? What for?' I say, shifting my head to look up at him in shock.

Dylan rolls his eyes. 'I think Marcus was acting out because the therapy was digging up things he couldn't cope with, personally. But yes, Javier and Luke were having an argument about something and Marcus got involved.'

'Bloody hell.'

'I know. So I cut him off. My therapist said she thought it would help, and . . . it did, for both of us, I think. So for the last year, Marcus and I haven't spoken. Not until I called him and asked if he wanted to travel to the wedding together.'

'Because you heard . . .'

'Everyone was saying it. *He's changing. He's trying.* He apologised to almost everyone – just me and Grace left. Well. And you.'

I smile slightly. 'I'm not sure I have your knack for forgiveness. I think it'll take me a while to . . .'

He presses his lips to the top of my head. 'Of course. I'd understand if you never wanted him back in your life. Of course I would.'

I shift away from him for a moment. It feels so good to be in his arms, but—

'We should . . .'

'Yes. Right. Rodney.'

When we eventually find the bridal preparation chamber, it doesn't look very torturous. One wall is covered in satin roses, floor to ceiling, and the others are decked out in the same expensive-looking pink wallpaper from the corridor. Everything is ornate. This is kind of how I imagine Marie Antoinette lived.

It's *so* Cherry. She comes to greet us in a billow of white satin and perfume.

'Come in! Come in! Help!' she says.

'Can I start now?' the hairdresser asks Cherry. 'The ceremony is in half an hour and I don't want to panic you, but normally I like to do hair before the bride puts on her dress, and you still need to speak to the registrar, and . . .'

'Don't worry,' Cherry says, 'I'm already at peak panic.' She sits down with a sigh and a flurry of fabric. Her dress is amazing: a pure white ballgown, corseted to her body at the waist, with enormous petals of satin blossoming around the bust, and her shoulders left bare. There's a red sari carefully folded on the table behind her, covered in countless gems and woven through with ornate gold thread. I run a gentle finger along its hem. It's *beautiful.*

'For the party,' Cherry says, watching me. 'Isn't it gorgeous? Krish's mum had it made for me.'

It's the calmest she's sounded all day. I should have realised fashion was the way to chill Cherry out.

'Have you got anything I could borrow to wear?' I ask her.

Behind me, Marcus, Deb, Kevin and Dylan debate the best way to tie a man up when you only have wedding table runners to work with. Dylan shoots me a quick smile when he catches me looking at him. He claps Marcus on the shoulder, one of those manly hug-type gestures guys do when they can't talk about their feelings.

Cherry's eyes focus on me. 'Oh, God, yeah, you *can't* wear that!' she says, horrified. 'Go into the bathroom, my honeymoon suitcase is in there. I'll help.'

'No,' the hairdresser says, then looks surprised at her own assertiveness. She fidgets nervously on the spot. 'Sorry. I just mean, can you sit still and let me take your rollers out? Please?'

Cherry harrumphs but sits back down. 'Try the bright blue dress, Ads,' she says. 'And give Deb the little red number, if she wants to pull tonight.'

'I do,' Deb calls, testing the tightness of a knot as she does so. 'Krishna promised me single men.'

'Bucketloads,' Cherry says, as the hairdresser begins to undo her rollers. 'The place is seething with them – that red dress will be like blood in the water. Ooh, that simile was surprisingly graphic. Who are you, by the way?'

'Kevin,' Kevin supplies. 'Hi. Happy wedding day. Thanks for having me.'

'God, you totally can't be here, we're already over the health and safety regulation numbers and we've definitely not got enough food. Addie? Does the blue work?'

I've barely got to the suitcase yet. This bathroom is about the size of my parents' living room, with a claw-foot tub sitting beneath an enormous window. The floor is grey flagstones. Cherry's suitcase is abandoned beside the shower, tilted on its side. It's big enough that I could comfortably get in it and go to Thailand with them both on their honeymoon.

'Am I meant to be leaving?' I hear Kevin mutter to someone on the other side of the door.

'Nah,' Deb says. 'I don't think she really meant it. Just try to look less conspicuous. Put on a top hat or something.'

'Well?' Cherry calls. 'Addie?'

'One second!' I shout, scrabbling through the suitcase.

I go still when I reach the blue dress. It's not just a blue dress, it's . . . *art*. Spaghetti straps, satin. There's something a little nineties about the style – it reminds me of the dress Julia Stiles wears to prom in *10 Things I Hate About You*.

I slip out of my white dress and slide into the blue gown. The sheath style would cling to Cherry's curves, but it tumbles past mine without hardly noticing. I love that. It's full length on me, too, where it'd be midi length on Cherry.

'The barely-there silver heels!' Cherry yells through the door, before I've even asked the question.

I pull them on with difficulty, trying not to tug with my injured hand. These shoes are too big for me and they're going to hurt like hell, but right now I don't care. I feel fierce and bright and beautiful. Obviously ideally I'd have had time for a shower, but still.

I open the bathroom door just as somebody knocks at the door to the bridal suite. We all freeze. Dylan's eyes flick to mine, and the air goes hot between us. I remember how it felt that summer in France. I almost *feel* the Provence sun, hear the crickets. Dylan's eyes are fiery. He's not looking at me like he's never seen me before – he's looking at me like he's never seen anyone else.

'Cherry!' Rodney calls through the door. 'Cherry, please open the door!'

Dylan's gaze snaps away from mine as Cherry stands and bundles everyone into the bathroom. I back in to give everyone space, and Deb carefully clicks the door closed behind her. My heart is beating too fast. I can't tell if it's the stalker outside the room, or Dylan being inside this one. I don't need to look at him to feel that tug between us. The link that never really broke.

'Talk to me, Cherry,' Rodney begs through the door. 'Please, let me in!'

We huddle by the door. Even Marcus looks serious. Deb and Kevin are between me and Dylan now, but I can still feel his gaze flicking towards me as we crouch, ears against the door.

Cherry lets Rodney into the room.

'You really shouldn't be here,' she says.

'How could I be anywhere else?'

Dylan's hand is on the doorknob, ready for us to burst out.

'I'm not going anywhere until you've realised this wedding is a mistake, Cherry!'

It's so over the top, like he thinks he's in a play. I'm not surprised to hear Cherry laugh.

'Rodney. Please. How on earth can you think that?'

'Does he really make you happy? Does he?'

'Nobody has ever come *close* to making me as happy as Krishna makes me,' Cherry says, more serious now. 'He is everything to me. I have never been in love like this. And Rodney – I have never been in love with you.'

There's movement. We brace. I think she's moved towards him, holding the door open, maybe?

'We belong together, Cherry!' Rodney says, sounding more desperate than ever. 'We're like – we're like Dylan and Addie!'

I startle. Everyone looks at me.

'Dylan lost Addie, but he didn't give up, and he got her back.'

The silence stretches for so long it hurts.

'Dylan never really lost Addie, Rodney. And you really never had me. It's not the same.'

'I'm not letting you do it,' Rodney says. 'I'll – I'll – I'll . . . stand here, in this doorway! For ever!'

'Oh, for God's sake,' Deb says, full volume. 'We don't have time for this shit.'

She opens the door and we all tumble through.

'Hey!' Rodney yells as we bear down on him. Dylan gets him by one arm, Kevin by the other.

'Come on, Rodney, sit yourself down,' Marcus says, reaching for the chair.

'What are you doing!'

'Tying you up,' Deb says.

'What!'

Rodney starts to struggle. He's surprisingly strong. Me, Deb and Marcus all move in to help Dylan and Kevin. I'm not really adding much value. I feel a bit like the extra person trying to get involved in moving furniture: holding on to a side, not really taking any of the weight.

Somehow, with an awful lot of *oofs* and swear words and kicks and dodged fists, we get Rodney sat down and tied up.

'I can't believe you're doing this,' he says, staring down at his tied wrists and ankles in amazement. 'This is ridiculous!'

'Good, isn't it?' Marcus says, tightening the knot on Rodney's left ankle. 'Never done *this* before.'

'What if I scream and someone comes to save me?' Rodney says, yanking at his wrists.

'Hmm, good point,' Deb says. 'Shall we gag him?'

We all stare at her.

'I won't scream,' Rodney says quickly. 'I'll just sit here.'

'You could listen to an audiobook,' Kevin suggests. 'They really help to pass the time on long drives.'

'He's not a very fearsome villain, is he?' Cherry says, inspecting Rodney. She's stayed out of the fray to protect her dress. 'If I was going to have a man try to stop me from getting married on my wedding day, I wouldn't choose Rodney. No offence, Rodney.'

Rodney looks wounded. 'I still love you,' he says. 'Though maybe a *bit* less now,' he adds, looking down at his tied-up ankles.

Cherry pats him on the head. 'You don't love me, Rodney, but you *do* have some issues you should probably examine when this is all over. Marcus, download him an audiobook, will you? His phone's in his pocket, make sure you leave it out of reach. All good, everyone? Addie? I'd better go meet the registrar.'

'Hang on.' I reach for a pen and paper on the dressing table and scribble a message.

Keep out! This room is reserved for the bride and groom, wink wink!

'Don't want anyone discovering the hostage in here.' I stick it to the outside of the door. 'Right. Go get married then.' I kiss Cherry on the cheek.

She beams at us all, and then notices the hairdresser gawping at us from the corner.

Hmm. Forgot about the hairdresser.

'Sorry,' Cherry says, giving her a bright smile. 'Exes, you know?'

Dylan

Krish and Cherry have their ceremony up on the roof of the castle; the battlements are adorned with waterfalls of intricately arranged flowers, and behind it all stretches an endless, azure sky. The wind touches the shining satin of Cherry's dress as her father leads her down the aisle, his face twisted with emotion. He beams tearfully at Krish when he kisses Cherry's cheek and lets her go, but Krish isn't looking: his eyes are on Cherry, and they're wide and bright with wonder. He loves her the way I love Addie, you can just see it in his face.

Krish and Cherry decided on a shortened, adapted version of the traditional Hindu ceremony. There's a small fire carefully laid within a circle of flints at the end of the aisle, beneath a tall arch of greenery and roses, and the pandit patiently translates everything he can from Sanskrit to English as puffed rice and spices are thrown into its orange flames.

I weep like a baby when Krish reverently bows his head and Cherry lays a garland of bright flowers around his neck, then dips her head so he can do the same. By the time they finish their seven ceremonial rounds of the fire, their wrists tied with a ribbon of deep red silk, there are tears dripping off my chin.

'You are a hopeless romantic,' Addie whispers to me as I wipe my cheeks.

I open my mouth to answer.

'I'm so glad that's not changed,' she says, and there's that cannon-fire explosion in my chest again. The poem I began almost four hundred miles ago is still growing, and as Addie smiles at me I decide that the words *unchanged and changed* will come back as a riff, a motif, like the same wish you make every time you blow out candles or lose an eyelash.

The wedding dinner is a feast of countless curries, and the desserts are piled on enormous tables like jewels spilling from treasure chests, balanced in overflowing piles: mango barfi and fig halwa heaped beside strawberry truffles and miniature jars of feather-light white-chocolate mousse. The fact that Cherry didn't think they'd have enough food for Kevin is absolutely laughable.

Our table is by far the most raucous, mainly thanks to Kevin. For the first few hours he followed Deb around with pining eyes; then he was introduced to my uncle Terry, and the two of them instantly formed what appears to be a very intense and sudden bromance. Deb's been entirely forgotten; Terry and Kevin are currently doing shots and slapping one another on the back, laughing so loudly even Marcus is wincing. I'm pretty sure Terry isn't meant to be on our table, but then, neither is Kevin, I suppose – the meticulously organised seating plan has clearly gone to pot.

It's all undeniably heart-warming. But it's nothing compared to the feeling of being near Addie. She's across the table from me, but our eyes keep meeting over the enormous centrepiece, and every time it happens there's a little spark lit in my stomach, as though we're touching hands, not just meeting each other's eyes. I'm so busy staring at her across the table I don't notice Cherry approaching until she waves a hand in front of my face.

'Hello!' she says. 'Bride here!'

'Oh, sorry, hi,' I say, swivelling to look at her as she ducks down beside me. 'You got married!'

'I know! Wild! Hey, have you seen your brother?'

I've been worrying about Luke too. 'No, nor Javier.'

Cherry makes a thoughtful face. 'Huh. Maybe they messaged – my phone's in Krish's pocket.'

I check my mobile – still nothing from Luke, even though I've called him a few times now. I frown.

'Can I ask you a favour?' Cherry says.

'Of course. Name it.' I slip my phone back in my pocket.

'Will you and Ads go collect my sari and Krish's tux? They're in the room with Rodney and I *might* have mentioned to Krishna that we tied a stalker up in that room and now he's being delightfully domineering and telling me I am absolutely not allowed to go in there. But we want to change into our evening outfits, and we need a good lead-time, because I can*not* get into that sari without Krish's mum's help.'

I choose not to point out that it is clearly not a two-person task to collect two garments from a room, and instead lean forward to give my friend a kiss on the forehead.

'Yes,' I tell her. 'Thank you.'

'No rush,' Cherry says, winking at me. 'Oh, and maybe take Rodney a plate of food? What, why are you giving me that face? Not even a pudding?'

'You should be organising a restraining order for the man, not dessert,' I tell her, and she pouts.

'Nobody's irredeemable, Dylan!' she says, and she reaches over to ruffle Marcus's hair as she stands. Her dress billows around her.

'Excuse me,' Marcus says, leaning back. 'Please don't equate me with that sniffling excuse for a human being.'

'You're right,' Cherry says cheerfully over her shoulder as she heads for the next table. 'You were a much *sexier* creepy stalker man. Sexier and drunker. That's totally better!'

Marcus scowls and sinks down lower in his seat as the guests around us glance his way with interest. 'Ugh,' he says.

Deb leans in from the other side of me.

'Welcome to the standard system of morality, *darling*,' she says, pinching the last champagne chocolate truffle from Marcus's plate.

I look across the floor of the wedding breakfast, scanning for Luke and Javier – and my mother, come to think of it. Instead I spot a woman dressed in a dramatic yellow gown who is making her way over from another table of Cherry's friends; her hair is dyed pale purple, and her strapless dress shows off the rose tattoo on her shoulder. Grace.

'I feel . . .' Marcus gnaws at his lip.

'Guilty?' I suggest, looking back to him.

'Ugh,' he says.

'Ashamed?'

'Stop it,' he says, scrubbing his hands over his face. 'You sound like my therapist. What is the *upside* of this reforming lark?'

I glance back at Grace. She's had quite the journey of her own these last two years. A stint in rehab, a spiritual awakening, a bruised heart. It's changed her. Gone is the woman who sabotages the rare moments when she feels complete; never again will Grace settle for less than the whole heart of a man she loves.

But she's still Grace – she's still wearily glamorous, still a little too intense, still smarter than the rest of us put together. And her eyes are on Marcus, the way they always have been, even as she tried to make other love stories work for her. Even as Marcus's eyes were so often drawn to Addie. She never stopped looking at him that way. She never gave up on him, not completely.

'Dylan?' Marcus prompts me. 'Come on. What's the *point*?'

'I think, if you're very lucky, you might be about to find out,' I say.

Addie

'We've been in this corridor before,' I say, spinning around. 'I remember that portrait.'

I point to an old guy in a crown framed on the wall.

'Really?' Dylan tilts his head to the side. 'I'm fairly certain that's John O'Gaunt, and I think the last one was Richard the Second.'

'I forgot how much *stuff* you know,' I say, laughing. 'Well, left or right?'

'All entirely useless knowledge, I can assure you. Left,' Dylan says, already heading down the left-hand corridor.

I smile. He catches my expression.

'What?'

'Two years ago you'd have asked me to decide,' I tell him, as we make our way down a corridor I am one hundred per cent certain we've been down before. Not that I'm complaining. Getting lost is pretty much perfect right now.

'You always pushed me to make my own choices,' Dylan says, falling into step beside me. 'I never really noticed it until we were apart.'

His hand brushes mine and I take the chance to interlace our fingers. Holding hands is as far as we've got, like a pair of Year Sevens. The thought makes me smile. He looks so handsome – he and Marcus recovered their tuxedos from the car once we'd got the keys off Rodney, and the sight of Dylan in a tux is doing dangerous things to my imagination.

'Before you, I'd always had my father, or Marcus. Someone to tell me what to do,' Dylan says, rubbing his thumb across the back of my hand as we walk. We couldn't be walking much slower – clearly he's no more keen than I am to get these chocolate truffles to Rodney.

'And now?'

'Now I have a therapist to tell me what to do,' he says wryly, and I laugh. 'No, I'm getting there. I've built a life for myself. I'm working on my Masters dissertation; I moved into a little shoebox flat on Cooper Street.'

I've wondered so many times where he's living. Imagined bumping into him in Bishop's Palace Garden or having a drink at the Duke & Rye. Thought about how it would feel to stand in the same room as him again, wondered if I'd be able to do it without bursting into tears.

'I want to hear all about your dissertation,' I say. 'Will I understand the title?'

'I hope so, or I'm doing it wrong.' He smiles. 'I'm writing about the idea of the quest in Spenser's *The Faerie Queene* and the works of Philip Sidney. Journeys. Oh, hey, there's the door!'

Dylan points to a door with a note stuck on it in my handwriting. We have somehow managed to make our way to the bridal preparation chamber. We both hesitate slightly outside the door, and Dylan shoots me a look.

'Do you want . . . a minute? Before we go in?'

There's a sofa underneath the window to our left, a love seat. We sit down together, knees dialling towards one another. I don't let go of his hand.

'I want to ask . . .' Dylan clears his throat. He's looking down at our linked hands, our knees just touching. 'If you're able – if you want to tell me – what happened after I left, after we broke up . . .'

My eyes begin to prick and I steady my breathing carefully, but my heart is beating too fast already.

'I'm sorry,' Dylan says quickly. 'I just – I want you to know I want to talk about it. When you're ready. It kills me that I couldn't be there for you through that, and I . . .' He looks at me helplessly. 'I'm sorry.'

'I know.' I squeeze his hand. 'I left the school. I guess that's not a surprise. I have a new job now – you know the girls' school over Fishbourne way? Yeah, there. It's good, you know. *I'm* good.' I grin. 'I wasn't at first, but I am now.'

'You wouldn't have said *that* two years ago,' Dylan says, knocking his knee gently against mine.

'Well, I have the *World's Best Teacher* mug to prove it these days.' I sober. 'I tried dating. Jamie, actually – one of the teachers from Barwood.'

I hate how my voice still catches on the name of Etienne's school, and I push on as I feel my face heating. Dylan is very still.

'It was . . . a mess. He was a weird choice – another teacher from Barwood – I don't know. There was clearly something weird going on in my brain with that. And he knew about what happened to me – I don't know how, but he did.'

'I saw Etienne was suspended,' Dylan says quietly. 'But you didn't press charges?'

'No, I tried,' I say, arching an eyebrow. 'The police said there wasn't enough evidence. But there was enough for Moira to make sure the school got rid of him. She was . . . she was good to me.'

'And . . . Jamie?' Dylan says with difficulty.

'He was sweet.' I squeeze Dylan's hand. 'But there was never – it never really got anywhere. And it turns out sex after – what happened . . .'

My eyes are pricking again. Dylan moves a little closer, tentative, and then his arm is around me and I'm leaning against his shoulder. I laugh shakily.

'Let's just say it doesn't go the way it used to.'

His arm squeezes me almost convulsively, like it hurts him to hear it. We sit for a moment. He takes a steadying breath.

'Well, last time around we started with sex, didn't we?' he says. 'So perhaps this time around we . . .' He trails off, realising what he's said.

I shift back so I can look at him. He's got that tight look around the eyes that means he's embarrassed, and I smile.

'This time?' I say.

'I didn't mean to jump the gun,' he says. His voice is low. 'But . . . Addie . . .'

I swallow. His hand comes up in that gesture I know so well, brushing his hair out of his eyes even though it's too short to ever come close now.

'Addie, will you think about it? I understand if you – but – I've never stopped loving you,' he says in a rush. 'I've never stopped loving you, and I really don't think I ever will, you know, because I tried all sorts to make it go away and I've never been able to stop it. And I understand completely if you can't take me back after what I did. But I so desperately want you to know that telling you I wouldn't listen to your side of the story was the worst thing I have ever done, Addie, and the thing that I most despise about myself, and that if you give me another chance, I will never, ever walk away from you again. I'll always listen. I'll never turn my back on you. I swear it.'

I let it sink in. Just close my eyes and hear the words he's saying, the shake in his voice. The way his hand clutches mine like he'll never let me go.

'You'd have to trust me,' I whisper, so quiet he ducks closer to hear me. 'And I'd have to . . . earn that.'

'I trust you,' he says immediately, but I shake my head.

'I'll show you,' I say. 'I'd never – what happened with Etienne – I mean, what happened before . . .' I take a shaky, frustrated breath. 'The flirting, the texts. It was so stupid. I think I was afraid of the power you had over me. How much I loved you, how much it hurt when you chose Marcus. Etienne was an out. Proof someone else would want me. It was . . .'

'It was then,' Dylan says, pulling me against him. 'And this is now.'

I cry then, my face pressed into the stiff cotton of his collar and the warmth of his skin. He holds me, and the sensation of his arms around me is almost more than I can bear.

I shouldn't be letting him see me like this, some part of my brain says. But I've come a long way in the last year. I know better than to listen to that voice.

'I love you,' I say through the tears. 'I loved you even when I hated you. I loved you even when I wanted to do *anything* else. Dylan, I can't . . .' I sob into his shoulder. 'I can't bear it, the idea of having you, this, us . . . I couldn't live through it if it ended again.'

He holds me even tighter. 'Then we won't let it.'

'I'm not . . . I'm not the person I was,' I tell him, my voice thick with tears. 'I'm so different now.'

'I am too. At least I bloody well hope I am,' he says, making me laugh. 'So we'll get to know each other again. We'll date. I'll take you for dinner. It won't be like last time because I'm very poor now, you know, so that'll help.'

I'm really laughing now, and I sit back, because I'm in danger of getting snot on his tuxedo. Dylan pulls off the napkin we wrapped around a few truffles for Rodney and hands it to me. I take it gratefully.

'Can you hear someone talking?' Dylan says, cocking his head.

I pause. He's right: there's a quiet voice coming from inside the bridal preparation chamber. I stand, moving towards the door to hear better.

'Though the sea, with waves continual, does eat the earth . . .'

Dylan comes to stand beside me, a smile growing on his face.

'What?' I whisper.

'It's the audiobook,' Dylan whispers back. 'Marcus chose him the worst book he could think of.'

'What's that?'

'*The Faerie Queene*,' Dylan says, grinning. 'He's listening to *The Faerie Queene*.'

I lean in and catch a line –

'For there is nothing lost that may be found if sought.'

Dylan

Rodney is in quite good spirits, considering, though in rather urgent need of what Deb would call an extreme-desperation break. Once we've seen to our captive and met Cherry and Krishna in the wedding suite to give them the clothes they need, Addie and I head back to the main hall through a labyrinth of corridors, our fingers still interlinked.

We've barely let each other go all day. Never again will I take for granted the feeling of Addie Gilbert holding my hand in hers.

When we reach our table, Grace is sitting in my seat, leaning towards Marcus, who's talking, eyes on the floor, visibly uncomfortable. Addie and I hang back for a moment, watching them before they clock us. It's so good to see Grace looking healthy again – even a year ago, with her sitting like that, I'd have been able to see the harsh ridges of her spine.

'Do you think she's getting her apology?' Addie says to me quietly.

'I hope so.'

'Do you think . . . Marcus and Grace . . . ?'

'I don't know. I don't know if he's ready, yet, or, you know . . . worthy of her.' I glance sideways at Addie, suddenly conscious that

I'm talking about a woman I once slept with, here, but she nods her agreement, forehead puckered in a frown that makes me want to press a kiss to the space between her brows.

Grace spots us then; she rises and hugs Addie first – *Darling*, she says, *you look divine* – and they exclaim over one another's dresses and new hair and slip into the easy conversation of friends who've spent too long apart.

'Oh, my book?' Grace says, tilting her chin back as she laughs. 'Burned. Quite literally.'

'*Burned?*' Addie says, eyes widening. 'But you've been writing that book for – for the whole time I've known you! And hey, you told me I was in chapter seven!'

Grace reaches to rest her hand against Addie's cheek. 'Adeline. You deserve to be chapter one.'

Addie starts to laugh. 'How does everything you say sound so profound?'

'Expensive education,' Grace says, with a languid smile. 'No, the book had to go. I shan't say I'll never write another, but *that* book was never really about the summer of our lives. It was all about a man. And once I'd realised that, I simply couldn't stand to look at it.'

Addie tugs her further away from the table, where Terry is now singing what sounds like some sort of sea shanty with Kevin.

'I tried reworking, restarting, everything,' Grace continues. 'But it was still *his book*.'

She lifts her chin ever so slightly towards Marcus.

'Ah,' Addie says.

'Quite,' says Grace, with a sigh. 'And he certainly hasn't earned a whole book to himself, has he? So I burned it. I thought it might help with the . . .' She waves a hand at her chest.

'The loving him?' Addie supplies.

'Yes,' Grace says heavily. 'That. Because I'm quite *sick* of loving a man who's really just an absolutely massive tosser.'

Addie burst out laughing. 'Did you tell him that?'

'Well, I was all ready to,' Grace says, 'and then he *apologised. Marcus.* I have to confess to you, Addie, I've imagined this moment countless times, *countless*, and then, just when I give up hope . . .'

'Wishing you could unburn the book now?' Addie asks.

Grace laughs, head back. 'No,' she says firmly. 'Certainly not. I'm a very different woman now, and if he wants to play the hero . . . he's going to have to audition.'

Addie grins at her. 'I've missed you,' she says, and I smile, because that candour, that unguarded affection, it's new to her – or rather, it's new to me.

'And I've missed you, my darling girl. And what about you two?' Grace asks, glancing at me. 'I thought that ship had sailed, but . . . ? Where are you now?'

Addie bites her lip. I lace our fingers tighter.

'We're at chapter one,' I say.

The sound of someone getting too close to a microphone – that low, wincing shriek – cuts across Grace's reply, but her smile says enough. There's a twelve-piece band setting up, and the tables nearest the dance floor are being cleared by an army of industrious people wearing the wedding colours; Krish's best man manages to stop the microphone shrieking for long enough to announce that it's time for the first dance.

Deb joins us as we make our way closer to the dance floor. She holds her phone out to Addie; there's a picture of Riley on the screen, beaming toothlessly at the camera, his brown eyes wide. He's absolutely adorable; I have to try extremely hard to suppress the incoming wave of broodiness. One step at a time, I remind myself. I've never been particularly good at that.

'Just got off FaceTime with him and Dad,' Deb tells Addie. 'They've bought him some ridiculous bouncy chair thing that must have cost an arm and a leg. He's getting totally spoiled.'

She pulls a face, but she's glowing, the way people glow when they're not just happy, they're *whole*. I'll get to meet Riley, I realise – I'll get to be part of his life, and Deb's, and I'll get to know all the new facets of Addie's world.

'Dyl?' calls a voice from behind us.

The music starts up as I turn. Krish and Cherry's first dance song is Shania Twain's 'Forever and for Always' – I can only think that Krishna gave up on arguing about that one and let Cherry have her way.

It's Luke and Javier behind me. They both look like they've arrived in a hurry, and Luke's cheeks are flushed.

'Dyl,' Luke says quietly as they slot in beside us to watch the dance.

Krish is doing a remarkably good job of waltzing to Shania Twain, though his lips are moving a little as he counts the steps, and his expression of absolute concentration is somewhat comical.

'Dylan, Mum's left Dad,' Luke says in a low voice.

'*What?*'

I say it so loudly even Cherry and Krishna look our way.

'Everything all right?' Cherry calls to me as Krishna bends her over backwards.

'Fine!' I call. 'As you were! *What?*' I say to Luke.

'It was amazing!' Javier hisses. He's bouncing slightly on the spot; his hair, pulled up in a high ponytail, bounces with him. 'We'd just arrived at the moat, and your parents were coming to it at the same time, and Luke's dad tried to go the other way so he didn't have to cross paths with us – well, with me – and . . .'

'Mum just flipped out,' Luke says, shaking his head and smiling. 'She threw her hat at him. Told him she was damned if she was going to muddle through another social event pretending she loved her husband, and that it was breaking her heart not seeing her sons, and that she was done standing by him. We've just taken her to a hotel and got her settled. Here, I'll message you the details so you can go later – she's dying to see you.'

He gets his phone out. I alternate between staring at the waltzing Krish and Cherry and the exuberant Javier and Luke.

'Your mum just left your dad?' Addie says beside me. She gives Luke and Javier a shy smile. 'Hey again, you two.'

The moment when my brother and his fiancé belatedly clock that Addie and I are holding hands is truly beautiful. They both beam simultaneously, as if on cue, and Luke claps a hand on my shoulder.

'Oh *good*,' Javier says. 'Dylan writes very lovely poetry but I'm not sure how many poems about heartbreak I can take.'

I reach over to shove him and he giggles, hiding behind Luke.

'I can introduce you to my mum,' I say to Addie, looking down at her wonderingly. 'Without my dad there. That would actually be . . . nice.'

She smiles up at me. 'I'd like that.'

The first dance is done – or at least, Krishna would like it to be. He is gesturing his best man on to the dance floor with an air of slight desperation; eventually a few couples take pity and the crowd starts to move towards the bride and groom.

'May I have this dance?' I ask Addie as the music shifts. It's another slow-dance song, a slightly more conventional one: Jason Mraz, 'I Won't Give Up'.

We walk to the dance floor; Addie links her hands carefully behind my neck and I rest mine on her waist. I look into those river-blue eyes that caught me up from the very first moment I saw them. We sway together as the dance floor fills around us; I lift my head for a moment and see Deb dancing with Kevin, Luke with Javier. Behind them a young woman in a green and pink lehenga pulls a very proper middle-aged lady in a suit on to the dance floor with her, then Marcus is up, too, stretching a hand out to tempt Grace, and Cherry's father is dancing with Krish's mum, and it's a melee of colour and hats and bodies swaying like we're one moving part.

I look back at Addie's upturned face. I can hardly believe she's here; I feel suddenly compelled to count every freckle, to memorise the precise shade of her hair while I still can, and I have to remind myself that she told me she loves me. She's not going anywhere.

'What you said earlier about . . .' I press my lips together, and I watch her gaze shift down to my mouth. 'I know we said sex might need to be approached a little more carefully, this time, but . . . can I ask where you land on kissing, presently?'

She starts to smile. 'Kissing?'

'Just hypothetically.'

'Well. I haven't done a great deal of it lately,' she says, that slow smile growing. 'But I think I'd be all right with kissing.'

I lower my head just a little, and she lifts her chin in the same moment, as though the threads connecting us have been pulled taut.

'Want to give it a try?' I whisper, my lips inches from hers.

She closes the distance between us in answer. And there, on the dance floor, with the mess of our past behind us and a tangle of our friends around us, with her hair shining silver and my heart bright and bursting, I kiss Addie Gilbert for the second first time.

Acknowledgements

Thank you as always to Tanera Simons, who manages to be super-smart and savvy *and* incredibly kind and supportive. I am enormously grateful for all that you and the team at DAA do for me.

Cindy Hwang, Emma Capron, Cassie Browne – you have made this book so much stronger and deeper (and sexier – I'm looking at you, Emma). I feel so lucky to have you all on my team. To everyone at Quercus and Berkley: thank you for your passion and ingenuity, and for having faith in me. Special thanks to Hannah Robinson, who listened when it really, really mattered.

I have dedicated this novel to my wonderful bridesmaids, Ellen, Nups, Amanda, Maddy and Helen, who were sadly not able to walk with me down the aisle at my wedding, but whose love and support have informed all the sisterhoods in this book. Thank you, guys, for the countless heart-to-hearts, pick-me-ups and cups of tea over the years. I'm really lucky to have you all in my life.

A huge thank you to Gilly for the voice notes, the 43mb chats, and the important discussion of whose dog is big and whose dog is small. You kept me afloat in 2020. Thanks to Pooja for always being so excited when a new word doc lands in your inbox, and for your help with the details. And thanks to Tom, for whom this will always be The Mercedes Book – apologies for ignoring most of the information you gave me. Call it artistic licence.

I'm very grateful to the Taverners for giving such valuable feedback on early drafts of this book. Thanks also to Peter for brainstorming with me in Provence, where much of this story was born. Thank you to Phil, who answered odd questions, and Helen, aka Boob Consultant, who answered even odder ones. Thanks to Colin, who very patiently taught me how to drive. I'm also immeasurably grateful to my parents, who are always there for me, something that I just cannot appreciate enough.

Finally, thank you to my husband, Sam. I love you the way Addie loves Dylan, the way Dylan loves Addie, the way Molly loves pears. Here's to a lifetime together.

Discover more from *Sunday Times* bestselling author

BETH O'LEARY

Visit www.betholearyauthor.com for:

New Book Announcements

*

A Q&A with Beth

*

Book Extracts

*

And to Sign Up to Beth's Newsletter

Fuel your reading experience with Beth's ultimate *Road Trip* playlist! Scan the QR code to listen now and add some of your favourites, too: